Monaro by Alyn Marland

by his daughter, Mrs. Katharine Carr

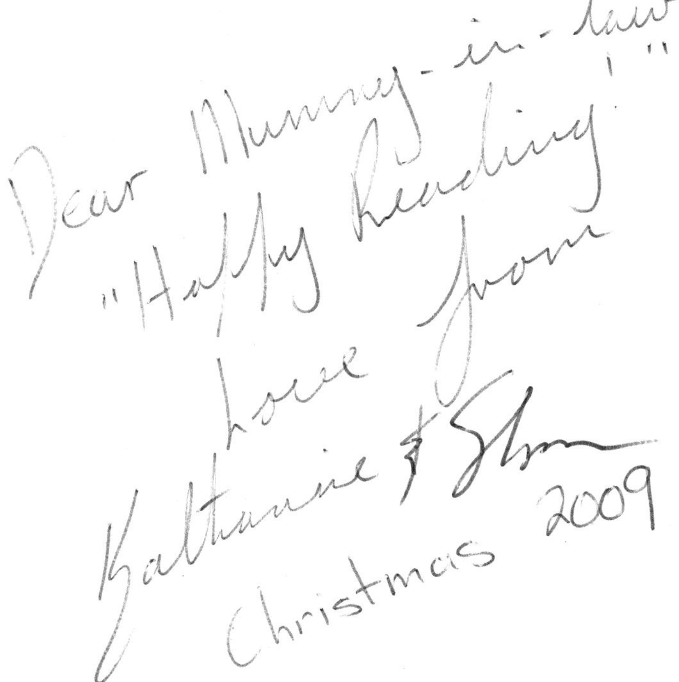

RoseDog Books
PITTSBURGH, PENNSYLVANIA 15222

ISBN: 978-1-4349-9524-7
Printed in the United States of America

First Printing

For more information or to order additional books, please contact:
RoseDog Books
701 Smithfield Street
Pittsburgh, Pennsylvania 15222
U.S.A.
1-800-834-1803
www.rosedogbookstore.com

CHAPTER I

Melbourne 1890

'Well Harry old man, there you are. I say, what a crowd! Hardly find a place to stand. What a day, couldn't have asked for better. Congratulations! Where is Madelaine by the way? Haven't sighted her yet. So young Harry finally took the plunge eh? Never thought he would. Hope, God rest her soul, always said he was the best catch in Melbourne. As they say, you may have lost a son but, good Lord, what a charmer you have for a daughter-in-law. Heavens, I do rattle on, my enduring fault, I am afraid.'

The year, 1890, on a fine autumn day in Melbourne. The place, the elegant drawing room of a fashionable Toorak mansion. The speaker, a tall, distinguished, middle aged man. His thick brown hair streaked with grey, had addressed his remarks to the Groom's father, Dr. Harry Wakefield, wealthy and respected physician to the town's well to do.

'James, my dear chap, so glad you could come. I know you legal fellows are always busy. Where have you been? It must be two months since I last saw you. Looked everywhere. Pity you missed the ceremony. Splendid turnout, the church was crowded.'

'Regret I missed it Harry. Truth is, I have been busy trying to reduce my financial exposure. Frankly, I fear this over -inflated bubble is about to burst.'

'Bad as that eh? I didn't know.'

His friend nodded. 'I am convinced, old man. Fortunately your position appears safe, you have always been cautious.'

'Well, I have always acted on your advice.'

'I know. Pity I haven't done the same.'

A waiter approached with a laden tray. 'Ah, something to drink- balm to the troubled soul.' He held his long stemmed glass to the light. 'Champagne, nectar of the Gods, but frankly, Harry, I could do with a Brandy. Hmm, not bad though, do ask that man to keep coming my way.'

The doctor eyed his friend ruefully. 'Be steady James, be steady. Now I must circulate. When you can, make your way to Madelaine, she constantly asks after you.'

'Of course, of course.' He touched his friend's arm. 'Before you leave me Harry, tell me, who is that delicious creature over by the piano? Look, you see? In the grey silk, talking to that old dragon, Lady Welton. By George, what a looker and who is that fat, pompous oaf slobbering over her? You must introduce me!'

'Oh you mean Ruth DeVries, a patient of mine and that "oaf", as you call him, is an Aide to the Governor. Really James, you are beyond redemption. I believe you do need a brandy. I will send you some.'

James Scully put his hand to his head. 'Good God, what some women will marry!'

Harry Wakefield chuckled. 'He is not her husband, James. Mrs. DeVries is a widow. Now old man, you must excuse me, we can talk later.' He moved slowly amongst the guests, goblet in one hand, cigar in the other, trailing a wisp of bluish, fragrant smoke. An imposing figure, tall and broad shouldered with neatly clipped black hair and beard. He looked down and over those around him through deeply set, intensely blue eyes. Women found him enchanting.

After depositing his glass, he proffered his hand to the men, bowed to their wives and stooped to kiss the hand of those ladies known more intimately.

A fashionably gowned woman touched his sleeve. 'Oh Doctor Wakefield, I am so glad to have found you. I am so unhappy, I still have such horrible dreams. I am sure I am losing my mind!'

'Let us not talk of such things here Mrs. Paton. I thought you were much happier than when I saw you last. Come and see me tomorrow, we can talk about it then. Now, here,' he plucked a glass from the waiter's tray, 'have some champagne.' He bent low and whispered in her ear, 'doctor's orders. You will feel much better for it.'

With a smile he moved away. Yes, he knew her trouble all right. If only someone would shoot that bastard Paton, all would be well.

He stopped suddenly. 'Ah, there you are, Mr. and Mrs. Janson. So glad to see you. What a crush!'

The brides father, a solid, ruddy faced wheat farmer from the Mallee, shook hands. Mrs. Janson, a serenely dignified woman, gowned in bombasine, smiled shyly, fingering a gold pendant, her only concession to fashion. 'We have seen Madelaine, Doctor. She is over by the piano surrounded. I'm afraid she is worried, Harry and Rose are taking so long to appear.'

The doctor looked over the crowded faces, all seemed to be talking at once. 'I see my friend, Mr. Scully, has found her. I have just been talking to him. What a splendid wedding it was! Unfortunately, he was delayed, missed the ceremony, quite a pity.'

Mrs. Janson's face lit up. 'Oh yes, it was absolutely wonderful. Rose looked so beautiful.' She added hastily, 'and Harry looked so distinguished.'

The doctor motioned to a passing waiter. 'Are you managing? I see some of the guests have empty glasses.'

The man appeared a trifle flustered. 'I'm sorry doctor. I'm sure I am doing my best. It is so crowded.'

'I understand. Just do the best you can. Now Mr. Janson, another glass?'

The farmer shook his head. 'Not used to this sort of thing. Makes my head spin. Whisky man, myself.'

His wife politely refused. 'Please let us go to your wife and your dear mother. Madelaine appeared upset. Harry has said nothing of their plans. Perhaps you know what they intend doing.'

'I'm afraid I don't Mrs. Janson.' He offered his arm. 'Let us try and clear up this little mystery.'

Madelaine Wakefield, petite and charming, the centre of attention, sat on a small sofa surrounded by guests. Next to her a white haired old lady gravely surveyed the lively scene. The doctor's wife, always beautifully gowned, always charming, looked lovely. All eyes were upon her. Her dark brown hair piled up high, her large grey eyes with their thick dark brows set off her delicate, clear complexion. She sat with the folds of her cream silk gown carefully spread, fanning herself and trying to appear calm. At the sight of her husband, she looked up with evident relief. She spoke rapidly in French.

'Now my dear.' The doctor lightly kissed his wife, whispering the while. 'English my love, speak English.'

Madelaine smiled mistily. 'Please forgive me. I am so upset, waiting so long for Harry and Rose to come.'

Everyone smiled understandingly. James Scully bowed low, kissing her slender hand. 'Madelaine my dear, nothing to forgive. It is delightful dear lady, just to hear your charming accent.'

'What a fine gentleman.' Mrs. Janson whispered to her husband.

Madelaine's gaze rested on Mrs. DeVries. 'Ruth, I am so happy you are here. I looked for you at the church.'

Ruth smiled at her dearest friend. 'I came late Madelaine. I sat in the back row. It was so beautiful.'

James Scully stood back slightly, Madelaine reached out her hand. 'Ruth, may I present our guest and most faithful friend, Mr. James Scully.'

The lawyer bowed. 'Your servant ma'am.' He was about to speak when the buzz of conversation ceased suddenly. All eyes turned to the arched doorway leading into the drawing room. Standing in the doorway accompanied by a small group of friends, was the couple all had been waiting for.

The groom, a tall, thin, slightly stooped young man with curly, sandy coloured hair parted in the middle, stood, one hand nervously fingering his drooping moustache, worn in the fashion of the day. He bent to speak to his bride, she looked up smiling encouragement. Rose radiant in her wedding gown, came barely to his shoulder. Her veil, held back with a jewelled clasp, revealed blazing red hair, contrasting vividly with the blue of her eyes. For a moment they hesitated, then advanced slowly into the room.

Dr. Wakefield spoke clearly. 'Ladies and gentlemen, dear friends, may I beg your attention?' Smiling broadly, he waved his cigar in the direction of the newly weds. 'I see my son and his bride have arrived a little late, but I am sure, forgiven on this happy occasion.' He cleared his throat. 'Now they have arrived, I understand tables have been prepared in the ballroom. I trust you will find everything to your liking.'

Smiling and gossiping, the guests filed through the archway, with the exception of the old lady who refused to move. She sat patiently, her hands folded in her lap, having given instructions that the young couple were to come to her after the guests had departed.

James Scully bowed slightly to Mrs. DeVries. 'Madam may I have the honour?'

'Thank you Sir, you are very kind.' They moved slowly, the last to leave the room. 'Madelaine has often spoken of you. Mr. Scully.'

'Really ma'am, I trust she gave a good report.'

'Indeed she did. She said you are the doctors oldest friend.'

They stood a moment in the doorway. 'Your husband ma'am, could he not accompany you today?'

She looked down. 'I am a widow, Mr. Scully. My husband passed away last year. It was very sudden.'

'I am sorry, how clumsy of me. Please forgive me.'

They proceeded into the ballroom. 'And your wife, Mr. Scully, she could not be with you?'

He answered quietly. 'My dear wife passed away these two years past. The doctors could do nothing for her.'

For a moment they stood in silence. 'What a beautiful room,' whispered Mrs. DeVries. 'I have visited *Monterey* often but I have never seen the ballroom before.'

'I doubt it has been used since the old man died. Harry keeps it closed up. They are not given to entertaining in the "grand manner", unlike the old days. I believe this place was quite the centre of Melbourne society.' He smiled. 'Such as it is. Somehow I doubt it will ever be used again. Harry is their only child, as you know.'

The design of the ballroom had been left to an architect with a reputation for taste, who had been given carte blanche with regard to cost. Three walls of the vast rectangular room were washed a delicate green, their plain severity softened by a succession of small arched alcoves panelled in rich red cedar within which stood tall exquisite Japanese vases trailing masses of late roses. The fourth wall was almost entirely glass with French doors opening onto an enclosed formal garden. From the domed ceiling hung a magnificent Venetian chandelier, it's tinkling crystals reflecting myriad colours from the diffused autumn sunlight.

The warmth of the room, combined with ever flowing champagne and the heady scent of roses, lifted flagging spirits. To the rising murmur of gay laughter and banter, the thirty odd guests found their way to the tables arranged in a horseshoe. Each guest found their place by the cards Madelaine had carefully and diplomatically arranged.

Lady Welton surveyed the scene through her lorgnette. She was seated in a place of honour next to Madelaine. 'My dear, how perfectly splendid. I do envy you. We find colonial domestics quite impossible. Yet this would do justice to a London house of quality.' She sighed heavily. 'My dear gal, your home is really an oasis, a veritable oasis in this vulgar country. Thank God, Hubert's duty is almost finished and we shall soon return to England. One can only tolerate the crudities of the colonies for so long. So boring, so unutterably boring. Surely you must find it so?'

Madelaine smiled faintly. Lady Welton's observations had been over heard, an awkward silence descended on the gathering.

Dr. Wakefield rose to the occasion. Standing with hands spread for attention, he spoke in his most persuasive voice. 'Ladies and gentlemen will you please bear with me a moment. This is a most happy occasion for my wife and I. It is our most earnest desire that you join with us and enjoy this food and wine.' He smiled his disarming smile. 'Before the mandatory speeches begin of course.' He sat down amidst laughter and clapping, the tension broken.

Conversation buzzed, the wine flowed, busy waiters, hired for the day, plied their duty with skill and good humour. On a small raised platform a String Quartet played soft music.

Mrs. DeVries turned to her companion. 'Madelaine said you were the Doctor's oldest friend. Were you boys and young men together?'

'Yes, that we were. We went to the same school, Melbourne Grammar. I came from the country, my parents had a large holding. Wool paid very well in those days. Rather than face the long journey home, I often spent my holidays here. The old people, Harry's parents, were quite wonderful. The old chap drove around in one of the finest rigs in Melbourne. He would always open his purse and hand us a florin each. Sometimes he would take us into town for tea and cakes and a concert.' He sighed. 'What grand times we had then, what happy, carefree times. But I must be boring you with these school day reminiscences, dear lady.'

'Oh no, Mr Scully I find it fascinating. I often wish I could talk to the Doctor's mother, such a lovely old lady, she must know such wonderful things about the past.'

The lawyer helped himself from a proffered dish. 'Yes, a remarkable story, too long I'm afraid to tell here.' He ventured a little further. 'Perhaps you will allow me to call on you, at your convenience.'

She felt comfortable with this fine looking man. 'You would be most welcome.'

Before he could answer, the Doctor rose to his feet again. It was the moment when contentment settled upon the festive gathering. Ladies sighed and wished their corsets were a little looser, gentlemen secretly cursed their too tightly laced boots and longed for a cigar.

Smiling broadly, Dr. Wakefield's gaze swept the table. 'Again ladies and gentlemen, may I have your attention? May I, with your indulgence, propose a toast?' He held his glass high. 'To our dear son and his lovely bride, Harry and Rose - may their life together be long and joyful.'

The guests rose, glasses charged - 'Harry and Rose!'

Amidst cries of 'Speech Harry, Speech!' Harry stood to respond, the long fingers of one hand nervously stroking his moustache, the other resting lightly on his wife's shoulder. Shy and reserved, he spoke slowly. 'Ladies and gentlemen, my friends.' He glanced down at Rose. 'I should say, our friends.'

A smiling young man called from down the table. 'Louder Harry, louder, we can't hear you down here!'

The guests clapped, Harry now more at ease, smiled and began again. 'Ladies and gentlemen, dear friends, thank you for your kind and generous good wishes.' He paused a moment to cough briefly, then turning to his parents - 'from my heart, I thank my Mother and Father for the love and care they have given me and to you, Mr. and Mrs. Janson, for giving me Rose.' He reached for his wife's hand. 'The greatest gift any man could wish for.' More confident now, he smiled his disarming smile and repeated. 'Thank you all again.' He sat down to calls of 'Bravo, Good Health and Good Luck!'

The warm atmosphere, good food and wine combined to remove inhibitions. Conversation flowed, loud and animated, all seemed to talk one above the other. Small groups of the more mature excused themselves, some to gather in the drawing room, others to stroll in the garden to admire the roses and take a breath of fresh air.

The groom took his wife's hand, smiled, executed an elaborate bow and led her to the clear space in front of the podium. The Strings immediately broke into a lilting waltz. They danced gracefully, Rose leaning against Harry's encircling arm, one hand on his shoulder, the hem of her flowing wedding gown gathered in the other. The effect was electrifying. The younger guests, mimicking Harry's gallant gesture, led their partners onto the floor.

Ruth DeVries looked on, her eyes shining. James Scully glanced at the woman beside him with undisguised admiration. 'Shall we join them?' Without waiting for an answer, he took her hand, leading her to the floor. They moved easily and gracefully to the enchantment of the music. As they circled and reversed in perfect time, he whispered. 'Look who is joining us!' Dr. Wakefield and his wife had entered the room after farewelling a few early departing guests. He looked at her, she smiled and nodded, then with all eyes upon them, he took her in his arms and with the lightness of movement peculiar to big men, they swayed as one to the strains of the waltz.

The sun was low on the horizon before most of the guests made their farewells. A few intimate groups still stood around talking. Rose, her parents and Madelaine stood in earnest conversation.

Dr. Wakefield found his son in the company of two of his friends. 'We have been looking for you, Dad. Please meet two friends of mine, Mr. Roberts and Mr. McCubbin.'

They shook hands warmly. 'Harry's friends are always welcome in this house, gentlemen. I understand my son is a great admirer of your work. I trust a little of your talent rubs off.'

The artists laughed. 'No worry on that count, Sir Harry's is a unique talent, his use of light and colour show great promise and character.'

'That is heartening news indeed,' smiled the doctor. 'but you must forgive me, on the subject of art, I plead ignorance. I only know what I like, as the saying goes.'

They laughed again. 'Light is the great talking point of artists, Doctor. We argue its value endlessly.'

The Doctor smiled. 'I leave that subject in your hands, gentlemen, now if I may beg your patience for a moment, I would like a word with Harry.'

Dr. Wakefield drew his son aside. 'Harry my boy, Rose's parents are in a stew, your mother is frantic. What is this I hear? You and Rose going on a camping holiday? For Heaven's sake, tell me what this is all about!'

The young Wakefield looked ruefully at his father. 'Sorry I haven't mentioned this before Dad, but you know Mother, bound to raise a hundred objections. Tom has made the arrangements. We are going up to Heidelberg for a working holiday. Quite a party of us, in fact. We leave tonight, everything is ready, tents, equipment, all we could need.'

The Doctors expression grew serious. 'Camping, Harry, camping? Surely not, this is most worrying. You know, you have been warned, the slightest chill, a change in the weather, could lead to serious consequences for you. Your lungs simply will not tolerate such conditions!'

'Please Dad, don't worry. Rose and I have the use of a covered wagon. Very snug and comfortable.' He smiled. 'The fellows say, in honour of the honeymooners.'

'Well, I can't say I am not a little worried, but if this is what you and Rose want, then you have my blessing. Now, bring your friends, we should join the others.'

Now the news was out, the parents, if not happy, appeared reconciled to the newly weds plans. Mr. Janson thought it was a grand idea. Mrs. Janson said they must make sure to keep warm and eat well. Although, she added with a hint of pride, she was sure Rose would see to that. Madelaine had dried tears of disappointment, giving her blessing provided they would promise to travel to Europe when they returned.

Throughout this little scene, the old lady sat serene and still, her wise old eyes missing nothing. She now commanded the young couple to sit beside her and tell her of their plans.

The Jansons, despite being pressed to stay the night, insisted they must start back, as they had promised friends a visit on the way and wanted to arrive there before night set in.

James Scully confided to his host, he would see Mrs. DeVries safely home. She wished his advice regarding a small property matter and had sent her carriage ahead. 'You know Harry, I find her absolutely charming, so gracious.'

The doctor regarded his friend closely. 'Careful, old man, careful. We are extremely fond of Ruth. A beautiful woman. I am surprised, I thought you were past becoming involved.'

'Purely friendship Harry, believe me. But we must make a start.' He looked around. 'Now where is Madelaine? Ah yes, shall I see you at the Club for lunch tomorrow? Good, excuse me while I interrupt that little circus round your good wife and make my farewells.'

He bowed before Madelaine, lightly kissing her hand. 'Au revoir my dear, until we meet again, which I trust will be soon.'

She smiled at him. 'Au revoir James. I will ask Harry to keep you to your promise to visit again soon. I am so glad you are seeing Ruth home, she is a dear friend. And James, she is very lonely.' She added softly.

'You may be sure I will see her safely to her door. Now we must go. Until tomorrow Harry. Take good care of your lovely wife. Goodbye Mrs. Wakefield. So glad to see you again. Mr. and Mrs. Janson, Godspeed, a safe journey home.'

Harry's friends gathered around him. 'Good Lord, old man, shake a leg, look at the time, we really should get a move on. Give you twenty minutes to change. Hurry him along Rose. We are loaded and ready to go. Perfect time to travel, still plenty of light.'

The old lady held their hands. 'May the Lord bless you, my dears. I know you will be very happy.' She turned to Harry. 'And you, young man, have a girl with strength enough for both of you.'

A tear glistened on her lined cheek as she whispered to Rose. 'He is such a gentle creature, my dear. Take good care of him.' She opened a small chamois purse and took out a delicately carved jade brooch. 'My husband gave this to me when we were married.' She carefully fastened it to the girl's gown where it lay like a flower against the white silk.

Rose's hand caressed the lovely green gem stone. 'Thank you Grandmother Wakefield, I will keep it forever.' She smile at the old lady. 'Or until we have a daughter some day.'

Soon all were gone. Only the Doctor, his wife and mother remained. 'Bless them,' she murmured. 'they are so young, all is before them.'

Ruth DeVries seated comfortably in the Lawyer's carriage, gazed through the window at the trees lining the gravelled driveway. Maples and Limes, burnished red and gold with the first touch of frost, brought forth a sigh of pleasure. 'This place has always held a special charm for me, Mr. Scully.' She blushed. 'Does that sound a little too romantic?'

'Dear lady, I have been coming here since I was very young, *Monterey* was my second home. I have always felt the same.'

They sat without speaking, only the sound of the spinning wheels and the clap of the horses hooves breaking the silence. The lawyer summoning his courage turned to face her.

'Please tell me if I offend you. I have been tempted to use your Christian name but sadly my nerve has deserted me.'

She lifted her veil, smiling. 'I am not offended, I feel so comfortable with you Mr. Scully. Madelaine has spoken so often of you, I feel safe. I trust my feminine instincts.'

'Thank you dear lady. I am deeply honoured. I would be doubly honoured if you could bring yourself to use my own name. Am I asking too much?'

She spoke softly. 'Of course not, I would be glad to.'

He sighed. 'Strange is it not? We met so short a time ago, yet it seems so much longer.'

The traffic grew heavier, he leaned forward tapping the roof with his cane. 'One moment Gleeson.' Then looking out the window he asked, 'Now where is this property you wish me to see?'

Ruth DeVries reached into a small draw purse. 'Little Bourke Street and here,' handing him a note book, 'this is the number. I have not seen the property but my bank manager has a buyer. I would so appreciate your advice James. I know so little of these matters.'

Again he tapped the roof. 'Little Bourke Street, Gleeson.' There was a sharp sound of leather slapping the horses backs as the carriage reeled, gathering speed.

'May I ask about your husband Ruth?' Her name so new to him, came softly from his lips. 'I pray I do not appear to pry but I am consumed with curiosity.'

She sighed. 'I am sure you would have found my husband agreeable. He was a good, kind man.' She suddenly broke off, appearing withdrawn.

'Please,' he murmured, 'I feel I have upset you.'

'Oh no, you have not. Forgive me, my thoughts were back to the time I first met my husband. Not a happy period in my life.' She pinned back her veil.

In the dim light his heart turned at the sadness in her face, the pale beauty of her features. 'My dear Ruth, if you would rather not, some other time perhaps.'

Her mood changed, she smiled slightly. 'I do want to tell you, James, but will you, first, tell me about yourself and Dr. Wakefield?'

'Not a lot to tell, I'm afraid. We grew up together, a couple of young larrikins, at least I am sure that is how people saw us.'

'I find that hard to believe.'

'Thank you, but truth is we were a bit on the wild side.' He sighed. 'Brings back such pleasant memories. Hunting and fishing whenever holidays came round.'

'Did you know Dr. Wakefield's parent well? Especially dear old Mrs. Wakefield, she must have wonderful stories of those days.'

'There is not much I can tell you there either. I only know what Harry has told me, although I saw them quite often of course. Apparently he landed here during the gold rush. I am told people from all over the world swarmed over the fields.'

'Dr. Wakefield's father was a miner?'

'A miner? Good lord, no. He was trader. His wagons travelled the diggings supplying the miner's needs. He was an astute business man. He was paid mainly in gold and invested in property all over Melbourne.'

'How fascinating! How did he meet his wife?'

'I believe she was the daughter of a Californian miner. The men became close friends.' He looked at her closely. 'Are you tired Ruth? You appear a little pale, perhaps we could continue some later time.'

'Oh no, please go on.' She glanced away. 'I really must appear a little vulgar, prying like this.'

'Of course you are not. In any case there is little more to tell you. Her father died of the fever and she married Harry's father. The rest, well, he was a wealthy man, sold his business and retired to the city. Oh yes, and built *Monterey,* named in honour of his wife's birth place.'

'What a romantic story!'

'Yes I suppose it is. My own father was also a miner, one of the lucky ones. When he struck it rich, he left the fields and bought into sheep country. Wool was at premium, he became very prosperous.' He chuckled. 'Could only happen in the colonies! From raw Irish immigrant to landed gentry in a few short years. I say, gentry, advisedly. Politely received but never accepted. But such is the power of money, he married into a well known family.'

'You must be very proud of your parents, James.'

'Sadly, both my parents are dead. I have one sister. She and her husband now manage the old property.' Pulling the curtain aside, he peered through the small window. The carriage had slowed as the coachman reined in his horses.

'Little Bourke Street, Sir.'

The evening glow had given way to dusk. Dim lights poorly illuminated the narrow street. He rubbed the glass with his gloved hand. 'I am afraid we have left it too late, almost impossible to see. Perhaps tomorrow Ruth?'

'Thank you James. It was inconsiderate of me to take you so far out of your way. I am grateful to you.'

'Please,' he said, 'it is I who is grateful. Meeting you today, being with you, I feel as though I am alive again.' He dared not look at her. 'Have I said too much? If I have, I promise to say no more.'

She flushed a little, then smiled. 'No James, I confess to the same feeling.' She in turn looked out the window, 'Oh dear, it is dark! I really must hurry, my little boy misses me so.'

The lawyer looked at her in astonishment. 'Your little boy? I had no idea you had a child. Forgive me, I never dreamt!'

'He is so young and so dear to me. Are you surprised?'

'It just did not occur to me.' He sighed. 'My dear wife and I were not blessed with children.'

The coachman tapped at the door. 'Beg pardon, Sir, I must put out the riding lights. Where to now, Sir?'

The Lawyer gave the address. 'Make it smart, Gleeson.' The swaying carriage sped on through the night. He looked outside, it was now quite dark. 'Afraid I am lost, fortunately Gleeson knows every nook and cranny of this town.'

Ruth touched his arm. 'Please go on, forgive me if my curiosity is overtaking my manners.'

He smiled with pleasure at her touch. 'Well the time came when Harry and I were at an age when decisions had to be made. No one could agree. Harry's father would not hear of him going to England, why, I don't know, perhaps something to do with his past. My father expected me to go onto the land but I did not fancy myself a farmer. My dear old pater was disappointed but gave in. Said if I must become a gentleman, I should go to Ireland to be educated. My mother would not hear of it, she was sure I would become a priest,' he smiled, 'or even worse! You see, my father was Catholic my mother Protestant. Although I can truly say, I never heard them argue on account of religion. I am sure they respected each other's beliefs.

Yes, it was quite an impasse, but broken in the strangest way. That account is a story in itself, suffice to say, through the good offices of a mutual friend, we ended up in Edinburgh. A dull, old town but to two young bloods from the colonies, wildly exciting.'

At that instant the carriage stopped, the coachman called down to his master. 'This is the address, Sir. Shall I drive in?'

'Just a minute, Gleeson.' He opened the door to see friendly lighted windows shining through the trees. He turned to her. 'My dear Ruth, please spare me a few minutes, you have told me nothing of yourself.'

'Just a few minutes then, James, I must see my little boy before he goes to sleep.'

He tapped the roof. 'Drive slowly for a while Gleeson, I will tell you when to turn.'

'You have been so patient with me James. You may be surprised - I was born in India. My father was a Warrant Officer in the British Army, I never knew my mother, she died when I was young. I grew up in barracks and apart from an Indian servant, I was very much alone.'

'How lonely you must have been.'

'Yes I was until I went to school. I made friends, mostly Indian, whom I will always remember for their kindness and affection.'

'Surely your father must have been a comfort?'

'I seldom saw my father, he seemed always to be away. I don't think he ever noticed me, that is until I grew up. Then I became an encumbrance. He told me bluntly to look around for a suitable husband.'

'Good God, how heartless!'

'Please,' there was sadness in her voice, 'you do not understand. Non commissioned men, without private means, are paid a pittance. They are under constant financial stress. My poor father was, like I, a victim of a system that asks so much and gives so little.'

'Believe me, I meant no disrespect. Please go on.'

'No young man begged for my hand. I hoped no one would.'

'How unhappy you must have been.'

'Desperate at times, but not unhappy. I always dreamt something wonderful would happen to me.'

'Did your dream come true?'

'In a way I suppose. I answered an advertisement for a lady's travelling companion, not that I had the slightest idea what that entailed. I heard nothing for several days, then a message arrived to attend the Commanding Officers quarters. I was petrified. Whatever could he want with such a lowly person? I finally summoned up enough courage to go. He was kindness itself, made me feel at ease, then introduced me to his elderly Aunt, Lady Burrows. She was so gentle. She said she had heard so many good things about me and would I be interested in travelling back to England with her. James, I was walking on air, I, who had never been out of India!'

'Of course, I understand.'

'I must be brief. Within the week we left for Calcutta. Lady Burrows took me shopping. She said I must have warm clothes as it would be cold in England.' She gave an involuntary shudder. 'I could never have believed such cold!'

'Were you sad to leave?'

'Oh no, I thought of it as an escape.'

'So a new life was beginning.'

'Yes. I was just eighteen, I thought I would die of excitement! I had never seen a ship, let alone the ocean. Lady Burrows was so good to me. I had little to do apart from reading to her and making sure she was well wrapped when we went up on deck.' She paused to have a look through the window.

'Please,' he touched her arm, 'we must be almost there.'

She nodded. 'One day as I was reading to her, a ship's officer bade us good day. With him was a tall distinguished gentleman with grey hair but such merry blue eyes. He bowed and said he hoped we were enjoying the voyage. He had such a thick accent, but so charming and polite. I did not know it then James, but he was to be my future husband. Pieter was a gold and gem merchant from Amsterdam and often travelled to India on business.'

'Fate plays strange tricks on us poor mortals.'

She smiled. 'To be sure it does indeed.'

'So you arrived safely.'

'Yes, in February. It was raining. I can never forget the cold, after India, it was almost unbearable.'

'And the good Lady Burrows kept you with her?'

'Oh yes. Her house in Mayfair was so grand - so many servants! Such fine people came to visit. I felt insignificant, unless I was needed I kept to my room.'

'How lonely for you.'

'I was lonely, but I had a little spending money and on my afternoons off, I explored London. In my ignorance, I walked through parts of the city I wish I had never seen. After all, I had been told. It was shocking to me. Those wretched dreary streets, those poor pale people. I had seen terrible poverty in India, I did not expect to find it in England. Mercifully, I never went that way again.'

'Please, do not be troubled by past memories, just tell me what you wish.'

'A year, almost to the day of our arrival, Lady Burrows died. Oh James I was so frightened. I kept to my room and only crept down to the kitchen for meals.' The carriage stopped, she spoke hurriedly. 'This went on for almost two weeks until one day I was summoned to the library. I will never forget that day. Two men were in the room, one sat behind the desk reading papers. He looked up and beckoned me. He was so brusque - my services were no longer required. I had a week to find another position. It was so cold blooded!'

'My dear Ruth, you were well rid of the place.'

Her voice took on a note of bitterness. 'James, do you know what happens to penniless girls in London?'

The coachman called down. 'We are back at the house, Sir.'

'Just a moment Gleeson, just one moment. Please continue Ruth, I swear I shan't sleep a wink otherwise.'

Sometime during that fatal week, I was in my room in despair when I was told someone wished to see me. No doubt you have guessed, it was Pieter. He had heard of Lady Burrows death. He asked me to go driving with him. I think he was surprised how quickly I accepted.'

He touched her hand, so soft and warm. 'I understand.'

'Do not judge me harshly James. Pieter asked me to marry him. I said, yes, without hesitation.'

'Surely you did not love him?'

'Not in the romantic sense. We were married quietly the next day at a registry office.'

'And you came all the way to Australia?'

'Yes, Pieter loved to travel. After two years in Europe, he thought a sea voyage would be good for me.'

'And you decided to stay.'

'It was not planned that way. You see, I was carrying our baby and the doctor said it might be dangerous to travel any further.' She smiled. 'You have probably guessed - it was Dr. Wakefield.'

The carriage had moved slowly along the drive to the entrance of the house. The groom dismounted and stood respectfully at the door.

James Scully lightly touched her hand. 'Until tomorrow.'

'Thank you James, until tomorrow.' With a rustle of taffeta, she was gone, leaving behind a vague fragrance of lavender.

'Where to now, Sir?'

'The Club, Gleeson.' He sat back against the cushions, hands clasped on top of his cane. 'God, how long, how many life times since I felt like this?' A sudden fear gripped him. 'I must be deluding myself. How could she be attracted to me at my age?' Hope surged briefly within him. 'Her husband was old enough to be her father! Dammit, I won't think about it tonight. Put it out of my mind.' He groaned quietly. 'Until tomorrow, I won't think about it until tomorrow.'

CHAPTER II

Guests departed, Dr. Wakefield stood at the open door, savouring a last cigar. The thin blue smoke spiralled in the still, cool air. A light mist hung over the lily pond, an occasional bird noise came from the darkened trees. He frowned. 'There will be a chill in the air later, hope to God they keep warm.'

Behind him the butler coughed discreetly. 'Shall I lock up, Sir?'

'Thank you Benson, yes. Before you do, bring me a tray, any quail left?'

'Yes, Doctor.'

'Good. bring a couple, some caviar and a bottle of that Heidseicke.' Hands clasped behind his back, he paced slowly. 'Damn worrying, why in Hell must they go camping? Bloody ridiculous!' He laid down his cigar as the butler returned. 'Thank you, Benson. That will be all, you may retire.' Taking the tray with the roasted birds, a small dish of caviar resting on cracked ice and the wine in a silver bucket, he slowly mounted the elaborate curved staircase.

His wife sat in bed brushing her long dark brown hair. She looked up in surprise. 'Harry, what is this? Are you now the butler?' She laughed, that soft tinkling laugh, so pleasant to him.

He bowed gravely, a smile twitching at his lips. 'At your service, Madam.' Setting the tray on the bedside table, he took her hands in his. 'My dear little one, you made me so proud. Everyone admires you. The women clustered around you, the men adore you.'

She ran her fingers through his hair. 'And you Harry?'

He kissed her fingers. 'Your devoted slave, as ever.' He assumed a mock severity. 'Now Madam, I am here as your physician and your husband. Madelaine, do you not think I observed you today? Hardly a bite did you eat, hardly a drop passed your lips.' He poured the sparkling, golden wine. 'Now let us drink a toast to our loved ones. Then, I insist you eat. Here, a little caviar first.'

She smiled, taking the goblet. 'Harry, you treat me like one of your patients.'

'Nonsense my dear, I am very severe with my patients.'

'You seemed very sympathetic to Mrs. Paton today.'

'Good Lord, you miss nothing. I should tell you but Mrs. Paton is very unhappy. She is not physically ill, her husband is her trouble.'

Madelaine nibbled delicately at a quail. 'I know, she tells me.'

'Good God!' He put his hand to his forehead. 'Is nothing sacred? Really Madelaine, you should not talk to my patients. I trust she tells you nothing more.'

'Are you angry with me Harry?'

He laughed. 'Of course not. Come now, eat up. A little more wine? Now tell me, were you happy with the day?'

She hesitated. 'Yes only once was it - what is the English word - embarrass?'

'Embarrassing? When for Heaven's sake?'

'James was there. Lady Welton does not like him I think. She just looked at him through her lorgnette and turned away. James was not pleased.'

His laugh boomed out. 'The old dragon is quite harmless my dear. She feels it her duty to keep an eye on the colonials. Noblesse Oblige, you know. But you must not worry, James is quite immune to her antics.' He held his glass to the light. 'This Heidseicke is quite magnificent. Thank heaven I laid in good stock. Come now, finish that bird and drink your wine. It's good for you.'

She giggled, her hand to her mouth. 'Oh Harry, I will be drunk!'

'Then you will sleep. You must rest, you worry me, little one. You give so much - it is not good for you.'

'But I must Harry! All those little ragged children, they are hungry. Their mothers have nothing to give them.'

'I know my dear, I feel for them too. But you can't change the world. If there wasn't so much drunkenness and this dreadful strike, perhaps things might be better. Yes, I know the streets and alleys stream with unkempt urchins - and we, who love children so much–' he cut himself short.

Tears filled her eyes. 'Oh, Harry, I am so sorry.'

He soothed her. 'Hush, you must never say that. It is not your fault, it is as the good Lord decrees.' He stroked away her tears. 'We have a son, let us be thankful. We will have grandchildren to love one day, never fear.' He tilted back her chin. 'Now promise me you will sleep, I need you too, I am but a child with you.'

CHAPTER III

Autumn 1890 cast a spell on the land. Warm sunshine, crisp starry nights. Just a hint of frost in the lush paddocks. In the parks fallen leaves carpeted the grass. Immigrant trees blazed extravagant reds and gold. But those who live in this southern city know only too well how the scene can change. Cold cutting winds spring from nowhere, leaves swirl in the dust, leaden skies weep a thin freezing rain.

Such was the weather, when after five weeks the little band of artists returned. Supported by his friends, the young groom, flushed and coughing was helped from his covered wagon into the house.

His mother, who had witnessed this little procession from an upstairs window, rushed downstairs. She stood, hand to mouth. 'Mon Dieu, what is it, what has happened?'

One of the young men smiled reassuringly. 'Please don't be distressed, Mrs. Wakefield. Just a bad cold, nothing to worry about.' Helping Harry to a chair, he grinned. 'Terrible thing to happen on a honeymoon.'

Harry reached for his mother's hand. 'Don't fuss, Mother. Please be calm. Ask Benson to bring some brandy for my friends.' With his handkerchief he smothered a long breathless cough.

Echoes of the departing troop had barely died away before Harry was safely settled in the bedroom made ready for the newly weds homecoming. A hastily lit fire crackled in the grate, stone bottles filled with hot water wrapped in cloth, were packed around his feet. His mother closed the heavy drapes shutting out the sight of rain that splashed fitfully against the sills.

She touched her daughter-in-law's shoulder. 'Rose dear, you look so tired. Let us have some tea. Harry may sleep a little now.'

Harry squeezed his wife's hand. 'Do, darling.' He grinned weakly. 'First time I've been warm in days!'

In Madelaine's sitting room-her refuge-she called it, the women sat drinking tea, Rose close to the glowing fire.

'Are you happy Rose?'

'Happier than I ever thought I could be,' answered the girl.

'And Harry?'

'I think so,' she said softly. 'He enjoyed himself so much. Mother Wakefield you are so wise, please tell me how does a woman know if her man is happy?'

Madelaine smiled. 'Dear Rose, I don't think I am wiser than other women. I know people say we French have a flair for such things, but that is not true. I think one must be lucky in love, but I will tell you I have always loved and admired my husband. It was, as they say, love at first sight! I know, in my heart, it is so with you and Harry. He needs you Rose. He has always been delicate, he needs your strength.' Rising she crossed to the window, drawing aside the heavy drapes and brushing away the condensed moisture on the glass, she peered out into the dark. The dim lights of an approaching carriage came slowly along the drive. 'He is home, thank God!' She held out her hand. 'Come Rose, our doctor is home.'

Dr. Wakefield stood, feet apart, his back to the log fire glowing and crackling behind it's iron screen. His butler held a tray on which stood a decanter and soda water. 'Well,' he boomed, 'our ladies! What a pleasure for these tired eyes.' He folded his wife's hands in his, kissing her tenderly.

'Harry, you great bear, your hands are freezing!'

He laughed. 'And dear little Rose.' He kissed her cheek. 'Where is that husband of yours?'

Rose looked at her mother in law, nor sure whether she should speak first.

'Come, come ladies, what troubles you? Tell me please.'

'Harry is in bed, Dr. Wakefield. He wanted to rest, he can't stop coughing.'

'I see.' He took a cigar from a leather case, carefully nipping the ends. The butler applied a taper. 'Yes, understandable, this treacherous weather. Harry was always susceptible.'

The butler coughed discreetly. 'If you will excuse me, Doctor, Mr. Harry is awake now.'

'Thank you Benson.' He replaced his glass on the tray, throwing the barely smoked cigar into the fire. 'I will go upstairs, see what ails our patient.' He held out his hand. 'Now, if you please ladies, I will see him by myself. You may come up later. Now, I suggest you take a glass of sherry before dinner. Benson, sherry for the ladies.'

Dr. Wakefield entered the sick room and stood looking at his son. 'Well Harry, I didn't expect to find you here.'

Harry looked at him with relief. 'No dammit Dad. The last place I want to be. This blasted cough is enough to drive a man to drink.'

His father pulled a chair to the bedside, taking his son's wrist between his thumb and forefinger then bent and listened intently to the heaving chest. Suddenly he took the cloth from the sick man's grasp, examining it carefully.

Red spots splattered the snowy linen. He spoke quietly. 'How long has this been going on, Harry?'

'Has what been going on?'

'There is blood in your sputum. When did this start?'

'I don't know. I didn't know there was.'

'I see.' The doctor tucked the blankets around his son's chest. 'You slept well this afternoon, I believe?'

'Yes, I think so, I'm not sure.'

'Benson said he looked in on you, apparently he kept an eye on you. Good old Benson.'

'I expect Mother gave him instructions.'

'I suspect she did. Now old man, this cold, which I suspect is the 'flu, must be taken seriously.'

'Dad, I hoped to be up and about in a couple of days.'

'So you shall my boy, depending on your progress. For now, I want you to take plenty of fluid, Rose will see to that and tonight I want an inhaler kept going.' Standing up, hands behind his back, he thoughtfully studied one of his son's watercolours. 'Sorry your honeymoon had to end like this. Hard on Rose too. Damn season is so changeable.'

Harry struggled through a paroxysm of coughing, then fell back amongst the pillows, exhausted. A faint smile lit his face. 'Dreamt we were back in camp. The happiest days of my life, Dad. It was wonderful. I'm lucky to have such friends.'

'What of Rose, did she enjoy camping out?'

'Everyone loves Rose. She is the sweetest, most perfect woman. Why she married me I will never know.'

His father smiled. 'Perhaps you should ask her some time, I'm sure she will tell you. Personally I think she saw a good and decent young man.'

'I hope so. As for the camp, she loved every minute we were there. Those first weeks were so warm, the nights were chilly but our camp fire was the highlight of the evening. We kept it going with big logs. It was wonderful, sitting around on blankets and yarning. I learned so much just listening. I never realised how little I knew.'

'Surely you should have returned home when the rain started. Remember I warned you, Harry.'

'I know, Dad. A matter of being wise after the event, I suppose. Anyway, we would never have been wet if that damn canvas hadn't leaked. A hell of a lot of good that was. Still,' a smile crossed his face, 'it was warm under the blankets.'

'I imagine it was. Now, enough talk for the moment. The women will be frantic. You must listen to me Harry, and do as I say. Violent coughing brings on a slight haemorrhage, try to suppress it. You must have lots of fluid, I will send Rose up with soup to start with.'

Harry shook his head. 'I am so tired, Dad. I have no appetite.'

'You must try my boy. Here,' he withdrew a silver flask from inside his coat, 'a little brandy will help. Later I will give you some morphine, it will help you sleep through the night.' He stood waiting as his son sipped the amber fluid.

'Hmm, your colour is better already - hard to beat good brandy.'

Harry reached for his fathers hand. 'Before you go,' he tried desperately to suppress another violent bout of coughing, the cloth pressed to his lips. 'this is awful. Dad, I want you to do something for me, as a favour.'

'If it is within my power. You know you only have to ask.'

'There is someone I want you to help. A man we met at the camp, an artist, self taught but brilliant.'

'I see, sounds interesting. What can I do for him?'

'Will you please go and see him? He is sick, Dad, very sick. He used to wander in the late afternoon. He looked like a labourer but spoke like a gentlemen. He did a charcoal of the camp - it's magnificent! I could never do anything like it.'

His father nodded. 'Tell me later, you must conserve your strength, you are quite exhausted.'

'Please Dad, let me finish. When he didn't turn up last week, Rose and I went looking for him to say goodbye.'

'You found him I take it.'

'Dad, it was awful. I never dreamt such poverty existed. They live in a shack. He has a wife and three children.'

'Don't distress yourself.'

'He was in the kitchen, propped up in the chair before the stove, coughing his lungs out.' A weak grin crossed his face. 'Like me.'

'Has anyone been to see him?'

'His wife sent the eldest boy for the doctor.' His voice turned bitter. 'Can you believe, Dad? He wouldn't come without the money.'

'Sadly, that is typical. I hold such men in contempt.'

'He was glad to see us. I think he thought us little more friendly than the others. They were all so damn busy anyway. I pressed what money I had on his wife. She is young and looked so worn out. She didn't want to take it but I insisted. I said it was a loan to help Dan. His name is Dan McSweeney.' He fell back on the pillows, his face flushed, mottled with perspiration 'Will you go?'

'I promise, Harry. Now, I insist you rest, no more talking. Rose will give me directions, I will go tomorrow. You have my word.'

He left the room closing the door quietly behind him. He stood deep in thought. 'Like his mother, cursed with a gentle heart.' What he had heard in his son's chest troubled him. Composing himself, he slowly descended the stairs to his wife and daughter in law waiting below.

The women stood silent, waiting. The grandfather clock, sounding like a muffled bell, struck seven o'clock. Dr. Wakefield, with presence of mind born of long practice, linked arms with them. 'Come ladies, we must not keep dinner waiting.'

On a night during the second week, when a fitful wind found it's way, gently ruffling the heavy drapes, Madelaine sat knitting, watching over her failing son. Except for an occasional crackle from the fire, the house lay still and quiet.Only the wheezing of the sick man and the hiss of the gas jets intruded on her thoughts. She lifted her eyes gazing into the glowing coals. How strange it all seemed, living here in this strange land, far from her family and her native France. How long ago it seemed, the night her beloved father invited this promising young doctor to their house.'My young colleague,' he had smiled, 'he shows great promise.'This huge bearded man who spoke appalling French A smile hovered about her lips, as in her mind she lived it all over again. When he took her hand, she knew. Oh yes, she knew!Of course it did not happen straight away, Mama had seen to that! Poor Mama, always so worried, desperate that her daughters should make a 'good match'.Mama had airily dismissed romantic love as girlish indulgence, foolishness. One married for security and position. If one's husband strayed, providing he did so with discretion, one accepted such things.

But her father had nodded approvingly. 'A fine man little one. You will be happy.' And she had been, love mingled with tears.

Her eyes turned to her son - her only child. She heard the click of the door and her husband's footsteps. He stood, his hand resting on her shoulder. She reached up placing his large, strong hand against her wet cheek. 'Oh Harry, I am so afraid. Just when he was so happy -'

Gently he lifted her to her feet. 'Hush, you must not think such things. His condition is stationary, he is no worse. Tomorrow Dr. McKenzie is coming for consultation. He is the best chest man in Melbourne.' He kissed her gently. 'Now, please go to bed. Do not wake Rose, I will stay.' He wiped away her tears. 'Goodnight my dearest, sleep well.'

Promptly at ten the next morning, Dr. Jarvis McKenzie's smart landau clipped into the spacious portico before the front entrance. In his seventies, the old gentleman cut a splendid figure in his immaculate morning coat and shiny top hat. Throughout the city's medical fraternity, his reputation was highly respected.

Harry Wakefield met him at the steps. 'Thank you for coming, Doctor. I am indeed indebted to you.'

'Not at all Doctor, not at all. My pleasure.'

Inside the butler took his hat and cane.

'My wife, Dr. McKenzie. And our daughter-in-law, Rose.'

'Good morning ladies.' He bowed briefly, his great white beard shining like a flurry of snow. 'Perhaps now we might see the patient.'

In the sick room the examination was long and careful. At last straightening up, he took his younger colleague to the far side of the room. 'Dr. Wakefield, I do not think I can tell you anything that you do not already know.' He paused briefly. 'I believe it essential we tap the pleura immediately.' He paused again. 'If there is to be any hope.'

Two hours later the Doctors emerged from the bedroom, talking quietly. Dr. McKenzie stood adjusting his morning coat, then examined his watch. 'For today, that is the best we can do. He is sleeping soundly, his pulse appears to have steadied. I suggest you keep him mildly sedated for the next twenty four hours.' He added brusquely. 'I do not hold with poulticing. In my opinion it weakens the patient.' Adding in a more gentle tone. 'My dear chap, I have no doubt you are aware of your son's problems. Perhaps we can discuss that at a later date. Now I must take my leave, I will call again tomorrow and bring my nurse, you will need her in this situation.'

After the older man had left, Harry sought his wife and daughter in law. They sat quite still on the little couch in Madelaine's drawing room, not daring to speak, afraid of what they might hear. He looked from one to the other. 'He is sleeping.' His voice was a little husky. 'He is out of danger.'

'Thank God!' whispered Madelaine. Rose buried her face in her hands giving way to tears.

The following morning, Dr McKenzie arrived, bringing his nurse, a pleasant, no nonsense woman who knew her job. She immediately took charge and from that day Harry began his long road to recovery.

Some days later a letter from the old physician suggested his younger colleague call and discuss his son's case.

'You may recall, Doctor, on my first visit I suggested there were more serious symptoms evident during my examination.'

Harry Wakefield, who had heard the ominous crepitations during his own examination, nodded. 'Yes Doctor, I do. Do you agree, only the right lung is involved at this stage?'

'Indeed, however as you well know, tuberculosis, even at this early stage is serious, very serious.'

'I am anxious for your opinion, Doctor.'

'Dr. Wakefield, I have practiced medicine for almost fifty years. I have been through epidemics, I have seen many good men come and go.' He paused, seeming to examine his cigar. 'If I have learned one thing and only one thing, one should not always blindly accept the teaching of orthodox medicine.' He held up his hand. 'I do not for a moment suggest all procedures and practices are wrong, far from it. However, there comes a time when we think for ourselves.'

'I am not sure I follow, Doctor.'

'Let me explain. You know the honoured treatment for your sons condition. Mountain sanatoriums, absolute rest. Dr. Wakefield I have seen more patients die in such places than I care to remember.'

'Then what do you suggest, Sir?'

'A warm climate, a nutritious diet and pleasant surrounding.'

'A warm climate, Doctor? But surely -?'

'I know Doctor, I know. But that is my advice, you may take it or reject it.'

'But, how on earth - surely he is too weak to travel - do you mean to say-? What should I do?'

The old man rose from his chair, flicking ash from his beard. 'I have anticipated you, Doctor. I have a friend, a Director of a coastal shipping line. Do you know the east coast of Australia?'

'I am afraid not, Sir. Some years ago I travelled north to Sydney Town, a rackety place.'

'Indeed. When your son is well enough to travel, I believe I could arrange passage for him and his wife to Brisbane. You understand the further one travels the warmer the temperature. Think it over Doctor and let me know.'

Harry Wakefield, for the first time in his life, was utterly bewildered. At the door, the old man shook hands warmly. 'I do not think it necessary for me to call again, Doctor. Please let me know your decision. You know where to find me.'

That night Harry called his wife and daughter in law to the library. An unlit cigar in his hand, he waved them to the couch by the fire. 'Please ladies, sit down. There is much to talk about.' They sat silent, apprehensive. With tongs, he lifted a glowing coal from the fire and applied it to the tip of his cigar. 'Now,' he hesitated, 'I appreciate this has been a difficult time for you, for all of us, but there is a complication I have not yet told you. You see, during our examination we found signs of Tuberculosis in Harry's right lung.' Before they could speak, he held up his hand. 'Please, do not be distressed. He is responding well. In a few days we will have him walking around again. Thanks to the excellent care of Dr. McKenzie's nurse.'

'Does he know?' whispered Rose, her fingers clutching at the neck of her blouse.

'No, I have not told him yet.'

'But it is like a death sentence isn't it, Dr. Wakefield?'

He looked at her through a haze of cigar smoke. 'Rose my dear, I will tell Harry when I think it is appropriate. But it is not, as you think, a death sentence. Harry is young. Dr. McKenzie regards the prognosis as hopeful.'

His wife spoke quietly. 'What did Dr. McKenzie say that troubled you, Harry?'

'Troubled me my dear? Hardly that, he merely suggested a treatment somewhat different to time honoured procedures. He does not agree with mountain sanatoriums and I respect his judgement.'

'Harry, what can he mean? That is where they sent my uncle, remember?'

'Yes my dear, I do remember. And you will remember also, he died there. Dr. McKenzie recommends, and perhaps he is right, that Harry and Rose take a sea trip to a warmer climate.'

Rose, trying valiantly to control her emotions, hardly recognised her own voice. 'When will we leave? I feel so-'

Madelaine stood up. 'I will ring for some tea.'

'Thank you my dear, an excellent idea.' he turned to Rose. 'You are a brave girl. I will write to Dr. McKenzie when I judge Harry well enough to travel. I should think within the next three or four weeks.'

Her voice trembled. 'Will Harry recover completely, Dr. Wakefield?'

'I would be less than honest Rose, if I said, yes. I don't know, I simply don't know.'

'But sometimes,' she twisted her handkerchief around her fingers, 'they do, don't they?'

'Indeed they do. Often there is complete regression.'

'Could that happen to Harry?'

'Of course it could my dear. That is what we will pray for.'

In the silence that followed, he turned over in his mind how to break the sad news that he had so far kept to himself. 'Rose, you remember your friend, Dan McSweeney? You gave me directions to their house.'

'Yes.'

He paced the library for a few moments. The women watched, wondering. 'I am sorry to tell you, I could do nothing for him. I, nor any doctors, could have saved your friend. He died of pneumonia, although I discovered he also had advanced tuberculosis. Terrible though my words may sound, death was a friend in his case.'

Madelaine looking with concern at her husband, became aware of how tired he appeared.

'I did everything I could my dear. Arranged his burial, pressed some money on his wife.' He laughed. 'She was proud even then. I insisted she take it, they were on the point of starvation. That poor young woman had left her husband and children and tramped the streets of Melbourne begging for work. Mending torn sheets and pillow slips at hotels for the paltry sum of one shilling and sixpence for a days work. This,' he added bitterly 'in a land of plenty.'

His wife went to his side. 'My poor Harry, you have done so much. Rose and I will go tomorrow and do what we can to help them.'

'Thank you both, but please do not fret for me. Being a physician I just feel frustrated, I can do so little for my patients. If only we knew more. Yes, if only we did. Some day I am sure we will. Madelaine my dear, you probably don't know, but my mother had several properties in Prahan. One is an empty shop with rooms at the back. They are already there - at least warm and dry.'

'Harry you are wonderful.'

He nodded smiling. 'I have advanced Mrs. McSweeney one hundred pounds to stock the shop. She is inexperienced of course but I am sure with a little help, she will survive. You will find the children attractive. The older boy, Sean, is about five, I would guess. The other boy Dan, about three and the infant, a girl Ellen, just three months.'

'And Mrs. McSweeney, Harry, what of her?'

'Apparently, from what I could decently gather, her husband came from an old family, well connected. They disowned him when he married her.'

'But why Harry, why?'

'He was Irish Catholic, she Protestant. The old, sad story - unforgivable in the eyes of his family.'

'Would no one help them?'

'Obviously not, but please understand, I know little other than I have already told you.'

Placing his arms around the women's shoulders he led them to the door. 'Now my ladies, we have much to do. I have received a note from Dr. Clark, my waiting room is filled with patients every day. He is doing his best but begs me to return. His own practice is suffering.'

July came in blustery, cold and sunny. All June an incessant light rain had fallen. The immigrant trees had lost their leaves, their bare skeletal arms dark against the blue sky. Only grey green eucalypts relieved the monotony of this southern winter.

In the library at *Monterey*, father and son sat deep in conversation. Coffee had been bought, a fire glowed warming the large wood panelled room. 'More coffee, Harry?'

His son nodded. 'Thanks Dad. You know, I simply can't believe it, a baby! I thought surely Rose was mistaken.'

'No fear of that, old man. Dr. Clark has confirmed it. Matter of fact, I suspected, myself, these last weeks.'

'Good God, I'll be a father!'

'Is that so serious?'

'No, of course not. Just a bit overwhelming.'

'Well it seems to have acted as a tonic, you have made great progress.'

'Actually, I'm beginning to feel like a damn prisoner, cooped up in the house like this.'

'In that case you will be glad to know I heard from Dr. McKenzie this morning.' He handed Harry the letter.

'Next Tuesday - what a relief! What sort of boat is it?

'Quite comfortable I understand. These small coastal steamers have provision for a few passengers. I notice you have a deck cabin,'

'Will Rose be well enough to travel?'

'Your wife is a very healthy girl, Harry. I am sure she will bloom throughout this pregnancy.'

'What about me? Pity she didn't know I was such a wreck before she married me.'

'Never think like that. I know Rose has never regretted it.'

'Be honest with me, Dad. What are my prospects?'

His father answered gently. 'Let us cross each bridge as we come to it, old man. I won't pretend your troubles are over, but so far luck has been with you.'

'Not like poor Dan McSweeney. I feel sick at heart.'

'There are many like your friend, Harry.'

'Thank you for all you have done.'

'The best I could do under the circumstances. I did what any Christian would have done. In any case, your mother has taken them under her wing.'

They both smiled. 'Yes, Mother will be in her element.' Harry coughed a hard dry cough. 'I still have this bloody cough.'

From a desk drawer his father took a small blue bottle. 'This is morphine, old man. Before you leave I will give Rose a supply, with some other medicines, to take with you and instruct her in its use. But remember - to be used judiciously, only when you absolutely need it - should you experience chest pain.'

'Why haven't I had it before?'

'You have, only you didn't know at the time. It is not a cure. Morphine is just a crutch. Remember, I said use it judiciously.'

His son nodded. 'Now tell me all the news, Dad. I feel like Rip Van Winkle, the women tell me nothing.'

'Well, drink your coffee, it will buck you up, keep you awake.'

'Thanks, first decent coffee I've had since Lord knows when.'

His father smiled. 'Now let me see what news there is. Tell me, do you recall Mr. Scully and Mrs. DeVries at the reception?'

'Yes, they seemed to get on together.'

'They did indeed. They were married last week.'

'I'll be damned! He is years older than her, isn't he?'

'True, but I could not think of a better match. Mrs. DeVries, I should say Mrs. Scully, is expecting.'

'Expecting? Good God, really Dad, old James, as I have often heard you refer to him, obviously doesn't waste time!'

'It happens. Nature often doesn't wait on social niceties.'

'Well I'll be - really, I am happy for them. Please give them our best wishes when you see them next.'

'Glad to. Now I suggest you rest. There is much to do between now and Tuesday.'

His son nodded. 'Yes, I am beginning to feel excited at the prospect. Perhaps it is a good time to get out of Melbourne. Are things as bad as the papers say?'

'Bad all right. The country has never experienced a depression like this. Wool and wheat are unsaleable, investors will simply not risk their money here.'

'What is going to happen?'

'I don't know. Good men are unemployed, people are literally starving. Even people known to us who trusted their wealth to unscrupulous investors, have been ruined.'

'Good God! What of Rose's parents?'

'No worry there, your father-in-law is a hard-headed man.'

'Dad, it seems an odd thing to ask at this time-do you think we will ever be anything but a colony-become an independent Nation, I mean?'

'I am afraid that is a question I can't answer. Why do you ask?'

'Some of the fellows I know feel very strongly on the subject.'

'Perhaps, but that will be for you, your friends and your children to decide, not for my generation. Drink and gambling appear to be the great opiate of the ordinary people. I fail to see greatness built on such foundations.'

'You paint a dismal picture.'

His father sighed. 'Perhaps I do, but I see so many intelligent men leave here for more 'civilised' societies and those who stay-well, what can I say-settle into comfortable nothingness. Harry, don't strive to change the unchangeable. The local squattocracy regard themselves as a mere extension of English society. Take my advice my son, leave such matters to future generations.'

Later that night, Dr. Wakefield stood before his wardrobe pulling on his nightshirt. His wife sat in their huge canopied bed brushing her lustrous brown hair. Her husband regarded her with affection. 'Madelaine Wakefield you are a beautiful woman.'

'Monsieur Le Docteur, vous etes tres galant!'

He kissed her fondly.

'Tell me, Sir,' she murmured, her fingers rumpling his hair, 'did you talk with Harry today?'

He pressed her fingers to his lips. 'My love, what can I say? Rose's condition is obvious.' He looked smiling into his wife's dark eyes. 'There is much to be said for a covered wagon on a rainy night.'

She giggled, snuggling up to him. 'I am so happy, so very happy.'

CHAPTER IV

'Look here, can't we get aboard this tug? There are friends of ours aboard. We don't intend to waste this champagne!' A group of friends, a little worse for too much of the grape, tried vainly to press up the gangplank. A burly good humoured mate blocked their way.

'Sorry gentlemen, the plank's about to come alongside. We sail in ten minutes. May I take a message to your friends?'

'Message be damned! We want to see them. Hey,' one bellowed, 'Harry, Rose, where are you hiding? We can't get on board.'

At that moment Harry, swathed in greatcoat and muffler, with Rose by his side, emerged from a cabin on the upper deck. A minor pandemonium of shouting and ribald humour broke out.

'We are just leaving.' Harry croaked. 'Where the heck have you been?' He grinned broadly. 'I can see what held you up.' His voice broke, he coughed into his handkerchief.

'Well, bon voyage!' They shouted. 'Come back fit. Look after him Rosie, he is precious cargo.'

'Beg pardon, Sir. 'The mate approached. 'We are casting off, planks coming up now.'

The little steamer, engines throbbing, moved away from the wharf, the one tug gently easing her into the main channel.

'Goodbye Harry, goodbye Rosie.' The little group shouted again. 'Come back soon. Good luck. God speed!'

Hand in hand they stood by the rail, mistily waving until the people on the pier became mere dots, finally disappearing from view. As they moved towards their cabin, a white coated steward appeared. 'Beg pardon Sir, Captain's compliments, would Mr. and Mrs. Wakefield take dinner with him tonight?'

'Please thank the Captain, we would be happy to. By the way Steward, what is our first port of call?'

'Sydney town Sir, be there tomorrow. Johnson's the name, Sir. You and your wife are our only passengers this trip.'

'I see. Well, thank you Johnson. Incidentally, how long does the trip take - to Brisbane, I mean?'

'No set time Sir. Depends on how long it takes to pick up and unload.' His sea reddened face broke into a grin. 'Mark my words Sir, you'll start to feel it warm up a day or two out of Sydney.'

'Thank goodness for that.' Rose took her husband's arm. 'I think it's time we went inside Harry.'

They sat at the Captain's table in the dining room, the talk was comfortable. 'I understand you are an artist, Mr. Wakefield?'

'I try, Captain.'

Captain McIntyre, a weathered Scot, smiled across the table.

'Ach, I envy you. To have such talent is a great gift.' He well knew the purpose of his passengers voyage but studiously avoided the subject. 'Aye Mr. Wakefield, you will find the scenery up north pleasing to the eye, indeed.'

'Do you make the trip often Captain?'

'Only when the Cedar is available, Ma'am, but our main charge is provisions for the towns. My home base is Sydney Town, always glad to be back with my wife and daughters.' He went on, 'We should be two days in Sydney. Take the steam ferry to Manly Cove, lovely spot. You would appreciate it, Mr. Wakefield.'

They awoke next morning to a new sensation. The steamer no longer rocked and pitched. The engine still throbbed reassuringly but the boat glided with barely a shudder. Harry peered through the porthole. 'Rosie, quick. Look at this, we must be in Sydney. Will you look at that shoreline, those cliffs and the water - that blue! Glorious, isn't it?'

The two day stopover passed in bubbling excitement as they explored the brash, thrusting town. They explored streets that wound around the waters edge. Golden wattle, red Poinsettias blazed extravagantly over garden walls. Winter days can be very changeable around Sydney, the steward had warned them, and it would be best to be back on board before sunset. The steward, a wiser head than they suspected, had heard Harry's hard, dry cough.

The too short stay over, the little vessel made her way out of the harbour, her nose rising gently as she cleared the Heads, turning north.

Coaling at Newcastle occupied the whole of the following day. 'Rather we didn't go ashore Rosie, I feel bone weary.'

She looked into her husband's gaunt face. 'Yes Darling, let us just sit in these deckchairs. Johnson said this is the best place, away from that awful black dust.' They sat high on the top deck, pleasantly relaxed. She signed. 'It's so warm here and so lovely I hope it stays like this.'

'Of course it will Rosie, you can't destroy beauty.'

At dinner Harry broached the subject of the ship's progress. 'To tell the truth Captain, I wouldn't mind a few days on terra firma.'

'Aye, I quite understand, Mr. Wakefield. She does not sail like an ocean liner. We could put you off at our next port of call, Coff's Harbour, or if you could bear a little longer, at Myuna, right at the mouth of the Millewa. A magnificent river, we take on cedar there.'

'Thank you Captain, that sounds very attractive.'

On the third day the *S.S. Camira* nosed across the tricky bar of the big river and tied up at the busy wharf. 'Rosie, I must rest. I simply cannot stay another day on the boat. I wonder if Captain McIntyre can help us find a place to rest up a while.'

They stood arm in arm on the deck. From across the river a warm breeze wafted a sweet mysterious perfume. Rose whispered. 'It's the seventh of August, we have been married exactly four months.'

His arm encircled her. 'Good Lord Rosie, we are an old married couple!'

Their laughter caught the attention of Captain McIntyre. 'Well Mr. Wakefield, you seem to be feeling better today.'

'It's the prospect of getting our feet on dry land, Captain. Is there an hotel here, some place respectable?'

The Captain stroked his stiff white goatee. 'Well now, the wife of an old friend of mine, now sadly gone, keeps what you might call a boarding house. Mrs. Cochran, a fine woman. I would be glad to recommend you.'

That evening, as the sun set over the vast expanse of ocean, a wagon piled high with their luggage pulled up at gate of a large timber house, standing high on sturdy poles. A double flight of steps, one each side, led up to a wide landing. The brawny driver carried up their bags. Harry was breathing painfully when they reached the front door. 'Phew! Why do they build houses so high?'

'Floods, Mister. Couple of weeks good rain and the river runs a banker. 'Specially close to the water like this.'

'It's so beautiful, just like a picture. People must love to live here.'

'Sometimes, Missus.' The driver smiled grimly. 'Sometimes they don't.'

A woman's voice from the rear of the house answered their knock. 'Hold yer horses, won't be a minute.'

The door stood open, a wide timbered hallway appeared to run the full length of the house. A slight breeze carried the delicious smell of freshly baked bread.

Mrs. Cochran, a plump middle aged woman emerged from the far end of the hall. She smiled a welcome, smoothing her snowy apron. 'Good afternoon, you must be Mr. and Mrs. Wakefield, Captain McIntyre sent a message. Please come in. I have just taken the bread from the oven.'

'Thank you for taking us in, Mrs. Cochran. We are both a little tired of sea travel. I hope we are not inconveniencing you.'

'Mrs. Wakefield you are very welcome. I don't have a soul at the moment, just the men who come in for dinner. Come, I'll show you your room then I'm sure you could use a cup of tea.'

Their large airy room, lined from floor to ceiling with dark sawn timber with the floor scrubbed to an off white, was relieved only by a sheepskin rug beside a vast double bed. A wardrobe, a chest of drawers with an oval mirror and a well worn leather chair with a few strands of horse hair protruding from the arms, completed the furnishings.

The sweet smell of cedar wood pervaded the room. Mrs. Cochran pulled back the drapes from the window. 'From here you can look straight out onto the river. It's lovely first thing in the morning.' She stood smiling. 'If it's satisfactory would fifteen shillings a week suit?'

Harry smiled. 'Of course Mrs. Cochran, very suitable indeed.'

'Then, when you are ready come to the kitchen, the kettle is always on the hob.'

Harry sank into the chair, his long legs outstretched. 'Rosie,' he signed pleasurably, 'I think I am going to like it here.'

Meals were served in the kitchen on a massive wooden table, it's surface graced for the occasion with a simple cloth. Five young men, including the wagon driver, sat shyly intent on their dinner plates, seldom lifting their eyes except to steal the odd glance at the newcomers.

Mrs. Cochran sat at the head of the table. 'Gentlemen, this is Mr. and Mrs. Wakefield. They will be with us for a few days. I hope you will make them welcome.' There were murmured acknowledgments, then even more intense concentration on their meal. They seemed to finish as one and with hasty excuses retired to the large sitting room where by the light of kerosene lamps they played cards or read, ostensibly interested in whatever they were doing.

Harry smiled at his landlady. 'Everyone is very quiet Mrs. Cochran, I do hope we have not disturbed them.'

'You must excuse the lads, Mr. Wakefield, they work so hard and they seldom see new faces, at least not here.'

'Perfectly all right Mrs. Cochran, they seem very decent young fellows. May I say dinner was delicious? I have never tasted such fish!'

'Schnapper, Mr Wakefield. Fresh from the sea.'

'That rhubarb tart, so delicious!'

The lady of the house smiled. 'I can see you are eating for two Mrs. Wakefield. I do hope you stay a while.'

'Thank you, I hope we will. Now, if you think we are not intruding, we will join the others.'

The sitting room, lined with aromatic cedar was dimly lit by a green shaded hanging lamp. Against one wall were some chairs and a leather couch, also sprouting tufts of horse hair, from where numerous elbows had rested.

Along the opposite wall stood an upright piano, it's ivory keys faded to a deep yellow. Rose tentatively struck a key, then sitting on the wooden stool ran her fingers lightly over the keyboard. Suddenly five pairs of eyes swung in her direction. She looked up at her husband. 'It is out of tune but the tone is excellent.'

'Play something Rosie.' Harry leafed through some sheet music. 'Is this all right?'

'I don't need it Harry, it's so faded I can't read it anyway. I will just try this.' She settled herself and the room suddenly filled with melody from the old instrument. She stopped and turned, smiling. 'Am I disturbing you gentlemen!'

They rose as one and gathered round the piano. 'Mrs. Wakefield, that was wonderful. Please don't stop.' Gone was the reticence-a reticence which becomes part of a man's nature when forced to live far away from the teeming cities. They gazed in rapture at the beautiful young woman, the light from the swinging lamp falling softly on her hair and arms. She smiled at them. 'Has anyone a favourite tune? If I know it I will do my best.'

Someone lighted candles in brass holders. 'Anything Mrs. Wakefield, play anything at all.'

Later in their room, Harry yawned, pulling his nightshirt over his head. 'Rosie, I feel a hundred years old. I'm sure I will sleep forever.' He sighed as he slipped between the sheets. 'Rosie, this mattress! It must be pure down. Only kings sleep like this!'

She giggled. 'Or old seafarers. Darling, if it's all going to be like this, let's stay here forever.'

A hard dry cough woke Harry in the early hours. Careful not to disturb his sleeping wife, he felt for his slippers then tip toed quietly to the window. Before his gaze lay the full sweep of the mighty river. It's surface unflurried, glasslike, serene. Over the wooded banks of the far side, the first rays of the sun caught the folded topsails of a four master lying at anchor. Reluctantly he turned, Rose was lying on her side, her eyes wide open smiling at him. He sat down taking her hand. 'Tell me,' he grinned, 'how is the little mother to be this morning?'

'Hungry, Sir.' She smiled, glancing down at her swelling abdomen. 'We both are.'

He stood up and walked back to the window. 'Rosie, could we live here for a while, I mean, would you mind?'

'Mind? How could you think such a thing? Wherever you are happy, I will always be content. Let us have breakfast and go exploring!'

Mrs. Cochran counselled them. 'Be sure to keep an eye open for snakes. There are some lovely spots along the river. Just come back when you feel hungry.'

'Thank you Mrs. Cochran. I expect we are not likely to see anyone are we?'

'Not likely, Mr. Wakefield. The town is half a mile back.' She thought for a moment. 'Father Trendel, the Anglican priest, comes this way sometimes. He would be the only one.' She turned to Rose. 'Thank you for playing last night. Such music is so rare here. I haven't heard the piano played like that since the Captain's wife-' she hesitated. 'It was simply wonderful.' She turned suddenly. 'Please excuse me, I must get the bread in the oven.'

Rose's curiosity was piqued, she whispered to her husband. 'The Captain's wife, who is this mysterious lady? Mrs. Cochran seemed unwilling to say more.'

Harry squeezed her arm. 'No doubt we will find out in the fullness of time. Come on now, mind the step.'

The rutted track in front of the house swept left into a long curve obscuring the distant town, to the right it followed the river disappearing from view amongst majestic trees. In a cleared spot by the river's edge, they found a log half buried in the sand. Harry took his wife's hand. 'Rosie, such colour, such light! I could dream of painting here.'

'Then you must, Darling.'

With a piece of stick he lazily wrote their names in the sand. 'Rosie, what I said this morning - remember, about staying a while? I don't know why but I feel happy here but I worry for you.'

'I am happy, you goose!' She slipped her arm through his. 'Very, very happy, so you have nothing to worry about.'

He kissed her. 'What a warm hearted, loving creature you are.'

Happily they took to the track again stopping suddenly at the echo of horse's hooves moving at a sharp trot. Heralded by a cloud of dust, a black hooded sulky drew up beside them. The driver let the reins fall slack. 'Good morning-whoa there Betsy, take a breather.' The old mare, obviously used to waiting for her master, began cropping short grass by the trackside. A tall thin man, dressed in sober grey, sat looking down at them, his clerical collar shining white against the black of his stock. Perched on his head was a battered Panama hat, his only concession to the sub tropical climate. A smile creased his deeply tanned, lined face. 'You must be Mr. & Mrs. Wakefield, Captain McIntyre asked me to look out for you.' He leaned forward, hand outstretched. 'Father Trendel or Padre, if you prefer, Anglican priest to the district.' He shook hands firmly. 'Padre is not strictly correct you know, but the title has stuck so I see no reason to disturb a comfortable relationship between a priest and his flock.' The old horse moved suddenly seeking more succulent shoots. 'Whoa there Betsy, hold still. Now may I ask where you are heading? Rather a rough track for walking and not without it's hazards-snakes, you know.'

'Really just exploring Father. We only arrived yesterday, such a relief to stand on terra firma again and in such a beautiful place.'

'Indeed. Even more so further on, dear lady.' Again he checked his horse. 'Look, why not come with me? I am on my way to see a sick parishioner, about two miles along the river. I promise you will not be disappointed.'

'Thank you Padre, that is kind of you.' Harry helped his wife onto the sulky's step and climbed in after her. A slight slap of the reins and the mare broke into a comfortable trot.'

'So you are staying with Mrs. Cochran? A generous-hearted lady. I knew her husband well. Tragic business. No doubt you have met some of the young men who take their dinner there.'

'Oh yes.' Harry smiled. 'They were a little shy at first, as were we, until Rose sat down at the piano.'

Father Trendel chuckled. 'I'll warrant that broke the ice! Music is a real treat up here.'

'I only hope they did not notice the many off notes I struck.'

'My dear young lady, I am sure heavenly harps would not have sounded more delightful.'

Weaving in and out amongst the trees, glimpses of the great river came into view through little clearings where simple wharves had been constructed. At times they passed small shacks with smoke curling from corrugated iron chimneys. Occasionally a woman or a small child waved a greeting. The priest would wave with his whip. 'These people are the pioneers of this country. People of iron will and great courage. It is a hard life, especially for the women. I try to keep in touch with those of our faith, but you know, we are all Christians. In times of trouble we forget our differences. After all we all serve the one Christ.'

'It does seem a hard life Padre. Why do they come here?'

'Why, Mr. Wakefield? Well you might call them refugees from the grime and poverty of the cities. Most of the men work, you know, the depression may be crippling in other places but here in Myuna there is still work for those who seek it.'

At this point the track forked, the priest gently guided his horse to the right following through the thinning trees into a large cleared area. At the far boundary, a small white cottage stood high on stout poles, surrounded by a picket fence. A woman shielded by a white sun bonnet, bent hoeing weeds between rows of young cane.

The priest touched his hat as she looked up. 'The Dennis family, fine people, came here from Sydney three years ago. Mrs. Dennis taught music, Fred, a carpenter, lost his job because of the depression. The upshot was, they left the city and with a little money from his wife's mother's estate, settled here.'

'Have they ever regretted their decision?'

'Not for a moment. Their dream was always to live on the land. Alas, many others have had the same dream, sadly some with disastrous results.'

'Have they children, Reverend Trendel?'

'One child, Mrs. Wakefield. Alice, just turned fifteen, on the brink of womanhood. They have put everything they had into this land. They brought their treasures with them, I refer to their furniture and Kathy's piano.'

'It seems a precarious situation Padre. How will they manage?'

'They will Mr. Wakefield, with the help of the good Lord and the generosity of our parishioners.' He smiled. 'My basket is never empty.'

The woman pushed back her bonnet, smiling a welcome.

'Mrs. Dennis, how are you today? I see the cane is coming along nicely, nicely indeed.' He introduced Harry and Rose. 'Visitors to our part of the world, Mrs. Dennis, all the way from Melbourne.'

Mrs. Dennis, a not yet middle aged woman, smiled. 'I do hope you have time for some tea. Fred, my husband, will be so glad to see you.'

'Thank you Mrs. Dennis.'

On the verandah, a solid bearded man lay on a wicker sofa, his left leg heavily bandaged. He extended his hand. 'Ah Padre, I see you have brought visitors with you.'

'Mr. and Mrs. Wakefield, Fred.'

'How do you do? You are welcome indeed, we see so few people nowadays.' He pointed to his leg. 'Afraid I am temporarily beached, as they say.' He motioned to a homemade bench seat. 'Please sit down. I think I can hear my wife preparing tea.'

Mrs. Dennis appeared with a laden tray, followed by their daughter. Harry thought, looking at the girl - pretty as a picture postcard.

Alice wore her honey blonde hair in plaits, her blue eyes were shining with excitement at having visitors. Rose held out her hand, the girl came shyly to sit beside her, gazing in awe at such fashionable clothes.

Harry felt at ease with these natural people. 'I understand you are a carpenter, Mr. Dennis. '

'A good one too, if I say so myself, Mr. Wakefield. With luck and the good Padre's help, I will be working again soon. Yes, before this bit of trouble I had more work than I could handle.'

'I sincerely hope you will be on your feet again soon.'

'Thank you Sir. Frankly, I need to be.'

The Rev. Trendel drained his cup. 'Time for me to dress that leg Fred. I am sure your wife would like to show our guests over the property.'

When the time came to go, mother and daughter stood waving until the sulky was lost to sight amongst the trees.

'A sad business, Padre.'

'Indeed Mr. Wakefield. They still have their sulky but the horse had to be sold, as was Alice's pony.'

'What a shame!'

'Yes Mrs. Wakefield, to be ill and without funds can be disastrous.'

'But how do they live?'

'Christian charity Mrs. Wakefield. Sadly I can do little on my small stipend but our good parishioners make sure my basket is never empty.' He gave a gentle slap of the reins and the sulky gathered speed.

'How soon will Fred be able to work again, Padre?'

'Within two weeks I hope. Fortunately they owe no money.'

Rose sighed. 'Alice is a lovely girl, Rev. Trendel. She played for us, she is quite talented.'

'She is, Mrs. Wakefield. My wife and I are very fond of Alice.'

Harry touched the priest's arm. 'Padre, my wife and I feel we would like to stay a while - the place appeals. I would like to do some painting. I have never seen such clarity of air.'

'Understandable Mr. Wakefield. You would stay with Mrs. Cochran no doubt.'

'We had in mind a house of our own - perhaps you could help us?'

'Ah yes, naturally. That may prove difficult, housing in this town is a premium.'

'I see, have you any suggestions?'

For a moment the priest was silent. 'Perhaps we can discuss your problem further tomorrow Mr. Wakefield. I trust you will both be free?'

That night they lay in contentment discussing the day's events.

'Rosie, do you mind going with the old boy tomorrow? Should be interesting.'

'I like him. He is gentle and kind. I enjoy his company. But Harry are we being realistic? I mean the thought of living here - what would our parents and friends think? And, Darling, what of your health?'

'Believe me Rosie, I have a far better chance of surviving here than I ever would back there. Anyway, we're grown up people, time we made our own decisions.'

She pushed back the covers, went to the window and gazed out on the tranquil river-she murmured. 'So peaceful, I could live here for ever. But, Harry, what would we do when the baby comes, is there a doctor here?'

He sat up suddenly. 'God, Rosie, how stupid of me! When you were with Mrs. Dennis and Alice, Rev. Trendel told me there is a young American doctor here, came into the port on a world cruise. Sick at the time apparently, came ashore, fell in love with the place and set up practice. About three years ago.'

'That's wonderful! What's his name?'

'Dr. Coburn, Tom Coburn.'

'I wonder if he is competent.'

'Apparently the town's people swear by him.' He stretched out his arm. 'Come back to bed Rosie, and stop worrying.'

The Rev Trendel arrived promptly at nine the following morning. Not in a sulky but an elegant four wheeler with a glossy black hood. In the shafts a powerful gelding tossed at the bit, impatient to be on the way.

'Trust we haven't kept you waiting, Padre?'

'Not a bit of it, Mr. Wakefield. Ah, there you are Mrs. Cochran, thank you for the flowers on Sunday, the church looked splendid.'

Mrs. Cochran handed Rose a cloth covered basket. 'I know the Reverend, Mrs. Wakefield, he can go without food all day but others can't.'

Harry cast his eye over the horse. 'Resting Betsy today, Padre?'

'In a way yes, Mr. Wakefield. The rig is courtesy of one of my good friends, Ned Lightfoot, who keeps stables. Always generous when I am in need of transport.'

The big horse pulled willingly. The town left behind, they entered a steep incline, the road following the contours of the hills. The horse slowed to a walk, Harry looked back over the vast country. The mouth of the great river was clearly visible where it entered the sea.

'Magnificent country, Padre.'

'Indeed, Mr. Wakefield. When my wife and I first landed here, we were overwhelmed. Coming fresh from England with it's tiny ordered fields and hedges, well, we felt lost. So much space. Then to find our Parish almost as large as the land we left behind! Frankly, I feel unequal to the task, but after the initial shock, we settled in. For which I owe so much to my dear courageous wife.'

'So, no regrets Padre?'

'No Mr. Wakefield, I have learned to love this wild land. I hope to finish my days here.' He let the reins fall slack as the horse strained in the shafts. 'Yes, sometimes I think of England, but not always with affection.'

Around a bend, a creek bubbled across the road, crystal clear water flowing in swirls and eddies before falling in spray over the steeper side. On either bank there were the beginnings of brickwork where a bridge had been planned. The horse stopped, burying his nose in the cool stream.

'Padre, this must be one of your more difficult journeys. Do you have many parishioners this far from town?'

'Just one, Mr. Wakefield, just one and he is not a Christian. At least not in our terms, but if a pure and loving heart counts for anything, he is an example for us all.' He gently slapped the reins. 'All right Prince, you have had enough.'

The horse snorted briefly as the buggy forded the creek. The road turned briefly through a cutting then flattened out onto a plateau, running straight and wide through a canopy of rain forest. The horse, finding his wind, broke into a slow trot.

Harry looked back at the great plain running to the sea. 'Seems like the top of the world, Padre.'

'It does indeed, Mr. Wakefield.' The priest smiled at the young man. 'And this is our journey's end. This is *Monaro*.' He pointed with his whip to where two massive wrought iron gates barred their way. He handed Harry the reins. 'Would you please bring it through when I open the gates?'

Inside on the overgrown gravelled drive, the horse, as if from memory, pulled up in the shade of a spreading wild fig tree. The young couple stared in amazement at the sight before their eyes. On the verandah of a small stone cottage, a huge South Sea Islander, his white hair glistening wet, sat in a wooden tub, his legs draped over one side, pouring water over his body with a metal pitcher. Seeing the visitors, he stepped out, without the slightest embarrassment. wrapping a length of cloth about his loins. His hand extended, he approached the minister, his face creased in a dazzling smile.

'Rev. Trendel, Sir. Every day I look out for you. So long since you came.'

The priest wrung the proffered hand. 'Forgive me Abraham, time slips away so quickly. Has all been well?'

The old man nodded.

'I am glad, Abraham. Now please come and meet two young friends of mine, Mr. and Mrs. Wakefield.'

With a gentle smile, Abraham extended a long, muscled arm, speaking slowly with a quiet dignity. 'You are welcome. Rev. Trendel's friends are my friends.'

The priest took him aside. 'Abraham, please unharness Prince for me, tether him in the shade and give him a drink. I am going to take my young friends to see the house.'

Taking Mrs. Cochran's basket from the rear of the buggy, he picked up a large stock, advising Harry to do the same. 'Snakes, Mr. Wakefield, one can't be too careful.'

The carriageway curved gracefully through an avenue of trees, grass and weeds, evidence of long neglect thrust through the gravel. Stands of Bangalow palms and strange trees and shrubs they had never seen before, lined the borders. Overhead, brilliant, chattering parrots hung like jewels from exotic flowers. Clouds of little yellow butterflies rose in profusion as overhanging bushes were brushed aside. Occasionally wallabies stood staring with curious eyes, pausing for a moment before bounding away. The minister waved his stick at them. 'Lovely creatures. The place is infested with them, becoming a pest to the farmers sadly.'

Harry paused, breathless, his coat over his arm. 'Padre, this place is magical. Such peace, a feeling about it I can't express.'

'I think I understand. But come, there is so much more to see.'

They had come to where the drive was overhung with Tulip trees, trailing boughs of scarlet blossoms. Pushing further through the shrubbery, the house appeared, suddenly, dramatically. Gleaming white with long verandahs railed with lacy iron work from which hung bougainvillea in tangled profusion. To the right rose a round tower, white as the house with one wide curved window looking out to the sea far below. Glazed, blue roof tiles gleamed in the noonday sunlight.

The priest smiled at Harry's surprised gasp. 'Yes Mr. Wakefield, it does strike one rather forcibly the first time. But come, follow me.'

From the carriageway, continuing in a wide sweep to the rear of the building, a brick pathway led through a low stone wall, enclosing an area which had once been tended lawn, now waist high with weeds. Red and pink azaleas bordered the edges, making a carpet of petals beneath their feet. All around the warm air hung with the perfume of flowers. Rose held tight to her husband's hand. 'It's an enchanting place,' she whispered, 'just sleeping, waiting for someone to come.'

He grinned, squeezing her hand. 'Perhaps it's waiting for us, Rosie!'

Across the tiled lower verandah, a heavy oak door was set deep within a vestibule. Rev. Trendel inserted a long iron key into the lock which turned reluctantly. The door swung open, creaking on massive hinges.

'Appears it hasn't been opened for a long time, Padre.'

'I am afraid the whole house is sorely in need of maintenance. Fred Dennis usually attends to these matters for me. I am most anxious for him to begin work again.'

Inside, the young couple stood silently gazing in amazement. A spacious room stretched before them. Cool after the outside warmth, vaguely dim with long narrow windows hung with heavy drapes. Dotted around the polished oak floor were odd shapes of furniture hidden beneath linen covers. A wide curved staircase rose gracefully to the floor above.

The Rev. Trendel pointed. 'That staircase, Mr. Wakefield, was cut from one giant cedar tree. Cedar is the area's biggest export, one of God's gifts to mankind but I fear, being over harvested. Once gone, it can never be replaced.'

He released a latch, opening one of the windows. A breeze stirred the drapes, wafting in the delicate scent of the bush. Harry coughed into his handkerchief. Concerned, the priest touched his arm. 'Mr. Wakefield, I think we could do with a spell. Mrs. Cochran's basket always contains delectable morsels, let us go to the kitchen. I keep a small spirit stove there. We can explore further after lunch.'

At the rear of the house, a door opened into a large flagstone kitchen, well lighted from windows high in the walls, unfurnished, except for an oblong pinewood table, it's surface well scrubbed, with several high back chairs standing neatly arranged as if ready for the next day's baking and preparation. Recessed into one wall was a cooking range flanked by long wooden cupboards.

Rose stood incredulous. 'Rev. Trendel, one would think this was the kitchen of a large hotel.'

'My dear lady, at times it almost appeared to be. Now, please be seated. Mrs. Wakefield, kindly unpack the basket. I will have the tea ready by the time you do.'

They ate in silence, not a sound intruded from outside. Rose shivered a little. 'Rev. Trendel, forgive me if I seem foolish -I feel as if we are intruding, trespassing almost.'

The priest smiled reassuringly over his steaming cup. 'Don't be distressed Mrs. Wakefield, although this house has had a tragic history. Any spirits here would manifest only love and devotion.'

'I am sure you are right. I feel rather foolish now, I think I was a little over tired.'

The kindly man grew a little solemn. 'Yes, this house has a sad history and now because of a promise I made at a time of deep distress, is somewhat of a burden to me. If you wish, and only if you do, I will be glad to tell you all I know of this house and the people who once lived here.'

'Padre, with all my heart, and I am sure I speak for Rose, we would dearly like to know.'

'So be it Mr. Wakefield. Now where to begin. I think first I should tell you something of my own background. I was not a young man when I first came to Australia. My health was failing and my sermons were not acceptable to the Church. I was quietly advised to retire, I could not accept this. An old friend, My Bishop, bless his soul, suggested this far away Parish. A matter of out of sight out of mind. My wife and I never hesitated. We were starting a new life, a decision we have never regretted.'

'Forgive me Rev. Trendel - have you no children?'

'A daughter, Mrs. Wakefield, married to the Captain of one of our coastal ships.' He sighed. 'We see her but seldom, Sydney seems so far away. But we must not complain, she visits every Christmas and Easter. And we are blessed with a beautiful grand daughter. But I must not digress. Captain Slocum and his lady had arrived here some three years before I began my Ministry. They came to see me-you see, I was the only priest in the district. I remember that day so clearly. They asked me to marry them. I had never experienced a situation such as this but I accepted their word that there were no encumbrances to their marrying. I performed the ceremony without delay. You will understand Mrs. Wakefield-time was of the essence.'

'How fascinating Rev. Trendel. Did they tell you anything of their background?'

'Not at that time. It was a brief ceremony. My wife and the good Mrs. Cochran acted as witnesses. They returned to the ship and sailed in the early morning with the tide. I should mention, Abraham came with them. The first time I laid eyes on him, he was sitting impassively, like an ebony statue at the back of the room. I had noticed their ship for the first time, the previous morning. A beautifully turned out Brigantine, the *Blue Dolphin*, out of Boston.'

'But they returned, Padre?'

He nodded. 'Oh yes, three weeks to the day and with them a baby daughter.'

'Were they happy, Rev. Trendel?'

'I think as happy as two people could be.'

'Did you find out, I mean did they tell you why they came here to live?'

'Yes, an old story Mr. Wakefield. He was a young Mate when first they met. She was from an old established Boston family. Her future was planned, as is often the case in such situations. To cut the story short, she promised against all opposition, to wait for him. I know little of the unhappy details but, desperately in need of money, he turned to the slave trade, blackbirding they call it here, and soon had his own ship. He prospered but his actions haunted him for the rest of his days. You may not know but the practice of slave labour still exists in this country. Wealthy cane growers in North Queensland use these poor wretches, kidnapped from their island homes and forced to work under appalling conditions, many die of disease and loneliness. Some day this country must answer for such wickedness.'

'Padre, I did not know, I never dreamt such things could happen here.'

'Oh yes, Mr. Wakefield, and worse. They have tried to enslave the native people but you cannot enslave a proud people. Reliable travellers have told me they even shoot or poison them in some parts, resenting the Aboriginals indifference and, I believe, seeked to exterminate them. You may have noticed, there are very few in this district, they have simply vanished, leaving silently for where they can live in peace.' He sighed. 'Forgive me, I must not digress. Thank you for your patience, there are times I feel I must unburden myself.'

Rose touched his arm. 'Rev. Trendel, may I make you some more tea? I should like some and I am sure Harry would.'

'I would indeed, can you manage?'

'Of course, I was a country girl before we were married.'

The priest settled back in his chair. 'You are a fortunate young man, Mr. Wakefield. Now, let me recall - where was I? Oh yes, this house. As I have already told you, Captain Slocum and his lady had arrived some three years before my wife and I. The house was almost completed, the place a veritable hive of activity. Ships arrived with material from all over the world. During this time they lived on the ship, driving up two or three times a week to inspect progress.'

'The name puzzles me, Padre. As far as I know, *Monaro* is an area in the southern part of the country.'

'So I believe but the captain had looked at many places before settling here. I understand the word means, a high place, but like many aboriginal words is capable of other interpretations. Apparently it appealed to the captain, so *Monaro* came to be.' 'The house is quite exquisite, Padre. Obviously the architect was an imaginative man.'

'A French gentleman with a great knowledge of Colonial architecture. I am sure *Monaro* owes it's harmonious lines to him alone. The captain brought an engineer from America, a very talented man. So far from civilisation yet this house has every modern convenience.' He sipped the fresh tea, smiling his appreciation. 'Mr. Wakefield, of necessity I must leave out many details, suffice to say, the house was finished. The captain and his wife moved in and the next two years was a period the town will always remember with affection. They were popular with everyone. Mrs. Slocum was a veritable angel. There are few families here, who when in need, will every forget her kindness and help. I should tell you also, we owe the very existence of our little church to the captain's generosity.' He paused to finish his tea. 'We saw a good deal of them, my wife and I. The captain liked me to visit with them. He often asked my advice, but whether he took it or not, I am not sure.'

'Did they not have visitors, Padre?'

'They did indeed. Sometimes a ship would come in with old friends and acquaintances from another time in their lives. My wife and I were always invited. Abraham would call for us in the captain's carriage. In my mind's eye I can still see Mrs. Slocum in her white gown, holding her white parasol - such a beautiful lady. My wife kept close by her side, I think she had become a substitute mother.'

'What of the captain, Padre?'

'By nature a reserved man, Mr. Wakefield, but soon he asked me to accompany him to the tower, to his Bridge, I should say. That is where I heard their story. He trusted me I think, felt he could confide in me. It is restful up there, one can see everything below, detached yet part of it. At first I was not sure why he asked me to sit with him but under the influence of a bottle of his fine old brandy, it became apparent. A proud man, it must have been agony to unburden himself. I hope I listened with sympathy and understanding. We priests and our brethren, the physicians, bear a crushing responsibility. Entrusted with the innermost secrets of the human heart, it often seems too much to bear. It was it seems, the familiar story. Her family's rejection of him as a suitor for their daughter.' He cleared his throat. 'But I have already told you that part of the story.' He examined his watch. 'There is still plenty of time to show you the rest of the house.' He pointed. 'That green door leads to the cellar. Quite deep, it takes up half the area of the house and is literally filled with bottles of the finest wines and spirits from all over the world.'

'Good Lord, Padre. The captain was obviously a man of taste!'

'Yes Mr. Wakefield, the finest obtainable and I have the privilege of helping myself as the need arises. Fortunately my needs are modest.' He added hastily.

Harry coughed, hard, into his handkerchief.

'I fear I am tiring you, Mr. Wakefield.'

'No, no not a bit of it, just a tickle in the throat. Please go on.'

Looking a trifle concerned, the priest continued. 'On festive occasions when they entertained, the entire driveway was hung with magic lanterns. Have you seen magic lanterns, Mrs. Wakefield?'

'Never, Rev. Trendel. It must have been quite beautiful.'

'That it was. A magical scene at night. The captain told me they came from China. Beautifully painted little glass lamps, each with a candle inside.'

Rev. Trendel again consulted his watch, becoming suddenly serious, a sigh escaped him. 'Alas, that is the happier side of the story of two exceptional people whose only wish was to live their lives in peace.'

'Were they never lonely, did they not miss their homes and family?'

'No Mrs. Wakefield, this was their home. They lived for each other and their little daughter.'

'How lovely. What was the little girls name?'

'Helen, named after her mother.' He smiled slightly. 'I christened her and have the honour to be her godfather.' The priest paced the room, hands clasped behind his back. 'Please forgive me and appreciate I find difficulty in relating the end of this tragic story.'

The young couple sat in silence as he wrestled with his emotions, so quiet the sound of warbling magpies filtered through the high windows.

Gathering his composure he continued. 'First I should tell you, Mrs. Slocum's old nurse was brought out. A worthy woman, a Scots lady. She had sorely missed the lady she had cared for from infancy. She was utterly devoted to Mrs. Slocum and the baby. After the imported workers departed, the captain employed local people and they in turn were devoted to her. It was in truth a harmonious household.

Often on fine summer days the captain and his wife would go sailing on the river in their skiff, the *Gull*, with Abraham at the tiller as the Captain worked the sail. Occasionally they ventured out to the open sea but only when it was prudent to do so. One terrible day, and I will never understand the captain's one error of judgement, they were caught in a violent squall and dashed against the rocks.' He put his hand to his eyes as if trying to block out painful memories. 'They were all thrown into the water and the skiff smashed to matchwood. After a heroic struggle, Abraham dragged them to shore. It was heart rending. Mrs. Slocum, that beautiful, gentle lady was quite dead, the captain unconscious. Men came from everywhere. They placed him on a handcart and Abraham, tears streaming down his cheeks, carried Helen like a child to Dr. Coburn's house. I cannot tell you the grief that tragedy aroused. People wept openly.' The priest mopped his forehead. 'Forgive me, my dear friends, it does not do to dwell on such things.'

'How terrible Padre, the captain must have been devastated!'

'Although he was a man of great control, he became withdrawn, seldom spoke. He worried me greatly. I had no words that would comfort him. I was the only person he would tolerate. He insisted his wife be buried here at *Monaro.*' He picked up his hat. 'Come, I will show you.'

Through a back door from the kitchen, they entered a walled vegetable garden, ordered rows evident of skilful care. 'This is Abraham's domain. He still tends the garden as if nothing had changed.' He turned before unlatching a high wooden gate. 'I should tell you, the captain rescued the old man from a slaver and nursed him back to health.'

'But was he not in that same terrible trade?'

'He was, but as he confessed to me, he became sickened by the cruelty and injustice of it all. Abraham was a chief amongst his own people but he could never go back. He was utterly devoted to the captain.'

They passed into the bush outside. A wide cleared track led through tangled, overhanging rain forest. Pushing through spreading fronds of tree ferns, merging scarcely above their heads, the priest stopped. 'This is the place. I never come here without feeling a sense of great personal loss.'

Ahead in a clearing, stood a beautifully proportioned little chapel, surrounded by a waist high stone wall. 'This is where they lie, Helen and her husband, our dearest friends.'

Climbing a stile that straddled the wall, they stood in silence before two headstones carved simply with the names of the sleepers. Helen Elizabeth Slocum, beloved wife of Benjamin. On the other just a name - Benjamin Ulysses Slocum. Between, nestling on a bed of sea shells, a little outrigger canoe, complete with woven bamboo sail.

The priest spoke in a whisper. 'Abraham comes every day. He keeps the track clear and the grass cut low. Some call him pagan but I believe his God is as real as ours. Come, I would like to show you the chapel.'

Passing through the unlocked door, they stood within a small domed atrium. In the dim light, prayer books lay scattered on a shelf. A priest's vestments hung from a wooden peg. Pushing open stained cedar doors, he stood aside as they entered. A soft amber light suffused the chapel, streaming from leadlights above a simple altar draped with a lace cloth. On either side of a carved wooden cross, silver candlesticks held candles long unlit. Behind and to the side of the pews a font encased with mother of pearl shell, shimmered with myriad colours.

Rev. Trendel, with head bowed stood before the altar murmuring a prayer.

It was early afternoon as they retraced their steps along the track. Under a giant spreading fig tree the priest stopped, hands clasped behind his back. 'Please excuse me if I appear reflective. Helen loved to walk here, especially when the native orchids were in bloom. Look above, you can see them. In spring they flower, a sweet enchanting perfume.' He turned with concern as Harry coughed. 'Mr. Wakefield, I fear I have tired you. Perhaps we should return to town.'

Harry shook his head. 'No Padre, please, the spell would be broken.'

'Was the captain a strong Christian, Reverend?'

'Frankly I don't know Mrs. Wakefield. Deep down perhaps he was.'

'But he did build the chapel.'

He nodded. 'Yes, for his baby daughter to be christened.' He added in a softer voice. 'And for his wife. Helen often came alone, she found great comfort here.'

Inside the silent house the long drapes stirred, a gentle breeze had dispelled the mustiness of the room. Climbing the great staircase Harry, his wife holding his arm, paused every few steps to ease the tightness in his chest. The upper floor led to a series of closed doors to the left and to the right a wide gallery lit from above by glass windows set at an angle and forming a section of the roof.

Against a wall, shrouded in linen hung two oblong shapes. Rev. Trendel using a small footstool gently unfastened the fine cloth which fell to the floor.

As if taken by surprise, the face of Captain Slocum looked down at them. A strong, handsome face, square of jaw with smooth deeply tanned skin. With intensely blue eyes and dark hair lightly sprinkled with grey, it was the face of a man accustomed to giving orders and demanding obedience. They stood silent, mesmerised, half expecting this stern image to stretch out his hand and admonish them for intruding on his privacy.

The priest spoke softly. 'A fine gentleman. I believe I knew him as well as any man ever could.' He carefully removed the other cover. In the subdued light the portrait of Helen appeared, faintly smiling, hauntingly beautiful. The artist had captured every detail, her pale ivory skin, thick amber gold hair, soft brown eyes.

Her expression captivated the artist in Harry Wakefield. Once, long ago on a trip to his mother's homeland, he had been taken to the Louvre. There he had seen a faint, indefinable smile. No, this was different. So much softer, more feminine, more alluring. He moved so light could fall at a different angle. Wherever he stood, she was smiling down at them. Obviously dressed for the sitting, in a white silk gown, corsage de collette revealed the slender curve of her neck, encircled with a necklace of emeralds set in filigree silver. Spellbound, Harry turned to the minister. 'I hardly know what to say. This is the work of a Master!' He shook his head. 'But he has not signed either portrait.'

'It was the captain's wish, why I do not know. He once told me they were painted in Italy, shortly after they first fled Boston.'

The priest, after replacing the covers, again consulted his watch. 'Mr. Wakefield, it is but two thirty. If you feel up to it, I could show you the tower.'

'Yes please. I assure you, I feel quite well.'

A door at the far end of the gallery led to a spiral metal stair way open to the air. >From a landing at the top a door opened into the interior of a faithful replica of a ship's bridge. A binnacle containing a compass mounted on gimbals, a long brass telescope mounted on a tripod looked out on the world below. A swivel chair set where the viewer could manipulate the telescope, and around the circular walls were leather covered benches strewn with books and maps.

The priest spoke softly. 'The captain's retreat, always inviolably private. I believe I am the only man living who had the privilege to visit him here. Take a look through the telescope Mr. Wakefield.'

Harry pressed his eye to the lens. 'Good Lord, I can see every ship on the river-all the houses,' he smiled, 'even our own cosy retreat.' Spellbound, he swung the heavy instrument. Through the haze of sunlight, the peaks of the Great Divide leaped dramatically into view, shrouded in purple haze, sharply outlined against the blue of the sky.

In silence they retraced their steps through the great house to the carriageway below. At the gates the horse stood harnessed to the buggy and carefully tethered so that both were in the shade. Of Abraham there was no sign. 'He knows,' smiled the priest, 'he always knows, but where he is I have no idea.'

Comfortably seated, the slow descent to the town began, the horse stepping carefully over numerous washaways. Harry cleared his throat. 'The captain, Padre, may I ask what happened?'

'Of course. I find it hard to bring myself to speak of the captain's suffering but if there is a hell, that man found it here on Earth.'

'But his little daughter, Reverend, surely she must have been a comfort to him.'

'She was, Mrs. Wakefield, of that I am sure. He loved his little one dearly. After Helen was laid to rest, he came to me and we talked long and earnestly. I did not waste idle words of comfort or sympathy, he was beyond that. I found he had charged the First Mate of his vessel, a man absolutely loyal to him, to return to Boston with his daughter and her nurse. He was to return them to his wife's mother. I learned at the time, she was the only person who every regarded the captain kindly.'

They had come to the creek again, the priest let the reins hang loose as the big horse had his drink. 'Yes, my dear friends, it was a harrowing time. I had assumed he would go on living at *Monaro* but no, he told me he would be going away and wished to sell the property. He begged me to find a suitable buyer and gave me the name of his Sydney solicitor. There was one stipulation, I must personally approve of the purchaser, he must be a Christian gentleman. He also said that should I not find such a purchaser, the property, in its entirety was to be gifted to the church.' He gently slapped the reins. 'Come on old boy, that's enough, we must keep going.' He touched Harry's arm. 'Are you that Christian gentleman, Mr. Wakefield?'

For a moment Harry was speechless. 'How on earth could you know-how could you guess what was in my mind?'

He chuckled. 'I saw the expression on your face when we stood under the Tulip trees this morning. But you have not answered to the captain's stipulation.'

'I can't with honesty answer that question, Padre. I adhere to Christian precepts and principals but I am not a regular church goer I'm afraid. I suppose, deep down, I consider myself a free thinker.'

'You are an honest man, Mr. Wakefield. Should it come to pass you are interested in buying *Monaro*, you have my sincere recommendation. Now, I think you should know the end of the story as far as my knowledge of the affair goes.'

They had left the high country, and were following the well worn track towards the town. 'Forgive me for digressing, but whenever I travel this vast expanse of country, I ponder it's future. Look at these tiny farms, cut from the bush with little but hope. So isolated at times I feel overwhelmed by it all, but if the spirit of the human heart counts for anything, there must be a future. Don't you agree?'

'I am ashamed to confess I have never given the matter serious thought, Padre.'

The minister slapped the reins. 'Come along, Prince. An hour more of daylight will just see us home.'

Harry and Rose sat silent, waiting for him to continue.

'Well now, after the captain charged me with that responsibility, which I accepted with some reluctance, he returned to *Monaro* never to be seen alive again. It is all so clear to me now, but how was I to read what was in his mind.

I find it difficult to tell you-it was so bizarre, so pagan, so beyond our concept of Christian thinking and yet my heart goes out to him even now.

I think it was about a week after I last saw him, I was awakened by loud knocking at our door. Two of our parishioners stood there, agitated, frightened. I calmed them down as best I could. They had been fishing from the beach, a favourite spot by the northern headland, they saw a fire and naturally investigated. They were astounded to see the captain and Abraham-the captain in full dress uniform, Abraham clad only in a loin cloth. They thought it strange and kept their distance. On a flat rock Abraham had placed a small carved figure and in his deep voice he sang a strange, slow chant that seemed to carry far out over the sea. Later he told me it was a warning to the sharks.

The men watching were too afraid to interfere, they hid behind bushes and watched. To their horror, the captain suddenly stood and walked slowly into the water. There was a full moon that night, the waves were, as they say here, lazy. That is they roll in gently, without breaking until they reach the shore. They told me, he slowly disappeared until only his cap floated on the water. All the time Abraham's chant grew louder and faster.'

Rose shuddered. 'How terrible!'

'Yes, I find it difficult to talk about even now. Thankfully, his body was washed up on the sand the following morning. He rests in peace now, side by side with his beloved wife. May God rest his tortured soul.'

'What of Abraham, Padre, why did he not join the captain?'

'Many have asked the same question. Abraham told me the captain ordered him to stay until the matter of *Monaro* was settled.'

'And what then?'

'That I don't know, Mr. Wakefield.'

Trotting briskly through the town, then following along the sandy riverside track, it wasn't long before Mrs. Cochran's house came into view. The minister looked with concern as Harry began to cough. 'I trust the day has not been too tiring for you?'

'I must confess to being a little tired, Padre, but I feel elated. Light headed even!' He smiled. 'This could be the most significant day of our lives.'

'Perhaps, Mr. Wakefield, we shall see. Ah, I see your good landlady waiting for you.'

Mrs. Cochran stood waiting by the gate, her apron gathered in one hand, a bucket in the other.

Harry helped his wife down from the carriage. 'Forgive me for keeping you, Padre, I am most anxious to discuss this matter further and if you please, could you direct us to the stables you mentioned? I think we would like to hire a reliable horse and sulky.'

'I have anticipated you, Mr. Wakefield, if convenient I shall call for you and your good lady tomorrow after lunch.'

He smiled, raising his hat to Mrs. Cochran. 'Goodbye for the moment.' A flick of the whip and Prince wheeled, heading back towards the town.

Mrs. Cochran shepherded her guests up the stairs. 'You do look tired, Mr. Wakefield and so do you Mrs. Wakefield. I will bring you some tea directly and if you wish, dinner in your room. I do hope you like oysters and lobster. Mr. Trimble, our fisherman, brought them, fresh today.'

Harry, holding on to his wife's arm, smiled his appreciation. 'Mrs. Cochran, you are a jewel. Such food is fit for a king - what more can I say?'

That night in bed, they talked long and earnestly. Harry lay propped up with pillows, his thin body racked from time to time with paroxysms of coughing. Each time he examined the cloth he held to his mouth. 'No sign of blood, Rosie, not a speck, thank God!'

'You are overtired, Darling. Let me read to you, that always helps.'

'In this light? Anyway, I want to talk. My mind is in a whirl. Tell me what you think. Not what I might want to hear, honestly, what do you think?'

She fixed her clear gaze on her husband. 'I don't know exactly how I feel, Harry, my feelings are mixed. *Monaro* is beautiful, but so strange.'

'Strange?'

'I know it sounds silly but I felt we were not alone there.'

'What do you mean?'

'Sheer imagination I know. I felt drawn to the place. As if, well, as if something or someone, was asking us to stay. Does that sound ridiculous?'

'Ridiculous! Rosie, I swear I felt the same.'

She took his hand. 'I think they felt we were kindred spirits.'

In the faint glow cast by the oil lamp, they smiled at each other. 'Tomorrow I must ask the Padre for more details.'

'That's for tomorrow Harry, now you must rest.'

'Rest, how on earth can I rest, let alone sleep? All the excitement and this damn cough, Rosie, I swear I won't close my eyes tonight.'

'You must Harry, remember what Dr. McKenzie said.' She went to her travelling case on the cedar chest, returning with a small green bottle.

'What is this Rosie - some new perfume?'

'Something your father gave me for times like this.'

He closely examined the bottle. 'Chloral Hydrate. Oh Rosie, I have had it before, tastes like poison - must I?'

She carefully measured out a small portion. 'Open up young man.'

Harry spluttered with distaste. 'God, it's vile!'

Rose sat gently stroking his head while the sedative took effect, then after extinguishing the lamp she lay beside him, fighting the doubts that clouded her mind.

Standing arm in arm, they waited for Rev. Trendel, sheltering from the sun under Rose's parasol. 'Am I dreaming of the impossible Rosie? I haven't even asked the price of the property. You know my father is a wealthy man and I am the sole beneficiary under my grandmother's will. I have no idea how much is involved there but you know me - I have never worried about money.' He gave a short laugh. 'Typical of the cavalier attitude of one who has never known want.'

'Where and how we are born, is how fate decrees, Harry.'

'Perhaps you are right old girl. Look here comes the padre.'

The Rev. Trendel, in his old four wheeler, raised his hat. Faithful Betsy cropped placidly at the grassy verge. 'Hope I have not kept you waiting. Whoa there Betsy. Dear oh dear, this horse has a mind of her own!'

'Good of you to call for us Padre, there is so much we wish to discuss, so much we would like to do and see.'

'Well then, we had best be on our way. To the stables if my memory serves me aright.' He chuckled, looking sideways. 'I must say you both look very well, Mrs. Cochran's cooking, no doubt.'

'I must confess to her skill, Padre. The food is quite magnificent.'

'Before she and her husband came up here, she was in great demand, she worked for the best hotels in Sydney. Yes indeed, she would often be called up to *Monaro* when the captain and his wife entertained. Now, if you are ready, I think we should be on our way.'

Rose gathered her skirts in her hand and taking her husband's hand, climbed up onto the seat. Harry followed. 'I hope we are not interfering with your work, Padre.'

'Not today Mr. Wakefield. I am entirely at your disposal.' He slapped the reins and the horse broke into a trot.

Emerging suddenly from the bush, the first straggle of shacks appeared. Occasionally an aproned woman, with children clinging to her skirts, waved a greeting to the familiar figure. 'A lonely life for many.' There was a touch a sadness in the priest's voice. 'Yes, it can be so. Especially for the womenfolk.' He gave another gentle slap of the reins. 'With your permission, before we see Ned at the stables, I would very much like you to visit the Vicarage.' He smiled. 'Such as it is. And my wife would be happy to meet a fellow artist.'

'Your wife paints, Padre?'

'Water colours, Mr. Wakefield. Painting and gardening are a great comfort to her.'

Mrs. Trendel, a tranquil, grey haired lady, met them at the door of a simple cottage adjoining a small white church. 'I understand my husband is taking you to the stables. I hope you will take tea first.'

The sitting room floor, bare of coverings, gave off a faint odour of beeswax from well polished tallowwood planks. A well worn settee and several chairs upholstered in heavy brocade, with a small occasional table, made up the furnishings. On the mantelpiece stood a vase of pink cosmos.

A young girl brought in the tea tray. 'Thank you Elsie, this is Mr. and Mrs. Wakefield.' The girl bobbed an awkward curtsy, smiling shyly.

'Thank you, Dear. Tell your mother I will be along to see her later.' Mrs. Trendel sighed as she poured the tea. 'Elsie is a dear little thing. She is from a large family. Her father makes very little and her mother is not well, another child is due. We do what we can but you know, we are so limited.'

Harry's eyes roamed the room. 'Your husband said you paint, Mrs. Trendel. May I?' He stood, examining the several watercolours. 'These are truly excellent, beautiful tonings.'

'I am afraid my talent is small, Mr. Wakefield, but painting is the one luxury I allow myself. I would so value your opinion of my work.'

'I would be honoured, Mrs. Trendel, but from what I have seen here there is little I could show you.'

Ned Lightfoot kept the stables. An ex-jockey from the south, he ran a thriving business. He greatly admired and respected the minister.

'Mr. and Mrs. Wakefield, Ned.'

Ned touched his cap. 'Glad to meet you.'

'Mr. Wakefield wishes to hire a reliable horse and sulky, Ned.'

'Well Reverend, no trouble there. Got nothin fancy mind you.' He took the reins, hitching Betsy to the rail fence. 'Better come have a look.' The stableman's shed appeared to be overfilled with a variety of vehicles. He lifted the shafts of a well worn sulky. 'What about this one, Reverend? She's solid, spoke's good, fitted a couple of new one's when she came in.'

'The seat looks a bit worse for wear, Ned.'

'Missus patched it up, Reverend, just needs a blanket. What do you think, Sir?' He asked Harry.

'Not bad Mr. Lightfoot but I need a horse and harness as well, you know.'

'Ah yes.' Ned rubbed his chin. 'Tell you what, got an old roan mare out back, she's strong. Not fast, I'll grant, but willing. With harness, what would you say sir - how does twenty five sound?'

'Ned!' Rev Trendel called softly from the back of the shed.

'Well, how does twenty sound, Mr. Wakefield?'

'Sold Mr. Lightfoot. When can we take delivery?'

'Tomorrow all right sir? Got to check the old girl's shoes.'

'Now, could you bring it out to us? We are staying with Mrs. Cochran along the river.'

'No trouble, sir. First thing tomorrow.'

About to leave, Harry turned again to the little man. 'Mr. Lightfoot, would you by any chance have a pony I could buy?'

'A pony you say sir. Well there is a little grey out in the paddock. Very poor condition. God knows, beggin' your pardon Reverend, what's happened to him, looks like he's been worked hard, cracked legs. Gave a bloke ten bob for him. Have a look if you like.'

The little horse stood facing the slip rails, head down, his tail flicking at the flies clustered around the sores on his hind legs. The priest, with a strange expression on his face, ran a practiced hand down the pony's flanks.

'You're welcome for what I gave for him Mr. Wakefield, ten bob.'

'Make it thirty shillings Mr. Lightfoot and throw in a bridle. Oh yes, and salve for his legs and a couple of bags of feed.'

'Right you are sir. Fix it all up tomorrow.'

Leaving the stables they drove for a while in silence. Then the priest, looking hard at his young friend, said 'Mr. Wakefield, a day ago you told me you were a free thinker, which I took to mean you are an agnostic. My dear friend, you are a Christian in the true sense of the word. I believe I know for whom you intend this pony. I knew that little horse straight away. Yes, that's poor little Neddy. Alice will be beside herself with joy!'

Harry laughed, then coughed into his handkerchief. 'Do you think her parents will be offended, Padre?'

'Coming from you, I doubt it.'

Soon Mrs. Cochran's high stilted house came into view. The priest eased the old horse into a walk. 'A satisfactory day, Mr. Wakefield.'

'Very satisfactory, Padre. If we are not imposing on your time, can you spare an extra few minutes?'

The horse, feeling the slack rein stopped by the picket fence.

'Of course.'

'My wife and I have thought long and earnestly regarding *Monaro*. Probably the most important decision we will ever make. We are both attracted to the idea but there is so much to consider. For instance, you have not mentioned the asking price for the property.'

'Ah yes, I am aware of that but you see, I don't know. That is a matter you must discuss with the captain's solicitors - Messrs. Erwin, Erwin and Hennesy in Sydney.'

'I see. So I must journey to Sydney.'

'I am afraid so, Mr. Wakefield.' He removed an envelope from his coat pocket. 'Here you see I have already written a Letter of Recommendation. That is of course, should you consider further.'

Harry smiled. 'My mind is quite made up, I think you already knew Padre. I believe the *Camira* is still loading, I will see Captain McIntyre in the morning.'

The priest smiled in turn. 'I confess I did think so, at least I hoped you would.'

After helping his wife down, they stood as the buggy wheeled and headed back to town.

That night, snug in their down mattress, Harry told his wife, 'You must stay here, Rosie, it is best I go alone. Remember Dr. Clark ordered rest and lots of nourishing food. Mrs. Cochran will see to that.'

She was crying quietly. 'I will worry every minute you are away.'

'And I would worry more if you came with me, so please be my dear girl and understand.'

In the early morn the stable man sat waiting outside the house.

'Thank you Mr. Lightfoot, put the pony under the house if you please. Now, if you have time could you drive me to the wharves? I wish to see Captain McIntyre. Oh, of course I'll pay you for your trouble.'

'No need for that, Sir. Give you a chance to get used to the old rig.'

Captain McIntyre stood on the bridge supervising his vessel. 'We sail with the flood on Wednesday, Mr. Wakefield.'

'I see. Thank you, Captain. I will be here Tuesday night.'

Returning to the boarding house, he told Rose of the arrangements. 'We have two whole days to fill, Rosie. What shall we do?' She smiled. 'The Dennis' first of course. Then we can get the key from Rev. Trendel. What do you think?'

He grinned. 'You have read my mind again, Rosie.'

She held tightly to his arm. 'Sorry I was silly last night.'

He kissed her. 'Darling Rosie, you could never be silly - leave that to me.'

With the sun well up, they headed along the river track at a slow trot, the grey pony tethered behind. Harry peered around him. 'Damned if I know, Rosie, it all looks the same to me. Do you remember where we turn off?'

'Of course I do, I was a bush girl remember. Just watch for an old fire blackened tree.'

Harry laughed. 'Right you are, I should have known.'

Fred Dennis stood on his tiny verandah shading his eyes as the sulky approached. His face creased into a welcoming smile. 'Mr. and Mrs. Wakefield, how good to see you.'

His wife and daughter came to the door, Mrs. Dennis brushing flour from her arms. 'Just put the bread in the oven. Please come in and have some tea.'

Alice suddenly left her mother's side, running quickly to where the pony stood, head down, exhausted. She flung her arms around the little horse's neck and burst into tears. 'It's Neddy. Oh Neddy what have they done to you?'

'Alice,' her father called sharply, 'whatever are you doing? Apologise to Mr. and Mrs. Wakefield if you please.' He turned to Harry 'I can't think what has come over the lass.'

His wife took his arm, her voice low. 'Don't you see Fred? It's her old pony!'

Rose put her arm around the girl's shoulder. 'Alice don't cry, please don't. Rev. Trendel told us he was once yours. I am sure he is happy to be home again.'

Alice turned her tear stained face to Rose. 'I love him, Mrs. Wakefield, I've missed him every day.'

'You will always have him now Alice, I promise.' The pony was nuzzling the young girl. 'Now, why don't you walk him around? My husband wants to talk to your parents.' She gently wiped away the girls tears.

Over steaming cups, Harry came to the purpose of their visit.

'Mr. Dennis, I understand you know of the property in the hills above the town. I refer of course to *Monaro*.'

'Indeed I do sir, as does everyone in the district. I have done some work there for Father Trendel.'

Harry nodded. 'It is possible that my wife and I may purchase *Monaro* Mr. Dennis, but if for some reason we are unable to do so, we intend to build a house. You see, I do not enjoy the best of health, yet this climate, the whole area in fact, seems to benefit me greatly. Mr. Dennis, would you consider working for me? When you are able of course.'

Fred Dennis' face lit up with relief and pleasure. 'I would consider it a privilege Mr. Wakefield.'

Harry stood smiling, extending his hand. 'Then the matter is settled. As from this minute, you are in my employ.' He counted out a number of banknotes. 'Please consider this an advance Mr. Dennis, we can discuss the correct rate later.'

'Mr. Wakefield,' Fred Dennis' voice was husky with emotion. 'I don't know what to say- how to thank you. God knows this will be a saver for us.'

Harry clasped the man's hand. 'I am happy too Mr. Dennis. We will be in touch in due course. Now we must take our leave, we have much to attend to.'

At the gate Alice held tightly to Rose's hand. She kissed the girl affectionately before climbing up beside her husband. 'I hope we will see you again soon Alice.' She smiled. 'I am sure Neddy will be as happy as his mistress.'

That night Harry rested, taking his dinner in their bedroom, hiding from his wife a cough that at times racked his body. Lying back on the pillows, he smiled as chorus after chorus rang through the old frame house. No wonder everyone loves her, she gives so much of herself. How fortunate can one man be?

The days passed quickly, too quickly. The return visit to *Monaro* affected Harry deeply. The very air of the rooms, saturated with a powerful silence, so comforting, so satisfying to the artist in his being. He felt overcome with an almost mystical desire that he must return to them, live in them, to embrace the beauty that rolled away from the tower window like an unfolding picture.

They wandered again the wide bush track to the little chapel, standing in silence before the two headstones. Tears came to Rose's eye's.

He gently wiped them away. 'Don't grieve for them, my dearest. Wherever they are, I'm sure they are happy.'

CHAPTER V

The voyage to Sydney left Harry miserable. The little ship shuddered and bucked in the choppy seas. He left his cabin only when they entered the calm of the harbour. The bustle of the town appalled him. He thought, good lord it's little over a week since we were here. He swore once he got back to Myuna he would never leave again. He sought out Captain McIntyre. 'Captain, I feel I could not cope with continuing on to Melbourne, could I impose upon you to have some papers delivered to my father?'

'Aye, that you can Mr. Wakefield.' He fingered his beard. 'Matters are a little uncertain at the moment, however. I understand the seamen are on strike at most major ports.' He lowered his voice. 'Frankly I cannot blame them, most are little more than slaves.'

'But the *Camira* appears a contented ship, Captain.'

'Aye, fortunately there are a few civilised owners.'

'What is to be done then?'

'I can unload here, Mr. Wakefield, all the cedar - even that consigned to Melbourne - and with luck provision her for the return trip.'

'You won't be held up, I refer to Melbourne, of course?'

'No chance of that, Mr. Wakefield, but I must report to my supervisors.' A brief smile creased his grizzled countenance. 'Fret not, Mr. Wakefield, I will have you back in Myuna, my word on it!'

'How long do you expect to be, Sir?'

'No more than a week, ten days perhaps.'

'Good lord-it never crossed my mind-can you recommend a good hotel?'

'Aye, the Metropole, a civilised oasis in this unruly town.'

Harry took a hansom cab to the hotel, a dignified retreat from the drunken squalor of the streets. The day still early, he directed his cab to Erwin, Erwin and Hennesy. A well polished brass plate at the doorway of a substantial sandstone building, proclaimed the firm's name.

A sallow looking clerk took his card. 'Please be seated, Sir. Mr. Mann should see you directly.'

Sitting on a hard leather backless seat, Harry's eyes wandered the room. On the wall hung pen sketches of judicial luminaries, past and present. He thought - how absurd, how ridiculous-thin, humourless faces, sly fat faces, peering out through great horsehair wigs. Some stood posing in flowing robes. All seemed to say, I am here to judge you, no matter if you are a murderer, a lecher. If your purse is fat they will plea earnestly on your behalf and I may be sympathetic. But if you have no money-. Harry wiped his brow-God, what am I thinking? James Scully must have been joking, surely there must be good and decent men!

His reverie was cut short. 'Mr. Mann will see you now, Sir.'

Seated behind a roll top oak desk, a little grey wizened man shuffled some papers. Close to his left hand, a gold watch and chain gleamed oddly against the unpolished desk top. In an ash tray, a pungent black cheroot, spiralled smoke. He spoke to the clerk. 'A chair, Peters. Now leave us please.'

'Ah yes, Mr. Wakefield, in this matter of the property *Monaro*. You have a letter from the Rev. Trendel?' Peering through half glasses he read and reread the priest's letter. Picking up the cheroot, he regarded Harry closely. 'You come highly recommended, Sir. I trust you are familiar with the terms and conditions in this matter?'

'Well, yes and no, Sir, not entirely.'

'I see. It is required of the purchaser, that he assumes responsibility for the care and well being of the Islander, Abraham.'

'Of course Mr. Mann. It goes without saying. We, that is my wife and I would consider it our duty.'

'Quite,' said the lawyer dryly. 'Now the question is, Mr. Wakefield, are you in position, financially to complete this purchase?'

Harry stammered a little. 'I, I believe so Sir, my father is a man of some wealth.'

'I see, I see,' murmured the little man. 'Then you are aware of the asking price?'

'Well no sir, I am not.'

'Mr. Wakefield, the sum involved for the house called *Monaro*, the complete contents and attached lands is five thousand guineas.'

Harry gasped. 'Good Lord sir, that seems a great deal of money!'

The lawyer appeared impatient. 'That property, Mr. Wakefield, is, in our opinion, worth four times that sum. Now,' he stood picking up his watch, 'if you are not interested, we should not waste each others time.'

'Oh but I am, forgive me if I am surprised. You see Mr. Mann, I have never had to deal with money matters in my life. I simply had no idea of values.'

The lawyer sat down again. 'Indeed Mr. Wakefield, then if you are quite sure, I will prepare the necessary documents. The name of your solicitors please?'

'Messrs. Scully and Latimore, Collins Street, Melbourne.'

The lawyer pressed his fingertips together. 'Hmm, that may prove awkward, unless time is not important to you.'

'But it is Mr. Mann, it is most important. I am anxious to conclude this matter.' He hesitated. 'Would it be possible for you to act for me?'

A wry smile creased the little man's face. 'Quite impossible Mr. Wakefield. I see you have little knowledge of the law. Perhaps I should not say this but there is a quite competent firm in this building. Try the second floor, Mr. Wakefield.'

Ten days after landing in Sydney, Harry stood with Captain McIntyre in the wheelhouse of the S.S. *Camira* as she cleared the harbour heads.

'So all went well Mr. Wakefield?'

Harry sighed. 'Very well indeed, Captain. A few anxious moments but happily, my wife and I are now the owners of *Monaro.*'

'How did you find Sydney town?'

'I thank God I am leaving-Captain, I could never have imagined such violence and the drunken behaviour, even amongst men who appeared, on the surface, to be civilised! We did not see any of that during our two day stopover on the way north.'

'Aye, but you went to Manly Mr. Wakefield and kept to the better harbour suburbs. It is the drink, that is the problem. Most of it cheap, some of it downright poison.'

Harry coughed hard into his handkerchief. 'If you will excuse me Captain, I think I should go to my cabin.'

'That might be wise, Mr. Wakefield.'

At the wheelhouse door, Harry turned. 'Captain McIntyre, I was surprised - before leaving, Mr. Mann the lawyer, asked me convey his regards to the Rev. Trendel.'

'Not surprising Mr. Wakefield, we carried him on two occasions to Myuna. Yes, he knows the good parson as well as he knew Captain Slocum.'

Lying on his bunk, Harry reread his father's letter. He was disappointed, but understood, that his son had not been able to come on to Melbourne. But for the strike which is paralysing the city, he and his mother would have come up to Sydney. *Monaro* seems a wondrous place indeed. If it agrees with your health, that is all that matters. The money is of no consequence. This draft for six thousand will meet your immediate needs and give you working capital. Harry must let him know if there is a reliable bank available so that further funds may be transferred, otherwise other arrangements will be made. He ended by begging Harry to be sure Rose was in care of a competent physician and asking to convey their dearest wishes. When things return to normal they were sure to make the trip north to see them.

Harry wiped away the tears that welled in his eyes - never a question as to the wisdom of his actions, not even a note of warning. He felt a sense of undying gratitude and devotion to the two people he loved next to his wife.

Myuna on a warm August morning. Harry peered through his cabin port hole. With the aid of a half bottle of whisky he had slept the night through. His fingers massaged the ache in his forehead, as his eyes adjusted to the view outside. His heart leapt, there she was, sitting in the familiar buggy with the Rev. Trendel. 'I'm home, thank God I'm home!'

Days passed in the feverish activity. Rose engaged a strong reliable girl, glad to leave the drudgery of farm life, to earn a little money, the first she had ever known. Fred Dennis, hobbling on crutches, brought in a team of helpers. Overgrown shrubs and trees were pruned back, the grass scythed to the velvety smoothness. Investigation of the coachhouse revealed Captain Slocum's own landau. Under the expert care of Ned Lightfoot, it was returned, gleaming under a new coat of varnish. With a lively black gelding in the shafts, it replaced their sulky which was accepted by Fred with heartfelt gratitude.

Abraham was not to be found. Harry took his worry to the Rev. Trendel. The priest appeared little concerned. 'Don't worry Mr. Wakefield, he is an independent spirit. When Abraham deems the time is right, he will return. Mark my words.'

The following week, returning home from their first meeting with Dr. Thomas Coburn, they chatted happily as the big horse made light work of the uphill track. 'You liked him Rosie?

'Yes I did, Darling. He said I was in blooming health.'

He laughed. 'Well that sounds encouraging.' Harry had taken an instant liking to the tall, good looking, young American.'

'I am glad someone has taken over the old place.' His handshake was firm. 'I hope I may have the privilege of visiting occasionally.'

'Of course, Doctor, we will look forward to seeing you.'

The afternoon was well advanced. Shadows from tall trees lengthened as the sun dipped just below the higher peaks of purple ranges. Harry peered through the fading light. 'Well, I'll be damned.' Standing by the metal gates, the massive figure of Abraham, dressed in his sail cloth, beaming a smile of welcome.

The weeks flew by. Harry set up his easel in the tower. Mrs. Trendel taught him the basics of landscape technique. Secretly he worked with a passion that consumed him. Passion for colour - great daubs of colour, filling canvas after canvas, each hidden where only he knew. Looking out to the distant sea, he thought - thank God, she can't hear my coughing up here.

At night in the great canopied bed, Rose would ask him if he was happy, had he ever regretted coming so far away from all they had known?

'Never, Rosie. I only worry that you might sometimes.'

'I came with my husband. I have never regretted one moment.'

The rather pretentious landau was stabled, replaced by a light sulky found hidden under canvas at the back of the coachhouse.

The girl, Emma, became a fixture of the house. Harry smiled at his wife. 'Rosie, you have a treasure there. Bless her soul, she brings my lunch to the tower, knocks discreetly and leaves the tray outside.'

'I am so fond of her, Harry. I could never manage without Emma. The poor girl has only known hard work all of her life. The look on her face when I gave her some of my dresses!' She smiled, ruefully. 'I'm afraid they no longer fit me.'

The weather grew warmer, Christmas was upon them almost before they realised. Harry, dressed always in cool white with his wide brimmed Panama hat, became well known and liked among the towns people.

He called on Dr. Coburn - would he consider spending Christmas Day with them? He certainly would, the previous few festive seasons had been rather lonely for him. That night, Harry confided to his wife. 'I am most impressed with him Rosie. I think we have a good friend in Tom Coburn.'

Christmas passed. The New Year, 1891 dawned hot and sultry. Harry painted, driven by a strange energy. Rose grew larger by the week.

Early in March, Mrs. Trendel, a regular visitor, offered to stay with Rose during this difficult period. The weather turned, heavy rain and gale force winds swept the coast. When the first spasms started Harry harnessed up the sulky. At the gate, to his surprise, Abraham was waiting. With a smile he motioned Harry to move over and took the reins in his huge hands. Drowning out the drumming of the torrential rain on the oiled canvas hood, there echoed a menacing thunderous roar. Coming out of the cutting, they stopped in dismay. The once charming, fordable creek, was now a brown swirling racing torrent. At least fifty yards wide, it carried all before it. Tree branches and rocks that could smash the sulky to matchwood and doubtless wash them over the steep hillside with it.

Harry looked at Abraham. The Islander slowly shook his head, crossing over was impossible. He turned the sulky back to *Monaro.* Harry sat hunched, fear clutching at his heart. At the gate in the stone wall the old man spoke for the first time. 'Abraham take care of the horse, Captain.'

Inside the house Harry, panting painfully, climbed the stairs to the bedroom. Emma met him at the door, her sleeves rolled to the elbows. By God, he thought, she has seen it all before. As in a dream, he heard her say. 'Mrs. Trendel says will you keep plenty of wood in the stove, Sir.'

For hours it seemed, he sat before the great kitchen range, his wet clothes drying in the heat. He did not hear Emma come, just her touch on his shoulder. She was smiling. 'Mrs. Trendel says for you to come now.'

In the bed, Rose lay propped up with pillows, a pink bundle at her breast. She smiled at him, a warm triumphant smile. He fell to his knees, tears in his eyes. Her hand smoothed his hair. 'A boy, Darling. A beautiful boy.'

Mrs. Trendel spoke quietly. 'Your wife must rest now, Mr. Wakefield, and I think, so should you.'

Harry stumbled through the picture gallery and up the winding stairs to the tower. From a cupboard he took a bottle of the Captain's fine old cognac. His mind torn between joy and concern for his wife, he drank steadily and sank thankfully onto the leather couch. He knew nothing more until Emma's knock roused him. 'Dinner is ready Sir.'

A week passed, the rain stopped and Dr. Coburn arrived on horseback. After his examination, he joined Harry in the library. 'You are fortunate to have had two such practical women here. Both your wife and son are doing well'

During the drowsy afternoon, Rose still a little weak, sat knitting, the baby in his cradle close by. Through a lattice of extravagantly blossoming bougainvillea, her eyes swept over the green lawn to the stone wall where Fred Dennis had planted zinnias and cannas, now ablaze with colour. She surrendered her thoughts to her life in this strange beautiful place. At times it seemed a dream, so much happiness, yet always that cloud that hung so darkly when she allowed herself to think of it.

Aroused from her reverie by the sound of spinning wheels, she looked up as Harry, with Abraham at the reins, swept around the bend under the tulip trees. He sat smiling at her, his old familiar grin, holding aloft a bundle of letters. He kissed her, then he lifted the net to look at his son. 'No doubt about it Rosie, he has your looks, not a bit like me, thank God!'

She laughed. 'All right flatterer, pull up a chair and read me the letters.' She looked up suddenly at a slight scratching sound. 'Harry what on earth have you got in that basket?'

'Shut your eyes Rosie, a little surprise for you!'

'Oh Harry! Isn't it lovely?' In his arms he held a black Persian kitten. 'Where did it come from?' She held out her arms. 'Let me hold him.'

'It's not a 'he' Rose, it's a 'she'. Given to me by the Padre. One of his flock had sent it from Sydney for his wife. Made her sneeze.'

The kitten settled on Rose's lap, purring. 'Harry, what shall we call her?'

'She is already named old girl. Ebony, Rev. Trendel suggests, Ebby, would be easier to say. And you know, full grown Persian are ferocious killers, that's why I was glad to take her. Snakes haven't got a chance with cats like these.'

The door opened, Emma appeared pushing a laden trolley. 'I saw you coming Mr. Wakefield, I knew you would want your tea,'

'You are a treasure Emma, you read my mind.' He gave a start, a flaxen haired girl followed Emma carrying a plate of scones. 'Alice! what a pleasant surprise. When did you arrive?'

'Just today Mr. Wakefield. Mrs. Wakefield said I could stay for a few days and help Emma with the baby.'

'Of course you are welcome to stay as long as you wish.'

Emma picked up the baby. 'He won't sleep tonight if he goes any longer Mrs. Wakefield. Alice will mind him while I do my work.'

Stroking the kitten, Rose waited for her husband to read through the mail. 'Damn! Listen to this Rosie-they can't come. The *Camira* just got out this time but there is no guarantee it will be allowed back in. The seaman's strike is worsening.' He shuffled the pages. 'And now the shearers and miners have joined them.' He leaned over gently scratching the kittens head. 'Don't worry old girl, it probably won't last long. My father says sympathy is with the men. There is talk of the workers forming their own political party.' He folded the letter and put it in his pocket.

'What will happen Harry, will everyone go on strike?'

'No, the padre says Myuna is too isolated, Rosie and on the whole, people here give a fair days work for a fair days pay.' He grinned. 'That's what the padre says anyway.' He replaced his cup on the tray and stood stretching. 'Just the right time to catch the light. I will be down for dinner.'

Her hand restrained him. 'Harry, I must talk to you, please sit down.'

He smiled at her. 'This must be important, or serious - perhaps both?'

'Harry, please listen to me. I see so little of you, you are either in the tower or you go into town. We don't talk like we used to.'

'I am sorry Rosie. I know I'm a thoughtless hound. Please forgive me.'

She took his hand. 'Darling, we must decide on a name for the baby and we must speak to the Rev. Trendel about the Christening.'

He nodded. 'Of course. We were going to do that when the Grandparents arrived. Yes, I see what you mean, we must do it ourselves now. Well,' his infectious grin again, 'have you picked out a name for him?'

'Harry, of course, Darling.'

He groaned. 'Oh Lord no, not another Harry! Look, why not Ben, after the Captain? Benjamin Wakefield-sounds just right somehow.'

'If that's what you want.'

'Don't you like it Rosie?'

She smiled.'I do, if you do. Will you see the Rev. Trendel?'

'Tomorrow old girl.' He kissed the top of her head. 'Now I must go. Leave you to read your mother's letter in peace and to spoil that cat.'

Rose watched the tall, pitifully thin man she loved walk away with his shambling uncertain steps. Her heart contracted within her.

Out of sight, he took his father's letter from his pocket. Rose must never be worried with all it contained. 'Chaos reigns in the City, old established businesses have gone to the wall. The boom days are over, Harry. Gone forever, some say. Gold and wool have fallen disastrously. There are strikes-shearers burning wool sheds. Erik Jansen has escaped their wrath, thank God, but then he has always treated men fairly. James Scully has heard nothing of his old place but they are decent people, so we pray all is well there. The Bunyip

Aristocracy are determined to break the shearers and I have no doubt they will. I wonder what the elegant gentlemen of my club would say if they knew where my sympathies lay. Mark my words Harry, seeds of deep bitterness will be sown over this business and they will flourish and grow. I fear we are drifting into unknown waters. We are sound, thank God. I must hurry and finish this now. The good Captain McIntyre will see it reaches you safely. Your mother sends her love, as do I, to both you and Rose and the little newcomer we wait with impatience to see. You must tell Rose, Ruth Scully gave birth to a healthy boy. Your loving father. P.S. In strictest confidence Harry - Mrs. Jansen has seen Dr. Clark. He suspects congestion of the heart. Say nothing to Rose.'

A cough shook his body. With streaming eyes he examined his handkerchief. A little spray of blood speckled its snowy surface.

With Abraham at the reins, Harry left for town early the following morning when the sun was just pleasantly warm.

Suddenly the Islander turned to him, searching his face. 'You are sick, Captain.'

Momentarily lost for words, Harry sat silently as Abraham turned his attention back to the road.

'Yes Abraham, very sick I'm afraid.'

'Abraham knows.' He held the reins between his knees as he lit a short black pipe. 'Every day I will bring oysters. You will then see.'

'Thank you Abraham, I would like that.' He paused then, 'Abraham, why do you call me Captain?'

'You are Captain, now.'

'You do me great honour.' This was the first sign of intimacy he had observed in the old man. 'Abraham, don't tell me if you don't wish to, I don't mean to intrude-would you tell me where you go when you leave us sometimes?'

'Away along the river, Captain.'

'Do you go fishing?'

He nodded. 'For some black people, too old to go with others. I help, we are friends.'

Harry murmured a silent prayer. 'God forgive us our sins against the helpless.'

Keeping at a brisk clip, they soon entered the town's dusty streets finally pulling up outside the doctors surgery.

'I don't know how long I'll be here, Abraham. Perhaps you might visit your friends.' Harry took a note from his wallet. 'I would like to help, Abraham.'

The old man shook his head. 'No money, Captain, no money.' He relit his pipe. 'Abraham be here. You see the doctor, Abraham wait.'

Tom Coburn answered the door. 'Harry, how good to see you. Come in, man, come in. Just in time for some tea.' He rang a little bell. 'Mary, some tea please and some of those raisin muffins. So,' he sat back keenly eyeing his new friend, 'to what do I owe the honour of this visit?'

'Just a visit Tom. The baby is to be Christened next week, Rose hoped you might have time to come up.'

The maid entered, unannounced, with a laden tray. 'Thank you Mary.' He poured the steaming aromatic tea. 'Try one of these, Harry. Mrs. Coburn's finest.'

'Just the tea thanks, Tom. Just what I need.'

Tom Coburn came to the point. He spoke gently. 'Rose has already invited me Harry. Now are you going to tell me why this unexpected visit?'

Harry ran his fingers through his damp hair. 'I have had a bit of a scare Tom.'

'I see, can you tell me about it?'

Harry told of the blood that had speckled his handkerchief. 'Should have seen you before this.'

In the surgery attached to the house, the young physician thoughtfully folded his stethoscope.

Harry dressed slowly. 'Well Tom, give me the bad news.'

Tom Coburn sat down at has desk, fingers pressed together. 'I will be honest with you Harry - both your lungs are involved.'

'How long Tom?'

'I can't say exactly. With complete rest, three perhaps four years.'

'You mean I must give up my painting?'

'Of course not, but this frantic pace you keep Harry. You work like a man possessed.'

'Perhaps I am possessed.'

'By what for heaven's sake?'

'*Monaro* - the portrait in the gallery - the very essence of the place.'

'You are an artist, Harry. Artists are romantics. Truly I envy you.'

'Thank you Tom.' He stood, pushing aside the curtains. 'I see patient Abraham is waiting for me. So I must rest you say. Well I can only promise to do my best.' They shook hands. 'Goodbye for now, old man.'

CHAPTER VI

Husband and wife, with their small son playing beside them, sat in the cool shade of the vine covered verandah. The black Persian, now fully grown, stretched in luxurious contentment amongst a litter of fallen leaves, lifting her head occasionally to investigate the odd mysterious rustle.

'Happy, old girl?'

Rose smiled taking his hand, not daring to reveal her feelings. 'I am so looking forward to seeing them, Darling. Do you think - I mean, Alice is so young!'

'Eighteen today Rosie. Good Lord, girls marry here at fifteen. At any rate, Tom has never so much as hinted to me.'

'He wouldn't, Dear. Men never talk about these things.'

With a wide grin, he stood listening, one hand to his ear.

She held her emotions in check, at the skeletal frame so clearly visible through his thin linen coat.

'Unless I'm mistaken, they are on the carriageway now.'

Moments later, Tom Coburn's light sulky rounded the last bend in a shower of gravel. Tom, in a striped blazer and jaunty boater, Alice in white muslin, her fair hair piled high under a little straw hat. She smiled down at them.

Harry stepped forward, his hand outstretched to help the young girl step down. 'Alice, happy birthday to you. Sit in the shade while I give Tom a hand with the rig.'

Rose patted the chair beside her. 'Alice, come sit by me. You look lovely.' She fondly kissed the girl.

Smiling, Alice unpinned her hat. 'You are both so kind to me, Mrs. Wakefield, I can never thank you enough.' She took little Ben by the hand. 'It seems such a short time since he was a baby, now just look how he toddles around.'

Tethering the horse in the shade, Harry took the young doctor's arm. 'Spare a few moments with me, Tom. Something I want you to see.' He called back. 'Won't be long, Rosie - back in time for Emma's cake.'

'Your boy is coming along, Harry. Good strong stock there.'

'Obviously not from my side.'

'Listen,' Tom stopped, eyeing his friend steadily, 'if he inherits his father's sweetness of nature, his eye for beauty, then he is blessed indeed.'

'Thank you, Tom. You do have a way with the right words.'

He led the way off the driveway to Abraham's little house. 'Just look at this will you.' Under a thatched cover, a beautifully crafted outrigger canoe rested on two solid blocks of Tallowwood.

'Good Lord, what a marvellous piece of work!'

'For the 'little Captain', I was told. Remarkable isn't it, from one solid Cedar log.'

'Remarkable! I have never seen workmanship like it.'

'I wanted you to see it, Tom. Truth is, I haven't seen the old fellow in weeks, God knows where he has got to.'

'For what it is worth, Harry, one of the fishermen mentioned he is camped along the river building a raft.'

'A raft, what on earth for?'

'God knows, old man. Abraham, so I'm told, never gives a reason for anything he does.'

Harry nodded. 'Yes, I can attest to that.'

They turned back toward the house. 'So Emma has made a cake for Alice's birthday? You have a treasure in Emma.'

'We regard her as one of the family. You know what a Godsend she has been to us.'

'I certainly do. Been spoken for, I hear. Young Greg Wardrop, one of Mrs. Cochran's young men.'

'Spoken for, yes, but Emma has a mind of her own. Says she will marry him when she is good and ready.'

'Good for Emma! I wish them well.' Tom stopped, taking his friend's arm. 'I was saddened by the news of the death of Rose's mother. How is she taking it?'

'Rather badly, but you know how controlled she is Tom. Rose hides her feelings, God bless her.'

'That she does. A remarkable woman, your wife.' They strolled on. 'I was most impressed with your parents Harry. Your father is one of the old school. Nothing much escapes him.'

'Apparently not. They will be here again at Christmas. In time to say a final goodbye, no doubt.'

'Harry, look we are in sight of the women. Before we join them let me remind you of our pact. Remember, we never discuss that, you agreed. Enjoy what you have, every moment of every day.'

On the verandah, Emma smiling a welcome, stood triumphant behind the tea trolley. On a silver stand stood an iced birthday cake adorned with a corona of thin wax candles. The little group clapped. 'Bravo Emma - what a magnificent cake!'

Emma blushed with pleasure. Alice embraced her friend. 'Dear Emma, thank you. It's beautiful.'

Tom looked fondly at the young girl. 'If Alice will cut the cake, we can all sing Happy Birthday!'

Alice did not seem to hear, her eyes were fixed on Ben. The child, unnoticed, had wandered from the verandah and now toddled as fast as his little legs would carry him, across the newly cut grass, intent on a glittering object menacingly coiled in the warm sunshine. They watched speechless, as she leapt from her chair, running like one possessed. Her hair streaming behind her, her arms outstretched. They watched in horror, as Ben reaching for the object of his curiosity, was snatched into the girl's arms. The huge aggressive tiger snake, now aroused struck, recoiled and struck again. Streams of pale amber venom ran down the hem of the girl's skirt. Desperately she stumbled backwards, the baby clutched in her arms, the snake now thoroughly aroused, coiled towards her.

Tom, moving a split second after Alice, running with fear and desperation clutching at his heart, snatched them both in his arms and moved backwards the reptile slithering after them. Barely comprehending what they now witnessed, they saw a hissing ball of black fur leap upon the snake. Long curved claws sank deep into it's body, sharp incisors closed with the instinct of countless generations of wild hunters, deep into the neck, severing the spinal cord. Again and again she bit until her victim lay quivering in it's death throes. Beyond the power of speech, they watched as Ebony, head held high, her great tail fully extended, dragged her prize towards them dropping it casually at the foot of the stairs and then rubbed herself gently against Harry's legs.

Rose found her voice. She stood her hand to her mouth. 'Oh my God - my God, Harry, it is dead?'

Tom picked up a spade left by the gardener and severed the reptile's head. 'It is now, Rose.'

Trembling, she took the child in her arms. 'You saved my baby, Alice, you saved my baby!'

Alice, her face white with fear and exhaustion, sat limp, her head against Tom's shoulder. He voice quavered. 'Could I change my dress?' She pointed with disgust at the stains of venom still damp on the material.

The ever practical Emma, took her hand. 'Come with me Alice. I have something nice that will fit you.' She gave a shudder. 'I hate those blasted snakes!'

Harry wiped his streaming face. 'There is only one place they can get in - through the wall. Tomorrow by God, I'll have Fred make a gate so tight not even a mouse can get through.'

Emma returned, hand in hand with Alice. 'I had better make some fresh tea, Mr. Wakefield. Can't let a snake spoil Alice's birthday.'

'God bless you Emma, that's what we need - good strong tea!'

Tom stroked the black cat and laughed a little unsteadily. 'The heroine of the hour, Harry!'

That night they sat at dinner at under the soft glow of acetylene lamps hung from the ceiling.

'A delightful dinner, Rose. Emma is a splendid cook.'

'Yes, she leaves everything ready to serve. Greg called for her early tonight.'

'I know I am prying, but where do they go - or shouldn't I ask?'

Rose laughed. 'Fishing, Tom. I think they are just happy in each other's company.'

'Well I think Greg is a lucky man.' He looked around the table. 'This seems a good time as any to tell our dear friends.' He reached for Alice's hand. 'Today Alice did me the honour of agreeing to be my wife!'

Alice, her cheeks glowing, a languorous expression on her face, listened to every word her new fiance spoke. She lifted her left hand, there on the third finger, the dull glow of a gold ring.

Tom smiled. 'It was my mother's. I've been carrying it around for weeks trying to pluck up the courage to ask her.'

Harry, his eyes bright from the morphine he had received earlier, looked from one to the other. 'I know Rose feels as I do - we are happy for you.' He lifted his glass. 'May your lives be long and exceedingly happy!'

'Thank you Harry, thank you very much.'

Harry continued. 'When the ladies make coffee, I think it would be pleasant to have it on the top verandah.' He waited as the women excused themselves. 'So Tom, when is the happy event to take place?'

'April I hope. I haven't mentioned it to her but I want to take Alice on a world tour.'

'What of your practice? You will be badly missed.'

'That did worry me until a week ago. A new man is starting up here. Charles Hawkes. Young well-qualified. We hit it off right away. By the time we are ready to leave he should know the ropes pretty well.'

'I hope for the town's sake, you don't discover greener fields.'

'You mean leave Myuna?' Tom shook his head. 'The thought may have crossed my mind the first few months here, Harry, but not now. No, I hope and expect to spend my life here.'

'You don't miss your native land?'

'America? Yes, I will always have a lingering affection, tinged with feelings of sadness at times. I was very young when my parents died during a typhoid epidemic. I was an only child. They had no family where we were in the mid west, so I was shipped east into the care of two maiden aunts.' He smiled. 'Dear old souls, they knew nothing about raising a small boy. But I survived.'

'And why medicine?'

'Expected of me. My father was a doctor.'

'So you decided to see the world.'

'Yes, when my aunts passed away.' He smiled. 'They were twins, when the one died the other did not last long - often the case, you know. To cut a long story short, I was in New York at the time, at a large hospital. I think that was when I realized big cities were not for me. Fortunately I was left in a good position financially, so I packed my bags and booked on the first steamer out.' He sniffed the air. 'Ah, coffee! This is the only place I have tasted coffee, I mean real coffee since I left home.'

Harry smiled at the gasps of pleasure from the women. Below in the velvety darkness the softly glowing magic lanterns lined the carriageway. 'Harry, how beautiful! When did you do this?'

'Thanks to Greg, Rosie. He unpacked and cleaned them up. That's why he and Emma left early. To hang them up and light them. It's for Alice's birthday.'

Alice, her voice barely a whisper, clung tightly to her lover's hand. 'It's the most beautiful sight I have ever seen.' A shooting star blazed across the eastern sky. 'An omen, I know it's an omen for good luck!'

Harry laughed 'I'm sure it is, Alice. Now, here is something to complete the evening.' From a bucket of cracked ice he took a long bottle of champagne, unscrewing the cork with a pop that sounded thunderous in the quiet night. 'Now where did I put those glasses? Ah here they are, with your help if you please, Tom.'

Laughing, they clicked their glasses and sipped bubbling amber wine. Harry held his glass high. 'I propose a toast - to Tom and Alice! A long and loving life.'

Alice put her hand to her mouth, a giggle escaped her. 'Oh dear, excuse me - I've never had champagne before.'

CHAPTER VII

Christmas, 1893

Dr. and Mrs. Wakefield with Hiram Jansen, stepped ashore from the *S.S. Camira*. The landau was brought into service with Abraham at the reins. Rose's father showed his age, like a child he clung to his daughter's arm. 'I am lost without her, Rose. I don't do much now adays. The farm is well managed. I have made my will, daughter. Everything goes to you, in keeping for the little one. Now, don't fuss but this, I fear, will be my last trip.'

'Never say that, Dad.'

'Aye, but I do say, child. Now Harry has promised me some good whisky, let us not talk about this any more.'

'Dr. Wakefield had met his young colleague on his previous trip. He sought him out. 'Your opinion, Doctor?'

'I can scarcely bring myself to say, Sir, but weeks - perhaps two months I would think, no longer.'

'He should have rested. Bed would have given him more time.'

'You know your son, Sir. Harry is his own man. He drives himself mercilessly. He paints as a man possessed.'

'Typical of his condition, Doctor. His collapse when it comes will be complete, would you not agree?'

The younger man nodded. 'I have been expecting it for some time. He practically lives on morphine and alcohol.'

Christmas passed. The New Year, 1894 dawned. Harry's frail grasp on life began inevitably to fade. No longer sleeping in the same room as Rose, he would slip quietly out of his bed when a paroxysm of coughing racked his body. Moving silently, so not to disturb her, never suspecting she lay awake grieving, he would take an oil lamp and go along the picture gallery to the steps to the tower. Always he paused before the portrait of the woman whose haunting beauty possessed his soul. Then struggled up the spiral staircase to where the ever-ready bottle of Cognac soothed and calmed his trembling limbs.

There in the warm night he kept his solitary vigil, waiting sleepless until the first rays of the sun spilled over the land, over the forest and the distant ocean shimmering like burnished copper.

Often he wept silently. 'Is this the will of God, or whatever there is, that I am to be denied this forever? Never to see my son grow up, never to see those I love again? So Damn life, if this is all there is-one moment of beauty, one short moment of happiness!'

The days passed. Harry too weak to resist, took to his bed, resigned, uncomplaining. The doctors whispered outside the bedroom door. 'In extremis, I fear Dr. Wakefield. He has lost so much blood, his breathing is shallow, the heart is failing.'

'Yes, yes, his heart. Digitalis, what do you say, Doctor?'

Tom shook his head. 'Why prolong his agony, Sir?'

Once Harry roused to find the Rev. Trendel sitting by his bed. 'You here, Padre,' he whispered.

'All who love you, my dear Harry.' The priest's voice was heavy with grief for the young life slipping away. 'Let me say the 23rd Psalm for you.'

Harry managed a fleeting smile. 'The Lord is my shepherd.' Tears glistened in his eyes.

On a night when only his wife sat holding his hand, his eyes opened wide, his whisper barely audible. 'Dear Rosie, what a man you got for a husband.'

'The only one I ever wanted,' she answered. 'The only one.'

He struggled for breath. 'You must promise me, Rosie.'

She leaned over to hear him. 'Anything, Darling, anything.' She laid his hand against her wet cheek.

'Keep *Monaro* for Ben. Never let it go, my dear patient Rosie.'

Rose sat until first dawn streaked the sky. A Mopoke answered her mate from the dark woods. Harry opened his eyes briefly. 'A Mopoke, Rosie.' His head turned to the window as his life's blood stained the pillow. Harry Wakefield had suffered a massive haemorrhage, dying quietly without murmuring a word.

'My dear Rose, you should return to Melbourne with us. You must not stay here alone. I understand your loyalty to Harry's memory but think of the child and yourself - a woman alone in this far away place.'

'I will never leave here, Dr. Wakefield. I made a promise to my husband. A promise I will keep.' She spoke with firm determination, her eyes beyond tears.

Madelaine with her Gallic common sense, her own grief locked within her, took Rose's arm. 'Come Rose, let us go inside, we have much to talk about.'

Dr. Harry Wakefield held his grandson in his arms. 'Perhaps it is best for the moment, my little man. Your mother has courage - perhaps it is best for the moment.'

Several weeks had passed since Harry had been laid to rest in the walled enclosure by the chapel. Only the newly turned earth next to Captain Slocum's headstone marked the place. Rev. Trendel had spoken the words, his voice heavy with anguish. He loved Harry as his own.

After the sorrowing parents had departed Rose steeled herself to face the future. She found no consolation only a bitter determination to carry on as her husband would have wished. With her practical common sense, she entered into an agreement with Fred Dennis to extend the acreage under cane, sharing the profit as the demand and price for sugar rose.

At times in the empty house, while Ben slept, she fought the loneliness that engulfed her. She looked out on the unkempt garden, the grass, once so neat, waving on long seeding stalks. 'I must get the gardener back, I must keep the place as Harry would have it.' With a rush of gratitude, she thought of Emma. 'Dear Emma, thank God for her!'

She hurried down to the kitchen. Emma, flour to her elbows, looked up, gravely regarding her mistress.

'Emma, forgive me, I haven't been down to see you for so long. It's been so bad.' Her voiced trailed away.

'Don't worry Mrs. Wakefield, I understand. He was the finest, gentleman I ever knew.'

'Thank you. You will stay with us? Ben and I need you so much.'

'Wouldn't want to be anywhere else, Mrs. Wakefield.'

Rose sat on one of the stiff backed chairs. 'Perhaps we could have tea. The way we used to.'

As Emma poured the fragrant brew, Rose chose her words very carefully. 'Emma, I know I have no right to ask, but it is important to me. When did you and Greg plan to marry?'

Emma smiled over her steaming cup. 'I have told him he will have to wait. He has to finish clearing the fifty acres you and Mr. Wakefield gave for our engagement and then build a house for us.'

'That is rather hard on Greg, isn't it Emma?'

'I told him, take it or leave it, Mrs. Wakefield.'

Rose smiled in spite of herself. 'I am sure he will take it, Emma.'

Later, about to leave, she paused at the door. 'I am a little worried, Emma, have you seen Abraham lately? He has been gone longer this time than ever before.'

The girl coloured, looking a trifle uncomfortable. 'I did see him one night, just after -,'

'Yes, Emma, go on.'

'I heard him singing, you know his sort of singing. Scared the life out of me. It was so strange.'

Rose smiled gently. 'Go on Emma, tell me. I should know.'

'Oh Mrs. Wakefield.' She spoke in a small voice. 'I peeked in his window, he was naked, just that little bit of cloth he wears sometimes.' She drew a deep breath. 'He was sitting on his mat, singing to a strange little doll.' She shivered. 'Fair gave me the creeps.'

After her talk with Emma, Rose determined to find out what she could. She drove herself in the light sulky with Ben secure in a wicker basket on the seat beside her. She found the bay where the fishermen moored their boats. They were polite - no they had not seen the old Islander but would ask around.

She called, as always, on Tom Coburn and unburdened her anxiety.

'Leave it to me, Rose. One of my patients is sure to have seen him.'

Days later, working in the garden, she lifted her head at the sound of wheels on the carriageway. A battered sulky padded around the bend. A weather beaten river man touched his hat. 'G'day Missus. Believe you have been lookin' for old Abe.'

Rose stood, trowel in hand. 'Why yes, Mr. -,' she hesitated.

'Clem Golding, Missus. Yeah, I seen him 'bout two weeks ago.'

'Oh Mr. Golding, thank you very much. Do you know where he is now?'

'Haven't seen him since. He went down the river on that raft of his went out on the rip, over the bar.'

Rose felt faint. 'But Mr. Golding, didn't anyone try to stop him?'

The man looked slightly surprised. 'Stop old Abe? No Missus, I reckon he knew what he was doin'.'

Rose's hand went to her mouth. 'Oh my God!'

The man touched his horse with the whip, turning in the carriageway. 'Sorry Missus, that's all I can tell you.'

Rose ran after him. 'But Mr. Golding, he would have gone out to the open sea!'

He touched his hat. 'That's all I know Missus. Good day to you.'

Weeks later Rose heard a coastal packet had sighted the waterlogged raft. Abraham had gone home, his duty done.

April came. Tom Coburn married Alice May Dennis in the little chapel. The Rev. Trendel officiated. Only Alice's parents, Emma and a few close friends were present. The photographer came from the town. Emma's wedding cake was voted the finest ever seen.

Later in the cool evening they all sat quietly together. Emma excused herself and slipped away with Greg. Below, the carriageway glowed with soft colours, magic lanterns turning with each little breeze. Alice murmured to her new husband. 'I will remember this for the rest of my life.'

Tom uncorked a bottle of champagne and carefully poured it into the tall thin flutes. Then standing, held his glass aloft. 'A toast, dear friends, to one no longer with us.' Then turning to Rose. 'And to you, dear Rose, our heartfelt love and gratitude.' After the last sulky had disappeared along the line of glowing lights, Rose sat dreaming. She knew Emma and Greg had returned as lantern after lantern was snuffed out. She was alone, only the stars in the velvety blackness of the night to keep her company.

CHAPTER VIII

The years passed, Rose's baby son grew to a strong carefree boy, paddling his canoe to the far reaches of the river's north arm, to deep pools where, in the pure clear water, great Silver Perch lay quiet, only the slow sway of their tails keeping them front to the current. Here he would sit, patiently waiting until one of the big fish rose to the bait.

Everyday, for four hours, he sat in a small room at the Vicarage where the Rev. Trendel tutored him in the basics of education.

'He must be ready for school, Mrs, Wakefield. I know he dislikes Latin but I am sure you agree, he must be ready.'

Rose had tried not to think about school but she knew that some day that reality would have to be faced.

Emma and Greg had married in a quiet ceremony at the church in Myuna. Rose presented them with a cheque for two hundred pounds to furnish their house.

'If you still want me, Mrs. Wakefield, I would like to keep working for you,' adding shyly, 'don't think we are going to have any young ones. We've tried but nothing's happened.'

'Emma dear, if Greg doesn't mind, I would be so happy if you would.' She looked fondly at the young woman. 'You are very dear to us, Emma.'

It was the turn of the century. Myuna quietly celebrated. Rose read the newspapers that came with the mail. Such great events - Marconi's wireless, by which sound could be sent over great distances. A man named Edison had invented electric lamps and pictures that actually moved. It was even rumoured that men had made machines that flew through the air.

Rose remained unmoved. Her life was her son, *Monaro* and sugar cane. Her ever increasing acreage which had to be planted and nurtured until ready to be burnt off and harvested. Gangs of men toiled with flashing cane knives finishing each day black with soot and prodigious thirsts.

She read of a war against the Boers, who they were she had no idea, they were a world away. To her surprise, Greg, grown relatively prosperous, had the previous year left with other men to enlist. Emma, with typical common sense, accepted the matter philosophically. 'I suppose he just got tired of being married. I didn't try to stop him.' Six months after her husband departed, she gave birth to a baby girl.

'She is a beauty.' Tom Coburn said, holding the baby aloft. 'Congratulations Emma!'

After what seemed an eternity Greg returned to the little town. The Rev. Trendel, who had been informed of his arrival, met him at the wharf. He was bone thin, his left leg missing from the knee down. The old priest, too wise to ask questions, spoke in generalities as they travelled familiar streets.

That night Greg sat beside their bed, his head bent low, holding tight to his wife's hands. Emma had never seen him cry before. She gently stroked his hair until he could find his voice. 'I swear I will never leave you again Em! God, if we had only known! The poor beggars are farmers, just like us. I've no respect for the British, especially the officers - to them we are just Colonials.' A bitter smile crossed his face. 'They knew where to use us though! But you know Em, those Boers beat the British in every battle, but in the end they just had nothing to fight with. Poor devils. I think about them all the time.'

'Don't worry about it any more Greg. You are home and safe now and you have a daughter. Isn't she lovely?'

Greg touched the baby's hand. 'She's a beauty all right Em and a bloody sight better off than those little Boer kids I saw.'

'Oh Greg how awful. What happened to them?'

'The British herded them and the women into big barbwired camps, last I saw.'

'How terrible! Then what happened?'

'God knows, Em. I hate to think.' He picked up his crutch, awkwardly moving to the kitchen. 'Em please make me a cup of tea. If only you knew how I dreamt of good strong tea and of just you and me together again.'

Christmas brought Dr. Wakefield and Madelaine again to *Monaro*. To Rose, her father in law seemed taller and more heavy set than ever. His hair and beard, once so black, were now streaked with grey. He stood hands clasped behind, staring out the window. 'It is the right thing to do my dear. The boy is of an age now when he needs proper schooling. I have spoken to the headmaster at Melbourne Grammar, a fine school, you won't find better.' He turned. 'But Rose, Ben is your son, it will be your decision.'

She was tearful. 'I have never liked the thought of children living at a school. It seems so impersonal, so lonely for them.'

Madelaine, sitting beside her, linked arms. 'But no Rose, he will live with us. He will be a day boy, I think they call it.'

The doctor laid his hand gently on her shoulder. 'You are not losing him Rose. He loves you, never doubt it but you must think of his future.' He lit a cigar, going back to the window. 'Lord, what tranquillity, so little has changed, here one would never know - the great depression has brought such misery. So many bankruptcies, so many fine old institutions gone. Frankly my dear, without James Scully's advice and my mother's money - well, it was close, very close.'

'My poor father.' Rose's voice faltered. 'To die so lonely.'

'I spoke to the doctor who attended him. Rose, my dear, you must not grieve. It was very sudden. He was working with the men when it happened. And you must not worry, James, on your instructions, has seen to efficient management of the property.'

Madelaine looked up at her husband, skilfully changing the subject. 'Ellen McSweeney, Harry, you must tell Rose.'

The doctor found his chair. 'Yes, a strange business, in many ways a sad business. The father knowing nothing of his son's death, apparently had a change of heart and came looking for him. Eventually he found the priest who had buried the poor young fellow. The priest referred him to me. I have never seen a man so completely devastated. I imagine the whole matter had weighed heavy upon him. Fine stamp of a man, Irish of course. Breeds racing stock. The upshot was he visited the wife. Of their meeting, I know little. He called on me before he left, still shaken but captivated by his grandchildren. I understand Mrs. McSweeney is now in very comfortable circumstances. They reached an agreement - the boys to attend a Catholic College, the girl, in deference to Mrs. McSweeney, to be educated at a Protestant Ladies School.' He puffed thoughtfully on his cigar. 'His wife will not meet with her nor does she wish to see her grandchildren. It is sad but true my dears, in matters of religious persuasion, women are often the least tolerant.'

On Christmas Day 1900, Dr. Tom Coburn with his wife, came to lunch. Later the two men repaired to the tower. Dr. Wakefield lazed back in the captain's swivel chair, a glass of golden Cognac in his hand.

'Strange, is it not Doctor, so much has happened since my poor son died. Forgive me, I know I am going over old ground, I will never know if I was right. Perhaps he would have survived in a sanatorium, but as you know, I took the advice of a man I consider the best in Melbourne. God knows, who can tell?'

Tom smiled gently. 'I was very close to Harry. I am absolutely sure he knew, but here he lived and savoured every moment of his life. Here, I believe with all my heart, he was truly happy.'

'Thank you, Doctor, thank you. Here, allow me to top up your glass.' He swung around in his chair, gazing down on the scene below. The three women, parasols extended, strolled amongst the flower beds. 'I must confess to a worry that occupies my mind. Rose is still a young woman, an indomitable spirit I grant you, but all alone now. Ben is coming to Melbourne with us - she has agreed. She must be lonely.'

Tom answered mildly. 'I doubt it, Sir. Her promise to Harry she regards as a sacred vow. Her life is dedicated to *Monaro* and to her son. Frankly, I doubt she has the time to feel lonely.'

'Yes Doctor, quite so. But as a physician, you will know to what I refer. A woman has certain biological needs.'

Tom thoughtfully studied his glass. 'I understand, Sir. May I say I was fairly close to Harry and Rose. I formed certain conclusions.'

'You don't suggest Rose is frigid?'

'No Sir, I do not. I do know certain women will tolerate one man only. That man, Sir, was your son.'

'You are a very astute physician, young man.'

'Thank you.'

The older man quickly changed the subject. 'May I ask how life is treating you here, Doctor?'

'I find life very satisfying, Sir. The practice is growing, my opposition has joined me - a godsend for both of us.'

'I believe you have a daughter.'

'Yes, Doctor. Jane came rather unexpectedly, just after we returned from overseas.'

'A pleasant trip, I trust?'

'Yes, on the whole but frankly we were glad to get back. Europe holds no charm for me. Such poverty, such a void between the rich and those who virtually starve in the streets.' He smiled. 'Alice was captivated, of course. We took in the museums, art galleries, the usual things tourists do.'

Dr. Wakefield nodded. 'My wife and I went back to Paris some eighteen months ago, I think for the last time. My wife is not strong, I would not risk another voyage.' He sipped from his glass. 'Yes, I must agree with your views on Europe. That cauldron seethes with the intrigue, with power play. Some day it will explode. There are powerful forces at work there, Doctor, misplaced national ambitions. Thank God we are well away from it.

Tell me,' he continued, 'have you ever travelled out west, to the hinterland?'

'Apart from Sydney, this is the only part of the country I know.'

Dr. Wakefield stroked his beard. 'I hope one day you may. The vastness of this country, virtually unpopulated,' he smiled, 'unless you count the sheep and cattle, and the flies - those accursed flies. Enough to drive a man to drink! Yes, my young friend, it takes a very special type of man to pioneer such country. But there is a certain charm there, it weaves a spell on those who embrace.'

'Similar to the American West, I imagine.'

'That I can't say, never having seen that part of the world but I do know something of this country. When I was a young man, before leaving for Europe with my friend James Scully, we determined to see all we could. I was anxious to see the gold fields where my dear old mother lived as a young girl.' He sighed. 'That journey left an indelible impression on us both. The terrible hardships men endure to carve out a home of sorts, yet no matter how hard their lot, they hide their despair behind a smile and a handshake.'

Tom remained silent.

'Yes Doctor, city folk could never understand. I have a friend who told me of his meeting some time ago, with a man, a man who seems to have captured the spirit of the Outback. Fellow by the name of Lawson, Henry Lawson. Met him one night at a country pub, a little the worse for drink at the time, but lucid. He was spellbound by his stories, his verse. Doggerel I suppose but in it the spirit of the bush. My friend said the man had a sadness about him that touched his heart.'

He rose, glass and cigar in hand, to look out the window. 'You must forgive me - this Cognac has made me a trifle more loquacious than usual. I believe we are expected below, Doctor.'

Monaro 1901. Great events hardly disturbed the even tenor of the burgeoning town. The news of Federation was accepted with mild enthusiasm. Some English Earl or Duke, later revealed as Lord Hopetoun, a sickly man, was to be the country's Governor General. Really, it was said, it was right to have a man of such nobility to preside over the new Commonwealth. Otherwise, why would their glorious Queen appoint him?

Rose wondered whether her father in law would be involved in such a historic event. She learned later that he had attended a few dinners for citizens of quality, refusing a certain Honour, then quietly retired to his busy practice, politely refusing further invitations. He had, however, taken time to take his grandson to Sydney for the celebrations. The like of which had never been seen in the Colony before.

Rose scarcely noticed the time pass. One year was very like the other. Emma brought her younger sister, Lucy, carefully instructing her in her duties. Much of the big house was closed up, leaving just enough for comfortable living. She appointed Greg to assist Fred Dennis, the two were old friends. Under their stewardship her interests flourished.

At times black despair gripped her as she waited with growing anticipation for her son to return for his holidays.

Home for Christmas, Ben rushed to his mother's arms. A quick embrace then away like a captive bird released from it's cage. The canoe was launched and little more was seen of him until Christmas Day. Rose felt pangs of jealousy - I am losing him! The tears glistened in her eyes. She confided in Tom. 'I doubt he is interested in seeing me.'

'My dear Rose, you are not losing him! Ben is a boy. He loves you, never doubt it.' He smiled reassuringly. 'Life for a boy his age is for living. The weeks he spends here, you can be sure he stores like treasure all year long.'

The next few years brought a series of disasters to Myuna. Heavy rains brought floods that destroyed crops, and Banks failed. Rose on her father in laws advice, banked with the oldest Bank in the Commonwealth which rode out the storm as others closed their doors.

She eagerly awaited her son's letters. How they had changed over the years, no longer letters from a small boy, Ben was growing up. Now he brought his friends to share the holidays.

CHAPTER IX

On a sunny afternoon in 1913, the clipped lawns and leafy trees surrounding *Monterey* echoed to the happy chatter and laughter of a group of gaily dressed young people. Men in striped blazers and white flannels, girls in summer frocks, carrying furled parasols. It made for a pleasant scene. Some lazed in the shade or strolled in groups greeting each other as only close friends do.

The slim dark suited figure of a young priest contrasted oddly with the others although it was obvious by his pausing here and there, he was well know to many of them. He stopped suddenly, his face breaking into a smile. 'Ben, there you are, I've looked everywhere for you.' He shook hands warmly. 'Congratulations, old friend, congratulations. So now it's Benjamin Harry Wakefield, Doctor of Medicine! We are proud of you, all of us.'

'Thanks Dan. Coming from you, that's a genuine compliment.' Ben, slim of build, tall as his grandfather, smiled with pleasure. 'It seems so long Dan, it's a tonic to see you.' He took the priest's arm. 'Please stay with me a while. Truth is, I don't know half these people.'

'Mostly friends of my sister I think. You don't mind?'

'Mind? I should say not. When Grandfather gives a soiree, the world is welcome,' he grinned.

'So he got what he always wanted of you, Ben. Do you mind?'

'I wasn't always the most enthusiastic pupil, but yes, I'm happy enough now. How about yourself?'

'I think you know, Ben, I never wanted to enter the priesthood,' he sighed, 'but that was part of the bargain struck between my poor mother and my paternal grandfather.'

'I am truly sorry. Can't you resign, is there no way?'

'No, Ben. Priest I am and priest I remain while ever I live.'

'What of Sean?'

'Absolutely dedicated. He is married to the Church, there will never be a rival.'

'Never mind. Come on, let's find the rest of the old gang, we can reminisce about *Monaro.* Those wonderful holidays when we were so young, growing up, so full of life. Remember my canoe? Remember the day it sank with all aboard? And Sean, dear old Sean pulling us out and then diving for the canoe.'

Dan laughed. 'Remember? I remember as if it was yesterday. Whenever I'm sad, I think of *Monaro* and your mother, that sweet, patient woman.'

Ben stopped, pointing ahead. 'I say, isn't that Pieter DeVries? Look under that tree, fussing over your sister as usual.'

'By George, so it is, although I must confess she doesn't appear to mind.'

Ben grinned. 'Afraid he's a gone man, our Pieter.'

The young lawyer suddenly became aware they were under scrutiny. With Ellen McSweeney on his arm, he strolled towards them, with a wide smile of recognition. 'Well Ben, a medico at last.' He rolled his eyes in mock despair. 'Heaven preserve us all!'

'True Pieter, if only I had known what slavery I was in for, I would have become a cane planter.'

'Over your grandfather's dead body, my boy. How are you, Dan?' They shook hands. 'How is the religious business?'

'Save your soul for fifty quid, Pete.'

'Done!'

They hooted with laughter.

'Ellen, you are prettier every time I see you. How is your singing coming along?'

'I go to Europe for more training next year, Ben.' She smiled at her companion. 'Unless Pieter objects.'

Pieter put his arm around her. 'Not the slightest objection my love, providing you marry me first.'

Ben broke in. 'Cut it out, you two. We've been talking about the old days at *Monaro.*'

Ellen smiled with the pleasure of memory. 'I will always remember Mr. Wardrop meeting us.' She sighed, 'Oh what wonderful, beautiful times we had. Ben, why did we have to grow up? I think of your dear mother so often, how good she was to us. I do wish she was here today.'

'So do I, Ellie, but you know she never leaves *Monaro*.'

Tears glistened in the girl's eyes, she took Ben's hands in hers. 'We will always be friends won't we, always and always.' She turned to her lover. 'We will, won't we, Pieter?'

Pieter made light of the situation. 'I vow my love. I will prepare affidavits of loyalty for all to sign!' He looked toward the house, one hand shading his eyes. He spoke with mock solemnity. 'Spare our souls, here comes Sean.'

They stood silently as the tall thin priest approached. His deep voice intoned a mock severity. 'So, at last I find you sinners!' A broad smile creased his face. 'Congratulations young Benjamin. I know you will be a credit to your profession.'

They all had a deep affection for the grave ascetic man whose sweetness of nature and dry sense of humour lay hidden under a quiet reserve. He gestured toward a large striped marquee. 'I come with glad tidings children - iced Champagne and excellent fare awaits.'

Pieter made an elaborate bow, the others followed suit. 'Lead on, oh Moses, to the manna you promise. We have all wandered too long in this desert and our throats are parched.' Linking arms, they set out, laughing, for the marquee.

From a drawing room window two elderly gentlemen looked down on the colourful gathering. 'Not a care in the world, James. They know nothing of life. My only wish is that it will be kind to them.' He brushed cigar ash from his waistcoat. 'Good God, where have the years gone?'

James Scully patted his friend's shoulder. 'Often wonder myself, Harry. Seems only yesterday when we were young, full of life.'

Dr. Wakefield, still an imposing figure, his hair and beard heavy with grey, nodded. He waved his cigar toward the laughing crowd milling around the marquee. 'Today's youth, eh. Live for the moment!'

'As did we, old friend.'

'That we did, James, that we did. You know, I'm so out of touch these days. I don't know half of what goes on. I haven't seen your youngest son in years, it seems.'

'Articled to old Pearson, solid man, looks after Ruth's interests. He will do well there. Full of life, quite the ladies man.'

'Chip off the old block, eh?'

They chuckled, comfortable in each others company.

'Pieter is with you, of course.'

'Yes, thank God for Pieter! Takes most of the work off my shoulders.'

'Hear he is sweet on the young McSweeney girl.'

'So Ruth tells me. Rum business that, Harry. The two boys Catholic priests and the girl brought up Protestant.'

The doctor laughed. 'You may have a couple of priests in the family good for your soul, you old sinner!'

'Too old and too late to worry about religious nonsense at my age. Tell me, what of that young grandson of yours?'

'Oh he will make a doctor all right James. Full of these new fangled notions they teach nowadays, but he's careful and he listens.'

'Not in practice yet?'

'No, he leaves tomorrow for *Monaro*. I am hoping Tom Coburn might find use for him.'

'And what news of your daughter in law? Never married again? What a waste.'

'No doubt she has been approached but Harry was the only great passion in her life.'

'Damned if I will ever understand women.'

Harry chuckled. 'For reasons beyond my comprehension, they seem to understand you James. Your irresistible Irish charm, no doubt.' He took his friend's arm. 'Come on, I have been expressly ordered to bring you to the ladies for tea.'

'Good God not tea - ruin my constitution!'

'Patience old chap. First we must pay our respects, then to the library.'

James sighed. 'Just a quick how d'ye do then Harry. I believe you mentioned iced champagne?'

On a cold morning in August 1914, Dr. Wakefield and his wife sat at breakfast in their cosy dining room. They exchanged few words, the silence broken only by the crackling of the fire in the grate and the rustle of the newspaper. The doctor put down the page he had been examining and reached for his wife's hand. 'Never fear my dear, it is only newspaper talk. The whole thing will blow over in six weeks, believe me.'

'But for such a foolish action, Harry - the shooting of the duke. It was a duke was it not?'

'An archduke I think, but you must not worry my dear. They are always within an ace of going to war, especially if they feel their position strong enough. Anything will do, a word, an action such as the assassination of this duke.' He sighed. 'Such I am afraid is human nature. In any case,' he smiled gently, 'France is well defended and safe.' He was interrupted by the entrance of their butler.

'The mail, Doctor.'

'Thank you, Benson.' He sorted through the sheaf of envelopes, selecting one, putting the others aside. 'Well, a minor miracle! At long last a letter from our errant grandson.' From his waistcoat he fished for his pinze nez attached to it's black velvet ribbon. 'He has to say, let me see - *Dearest Grans* - for Heavens sake, Grans, whatever next. However - *Sorry I have been so derelict in my promise, but you know how I hate letter writing. Believe me, a day never passes I don't think of you and miss you both.*' Dr. Wakefield peered over his spectacles at his wife, smiling in anticipation. 'At least that is comforting to know. This is the only letter the young hound has written these last three months.' He tilted back in his chair, the better to read the closely written scrawl. '*Mother is well, busy from morning to night. Seen some of my old friends, go fishing every opportunity. Dr. Coburn keeps me at it, says I will probably make a passable surgeon one day. What do you make of all this talk of war in Europe? What an adventure should it ever happen.*' The doctor turned the crumpled envelope over. 'Hm, I'll warrant this was written weeks ago, probably carried it around in his pocket until he thought to post it.' He handed the letter to his wife. 'You read the rest my dear.' He rose from the table. 'I really must be off.' Pausing at the door, he smiled at her. 'Promise me now, you will not worry. Promise me.'

'I promise, Harry.' Her voice was so low he barely heard her. His thoughts were mixed as he left his home, muttering to himself. 'Damn and blast this bloody war. I'd lay odds, Ben himself will turn up any day now. Adventure, he said! God help us.'

Dr. Wakefield's prediction proved correct. Some three weeks later their grandson arrived unannounced in the uniform of a Captain in the Australian Medical Corps.

Over dinner that evening Ben gazed affectionately from one grandparent to the other.

Dr. Wakefield clearing his throat, broke the silence. 'So Ben, what is the feeling in the country?'

'Wildly enthusiastic, Sir. All the young men,' he grinned, 'and not so young, are rushing to enlist.'

'Hm, escape from boredom and responsibility eh?'

Ben hesitated. 'Yes, perhaps you're right. Old Mr. Wardrop told them they are all bloody fools.' He kissed his grandmother's cheek. 'Forgive the language, Gran?'

Madelaine smiled, her eyes soft with affection. 'How like your father you are mon cher, so gentle.' She stood, taking his arm. 'Come, let us take coffee.'

Monaro, December 1915

Rose sitting in the shade of the verandah breathlessly pulled at her bonnet strings, her cheeks flushed in anticipation of the letter lying beside her on the little cane table. '*Dearest Mother, a brief note to let you know I am all right. I say with some reservations, having fallen victim to the 'flu raging at present. No doubt you have read the news, more about that when I see you again, which I pray won't be too long. Seems the whole world is over here. London is drab but very exciting. Had supper with one of your favourite young ladies the other night (of course I am privileged). She is the toast of the town, entertaining the troops and on the stage. She has a beautiful voice. Believe Dan is over here as a Chaplain, looking forward to seeing him. All for now Dearest, must rush. May be going to France shortly, don't know for sure, will let you know. Sorry to hear about Great Grandmother. What a wonderful old lady she was. Miss you and Monaro terribly. All my love, Ben. P.S. Please let the Grans know you have heard from me.*'

Rose gazed out over the landscape shimmering in the noonday heat. She whispered, clutching the letter to her, 'God keep you safe my darling.'

CHAPTER X

The action at Fromelle raged with terrible ferocity, a diversion, a feint before the hell that was Pozieres, a monument to the incompetence the sheer stupidity of the High Command. In less than twenty four hours five thousand troops lay dead.

Working feverishly in a forward dressing station amongst torn and mutilated flesh of his countrymen, Ben cursed the war and the criminality of the fools responsible for it. Working without sleep, unaware of the passage of time, he moved from stretcher to stretcher crammed closely together. Outside wounded lay in rows silent or moaning quietly, patiently waiting for what little help he could give.

In the dust and clamour of battle, later, he could never remember just when he became aware his fellow surgeon had dropped the instrument he had been using and stood staring through the half open tent flap-'Jesus Christ, Ben!' His voice was hoarse with fatigue. 'Don't move, we've been over run!'

As in a dream, Ben followed his gaze. Grey clad soldiers, their long bayonets extended rushed towards them. Ben rushed out, his arms outstretched.'Doctor, Doctor,' he s'creamed. A soldier, hardened in the art of battle, lunged at him slashing him from chest to rib cage. In mortal terror that would forever haunt his dreams, he staggered backwards through a tangle of ropes and stretchers. Falling to his knees waiting for the final thrust, he whispered his mother's name. The soldier followed slowly, kicking aside the debris blocking his way.

Under the effort of his terror Ben blindly scrabbled backwards in the dust. Half hidden where they had fallen, his groping fingers felt the smooth butt of a discarded rifle. With instinct born of his boyhood hunting days, he slid home the bolt and without aiming, shot his tormentor point blank through the chest. The German soldier stopped suddenly a surprised, almost pleading look on his face. He fell heavily, the rifle sliding before him. Vomiting and shivering Ben dropped the rifle, clutching at his chest, incredulously watching blood ooze between his fingers. As his eyes glazed over he was dimly aware of shouting khaki clad figures milling round him and the sound of unmistakable Australian oaths.

Slowly as his eyes groped for light, he found he was lying securely strapped to a stretcher in a swaying ambulance, each movement a searing pain. He desperately tried to recall the previous hours.

'A drink, Sir?' A British orderly bent over him, holding a water bottle to his lips. Ben gulped greedily then fell back with a groan.

'Where are we?' His voice a harsh whisper.

'Have you back in Blighty in no time, Sir. Back over the Channel tonight.'

His hands wandered over his heavily bandaged chest, he begged for more water and then drifted back into oblivion.

He woke suddenly. The ambulance had stopped. He heard voices, orders being given, and smelled the strong sweet smell of the sea. The door opened, he heard an Australian voice. 'Just a minute, men. I'll take a look before you shift any of them.' The medical officer, a much older man, made a swift examination. Ben was the last to be moved.

'Well young fellow, what have you been doing to yourself?'

Ben mumbled incoherently.

'Well never mind,' came the practiced, comforting voice. 'We'll give you a good shot of morphine, you won't notice the crossing.'

Ben woke from his drugged sleep as he was being carefully placed in another ambulance, this time on English soil. The driver, a mere girl, was tucking a heavy blanket around him. He looked up into the bluest eyes he had ever seen. From under her cap, brown hair fell in strands around her face. For the first time since the action he grinned weakly. 'Is this Heaven?'

She looked at him blushing, 'Afraid not, Sir. Now please just lie still.' She made a final tuck of the blanket before gently closing the door.

'It is highly irregular young lady, out of visiting hours. Why do you wish to see this patient?'

The girl's voice faltered as she stood before the authoritative figure of the hospital matron. 'He was in my ambulance, Matron.' She held out a leather wallet. 'I think this is his. The name inside is Dr. Wakefield.'

'Well leave it with me, I will see he gets it. Now if you will excuse me?'

The girl blushed slightly. 'May I please give it to him myself, Matron?'

Matron Jones' expression, normally unyielding, softened a little as she glanced at the young woman. She sighed, closing her record book with a bang. 'Well, if you must. Come along with me.' For a large woman the matron moved quickly, leading the way through wards of wounded. As they passed, some gave a cherry wave, others lay still, quiet resignation written on their faces. She stopped before two large swinging doors. 'The officers ward, Miss.' She pointed. 'There you are, Number 3 Dr. Wakefield.'

She hesitated. 'It seems so strange to see a doctor sick in bed.'

Matron Jones allowed herself a brief smile. 'They are human like everyone else, my dear, and' she emphasised the word, 'they make the worse patients.'

Ben lay in a half sitting position, reading. He looked up as she approached, the book falling to his lap. He smiled in disbelief. 'Well, so it was not a dream. The beautiful blue eyed lady herself!'

Matron looked severe. 'Five minutes, Doctor, no more.'

The girl spoke shyly. 'I hope you don't mind my coming.' She held out the small leather pouch. 'I found your wallet in my ambulance.'

'Mind your coming? I have thought about you every day I have been lying here.' He shook his head. 'I really began to believe - please tell me I am not still asleep.'

She blushed to the roots of her hair. 'I really must go now, Doctor. I hope you feel better soon.'

'Oh no, please don't go.' He winced as he held out his hand. 'I haven't even thanked you yet. Please tell me your name.'

She hesitated. 'Frances, Frances Chapman.'

He held tightly to her hand. 'Ben Wakefield. You're an Aussie, aren't you?

She sat on the chair by his bed. 'Yes, all the way from Wangaratta.'

'Good Lord! That's near where my mother comes from.'

'It's lovely country round there. Afraid I am often homesick for the sunshine.'

'I know. But what is a beautiful girl like you doing all the way over here in this mess?'

'I was over here with my parents when the war broke out. You know - the Grand Tour!' She smiled, pushing the errant curls back under her cap. 'They had to go back. Dad was worried about the farm.'

'They let you stay?'

'Yes,' she smiled, 'not without a scene through.'

He hadn't taken his eyes from her face. 'I can imagine. So you volunteered and became an ambulance driver.'

'Yes.' She tried to withdraw her hand. 'I really must go, Doctor. Matron will be back.'

'Ben, please call me Ben.' He released her fingers. 'Promise you will come and see me again soon. Will you, Frances?'

She rose and moved to the doorway, turning as she left. 'All right, I'll try next time I'm off. Must fly, I can hear Matron coming.'

Matron Jones entered, followed by the ward Sister and an orderly pushing a trolley. 'All right gentlemen, time for dressings.' She spoke quietly in an aside to the Sister. 'Hurry it up, Madge, there is a new lot arriving.' She stopped briefly by Ben's bed. 'Dr. Wakefield, I only allowed that young person to visit out of hours because she had some personal property of yours.'

Ben grinned up at her. 'You're a brick Matron.' He grimaced as he held out his arm to hold her attention. 'Please let her in when she comes next time. You know she can't choose when she can get off. Please?'

Matron looked hard at her patient. 'Hm'm, we'll see.' She turned to leave. 'All right gentlemen, don't waste Sister's time, get on with it.'

In the days that followed Ben waited with growing impatience. A week passed. His anxiety increased, waiting became intolerable, anxiety turned to self pity. She had obviously done what she considered her duty, returning his wallet. He found a dozen reasons why she could never be interested in a wreck like himself. Matron did not wait for his inquiry whenever she entered the ward. 'I am sorry, Doctor, she hasn't been back.'

Now in a wheelchair, Ben lapsed into a sombre melancholy. He tried reading, occasionally talked to fellow patients, increasingly spent any fine day in the garden behind the hospital. It was there Frances found him, dozing, a book open on his knees. At her soft greeting his heart leapt. He looked up, she was standing there, a bunch of blue cornflowers in her hand. His voice seemed to come from far away. 'I thought you had forgotten. I thought you would never come again.'

She smiled. 'I had not forgotten, Ben.' She spoke his name shyly. 'It has been so hard to get away. We have been terribly busy.'

He gazed at her, 'Oh Frances, if you only knew how I have wished for this.' He stopped conscious he was going too fast. He reached for her hand. 'I am so glad you've come.'

She did not draw back. He felt how soft and cool it was. She took off her cap and loosened her hair, flushing slightly.

'Frances, you are the prettiest girl I have every seen.'

'Please Ben. You must not say that.'

'But I must. I mean it with all my heart!'

She wheeled the chair to a little garden table and sat facing him. 'You only say that because you are lonely. I am just an ordinary girl, you need someone to talk to.'

Ben drew a deep breath. 'I am walking now, you know. I only use the chair to loaf. Stitches come out tomorrow.'

'Oh Ben, are you really that much better?' To hide her confusion she looked around. 'What a dear little garden.'

He didn't seem to hear her. 'Frances, I'll be back at work in a couple of weeks. I'll be up and about again.'

She looked down, he held tightly to her hand. 'Saturday week Frances, will you have dinner with me? I know a good spot, and then we can see a show. I have an old friend, I can get tickets. Or do whatever you like.'

Her answer was barely audible. 'If you really want to Ben.' She glanced at her watch. 'I must go now.'

He stood up. 'What time? Where?'

She gave the address.

'All right, six o'clock sharp. I'll be there.' He watched as her slim figure walked away, pausing briefly to turn and smile before disappearing.

Ben's relationship with Matron Jones blossomed. He learnt she was a widow, her husband had died in an accident on the wharves. Their only child, a daughter was married, living in Sydney. 'You are a sport, Matron, letting Frances in after hours.'

'Well I must admit, for a slip of a girl like that, she's got courage. I know the sort of work they do.'

'I'm going to marry her.'

Matron Jones stared at him in astonishment. 'Marry her? For Heavens sake, when did you ask her? The girl has only been here twice to my knowledge.'

'Oh I haven't asked her yet.'

'You haven't eh, and what makes you think she will have you?'

Ben wheeled his chair round. 'I haven't the foggiest idea but I am going to ask her and keep asking until she says yes.'

Matron slowly shook her head. 'Well if this doesn't beat the band. I think I have heard everything now. Here sit still, I'll wheel you back inside.'

'Wheel be buggered, I'm walking now.' He took the older woman's arm. 'You are a pretty good sort, Jonesy.' He stooped to pick up the flowers from the table. 'Like her eyes aren't they?'

Matron merely smiled.

Ben told the driver to wait and entered through a wrought iron gate to a small flight of stairs leading to a heavy door, it's shiny brass knocker gleaming in the dim gaslight. A pleasant- faced woman answered his knock. 'Does Miss Chapman live here?'

'Oh yes, Sir. Please come in she is expecting you.'

He followed into a cosy dimly lit parlour smelling faintly of lavender. At his entrance, a tall broad shouldered man, who had been standing by the window watching the street, turned to face him. Ben's heart sank, he groaned to himself-I might have known! The stranger in the uniform of an Australian Army officer, leaned heavily on a walking stick favouring his left leg. He smiled, extending his hand. 'Looks like we are waiting for the same lady.'

'Ah, yes.' Ben took the proffered hand. 'I think we are.'

A broad smile creased the man's face, a handsome face, deeply lined thick brown curly hair and a clipped moustache. 'Frank Chapman, Francie's brother.'

Ben felt a surge of relief and slightly light headed. 'Ben Wakefield, I didn't know Frances had a brother.' He stopped. 'Good Lord, you must think me an idiot - we have only met twice.'

'Don't worry, she has already told me all about you. Believe you have seen a rough time.'

'More lucky than rough, I'd say.' He glanced at the other's stiff dragging leg. 'France?'

'No, Gallipolli. Second week ashore.'

'Appalling.'

Ben nodded. 'Sounds like this whole bloody war.'

'Yes, thanks to the stupidity of the bastards running the show. We ran straight into the trap the Turks set for us.'

They were interrupted by light footsteps on the stairs to the upper rooms. Ben stared. Could this be the same girl? Dressed in civilian clothes - blue linen with her shining brown hair tied back with a blue beaded headband. He stood speechless.

Frances kissed her brother and turned smiling to Ben. 'I see you two have already met.'

Frank laughed. 'Hard to miss each other in a room this size.' He put his arm around his sister's waist. 'Trust you have been behaving yourself, young lady.' He grinned at Ben. 'Promised to keep an eye on her. However,' He smiled, 'I see you are in good hands.'

She lightly kissed him again. 'Thanks for coming, Frank. Ben's taking me out to dinner.'

Ben took her arm. 'I have a cab waiting Frank, can we give you a lift?'

'You can, old man, far as Piccadilly. If that is not out of your way. I'm meeting friends later.'

As the evening wore on, Ben and Frances joined the gay crowd at the Ritz. Dancing close together, mingling in a sea of uniformed men and beautifully gowned women. His lips close to her ear, he whispered. 'Francie, every man here is looking at you.'

She drew back, her wide, generous mouth curved in a smile.

'Francie, I'm in love with you hopelessly!'

'Ben, please, you mustn't say that.'

'Dearest Francie, will you marry me?' The music stopped and they returned to their table. He reached for her hand. 'Francie, if you won't marry me, I am lost.' For what seemed an eternity they sat in silence. Then, 'please Francie, put me out of my misery.'

She looked at him, a hint of tears in her eyes. 'Ben, I don't know what to say.'

'Can you feel anything for me?'

'Yes Ben, I do.'

His hand trembled as he poured the wine. 'I will love you with all my heart for as long as I live.'

On a sunny day in August, the war seemed far away. Their union was solemnised in a little Norman church. Frank acted as best man. A few friends were there. In a daze, Ben greeted them all. So dear, from the distant past, another world away. He introduced his bride with such happiness he never thought possible. Deliriously, they set up house in a pleasant cottage in Surrey. There was no time for a honeymoon, every surgeon was needed as the wounded came in a never ending stream. Ben was posted back to the same hospital he had himself been a patient in.

The summer passed, winter came with it's biting cold. For the soldiers bogged down in mud of No Man's Land, the bloody battles took a terrible toll, achieving little, a stalemate. Australian troops achieved everlasting glory with their furious onslaughts, earning faint praise from the British Brass who though grudgingly admiring them considered them insolent colonial upstarts.

The following summer Frances, who worked through the winter months, gave birth to a healthy boy. Ben, grey with fatigue, sat at her bedside holding her hand. 'So soon Francie, so soon. But I am glad you know. What are we going to call him?'

She smiled, cuddling the tiny bundle. 'Harry, I suppose darling.'

He shook his head. 'No more Harry's, not yet anyway. What about Frank?'

She shook her head. 'No that won't do either. Do you like Gareth for a name?'

'Gareth? Where on earth does that come from?'

'My father. Do you mind?'

He laughed out loud. 'Mind? Of course I don't mind. Gareth. What is it anyway - Welsh, Irish?'

'I don't know, but you know I love my dad dearly.'

He leaned over and kissed her tenderly. 'Yes I know that, dearest Francie. If you want Gareth, so do I.'

Frances made the little house a haven. She was silent when Ben came home looking old and haggard. She never probed, waiting until he was ready to talk. When he did, it came in a torrent.

'Francie, sometimes you must think me out of my mind, I know I do.' He would bury his face in his hands. 'I don't know how much more I can take. Francie, for Christ's sake they thank me, thank me for cutting off their shattered gangrenous limbs!' He would stand and pace the floor of their sitting room. 'They are glad to be out of it. But in God's name - why are we here, anyway?'

She would put her arm around him trying to sooth his anguish. 'You only do what you have to do darling.'

He would hold onto her like a drowning man. 'Some day I will take you to *Monaro* Francie. You belong there.' He would smile as his mind travelled through the endless distance. 'We will be so happy there, so happy. You just can't imagine.'

The little house became a lively meeting place, a refuge for homesick Australians. A few of the old gang came and stayed a while, leaving reluctantly and always returning when their duties allowed.

Pieter DeVries, a pilot in the Royal Flying Corps, was a regular. Ben secretly envied him. Dan McSweeney, now an Army Padre and Ellen his sister, found the house a refuge from her demanding role in the theatre and entertaining the troops. They came and left, always bringing small offerings of food or liquor. Whenever enough got together, the subject was always war. This curse of mankind, would it never end? They laughed, they argued, at times some wept for fallen comrades but endlessly they talked about their homeland. Their anger blazed at the conscription issue - the bloody thing had been defeated twice, two referenda 1916 and 1917. Who is this little creature over there furiously campaigning to send more Australians to the slaughter? Even the troops were against it. At this Ben kept quiet. From his mother he had learned his beloved Myuna had voted for conscription. Poor bloody fools, if only they knew. Living over there in their comfort and safety. Anyway they will know the cost one day, then perhaps their tune will change.

Frank returned from convalescing in the country, his wound healed. His natural impatience satisfied only when he was allowed to join the remnants of his old unit on the Western Front.

As the ghastly slaughter went on, the unthinkable began to dawn in the minds of the allied leaders - the war might soon be over, disastrously!

Two events occurred in 1918. One altered the course of the war, the other, the birth of another son to Ben and Frances.

General Pershings army of fresh American tipped the scales and Germany sued for peace.

Frank returned from France weary and bitter, his cheerful, infectious smile faded. He had been in the thick of a bitter battle for a little French town, Villiers-Bretonneaux. A decisive battle that had broken the German spirit and left fourteen hundred Australian dead on the blood soaked soil. Forever after that same town would honour and remember Australia with gratitude. Gratitude for men who would never see another sunrise.

The Armistice was duly signed, an armistice at the end of a war that cost millions in dead and wounded, left nations bankrupt. An armistice which marked the final chapter of the war to end all wars.

Hysterical delirium swept the country. People bound by a rigid class system, who would never pass the time of day with strangers, danced in the streets. Promises were made. A New World, a new world order where nations could talk out differences and man could live in freedom and comfort in nations fit for heroes.

When Frances was well enough for visitors, the house came to life again. 'Oh Ben, isn't he beautiful? I want to call him Gerald, do you mind?'

Ben smiled. 'You know I don't mind, whatever you want is good enough for me. Where did you get it from?'

'From Ethel, Matron Jones. She has been so good to me. She came every day while you were away. It was her husband's name. She was very fond of him, you know.'

'Of course, Darling. It's a fine name, I like it. Jonesy is the salt of the earth.'

After the celebrations subsided and a degree of normality returned, people began to count their losses. Many Alfs and Alberts did not come home to a heroes welcome. The hospitals overflowed with the shattered moaning relics of what had been men. Ben with other surgeons worked until they dropped. He spoke seldom, telling Frances little of the horror he witnessed every day. Once he told her of the terrible effects of gas. 'By God, if anything should be outlawed, it should be gas. How can civilised man inflict that on his fellow man?'

Evacuation began. The long painful procession of stretcher cases and walking wounded. The rows of caskets containing those who would never again see their native land. Those who had miraculously escaped injury, crowded the troop ships, one thought in mind. Home. Home to Australia, home to sunshine, home to security and peace. Many remained, too ill to be moved.

Ben walked the wards, his own impatience subordinated to his sense of loyalty to his country men.

By the end of 1919 a new terrible enemy arrived on the scene. A virulent strain of pneumonic influenza spread like an uncontrollable bushfire. People dropped in the streets. Men who had survived the holocaust died on the crowded troop ships. Ben's alarm grew as the plague spread like a dark shadow over the land. He heard from his grandfather that Melbourne was a city of fear, the infection having been bought back by returning troops. Few places escaped. Myuna had not recorded a single case. That was it, he reasoned, out of the fetid cities and big towns, out into the countryside.

Most of the old gang had gone, only Frank remained. A gaunt, silent figure, his old gaiety gone. He would sit for hours reading, staring into the fire or watching with tenderness, his sister and his two tiny nephews. When Ben's step at the door announced his arrival, Frank would look up with the semblance of a grin. 'Get out of the whisky, Francie. I think your better half will be ready for one.'

Ben would drop into his easy chair, shoulders hunched taking the proferred glass with gratitude. Frances would stand beside him her hand on his shoulder until with a sigh he relaxed, stretching out his long legs.

Privately, Ben unburdened himself to his brother in law. 'Frank, I'm worried, bloody scared in fact. This thing is not like ordinary 'flu, it's fatal. I want Frances and the kids out of here. You too, old chap. You know I could bring the germ home and infect all of you.'

Frank nodded. 'I know. It's been on my mind too. What can we do?'

'Well, I've got a bit of influence in the right quarters. There is a transport leaving on the first of next month, that's just over a week from now. I can get a cabin for Frances and the boys and luckily Matron Jones will be on the same boat.'

'Best bloody news I've heard in a long time. Will there be room for me?'

'That's been arranged too. You will have your own little cubicle.' He grinned. 'Not luxurious but adequate.'

'You have been pulling strings my boy.' They laughed, clinking glasses. 'Wonderful!' Frank pulled the cork from another bottle. 'I suddenly feel the sun has come out. Here's to happier days.'

Returning home the following evening, Ben found a visitor waiting. The man rose from the chair where he had been sitting close to the fire. Frances made the introduction. 'Ben, this is Professor Brelat, he has come over from Paris to see you.'

A small, neat man, his dark hair and moustache liberally sprinkled with gray, shook hands warmly. His English was impeccable. 'Thank you for receiving me, Doctor. I am a distant relative of your grandmother, Madame Wakefield.'

'Then you are very welcome here, Professor. Please be seated. May I offer you some wine.'

'Thank you.' He coughed into his handkerchief. 'The Somme, you understand, a little of the gas.'

'I understand.' Ben seated himself opposite his guest. 'How can I be of service to you?'

'First I must explain. I was, before the war, Professor of Music at the Sorbonne.' He paused, sipping his wine. 'Doctor, my wife and I wish to leave. Europe has little to offer now.' He put his hand to his mouth as he expressed a cough. 'Perhaps the clean air of your country will benefit me.'

'Professor Brelat, you may rest assured my grandparents will do everything in their power to assist you. I will write them immediately, you have my word on it.'

The Frenchman took his leave. 'I am forever grateful. It will be a joy to my wife who is delicate in health. Sadly we have no children.'

When Frank came in, he chuckled at the account of the visitor from across the Channel. 'A frog migrant eh? Well the more the merrier, I like them.'

As the time for departure drew near, Ben broke the news to his wife. 'Francie, please understand. I can't leave with you. I am needed here for a few more months. Frank is taking you and the boys straight to your parents place. Darling, you must not stay in Melbourne a moment and,' he emphasised, 'do not mix with the other passengers on the ship.' She protested violently, objecting to leaving him. 'But my love, it is the safe thing to do.' He grew serious, holding her firmly in his arms. 'I simply cannot expose you to the risk of staying here. It will only be for a little while. Frank will be there to support you, to get you safely home.' He smiled through the tears gathering in his own eyes. 'Dear old Jonesy will be there to look after you.'

Frances was crying. 'Please don't. We will think about each other every day. The time will pass so quickly, you will hardly notice. Promise now, no more tears. Soon as I get there we will go straight to *Monaro*.' He smoothed her hair and kissed her wet lashes. 'There is not much to pack, just our wedding presents.' He took her hand pulling her down to the couch. 'I'll end the lease here and move up to London. I'm sure I can find a place. Come on now, make us some tea, I must get back.'

Ben saw them off on a bitingly cold day, even the returning troops were muted. 'Keep warm my dear. Don't let the children out until you feel the warm wind from the Indian Ocean. Thanks old man.' He wrung Frank's hand. 'They are in your good keeping from now on. And you, you sinner, keep low until you get home!'

'Don't worry about me, Ben my boy, I have a case of Scotch stowed away. Guaranteed to keep anything at bay.'

'All right, I believe you. Good luck.' He kissed his wife again. 'Keep your spirits up, my dearest.' He held her to him. 'There's the last warning whistle. I must see Jonesy before I leave.' He found Matron Jones in the Sick Bay, unfussed as she supervised nurses and orderlies. Ben approached, playing his part correctly. 'May I have a word, Matron?'

She handed a list of instructions to a waiting Sister. 'Of course, Doctor. This way please.'

In the cubicle that served as an office, they talked long and earnestly. Leaving he squeezed her hand. 'Ethel, you're a brick. Worth your weight in gold!'

'Get out with you. You've more blarney than the Irish.' Then quietly as he left the room. 'Don't worry, I will keep an eye on them all the way.'

CHAPTER XI

After finding lodgings convenient to the hospital and his work load diminishing, Ben found time to relax and socialize with his fellows. The best clubs were open to officers of the Allied forces and here he formed a new friendship. On a bitter afternoon, lazing in the warmth and comfort of his favourite reading room, he sat in a deep armchair, a Scotch at his elbow, leafing through a magazine. An unmistakable American accent reached him. 'Mind if I join you?' Ben looked up, a solid shortish man, his dark hair greying at the temples, grinned at him. 'Sam Bush. I noticed the insignia on your jacket, one of the clan. Thank God. I am sick of talking to the uninitiated.'

Ben laughed. 'Ben Wakefield. Sit down by all means. Glad of your company.'

'Thanks. Like me, I guess, you don't care much for this place. Under normal circumstances, I do. I love the countryside.' He grinned. 'Except in Winter, of course. But I am ready to leave. Can't wait to get home. What do you do? Any speciality, private or general practice?'

'In truth before coming here over here I had precious little experience. What about you?'

'New York. I do quite well. I've learned more here than a hundred years pandering to wealthy matrons.'

Ben laughed. 'You put yourself down. Come on, let's continue this over dinner.'

In the cheerful warmth of the dining room they learned each other's story. Sam's had been uneventful up to the war. He had taken over his father's practice when the old man retired. He was married, happily, with two beautiful children. The photograph he pulled from his wallet showed two smiling girls. 'Twins Ben, runs in the family. My twin brother is in Urology.'

Ben held the photo to the light. 'They are beautiful, Sam. How old?'

'Fourteen. Yes, they are great kids.' Sam regarded his new friend through a haze of cigar smoke. 'This *Monaro* of yours sounds like a bit of Paradise. The mysterious Captain and his lady. Gad, what a story it would make.'

'Yes, I might try and find their relatives some day.'

'What did you say the names of the American lawyers were?'

'Rainford, Benson and Harrington, but they are in Boston.'

'Boston eh. Just a minute my friend, a thought just struck me. There is someone here who might know them.' He beckoned the waiter. 'Would you find Captain Willis for me please? I noticed him come in a short while ago. Ask him if he will kindly join us.'

'Certainly sir, at once.'

Shortly a tall, gangling, bespectacled young man appeared at their table. 'Ira, meet Ben Wakefield - another sawbones.'

They shook hands. 'Glad to meet you, Ben.' He caught the waiter's eye. 'Drinks on me, gents.'

'Looks like you have already had a skinful, Ira. Give your liver a break.'

'To hell with my liver! Now what can I do for you two?'

'Seeing you are in that fabled profession, loosely referred to as Law, Ben would like to know if you know of a firm of gold diggers by the name of - what was it again Ben? Oh yes, Rainford, Benson and Harrington.'

A wide grin creased the young lawyer's face. 'You speak of the creme de la creme of Boston's Law fraternity, my son!'

'You know of them then?'

'Of course. Famous old practice, hoary with age, ultra conservative. Strictly carriage trade.'

'Sounds formidable, thanks Ira. Care to join us for coffee?'

'Hell no. I have a lady waiting, very English and very charming.' He finished his drink. 'And I hope very kind.'

Ben laughed as the tall figure made his way through the tables. 'Quite a character, your friend.'

'One of the best. His men respect him, that's the real measure of a man.'

As the wards thinned, only the very ill remaining, the walking lame and stretcher cases were loaded on to the last transports. Watching them Ben wondered what their reception would be in the land of their birth. He saw a good deal of Sam Bush, meeting regularly for drinks or dinner when ever it could be managed. He found his new friend knowledgeable and a first rate surgeon.

They sat talking in a noisy pub, a favourite meeting place. 'So you are just about ready to leave, Ben?'

'Yes, thank the lord. What about you?'

'Within a month.' He beckoned the barman. 'Two more please. By the way I have something that might interest you.'

Ben waited.

'If you are so hellfired determined to find out about your Captain and his wife, I think I can help you.'

'Sorry Sam, I don't follow.'

'Well, the transports are winding down as you know. There is a Hospital ship sailing for Boston Wednesday. I can get you on as Assistant M.O.. You could see those lawyers and be back here within two weeks.'

'Christ, you mean it?' Ben sat back regarding his friend with astonishment. 'To say I am tempted would be an understatement. How the hell can you arrange all that?'

'That is my problem, old man, all you have to say is, yes.'

Ben gulped half the beer in his glass, then banged it down on the table. 'Sam, I'm probably certifiable, but I say yes. And thanks.'

Boston was snowy and cold, with a piercingly cold wind. Ben sat hunched in his great coat, in the back of a wheezing taxi. Through the fogged up windows he watched the unfolding scenery. Rather old fashioned like an old English city. The Grand Tour of his youth had not included Boston. He motioned to an open space. 'What's that, driver?'

'That's the common, Sir.'

'Hm'm, still a few sparrows hopping around, I see.'

'Yeah, guess they don't feel the cold.' He hesitated. 'Say are you one of these foreign soldiers, Sir?'

'Er, yes, I suppose you could say that.'

The driver thought a few moments. 'It's your funny accent, Sir. You speak American real good.'

Ben chuckled. 'It's a natural talent, I guess.'

Coming to a halt, he peered through the glass. 'This is the right address, driver?'

'Right on, Sir. See for yourself.'

By the entrance to a solid building a polished brass plate proclaimed the offices of Rainford, Benson and Harrington, Attorneys at Law. He thrust some bills into the cabby's hand. 'Call back for me in an hour. If I am not here wait.'

In the comfortable waiting room, tastefully hung with lithographs of country and hunting scenes, Ben approached a polished counter that ran the width of the room barring access to the inner offices.

Behind this barrier, a middle aged woman looked up from the new fangled Remington she had been pounding.

'I wish to see one of the partners, please.'

She looked startled. 'I'm sorry, Sir, Mr Benson is the only one here. And he sees no one without a prior appointment.'

Ben spoke firmly. 'Young lady, I have come a long way. I intend to wait here until I see your Mr. Benson or anyone else connected with this firm.'

She seemed completely captivated by Ben's accent and uniform. 'Please wait, I will see, Sir.' She smoothed her hair and blouse before timidly knocking at the door behind the counter. A high pitched, querulous voice issued forth. 'What is it, what is it Mrs. Hart?'

'There is a gentleman to see you, Sir. A foreign gentleman.'

The door burst open, a portly little man with the shock of unruly white hair, peered out. 'What foreign gentleman?'

'Excuse me, Sir.' Ben strode forward. 'My name is Wakefield. I have come over from England especially to see you. My time is limited, I leave almost immediately.'

The little man looked Ben over. 'Well, in that case, come in. Open the flap, Mrs. Hart, let the gentleman in. So, what can I do for you? Hm, I see you are a medical man.'

Ben told his story as quickly and simply as he could. 'You see, Sir, the fate of the little girl troubled my parents, whether she was well provided for. Fact is, I have often wondered myself. Perhaps you can tell me, give me a name.'

'I see.' The lawyer opened an elaborately carved little box and noisily inhaled a substantial pinch of snuff up each nostril. By the smile on his face, Ben suspected the snuff contained ingredients other than tobacco.

'The matter is unknown to me, but we shall see.' He rang a little brass bell on his desk. The inner door opened, an old, thin, permanently stooped clerk appeared. 'Pepper, there should be a file on Slocum, a Captain Benjamin Slocum, probably in the old room.' He fussed with the papers on his desk. 'Can't get clerks, our young men deserted us for this blasted war. No business of ours, young man. What business have your people being over there?'

Ben did not answer. The clerk returning, dropped a faded manilla folder tied with pink ribbon on the desk and left again without a word. 'Old fool, we had to bring him out of retirement. The world's gone mad I tell you, mad!' Untying the tape he scanned the contents. 'Afraid there is not much here, Captain. We acted on instructions from the attorneys in your country.' He looked sharply at Ben. 'There was a considerable fortune involved.' He read on. 'Yes, it was paid as instructed to the child's grandparents to be held in trust.' He closed the folder.

'That is all you can tell me?'

'I am afraid so.'

Ben felt baffled. 'Surely you can tell me the name of the grandparents, their address perhaps?'

'No, there is nothing more I can tell you.' He held out his hand. 'Good day to you, Captain. This is an old matter, but the instructions are quite clear. I am sure you understand.'

Outside in the snowy street as Ben walked toward the waiting taxi, he felt a light tap on his shoulder. The old clerk rugged up to his neck stood beside him. 'Good luck to you, Sir. The name you wanted is Carrington.'

Standing oblivious to the falling snow, Ben watched the gaunt figure shuffling away along the pavement. 'Well I'll be damned!'

CHAPTER XII

Monaro, August 1920

'Nothing has changed. Seems I only left here yesterday.' Ben sat between his wife and his mother on the verandah shaded by the trailing bougainvillea, now thicker than ever. He picked up his youngest child. 'And who has nick-named this rascal 'The Captain'?'

Frances smiled. 'Your grandfather I'm afraid, Darling.'

'And sober Gareth is still plain, Gareth, I take it.'

'Ben, Frances and I agree. I really don't think children should have nicknames, as you call them.'

He laughed. 'You don't, don't you Mother. Well we'll see.'

His mother looked at him closely. 'You look pale, Ben.'

'Don't fuss, Mum. I am perfectly all right. A little tired but that will soon pass.' He handed the boy to his wife and then stood, hands deep in his pockets. 'So there you are, my dears. I can't think of anything else to tell you.'

'You didn't tell us you were going to Boston.'

'There was no time, Francie. Spur of the moment.' He lit his pipe. 'I'll be ever grateful to Frank for bringing you up here.'

'Your grandmother didn't want us to leave. Madelaine loved the children. She was so upset when we left.'

'So I heard. Those distant relatives, the Brelats, arrived while I was there.' He smiled. 'I think she is well occupied for the moment. I couldn't wait to get away, but they are so dear to me - you understand Mum.'

Rose answered gently. 'Of course we do, Dear. You are worried about your grandfather, is he ill?'

'He looks so ill. Frankly, I was shocked. He must have had a hard time, the death of Mr. Scully affected him deeply. Damnation! I wish I could have been there.'

'You could not be in two places at once, Dear.'

He smiled wryly. 'No of course not. Now if you will excuse me, I'll take a stroll down the drive.' He sniffed. 'Just to smell the place.'

Rose called after him. 'Ben, you don't mind the welcome home planned for Saturday, do you? Everyone wants to see you.'

He hid his annoyance. 'If you must, Mother.'

'Many of them are grieving, Ben. They will want to know if you can tell them anything. You know most of them. Some might still be in hospital somewhere, you may have seen them.'

He answered shortly. 'I doubt it. They would have been notified by this.' He thought-I wonder if they would vote for conscription now? Like hell they would.

'Please Ben, Frances and I have brought out the magic lanterns and cleaned them.'

'All right, Mum, of course. It will be like old times.' Hands in pockets, he strode along the drive. 'What an ungrateful bastard I am! They give all and ask nothing.' His teeth clenched on his pipe stem. 'That bloody stinking war. Curse and blast it. I can't get it out of my mind.'

July 1921

'It's the last one Francie, so help me! Three boys, that's enough for any one family. I'll join a monastery, I'll practice celibacy!'

She laughed up at him from the hospital bed. 'Really darling! What about me?'

Ben grinned, kissing her fondly. 'All right then, if you find me so irresistible. But from now on we must be so damn careful, three is enough.' He stood up. 'I really must go - see you tonight. Have you decided what we are going to call him?'

'Harry, it must be Harry. Harry Franklyn. Oh Ben, he is so beautiful.'

Ben smiled. 'Of course he is. Did Tom say everything is all right? Got all his fingers and toes and things?'

'How can you say such a thing? He is perfect!'

He threw her a kiss from the doorway. 'Back later.'

The telegram was brief - *Dr. Wakefield passed away suddenly. Please wire instructions re funeral arrangements. Pieter.*

Ben sat hunched in his chair, his hands to his face as tears welled in his eyes. His mother sat close to him, cradling his head. 'He was an old man. Remember all the good times you had with him.'

He fought to control himself. 'Sorry Mum, but he was a father to me. I never really knew my own, I will always regret that.'

Rose kept her voice calm. 'I know. Now wash your face and tell Frances. You have a lot to do.'

Ben wired Pieter DeVries - Leaving first available train, appreciate you make necessary arrangements.'

'Well, they gave the old boy a good send off.'

'Thanks to you Pieter. Amazing how many people knew him.'

'Same as when my father, should say stepfather, went. They were well known in the city.' The solicitor eyed his friend carefully. 'Few things to discuss, Ben. Care for a drop?'

'Thanks I could do with one.'

'Here's health.' They lifted and clinked their glasses.

'About the will. You are the sole beneficiary, I suppose you know that.'

'No, I did not. What of my grandmother?'

'Well, the terms are fairly straightforward. She is to retain the house as long as she lives and of course, to have whatever funds she requires.'

'Of course. Dear old soul. She was so calm, so accepting. She refused to give way. Thank God she is surrounded by friends. Distant relatives are with her for the time being. I don't know what they intend to do. He was gassed at the Somme. Anyway, that's how it stands at the moment. What's new with you.'

'Something you couldn't know of course. Ellen and I were married in England.'

'I'll be damned! Why didn't you ask Frances and me?'

'You were away somewhere, I couldn't find you. Frances had already left.'

'Yes, unfortunately we lost touch for a while. How is Ellen?'

'Expected home this month.' He smiled. 'She's pregnant - wonderful isn't it?'

'Christ, you don't waste much time!'

'Love, old friend, love. Let me recharge that glass of yours.'

Ben grinned. 'Congratulations, anyway.'

For a while the lawyer fell silent, shuffling the papers on his desk. 'You seem preoccupied.'

Pieter sat back, hands behind his head. 'Trouble is, Ben, there is more to the will. I'm not sure where to start.'

'Afraid I don't follow, old man.'

The solicitor leaned forward. 'Ben, we have known each other a long time, a bloody long time. Agreed?'

'You rouse my interest, Pieter. Is there some skeleton in the cupboard you haven't told me about?'

'Hardly skeletons Ben. Did you suspect the old boys kept mistresses?'

'You mean - for God's sake, I'll be damned!'

'It's true enough all right. As sole executor of both wills it was my duty to pay substantial bequests to both ladies. You could of course, contest this but by any measure you are still a wealthy man.'

'Contest it? I would never do such a thing.'

'Nor would I. Even in death they are entitled to their privacy.'

'Mistresses!' Ben laughed, shaking his head. 'Of course they would, the old toffs.' He grew serious. 'Do you suppose the wives ever suspected?'

'My mother, no. But it was damn close. Your grandmother, well who knows, she is French of course. But I doubt it.'

'What do you mean, it was close with you mother?'

'Well, common knowledge is, the old man died of urinary trouble.'

'That's what I understood'

'Truth is, he died in his lady friend's bed. Flagrante Delicto, as it were.'

'For God's sake!'

'Your grandfather saved the day. Somehow they got him out of the house, into a cab. Young James Clark who has his surgery in this building signed the death certificate. I doubt your grandfather ever suspected I knew. In any case, he never let on.'

'So that's the story. I thought I knew him but I suppose I never did really. Would it be indelicate to enquire the lady's name?'

'Of course not, Mrs. Paton a charming old girl. Here, have a drop more scotch. Do we ever know anyone?'

'Thanks. Tell me Pete, what are your plans?' Ben looked around the spacious office. 'You look prosperous enough.'

'Frankly Ben, I'm bored. Money is not a problem, I could coast along here in comfort for the rest of my life but the war has left me restless.'

'What about Ellen, her singing career, all that?'

'Given it all up. Just wants to be a wife, she says.'

'And your young brother?'

'That is half the problem. Wants to come in with me, now the old man is gone.'

'What is wrong with that?'

'Oh I don't know. Set in my ways I suppose.' He leaned over the desk, refilling the glasses. 'He's a serious young man these days. The Flying Corps made him realise every day is a bonus.'

'Why not leave the whole thing to him?'

'What would I do?'

'Come up to Myuna. There's not a lawyer in the town. How would Ellen feel about it?'

Pieter eyed his friend gravely. 'Ben, you have just sowed a seed in my mind. By Heavens, you have!'

'And Ellen?'

'I think she would love it. She is still a country girl at heart. Come on let's have dinner. Talk more about this over a good meal.'

They emerged into the dusty, busy street. 'I love old Melbourne, Ben. There is something a little European about it, don't you agree?'

'There is, old friend. But a good place to be out of.'

'Dr. Coburn, I'm not sure what you mean. A partnership? I don't think I have the experience.'

'I don't intend retiring straight away, Ben.' He smiled briefly. 'But I am getting on you know. Time to ease up, have some time to ourselves.'

'Of course, Sir. I understand.'

'As for experience, if anything, you're over qualified for a country practice. You can come on rounds with me until you get your hand in again if you wish.'

'Thank you, Sir. Do you intend to stay here? In this house I mean.'

'No, Ben, far too big for us now with both daughters married. I think Alice spends more time with your mother than she does here.'

Ben smiled. 'It still has that comfortable, lived in feel about it.'

'Yes, we have been very happy here, which brings me to the point I wish to discuss with you.'

Ben waited.

'Would Frances mind living in the town?'

'I should think not. Why do you ask?'

'The practice has always been here Ben. The house is yours for a nominal rental. What do you say?'

'Apart from not knowing the words to thank you, Doctor, I think it would suit me perfectly.'

'That's settled then.' The older man stood as they shook hands. 'I hope you will be as happy here as we have been.'

The next few weeks were so full, Ben had hardly time to reflect on his shortcomings in dealing with civilian patients.

'You have the makings of a first rate doctor, Ben. Some men are haunted by the suffering they have seen, that's natural enough. Thankfully you have retained your balance.'

'Thank you, Doctor. I hope I never disappoint you.'

Tom Coburn laughed. 'I doubt you will. Come on, Alice is ready to pour the tea.'

CHAPTER XIII

1924

'Francie, not another one!'

'Oh Ben, she is a lovely girl. She teaches Gareth's class at the Primary School. She shares that little Mundy house with the two other teachers. Please say, yes.'

'When?'

'Tonight for dinner. Your mother is very fond of her.'

'Whatever you say, my dear. What's her name?'

'Miss Halsey, Muriel Halsey.'

'In these surrounding, how could I refuse?'

They sat at morning tea in the garden peacefully private from the street, behind a high, flowering Plumbago hedge. Ben leaned back, sighing. 'Thank God young Dave Aitken opened up here. At least I get a weekend to myself.' He sniffed the air. 'What is that beautiful perfume, Francie?'

'Verbena, Darling.'

He looked at the masses of pink and mauve flowers bordering the neat, well manicured beds. 'Very pleasant. I think from now on, my favourite flowers.' He pulled his Panama down over his eyes. 'Call me for lunch, my love.'

'So you teach one of our young rascals, Miss Halsey.'

Muriel Halsey, a petite, pretty brunette, smiled shyly. 'Gareth is a very quiet and serious boy, Doctor. One of my favourites.' Adding hastily. 'I know I should not have favourites. I honestly try not to.'

'I believe young Dave Truman, the police sergeant's son is in your class also, Miss Halsey.'

'Oh no, Doctor, Dave is in Gerald's class. They appear to be very special friends. He is a nice youngster, I often see them together.'

After coffee they sat in easy chairs on the verandah that ran three sides of the house. Ben filled his pipe, tamping the tobacco slowly into the bowl. 'How do you like our town Miss Halsey?'

'I'm feeling much happier now Doctor, since getting to know Frances and your mother. I never dreamt there was such a place on earth as *Monaro*. It is so beautiful.'

'Will you be going home for Christmas? Frances tells me you are from Sydney.'

'Not this year Doctor. My parents are hotel people, Christmas time is so rushed.'

'In that case, my dear young lady, you must spend Christmas with us at *Monaro.*'

'Please do Muriel, it would be wonderful. My brother Frank comes up every Christmas. Dr. and Mrs. Coburn will be here, so many friends drop in. You will stay the holidays, won't you?'

'Good Lord, I thought it would never end. Crowded again today.' Ben came from the surgery, closing the door behind him.

'Come and sit down darling, lunch is ready.' Frances poured from a jug nestling in a bed of cracked ice. 'Lemonade. There's a lemon tree in the garden, it's simply laden.'

'Just what I need.' He sipped slowly, smiling at his wife. 'Tell me Francie, how many surprises can you take at once? That is altogether.'

She stood behind his chair, her hands on his shoulders. 'That depends I wish I knew what you are talking about.'

He looked around. 'Where is my little Buddy?'

'Oh Ben, please stop that. Harry is asleep. All these names you give the children, they will grow up not knowing who they are.'

'All right. Just wait a minute till I finish this.'

Frances sat facing him, her chin in her hands.

Pushing back his plate, he carefully wiped his fingers. 'Two letters came in the mail today, Francie, both of them like bolts from the blue.'

'Ben will you please get on with it! Who were they from?'

'Well, one from my grandmother. The Brelats, you remember the French couple, want to get out of Melbourne. He was gassed you know. Anyway, they want to know if there are any prospects for a music teacher in the town.'

'That would be wonderful!'

'You think so?'

'Yes, I do. Gareth loves the violin but Mr. Wardrop says he can't take him any further. He needs a proper teacher.'

'What about the Captain, sorry love, Gerald?'

'Your mother does her best with him. He hates finger exercises, says he would rather go fishing. Music is sissy.'

Ben laughed. 'That I can believe. They are still very young, I wouldn't worry. I think the Brelats would find all they could handle here. Thank God they are not coming until after Christmas.'

'Ben, I'm just wondering - what about the old Walton place? You know, with those two big Norfolk Island pines at the front and those cactus plants along the drive. It's been empty since old Miss Walton died.'

'No idea, I'll look into it.' He smiled at her. 'You can't guess who the second one is from.'

'You know I can't. Tell me quickly before I burst.'

'Pieter, Pieter DeVries. They are coming for Christmas, with their little daughter, Dorothy, I think it is.' He grinned. 'I thought that might please you.'

Frances gave a cry of pleasure. 'Isn't that marvellous? This will be the most wonderful Christmas. I must tell your mother straight away.'

'Later my dear, later. You haven't heard all I have to tell.'

Her hand went to her lips, she faltered. 'It's nothing serious is it? Not bad news, I'm sure it's bad news.'

He came round, putting his arms around her. 'Only if you think buying a motor car is bad news.'

'Ben Wakefield, you are the most secretive man!'

'Not with you, Francie.'

'But you haven't said a word about it.'

'I wanted it to be a surprise. Motor cars are coming in now. Dave Aiken has one, Dr. Coburn was the first in town to have one.'

She was curious. 'Where will you get it? The stables only sell buggys and sulkys.'

'Brisbane my dear. I am going up next week. They will teach me to drive and then I will drive it all the way home. I'll be expert when I get back.'

'It sounds dangerous.'

'Don't be silly, Darling. If you can manage a horse you can drive a car. Now I have got my afternoon rounds to do.'

Frances followed him. 'What's to become of old Ringer and our lovely little sulky?'

'Ringer can go out to grass and the sulky into the coach house at *Monaro*.' He kissed her. 'I'm off now. Stop worrying.'

'Another Christmas, Frank, how quickly they come round. Glad you could find the time.'

'How quick indeed, Ben.' They sat talking quietly, old friends, comfortable with each other. Below, magic lanterns glowing like exotic flowers, lined the darkened driveway, disappearing into overhanging trees.

'This place fascinates me. I could live here.'

'You say that every year.'

'True enough, but since the old man died, I've never been busier. I must work, you know Ben, it's my nature.'

'Time you were married. Need a good woman to look after you.'

'Who travels alone - you know the rest.'

Ben chuckled. 'You never change. What do you think of Muriel Halsey by the way?'

'Nice girl.' He grinned in the darkness. 'Nice legs.'

'Yes, I noticed you noticed.'

'Well, I'm all for this new Flapper age. Time the girls came out. What does Rose think?'

'Oh Mum's all for it. Thinks they're wonderful. Wishes she was young again.'

'Remarkable woman, your mother.'

'Yes, I worry about her though. Don't think she is as well as she pretends to be.'

'Have you spoken to her?'

'Hell no. She would never tell me. Only old Doc. Coburn would know. That is if there is anything to worry about.'

'Can't you sound him out?'

'Bit delicate. Anyway, let's forget that for now. How's your glass?'

'Need you ask? Tops off a perfect dinner.' He rolled the golden liquor around his mouth. 'By God, this is a superb Cognac. How's your stock holding? Adequate, I hope.'

'Enough to float you in.'

'You know, he must have been a rum sort of a bloke, this captain.'

'Yes, wish I knew more about him. Found out damn little in Boston. All I know is what the old priest, Rev. Trendel, told my parents and you know all that.'

'Well, all I can say is, he had excellent taste.'

'I'll drink to that. So you are back building again?'

'More bloody work than I can handle. I was sorry to sell the old farm. We grew up there, Francie and I.'

'How do you like Sydney?'

'Place is growing like a weed. Plenty of money about. Ever been there, Ben?'

'Matter of fact I have, little over a month ago.'

'Really, what were you doing down there?'

'Looking for an old friend of ours. Remember Matron Jones? Jonesy we used to call her, when she wasn't there.'

'Yes, of course I remember her. Grand old sort. What do you want with her?'

'To come up here and work for me. Badly need an experienced woman in the surgery. You've no idea how careful you have to be with women patients.'

'You found her all right?'

'I did. She made a hell of a fuss over me. Be up here after Christmas. Caught her at the right moment, she's not very happy - family matters.'

'Didn't she have a daughter?'

'Married to an up and coming barrister. Doesn't see Jonesy fit into their social pattern. Ignores her.'

'Must be a prime prick.'

'Never met him, no desire to. The daughter is very nice though.'

'Life's strange - who would ever have thought? Brings back memories.'

For a few moments they sat in silence, each immersed in his own thoughts.

'Refill?'

'Thanks. Tell me, Ben, why would a man with all this,' he waved out into the darkness, 'all this and plenty of money, work as a country doctor?'

'If I said out of a noble desire to help my fellow man, you would call me a fraud, wouldn't you?'

'Knowing you, I'm not so sure.'

'Well if you did you'd be half right I suppose, but what else would I do with my life, Frank? This is my home. I know the people and I am happy here.'

'You seem to have a pretty big practice.'

'Too big. Young Dave Aitken is coming in with me, thank God.' He clipped the end of a long Havana, rolled it above his ear then after delicately savouring it's fragrance, applied a match. 'Thanks for these, old man. Nothing like a good cigar, one of the rarer pleasures in life.'

'Glad you like them, believe your grandfather did too.'

'He certainly did. I can close my eyes and remember cold, frosty mornings in Melbourne on my way to school and that sweet pungent smell of cigar smoke along the street.'

'Yes, they are good memories, takes the mind off other things.'

'You mean the war?'

'I've never told another soul Ben, it still haunts me. When I can't bear to think about it anymore, I go on a bender. For days sometimes.'

There was such bitterness in his voice, Ben was startled. 'Hold on old son, you've got to get it out of your mind. I see it every day, the limbless, blind, lungs ruined by gas. You've simply got to come to terms with it. Get on with your life. It's the only one you'll ever have.'

'Didn't this town vote for conscription?'

'Regrettably yes, one of the few places that did.'

'Makes you wonder. Sixty thousand, the cream of the crop, you might say, dead and God alone knows how many ruined physically. But the bitterness is still there, still simmers under the surface.'

'You know Frank, that funny little lawyer I saw in Boston asked me what business we had being over there. I often ask myself the same question. Let's not think about it any more, let's talk of more pleasant things. This Cognac is too good to waste on sad memories, after all I only see you once a year.'

'You're right, what a fool I am.' He pulled hard on his cigar. 'How is your friend DeVries settling in, Pieter and Ellen isn't it? That is one of my pleasant memories, such a beautiful voice. And that French music teacher?'

'You will meet them all tomorrow. The usual Christmas Eve get together.'

'Hope she will sing for us.'

'Probably will. As for Pieter, reckons it's the best decision he ever made. Only lawyer in the area. Built a very impressive home, red brick, white marble steps, all the trimmings.'

Frank chuckled. 'And you bought yourself a motor car at last.'

'I thought it about time. Drove it down from Brisbane myself. First Cadillac on the coast. Fine piece of machinery.'

'I'll be damned! For a horse man that was quite a conversion.'

'Got to keep up with the times. Now, how about another drop before we join the ladies?'

'Frank, meet Dave Truman, one of my oldest friends. Dave is the local police sergeant. And here is Jack Raywood and Hal Wynter.'

'How do you do?' Frank shook hands all round. 'Light Horse, Ben tells me, at least you didn't get your feet wet.'

All smiled with grim mirth. 'Don't you believe it, Frank. We were up to our hocks most of the time.' They stood in the shade of a giant Lilli Pilli inside the walled enclosure, the grass scythed low and raked for the occasion.

'Sorry boys, I've got to take care of him. Circulate amongst the ladies. He's the only bachelor out of captivity here, you know.'

They laughed. 'Lucky bugger! All these young flappers about, enough to make a man wish he was single again.'

'Be careful your wives don't hear you.' Ben grinned. 'Time you moved around yourselves. The women want to know what you all talk about when you get together.'

Dave Truman chuckled. 'I'll bet they do. All right, Ben, just one more beer and we'll be there.'

'So what do you think of my friends?'

For an instant Frank was silent. 'Salt of the earth, what else?'

'Those four are all that is left. Dave lost two brothers on the Somme, Hal's younger brother was killed in the battle for Windmill Hill at Pozieres, the apple of his mother's eye. The blinds of the house are still drawn. He was only eighteen. Many I never even knew are gone. Fortunately, most had children to carry their names.'

'Let's change the subject, Ben.'

'Right you are. Want you to meet Mr. Wardrop, taught me to fish, wonderful old chap. His wife brought me into the world. She and the minister's wife between them.'

'Look, there's Pieter, surrounded by women as usual.'

'So, what does he have? What do they call it these days? Sex appeal?'

'Something like that. And there is your mother, holding court with the ladies. God, Ben, I'm starting to sweat.'

'Take it easy, old son. They will all be gone by sundown. Only Muriel, Pieter and Ellen, Dr. and Mrs. Coburn and the Brelats will be staying.'

Twilight came quickly, the sun fell over the purple range, velvet dusk crept over the land. Eager hands lit the magic lanterns, lighting the way for spluttering motors and rubber-tyred buggys as they moved off homewards. The group remaining stood at the gate waving goodbye. Cries of 'Merry Christmas, see you New Years' rang from each crew as they passed.

Ben stood close to his mother. 'Well Mum, another Christmas.'

She took his arm. 'I wonder how many more for me.'

Ben fought to control the twinge of alarm that contracted his heart. He kissed her gently, looking closely into her eyes which seemed to have grown larger, more luminous with age.

'This is where your father and I used to stand. I think of him every day of my life. You are so like him, Ben.'

'You will still be here when I am an old man, dearest Mother. Now, come along the others have all gone inside.'

In the dining room, brilliant with festive lights, Rose carefully seated her guests, placed so conversation flowed unhindered. Her heart lifted as she glanced around the table - how things had changed. Her son married, a lovely wife, three beautiful children. If only Harry -.

Someone touched her arm. 'A penny for them, Rose.'

'Tom, forgive me. For a moment I was lost in thought.'

'Pleasant ones, I hope?'

'Mostly Tom,' she smiled, 'Mostly pleasant.'

He patted her hand. 'Just think of the good times, my dear.' He glanced up at the twin chandeliers. 'You know Rose, I think I preferred the gas light. So much kinder to old faces.' They both laughed.

'Your glass, Doctor.'

'Thank you, Ben. Excellent wine as always.'

'Mrs. Ellis excelled herself, Mother.'

'Yes, she is a treasure. She left everything prepared, the table was your young ladies doing.'

Ben smiled. 'I will propose a toast to them later.'

'Your brother in law seems very quiet, Ben.'

'I hadn't noticed, Doctor, probably tired after riding all morning.'

Frank sitting opposite Muriel Halsey, found his eyes drawn to her. In her green silk beaded dress, her dark hair bobbed, she looked radiant. She coloured each time she raised her eyes to find his gaze upon her.

'More wine, Frank?'

'Thanks, Ben, delightful drop.'

Ben moved around the table. 'Muriel, what's happened to your appetite? Here let me top up your glass.'

'Oh, please no, Doctor.' She smiled self consciously. 'I'm afraid I am not used to wine.'

He smiled back at her. 'Of course, my dear.' He glanced across the room. 'The children seem to be enjoying themselves. I think their bedtime is fast approaching.' He moved on. 'Pieter, your glass.'

'Ben my dear chap, thank you.'

'Your daughter seems to have calmed our ruffians at their table.'

'Naturally old man. The power of the female!'

A ripple of laughter erupted around the table. Rose smilingly folded her napkin. 'I think the gentlemen can now retire to the library, if they wish. We will see to the children. Coffee will be along a little later.'

'You will take brandy, Doctor?'

'Thank you Ben, yes.'

'And try one of these excellent cigars Frank brought with him.'

'Normally I smoke little but this is an occasion.'

Dr. Coburn settled back in his chair. 'Glad to see you could make your yearly pilgrimage Captain.'

'Wish I could make it more often Doctor. Time passes too quickly.'

'Indeed it does, especially if one is busy. When my wife and I moved to Lambruk, I had visions of a quiet life.' He smiled ruefully. 'Patients still turn up. Misguided loyalty, I suspect.'

Ben laughed. 'I wouldn't say that, Doctor.'

The older man turned to Pieter. 'How do you find country life, Mr. DeVries?'

'Very satisfying sir. The town has grown so much, quite remarkable. Of course Australia is riding a wave of prosperity at the moment.' He puffed gently on his cigar. 'I only hope it lasts. The only good thing that came out of the war, I'm afraid.'

Ben fought to control the bitterness in his voice. 'Nothing good came out of that frightful war. You've only to look around to see that.'

Dr. Coburn's soothing voice broke in. 'I believe you saw something of Europe before the war, Captain Chapman?'

'Yes Doctor. After University my father gave me a year to find my feet.'

'How did you find things over there?'

'A wonderful experience. My best friend came with me. We bought bicycles and explored the countryside.'

'Only the British Isles?'

'No, we managed France and Germany as well. It was a perfectly wonderful summer.' He laughed. 'Two young bloods doing on the cheap.'

'A pity Frances missed out.'

'Yes, sadly they landed in England just as war broke out.'

Dr. Coburn continued. 'What was your impression of Germany?'

'A paradox, Sir. On the whole the most kindly unselfish people. Democratic to a degree, class hardly counts. So unlike the fossilized rigidity of the English classes.'

'Then how do you account for their adventures in Europe?'

'I don't know. All I do know is that from childhood a German is taught to obey. Given a uniform he becomes an entirely different person.' He laughed. 'If that sounds all too simplistic, I am afraid you will just have to put it down to my ignorance.'

'God preserve us from it ever happening again.'

'I doubt it ever will, Doctor.' Pieter poured from the decanter with a practiced hand. 'A client of mine, a businessman recently returned, tells me the country is utterly devastated, abject poverty everywhere.'

'Perhaps the Allies terms were too hard, poverty breeds resentment.'

'I agree. America was prepared to be generous but Britain and France demanded their pound of flesh.' Pieter frowned a little. 'Frankly, who could blame them?'

Conversation ceased as the library door opened. The fragrant smell of coffee floated on the air. Pieter held the door aside for the trolley. 'Ah, at last the ladies join us.'

Ellen smiled at her husband. 'What have you gentlemen been talking about?'

'All manner of things, my dear. The old days when we were young. How much the town has changed.'

'Mother,' Ben held a chair ready, 'please sit here by Dr. and Mrs. Coburn.' He pulled his own chair closer. 'has the town changed that much?'

Rose smiled. 'It was only a village when your father and I arrived. There was really very little. Wasn't it so, Tom?'

Dr. Coburn nodded. 'Yes, they were pioneering days. People helped each other, in good times and in bad. I'm not sure that spirit still exists.'

Alice spoke up. 'Remember my pony, Rose? The piano lessons, the wonderful times we had?'

'Dear Alice, I often think of those times. I live them over again in my mind.'

Dr. Coburn polished his glasses. 'What was the town like in those days, you ask? I suppose the right word is, vibrant. It thrived on cedar and sugar. Sadly, most of the cedar has gone now, a great pity. Magnificent trees, felled without a thought for the future. Yes, the town has certainly changed. Many of the merchants and growers have become very prosperous indeed, very conscious of their position, too. They mix almost exclusively with one another these days.'

Frank laughed. 'A sort of bunyip society, Doctor.'

'Well put, Captain. Although I imagine the same is true of most prosperous country towns.'

'It certainly is amongst the wealthy squatters. They would dearly love a sort of antipodean aristocracy' He grinned. 'Perhaps, squattocracy, would be a better word.'

'You are not serious, Frank?'

'Never more so, Pieter. It's true enough, I've seen it working at first hand.'

'Will it ever happen, I mean, could that sort of thing happen here?'

'I doubt it. The ordinary Australian shows scant respect for rank or authority. You must have seen that yourself during the war.'

'I certainly did, been on the receiving end of it myself a few times.' Pieter chuckled. 'Yes, I think I agree with you, almost a classless society and thank God for that.'

Dr. Coburn looked at his watch, 'Well, it has been a most pleasant evening. Now if you will excuse us, my wife and I must make an early start tomorrow. Our daughters will be arriving.'

They all rose with him.'Tom, you won't forget New Year?'

'My dear Rose, how could I? We have been celebrating New Year's Eve together for - how many years?' He laughed. 'Best not to try to remember. Now we bid you all goodnight. The compliments of the season, ladies and gentlemen, it's almost Christmas Day.'

In the privacy of their bedroom, Frances watched her husband undress. She closed her eyes as he removed his shirt. Always she fought back tears at the sight of the terrible weals of the bayonet wounds, like great red cords across his chest.

From the mirror Ben watched her, slipping his coat on without a word, he stooped and kissed her. 'Merry Christmas, dearest Francie.'

She pulled him down. 'Oh Ben dear Ben. Don't go to sleep yet, talk to me.'

'For heaven's sake, at this hour? The children will be awake soon! What will we talk about?'

'You didn't say anything about Dan, did you?'

He sat straight up. 'How in tarnation do you know about that?'

'Ellen told me.'

'Women! You can never keep a secret can you? In any case, there is nothing definite. All I know is, the old priest is retiring and Dan hopes for the post.'

'Is it true he has tried to leave the priesthood?'

'Several times I believe, which is out of the question. Anyway, if he does get it, it will be because of Sean's influence. He is highly regarded by the Bishop.'

'It will be like old times for you.'

'Hardly Francie, we were children then. Don't forget we are still regarded by the R.C. church as separated brethren.'

'Ben.'

'What now?'

'Do you suppose Dr. Coburn and Alice ever had a great passion - you know?'

'Francie, how the hell would I know? They produced two daughters, didn't they? Now go to sleep.'

'I just can't sleep, wish I could.'

'Must be the full moon! Frank has taken Muriel to the tower to see the sights.'

For a moment she lay still. He heard her gasp. 'Ben how could you? Muriel is so young - so, so innocent!'

'What do you mean - how could I? They are both adults.' He grinned in the darkness. 'You are always telling me what a gentleman Frank is.'

Frances cuddled up close to him. 'You're impossible, Ben Wakefield.'

Soon only his gentle snoring broke the silence of the room.

Christmas and New Year passed. The last two months of summer brought little rain. The scorched grass crackled underfoot. Only the cool sea breeze at night made sleep possible. Ben and Frances returned to the house in town to the great relief of his young colleague.

The Brelats found the old Walton house charming. The elegant furniture to their liking. They had brought with them only his violin and her cello. He gently touched the keys of the piano, obviously unused for years, smiling as they watched. 'It is badly out of tune but soon, oh yes soon, I will have it perfect. And yes, you see, we speak only English now.'

Toward the end of February, Ethel Jones arrived, looking older than they remembered. Ben took her arm. 'Thank you for coming Ethel. Your room is ready and waiting for you. Now brace yourself, I think there is a welcoming committee waiting.'

Ethel walked toward the little group at the entrance to the wharf, her eyes glistening. She fought hard to keep her voice steady, embracing each in turn, then she stood back as if surveying her nurses those years ago. 'So here you are, all grown up and married, but my dears, just as I remember you.'

Unable to go on, she held onto Ben's arm. Frances came to the rescue. 'Ben, put Matron's luggage into the car. Tea will be ruined if we don't hurry.'

Sitting next to Frances, Matron whispered to her. 'Thank you Frances dear, you saved me from making a fool of myself.'

Some weeks later, on an afternoon heavy with the menace of a storm, Ben sat with his brother in law on the shaded side of the verandah. 'Looks like a bad one brewing, Frank.'

'If it cools down a bit, it's welcome.'

They sat watching the great cumulus clouds slashed with distant lightening, counting the seconds before each rumble of thunder.

'When are you going back, Frank?'

'Why, have I outstayed my welcome?'

'Don't be bloody ridiculous!'

'Sorry Ben. Yes, I have stayed longer this time.'

'Muriel?'

'In a way I suppose, but I'm not ready to become too involved. Not yet anyway.'

'How does she feel?'

'If I said the word, I think she would say yes.' He drained his glass of lemonade. 'This stuff is rotgut. When do we get a real drink?'

'Later, before dinner, Dave is on tonight, thank God.'

'Yes, Muriel is a lovely girl, everything I admire in a woman.'

'So?'

'She is an R.C. for a start. You know I am not religious but I'm buggered if I will go through all that rigmarole. Kids must be brought up Tykes, all that sort of stuff.'

'My grandmother is Catholic, goes to mass regularly every week.'

'Your grandmother is French, that's different.'

Ben left to ponder this, did not reply.

A sudden gust of wind brought great drops of rain pounding on the iron roof. Frank lay back in his chair. 'Ah, feel that breeze, relief at last.' He fished in his pocket for cigarette. 'Remember Christmas Eve, Ben? Muriel and I went up to the tower. Christ, talk about passion! I could have had her then. We went along the gallery, where the pictures are hung. That Captain, Jesus, those eyes! Sobered me up I can tell you. When I had my hand between her legs all I could see was those eyes. I swear, somehow the old bastard was watching me. Anyway, I'd have hated myself, she's as innocent as a new born lamb.'

'Thank God you didn't!'

'Amen to that.' He stood, watching the water cascading over the gutters. 'And that's the story.'

'What do you intend to do now?'

'Back to Sydney, clear up things then I'm off. If I leave it any longer I'll never see the bloody world.'

'Well, come on, I'll pour you that drink.?'

Life returned to normal. One morning, Ben, about to leave the surgery was surprised to find Dave Aitken waiting.

He sat down, lighting a cigarette. 'Jesus, Ben, there's a few things around here you didn't warn me about.'

'Like what, Dave?'

'I had to go the Ryan's today. You know, right up in the hills. I've never seen anything like it. Incest, Ben, two brothers fighting like dogs over a sister! I had to close up with horsehair, ran out of sutures.'

'Sorry Dave, I should have told you. When old Doc. Coburn first took me into the hills, I couldn't believe it myself. It's widespread, you know. There are more foetus' buried up there than there are trees.' Ben looked closely at his young colleague. 'Still want to stay in the bush?'

Dave grinned. 'You don't think I'd leave this little paradise, do you?'

Ben, who knew more than the young man suspected, smiled broadly. 'No, I didn't think you would.'

With the subtle changing of the seasons storms came in quick succession. The country steamed, creeks ran high, the flats heavy with cane, thick, lush and green spread down to the river, ready for harvest.

Driving to a call along the road to Lambruk, Ben pulled to the side of the road as a familiar conveyance approached from the opposite direction. There was no mistaking it, his mother and his wife in the rubber tyred sulky. Stepping onto the road, he held up his hand. 'Whoa there, boy.' He held the horse by the bridle. 'Well, what a pleasant surprise meeting two ladies I know on this lonely road. May I ask where you have been?'

His wife smiled. 'Oh just visiting, Ben. Where are you off to?'

'Me?' He feigned surprise. 'Making a call, of course. Why else would I be up here this time of day?'

'Benjamin,' his mother spoke quite sharply, 'we have been to see the Coburns, you know we haven't been up for ages.'

'But Mother, Dave or I would have driven you up if you had asked.'

'I'd rather use my sulky, thank you Ben. Now please let go the bridle we must be getting back. Muriel has the children.'

He grinned as he waved them goodbye, then sitting in the car, he made a quick decision. 'After the Flannery's I'll slip up and see the old man. It's not that much further. I know damn well this is not the first time they have been up there.'

The Flannery's house stood well back from the road. Unpainted, mossy with age, its saving grace was a huge Moreton Bay fig that shaded the house from the western sun. Mick Flannery, a sweat stained battler, came out to greet him. He walked dragging his left leg.

'Well Mick, how's the wife today?'

'Not the best, Doc. Thanks for coming all this way.'

'That's all right. How is the leg?'

'Still a bit crook but me job at the mill's OK. The boss puts me on the easy stuff.'

'Glad to hear it. George Carr is a decent bloke.'

Mick had been in the second futile wave ashore at Gallipolli. He was lucky to still have his left leg.

'I'm a bit rushed for time, Mick. I'd better go in and see how your wife is coming along.'

Mrs. Flannery, hardly more than a girl, lay propped up with pillows, a baby at her breast. Ben's practiced eye took in the pallor, the obvious signs of fatigue and anaemia. 'Well Mary, how are you today?'

Tears glistened on her cheeks. 'I'm so tired. Dr. Wakefield. I know it's the will of God, but I just can't cope. I can't eat, can you give me a tonic?'

He smiled his most comforting smile. 'We'll talk about that later, Mary. Let's have a look at you.' After the examination he closed his bag with a snap and sat on the side of the bed. 'Mary, you are very weak. You really shouldn't be feeding the baby. When is your sister coming?'

'Tomorrow, Doctor. Poor Mick, he tries but he can't work and look after the children.'

'I know. Now you must promise me, I'll leave a note for her, you simply must eat. Eggs and milk - I've heard your sister is a good cook, so do I have your promise? You will do as I say?'

Her voice was hardly audible. 'I promise.'

He smiled grimly as he closed the door behind him. Mick stood waiting at the foot of the verandah stairs, a child about twelve months old in his arms.

'How is she, Doc? Will she be all right?'

Ben took the man by the arm. 'Walk over to the car with me, Mick.' He sat behind the wheel and lit his pipe. He was brutally frank. 'If I'm not mistaken you've been married about seven years now, Mick.'

'Just about seven, Doc.'

'I've no doubt you love your wife.'

'Good God, Doc, of course I do. Mary is my whole life!'

'In that time you have had six children.'

Mick looked miserable. 'I know. I can't help it and it's costing me every penny I earn. God knows what would happen if I lost my job.'

Ben took the pipe from his mouth. 'Mick, if you still want your wife,' he shook his head, 'I'm sorry to tell you, there can be no more babies.'

'No more? I don't understand, what do you mean?'

'I mean another pregnancy will kill her.'

'Holy Mother of God! What am I going to do?'

'You can either live the life of a monk or use contraceptives.'

Mick drew back, a startled look on his face. 'Jesus, Doc, it's a mortal sin, I'd go to hell, Father Brian says so.'

'Well, you wouldn't be lonely. You'd find a lot of your mates there.' Ben knew this was an area where he must tread with great delicacy. He spoke quietly. 'I'm a doctor, Mick, not a priest. I can only speak from a medical viewpoint. What you do is between you and your conscience.'

Mick sighed deeply. 'But I couldn't go to that bastard Connors, Father Brian is always in there talking with him.'

'Well, he wouldn't keep them anyway but there is old Mr. Emery down the south end.'

'The old crippled chap?'

'Yes, he's a very decent man. Look,' he tore a sheet from his notebook, 'here's a note to Mr. Emery. All you have to do is hand it to him. Use the same note whenever you need them. There's no need even to talk to him.'

Mick took the folded paper. 'I don't know, Doc. I don't know what to do.'

Ben started the motor. 'I must be off, Mick. Whatever you do is your business.'

Half an hour later Ben pulled up outside the pleasant Coburn bungalow. He wondered how long it was since he had been here. How the wisteria had grown. The warm air was heavy with the perfume of roses.

Alice opened the door to his knock. 'Ben, what a lovely surprise. You haven't been up for ages. Please come in. I'll call Tom and you will stay for some tea, won't you?'

'Thanks Mrs. Coburn, I could do with some.'

Tom Coburn came in wiping his hands. 'Hullo there Ben, good to see you.' He smiled. 'You must excuse my appearance, Alice says I spend more time with my roses than I do with her.'

Ben smiled in return. 'I could smell the perfume when I pulled up outside. No wonder they are called the Queen of Flowers.'

'Ah yes, true enough. But I know you didn't come all this way to discuss roses. Come into the surgery.'

The old man sat in his high backed swivel chair behind the big cedar desk, finger tips pressed together. 'So Ben, to what do I owe the honour of this late visit?'

'Dr. Coburn, it may not be ethical, in the strict sense of the word, but may I ask you a question?'

'If I can answer it, yes.'

'I met Mother and Frances on the road up here today. Is there anything I should know?'

A gentle tap at the door announced the arrival of the tea tray. 'Thanks, my dear.' He waited until the door closed behind his wife. 'I have seen your mother several times, Ben. No need for alarm. There is a slight problem.'

Ben waited, sipping the hot tea.

'A touch of angina.' He held up his hand. 'Nothing to worry about for the moment. She is on medication.'

'I didn't know. I suspected something. What do you think?'

'In my opinion, providing she takes it steady, the prospects are excellent.'

Ben drained his cup. 'I appreciate your confidence, Doctor, of course I'll never let her know, she would never forgive me.'

The older man laughed. 'I've known your mother for, good Lord, how many years?' His eyes twinkled. 'Whatever your age is, Ben, that's how long.' He rose extending his hand. 'Drive carefully on the way back.' With his wife at his side, they bade Ben farewell at the front door. As an afterthought he followed Ben to the gate. 'I should mention, Ben, your wife may have something to tell you tonight. Goodnight now, remember, drive carefully.'

Bemused by these last cryptic words ringing in his ears, Ben pointed the black Cadillac down the long winding road to the town.

Later that night at dinner.

'You're very quiet tonight, Darling. You look tired.'

'I am Francie, it's been a long day. How are the children?'

Frances looked down, frowning slightly. 'I didn't want to worry you about it, but they are running wild. They live for the minute we go up to *Monaro* and Ben, I do love your mother, but she does spoil them.'

'It's natural my love, they are boys. You wouldn't want them any other way, would you?' He grinned. 'You'll be a grandmother yourself one day. How's the music coming along?'

'Professor Brelat says Gareth will make a fine violinist. Gerald hates the piano but he knows he has to practice so at least it's good discipline for him.'

'Well there you are. Don't worry, they'll grow up just fine.' He bent and kissed her. 'You'll be proud of them when they grow up.' He laughed. 'God help the poor girls they bring home!' He looked around. 'By the way, where is Ethel?'

'She and Dave have gone out to the Franklins. Mrs. Franklin started this morning. Dave said he will send for you if they need you. First babies are terrifying. I feel sorry for her, she's such a little thing.'

Ben surveyed his wife closely. 'I suppose you might say subsequent births are too.' He waited. 'Have you go something to tell me, Francie?'

'I didn't want to say anything yet. Dr. Coburn says I'm about three months.'

'God help us. I thought we had finished with that.'

She began to cry quietly. 'I'm sorry, Ben.'

He put his arms around her. 'It isn't your fault, Darling. One of those bloody things must have leaked or something.' He stroked her hair. 'Don't cry, it's not a calamity. Come on, let's have a smile.' He kissed her wet eyelids. 'Now, tell me you forgive me for being such an unfeeling bastard.'

In the warm darkness they lay on the bed with the covers thrown back, talking over the events of the day. The time they liked best.

'Francie, it's about time you had a car of your own.' Ben chuckled. 'All the leading lights of the town have one. You wouldn't want them to think your husband mean, would you?'

'I don't care what they think. Most of them are boring - mah jong, bridge, endless afternoon teas. They give themselves such dreadfully silly airs.'

'You have to accept, my dear, that you and Ellen are at the top of the pecking order. Doctors and solicitors wives, you know. Bloody silly isn't it? But that's high society, country style.'

A week later to the day, a little Chevrolet roadster was delivered to the house. Frances was charmed. 'But I can't drive!'

'Jack will teach you, won't you Jack?' Ben shook hands with the grinning agent behind the wheel.

'Have you expert in three days, Mrs. Wakefield.'

The season wore on. Easter came and with it Frank, dusty in his Buick tourer. 'Bloody roads, shook the guts out of me and the car.'

Ben gripped his hand. 'All you need is a stiff drink, a bath and a good dinner, in that order.'

Frank grinned through the grime on his face. 'Lead on, old son. God, it's good to see you, Francie!' He hugged her then held her off. 'What's this, another bun in the oven? Aren't you two ever going to stop?' He turned as Matron Jones came down the steps. 'Jonesy!' He gave her a great hug.

'You cheeky devil, Frank Chapman! You don't improve with keeping.'

'Well Francie, that dinner was absolutely delicious. Where did you get this red, Ben? As good as anything I've ever tasted.'

'Would it surprise you to know it's Australian? Amazing isn't it, we produce stuff like this,' he held his glass to the light, 'but if you tell the average Aussie you drink wine, he thinks you're strange.' Ben pushed back his chair. 'If the ladies will forgive us, Frank and I will have a cigar on the verandah.'

They sprawled into comfortable, deep cane chairs. 'You're lucky to have old Jonesy, Ben.'

'Lucky! You have no idea. She is one of the family. I tell you I couldn't survive without her.'

'What about the young bloke, Dave Aitkens?'

'A brick. I don't think the young bugger has any intention of marrying.' Ben laughed quietly. 'I suspect he does all right without the responsibility.'

They sat silent for a while.

'Thanks again for the Havanas. Where the hell do you get them?'

'Little shop in Pitt Street, keeps all the good stuff.'

Again they were silent.

'Funny bloody place, Australia.'

'How do you mean?'

'Well, just look at the map. A little Anglo Saxon enclave stuck out in the Pacific Ocean, light years from anywhere.'

'Maybe we are lucky because of that.'

Frank rubbed his chin. 'We need people. Open the doors, let them in. It's the only way we'll ever develop the place.'

'Perhaps you're right. Mother told me the old man, my grandfather once said, our trouble was we never produced a Thomas Paine or an Abraham Lincoln.'

'Bloody little chance of that. All we produce are opportunists. Offer them a knighthood, they'd sell their grandmother.'

'I haven't heard you talk like this before old friend. You sound serious.'

'No, I suppose you haven't Ben.' He sounded weary. 'I guess it was the war and all that. I'm taking an interest in politics now, in fact I'm involved to some extent.'

'You surprise me.'

'You shouldn't be. You know how I feel about this country.'

'I do, but don't let it depress you. Come on, a drop of brandy will cheer you up. We're all going up to *Monaro* for the Easter break. Muriel will be there.'

Frank stretched and yawned. 'I'm ready for that brandy and a good night's sleep. So young Muriel will be there will she? Nice girl that, Ben a very nice girl.'

'Nice to see you again, Muriel.'

'And you, Frank. What have you been doing with yourself?'

'Working very hard my dear. And you?'

'Oh, the usual, teaching. I really love my job.'

'Are we going riding again, like we did at Christmas?'

'I'd love to.'

'So would I. Now I must pay my respects to Ben's mother.' He took her arm. 'By the way, I promised to take the boys fishing this afternoon, care to come?'

'If you put the bait on my hook for me.'

'Agreed.' Smiling they strolled together into the house.

'I'm glad you could come up for Easter, Frank. How long can you stay?'

'About a week, Mrs. Wakefield. While I'm here, with your permission I would like to make some rough sketches of *Monaro* and take a few photographs.'

'There is no need to ask. Of course you may.'

'Then I'll get my sketch pad.' He smiled. 'Muriel can be my assistant, hold my crayons for me.' He looked outside. 'Yes, the light is ideal, I can get a full frontal view.'

They stood well back, near the stone wall that encircled the garden. A faint breeze brought heady perfume of late roses. Rozellas brilliant against the greenery, flashed screeching in blocks to the scarlet coral trees.

'It is so lovely here.' Muriel smiled up at him. 'Don't you think so?'

For a moment he was silent, stealing a glance at her over his pad. He thought - how lovely she is, so gentle.

'Yes my dear, it is beautiful, all of it, especially the house. As an architect, I am filled with envy.'

'I don't think you could ever be envious, Frank.'

He sighed. 'Believe me, Muriel, I am. I could never design anything like it.' He handed her his sketch pad. 'You see, already I'm plagiarizing his work, whoever he was.' Folding his pad, he took her arm. 'Let's walk a little, there is something I want to say to you.'

They stopped, standing face to face. 'I have been trying to pluck up courage to say this.'

They walked on slowly, close together.

'I owe you an apology.'

'I don't understand Frank.'

'Christmas Eve in the tower. I'm sorry Muriel, I had too much to drink.'

She took his hand. 'Please, don't say any more.' Her head was back, lips slightly parted. 'I am a grown woman you know.' He held her close, the pad fell to the grass.

'Uncle Frank, Uncle Frank!'

They broke apart. Across the lawn four children raced towards them, the little girl trailing behind. Breathlessly they clustered around, then recognizing Muriel, stopped suddenly except Dorothy who flung herself into Frank's arms.

'Good morning children.' Muriel struggled to regain her composure.

'Good morning Miss Halsey,' they chorused.

'Well now.' Frank set the little girl down. 'Are we still going fishing after lunch?'

Gareth piped up. 'We don't have to take Harry and Dorothy do we Uncle?'

'We'll see, we'll see. Now run along all of you.' He kissed the little girl. 'Never mind Dorothy, we'll have some fun later.'

After dinner Ben sat with his brother in law out on the high verandah.

'Ben, I'm beginning to understand why you don't leave this place.' He leaned forward. 'Those lanterns, how often do you light them?'

'Well, Christmas, Easter, any special occasion.' He held out his glass. 'If you're pouring yourself another, top mine up please.'

They sat in silence for a while, then 'So what's new between you and Muriel? Gareth told his mother he saw you kissing her today.'

'Bloody kids!' Frank laughed. 'They don't miss much.'

Again there was silence.

'Well?'

'I don't know Ben - buggered if I do.'

'You like her don't you?'

'Like her! Christ, I could eat her!' He stood pacing slowly. 'You know how I feel about marriage.' He gave a wry smile. 'Spoils a beautiful friendship.' He sat again. 'Seriously, we have discussed it of course, but damn it, this bloody religious thing keeps cropping up. To tell the truth, we have decided to wait. Give ourselves a chance to think it over.'

'Any set time, this waiting I mean?'

'Not really, but I have made a decision on one thing.'

'What's that?'

'I'm taking the year off. Going overseas, America, Europe, the whole thing.'

'Rather sudden, isn't it?'

'You know I've been thinking about it for some time. I'm not short of a quid. The old place brought a good price, half of which is Francie's of course, but I can well afford to indulge myself for a year, or more if necessary.'

'When do you leave?'

'Soon as I straighten things out in Sydney. Which reminds me, I must see Pieter before I leave. Get a few things in order.'

'I must say it all sounds very sudden. How does Muriel feel about it? Your going away I mean.'

'Bit upset but basically she agrees. To be honest, I feel a bit of a bloody heel.'

'I think you are doing the sensible thing. Muriel's young, she will either forget you, or - I don't know, time will tell.'

Not to prolong the agony, Frank left immediately after the Easter holidays. Muriel wept quietly as the car disappeared down the drive. Rose held the girl to her. 'Don't my dear, if he loves you and I am sure he does, he will be back.'

CHAPTER XIV

Frances rejoiced in the new freedom the little car gave her. With Harry secure in the seat beside her, whenever the opportunity arose, she headed for *Monaro*. As always, Rose waited for her on the lower verandah, sewing basket on her lap. She smiled with pleasure as the car pulled up. Coming down the steps to meet them, she took Harry by the hand. 'I always know it's you Frances. As soon as we hear you coming up the hill, Mrs. Ellis puts the kettle on.'

'Mother Wakefield, how are you? Are you obeying Dr. Coburn's orders?

'Oh Tom, such an alarmist, of course I am, dear. Now don't worry, come and sit down.'

A pleasant middle aged woman came through the doors with a laden tray.

'Thank you, Margaret.'

'How are you, Mrs. Ellis?'

'Well, thank you, Mrs. Wakefield.' She set the tray down. 'Will you pour?'

'Yes, thank you.'

They sipped their tea as Harry, cake in hand, chased butterflies along the tiles.

'He is a lovely, healthy child, Frances. What are you hoping for this time?'

'I don't mind really.' She laughed. 'A girl would be nice.'

Rose smiled. 'I went to the chapel this morning. It was our anniversary.'

Frances looked apprehensively at her mother in law. 'It must have been sad for you.'

'No my dear, not sad.' She sighed. 'That passed many years ago.'

'All these years by yourself, you must have been very lonely.'

'Not for a minute. I have had such dear friends. We managed you know. Yes, perhaps without those who stayed close to me I might have given way, but I gave my promise to Harry to keep *Monaro.* That was my strength.' She took

Frances' hand.. 'Frances my dear, my strength was renewed the day Ben brought you home. You are the daughter I would have chosen.'

Later as Frances drove away savouring the pleasant warmth of the autumn sunshine, her heart lifted within her. She glanced at her small son sound asleep amongst his cushions. She thought - I am the most fortunate of women.

That night in bed in their 'Conference Room' as they called it, where they talked in whispers and laughed quietly over the days events. 'I don't understand, I thought Jonesy was happy here. Is it the children?'

'She loves the children, you know how devoted she is to them and to you.'

'Then why move?'

'Oh Ben, it's only ten minutes away. Ethel is a very independent woman.'

He sighed. 'Well, where is it?'

'Just around the corner, Cudgee Street. You know the little cottage, it's been empty for months.'

'Has she rented or bought it?'

'She bought it. Pieter arranged everything.' Frances moved to ease the burden within her. 'Don't say anything darling. I think she wanted a place of her own, for her daughter's sake. Things are not very good in Sydney, her daughter may bring the girls up here for a while.'

He grunted. 'That I can understand although I have never met the man.'

'Promise you won't say anything.'

'Don't be silly, of course I won't say anything.' He turned to face her. 'Francie, why the hell am I the last person to hear anything around here?'

She snuggled up to him. 'Because I don't want to worry you with unimportant details.'

'Well I think - oh, what the hell! How's Muriel bearing up?'

'She's fine, darling. Mr. Worlby took her to the pictures Saturday night and he is taking her to the eisteddfod next week.'

'Well she's safe there.'

'What do you mean?'

'Adrian Worlby is homosexual, in vulgar parlance, a poof.'

'Oh dear, I didn't know!'

'No, I suppose you didn't. He married old Miss Walton, that's why he is so comfortable today. You know the Brelat's house? That belonged to him.'

Frances sounded shocked. 'But she was an old lady, she must have been at least sixty five, even older.'

'I guess she was, but she married him anyway. The family was furious.'

'What happened, he didn't kill her did he?'

'Cut it out Francie. Tom Coburn was her doctor, far as I know, she died of natural causes, heart trouble probably. Anyway, I believe she was happy just having him around.'

'I think it's horrible, men like that.'

Ben yawned. 'That's how God made him, my love. Now please no more chatter, it's after midnight.'

At breakfast next morning, Ben opened the mail. 'There you are, Frank has gone at last. Posted this just before he sailed.' He handed the letter to his wife. 'Good thing Francie, give them both time to sort things out.'

'Poor Muriel, she loves him so much.'

He rose, kissing her lightly. 'Don't worry old girl, she'll survive.' He wiped his forehead. 'Going to be a stinker today and I have to wear this damn tie.'

Ethel came in. 'Ben, Mick Flannery is outside. Came down on his horse. His wife is not too good. Can you come quickly?'

'Pack the bag, Ethel, I've got an idea we're in for trouble.'

Mary Flannery never stood a chance. She haemorrhaged badly, the child was stillborn. Towards noon Ben went outside to the husband sitting dejectedly on the wooden steps. A robust, ruddy cheeked young woman had the children. 'Sorry Mick, I'm truly sorry. Mary's gone, Matron Jones is attending to her now.'

Mick wept, his head in his hands. 'Oh dear God, my Mary, my poor darling Mary!'

Ben laid his hand on Mick's shoulder. 'Come and see me when things are settled.'

Two weeks later Mick turned up at the surgery. 'Thanks for everything Doc. Be all right if I pay a bit at a time?'

'There is no charge, Mick, you got it hard enough as it is.' Ben looked at him keenly. 'What are you going to do now?'

'That was Mary's sister you saw that day, Doc, she's going to look after the kids. Soon as it's right, we're getting married.'

'Sounds like a good idea. What is her attitude to contraception?'

'No kids for her, Doc. She said we'd have to use them things.'

'I'm glad to hear it. A practical young woman.'

'Mary wouldn't, reckoned it was a sin against God.'

Ben rose guiding him to the door. 'Well, good luck Mick. Remember I'm always here if you need me.'

Mick wrung his hand. 'Ain't many like you, Doc!'

Later Ben told Dave the details. 'They think we're Jesus Christ, Dave. It's frightening!'

Later in the year, Frances was delivered of a healthy male child.

Dr. Coburn shook Ben's hand. 'Perfect specimen, Ben. What are you going to call this one?'

Ben smiled. 'Ronald I believe, Doctor.'

'A noble name. You're a fortunate man.'

'My sincere thanks, Sir. Frances would only see you, you know.'

The older man chuckled. 'Well, retirement can be a little boring at times.'

They shook hands again. 'Call on me any time I can be useful, Ben.' He smiled. 'Keeps the brain cells working.'

Christmas 1926 at *Monaro* was the usual happy gathering of old friends. Rose claimed the new baby. 'He is beautiful, like the others Frances. I am so happy my dear, happier than I can remember. I promised Harry I would always keep *Monaro*, then when Ben went away to the war - well, there is no need to worry about that now.'

Frances touched the older woman's hand. 'I am glad you are happy, Mother Wakefield. Come on, we'll display him to all the others.'

Dave Aitken came up for the festivities. 'First time I've seen the place at night, Ben. Looks like fairyland.'

Frances nurtured the hope the young man might be interested in Muriel but he had more accommodating ladies in mind. Besides Muriel had been receiving regular cards from Frank and had found that absence does indeed make the heart grow fonder.

New Year came and passed. April brought a change from the depressing humidity of the summer months.

On a night with surgery over, the two partners sat talking. 'Thanks for dropping in, Dave. How's your patient?'

Dave rubbed his chin. 'Can't pick it, Ben, appreciate you having a look.'

'Gladly old chap, I'll drop in tomorrow after rounds.' He rose. 'Now I won't ask you to stay for a drink.' Grinning broadly he opened the door. 'I wouldn't want you to keep the delectable Widow Prentice waiting.'

'Good God! How do you know about that?'

'A little bird told me.'

Dave laughed as he crossed the verandah. 'A female bird I'll bet.'

Ben sat late, pouring over the details of the case in question. Male, age twenty, normally good health, presented Monday. Temperature 102 degrees, sever general aches and pains, presently in Infectious Annex at the hospital. Ben glanced at the calendar, now Thursday. General deterioration, patient comatose.

Might ask Tom Coburn's opinion. The old boy knows the game backwards. Went straight to it when Bill Ticker, the butcher, presented in extremis. Ben often sat late, finding the surgery comforting. Here he could ponder, think things out. Maybe Pieter was right. Why the hell kill yourself working as a country practitioner? He smiled to himself, knowing the answer - he belonged here. The buzz of the front door bell broke his reverie.

He glanced at his watch - almost midnight, Frances and the children were fast asleep. Groaning inwardly, he peered at the figure standing in the shadows.

'Aren't you going to ask me in?'

'Well I'll be - Dan!' He wrung the priest's hand. 'Come in, come in. Here, sit here. I was dozing. God help us! I thought I would never see you again, until I got your letter. Make yourself comfortable. This calls for a drink.' From the cupboard he brought a dusty bottle of Scotch and two glasses

'You haven't changed, Ben. A little older, a lot wiser no doubt.'

'Maybe. Now sit there and tell me everything. Where you've been, what you've been doing.' He smiled at his old friend. 'I'm curious, you know.'

Dan emptied half his glass. 'I needed that, Ben, after that train trip.'

'That I can believe. Where are you, at the Presbytery?'

'Yes, I've just come from there. Old Father Brian leaves next week, giving me the rounds before he goes.'

'How do you find him?'

Dan laughed. 'Typical country priest. Fire and brimstone. Basically not a bad old stick. Loves his booze by the look of his nose.'

'Yes I've noticed. But what about you, where have you been all this time?'

'Well, if you'll top up my glass, I'll tell you.'

'Good luck.' They held their glasses up.

'Now where do I start?'

'As they say, at the beginning.'

Dan settled back. 'For a start, you know I never wanted to enter the priesthood, but you know - the pressure put on my mother etc.'

Ben nodded.

'There was no chance of my getting out, the Church has ways of dealing with rebellious priests.'

'I can imagine.'

'Oh yes, they worked on me. To tell the truth Ben, I could have disappeared, gone to Europe or somewhere.'

'What stopped you?'

The young priest smiled. 'I think you can guess the reason.'

'Your brother?'

'Yes, Sean. A saint,' he grinned, 'a saint with a sense of humour.'

'That sounds like Sean all right.'

'What I put that dear brother of mine through. He stood by me through all my whingeing and whining.'

'You're a bit hard on yourself, aren't you?'

Dan slouched back in his chair. 'Oh I don't know, perhaps. I suppose I feel cheated in a way.'

'Anyway, you're here now, however you wangled that.'

'Sean again.' He reached for the bottle. 'May I?'

'Of course, I'll have a drop more myself.' Ben lit a cigar. 'Does the smoke bother you?'

'No, I love the aroma.' He fished for his cigarettes. 'Mmm, this is pure comfort.'

'Sean worked all this out for you?'

Dan nodded. 'He is held in such high regard, Ben, has the Bishop's ear. He could go anywhere in the Church, but you know Sean.'

'I saw him when I was in Sydney last year.'

'Yes, he told me. Sends his regards, and his blessing of course.'

'And now you are here. Will it make any difference to the way you feel?'

'I think so, time will tell. I'll probably alienate half the congregation within a week.'

'I doubt it. After Father Brian you will be like a breath of fresh air.'

'I hope so. Must be careful though, the diehards won't forgive too much fraternizing with the separated sheep.' They both laughed.

'Well, one for the road. How did you get here anyway?'

'The old boy's sulky. Doesn't believe in motorcars. Works of the Devil no doubt. Soon as he leaves I'm buying a car. I'm well fixed for money, thanks to my mother.'

Ben saw his friend to the gate. 'Come again soon, Dan. Frances will have a fit that I didn't wake her.'

'Rely on me. Doctors are exempt you know, especially if there isn't one of the faith in town.'

Next morning Ben, holding the baby on his knee, waited his chance.

'You had a late night visitor, darling? You look tired.'

'Did we wake you?'

'No, Ronnie stirred. I thought he felt hot. Feel him, Ben.'

His cool hand lightly pressed the baby's forehead. 'Nothing there, Francie. Slightly warm, all children run mild temperatures when their teeth are coming through.' The child nestled against his father. No wonder the women dote on him, he thought. He gently pushed back the blonde curls. 'He's got your eyes, Francie and those long dark lashes.'

Ronnie slid off his knee wanting to greet his brothers as they suddenly trouped into the room.

Ben smiled at his wife. 'There you are, right as rain. He has your nature too, old girl, even the kids love him.' He stood up. 'I must go. Have to make a call at the hospital before surgery.'

Frances held tight to the lapels of his coat. 'All right, Ben Wakefield, you've had your fun. Who was it?'

He looked down at her with mock surprise. 'Oh that, I thought you would never ask!'

'You are impossible! Come on, tell me.'

He told her of the events of the night before. She could hardly suppress her excitement. 'Dan! Isn't it wonderful? It will be like old times.'

'Now listen, Francie.' He grew serious. 'Dan is a Catholic priest. You know we can't fraternize, we'll have every bloody Catholic and Protestant down our throats. Leave it to Dan, you'll see him soon enough.'

'Your mother will want to see him.'

'Of course she will but knowing Dan, he will be very discreet.'

'It's all so silly, isn't it?'

'Bloody ridiculous.' He kissed her. 'Now I must be off.'

A grave faced Dave Aitken met him at the hospital.

'Trouble, Dave?'

'I've been here half the blasted night, Ben.'

'How's your patient?'

'Died this morning. I diagnosed meningitis, had all the earmarks. I'm not so sure now.'

'Why? Pretty straightforward surely?'

'Perhaps, but three more presented this morning. Two children and one young male about twenty.'

'Phew, we had better take a closer look.'

They were joined by Matron Truman. 'I'm glad you are here, Ben. We can't put any more on the verandah, we haven't any beds.'

'Let's not worry about that now, Matron. We will face that problem if it eventuates. Now, let us see the patients.'

Matron Faith Truman, a gentle caring woman who was the police sergeant's sister and a close friend of Ethel Jones from the war years, led the way.

Ben examined each patient with meticulous care. 'I'm pretty sure, Dave, but I would like Dr. Coburn's opinion. Almost certainly Poliomyelitis.'

'I've only ever seen one case, while I was Resident, Ben.'

'And pray you don't see any more.' Ben carefully washed his hands. 'What do you think, Matron?'

'I've seen cases in the city, Doctor. I'm afraid you are right.'

'Yes, it's something I don't like to believe, Dave. You had better go and have some rest. I'll do your rounds here. Matron will ring Ethel and put surgery off until this afternoon.'

Dr. Coburn arrived midmorning and quickly confirmed Ben's diagnosis.

'Just three, Doctor. I am not sure about Dave's patient.'

'We had better send samples to Sydney, as is required, Ben.' The older man looked serious. 'My experience is, you had better prepare yourself, this may be only the beginning.'

'I feel pretty helpless, Doctor, I'd appreciate your advice.'

'All we can do is wait. It's a mysterious disease, generally no more than a mild fever, patients recover quickly but you see people around here crippled from the last epidemic. That was before you time, of course.' he added.

'Were there any fatalities?'

'Yes, as I said, a strange disease. Some seem to shrug it off, others, well I think it's a matter of their susceptibility to the infection.'

The following weeks became a nightmare. Hot dry weather returned, fires burned out of control in the ranges and twelve more cases were confirmed. Ben closed the surgery and the three doctors, with Matrons Truman and Jones, held a council of war.

'Thank you for coming, Doctor.'

Dr Coburn nodded. 'So far it seems confined to the town, Ben. There could be a carrier.' He shook his head. 'We will never know because such people seldom develop symptoms and frankly, we know nothing of the disease itself.'

'Should we close the schools? All new cases are children, as you know?'

'A drastic step, Ben, but yes I would advise it.'

Frances met a weary husband at the front door. 'Ben, what is happening? They have closed the school and darling, people are asking why the surgery is closed.'

'How about a kiss for your old man? Ah, that's better. Now yes, as District Medical Advisor, I closed the schools on Dr. Coburn's advice. Believe me Francie, he knows what is best.'

'But the surgery, Ben, what shall I tell them? Ethel is at the hospital all the time now.'

He put his arm around her. 'Tell them to go to the hospital. I am having a notice put up anyway.'

They sat at late dinner, Ben having been called out on an urgent call, Frances had switched off the ceiling light and lit a lovely old oil lamp that had come with the house. It's green shade cast a comforting soft light.

'Who was it, Ben?'

He answered shortly. 'The Hansen's.'

She put her hand to her mouth. 'Not little Ruby?'

'Afraid so.' He leaned across, lightly gripping her arm. 'No more, Francie, I've had enough for one day.'

'But she is their only child.'

'Frances,' he spoke sharply, 'please.'

'I'm sorry, I know I shouldn't ask, but I am so worried.'

He smiled at her. 'Can we have some coffee now?'

She returned with the steaming pot. Ben waited until they had finished then pulled his chair closer to her. 'Sorry I was so sharp darling, I'm so tired and this is my only haven.' He sighed. 'Don't think I don't understand, I'm worried too my dear but we can't afford to show it. You know that don't you?'

She nodded. 'Yes I do.'

'Just keep going the way you are. Keep the children inside.'

The next few weeks saw fewer cases. Most of the children were discharged to convalesce at home. Some had died, including little Ruby Hansen. The remainder would be hopelessly crippled. Exhausted and haggard Ben broke the news to his wife.

'Oh my God, what will they do?'

He spoke quietly. 'What will the others do Francie? I've dreaded every minute of this. There isn't a doctor living who could have saved her.'

'But you said it was finished now.' She spoke accusingly. 'That's what you said Ben.'

'What are you talking about Francie?' At sight of her face, he stopped short. 'What is it?'

She was crying, trying desperately to control herself. 'Harry and Gerald are feverish and Ben, the baby is hot.' Her voice trembled. 'He won't take his food.'

Ben sank limply back in his chair. He looked up at her, so worn and tired her heart went out to him. She knelt and put her arms around him, her head on his chest. 'Oh Ben, I'm sorry, I'm so sorry.'

He smoothed her hair back from her forehead. 'I know Francie, I know. There's nothing to be sorry about.' He held her close. Finally he said, 'while you get me some dinner, I'll take a look at them. I'll bring Ethel back from the hospital tomorrow and open the surgery again. Time I did.'

They ate their dinner in silence. At last he pushed back his chair. 'Ben?'

He looked steadily at his wife. 'I don't know Francie. It could be anything. I'll ask Dr. Coburn to come tomorrow.' He slipped into his coat.

'Oh Ben, must you go out again?'

'Outpatients is full, darling. Now you get some rest. I'll be back as soon as I can.' He paused at the door. 'Gareth is perfectly normal, no temperature at all.'

The following day, Dr. Coburn made his examination. In the privacy of the surgery, he spoke in a low voice but the gravity of his tone was unmistakable. 'Your eldest boy Gareth, is unaffected. The others, Gerald and Harry, exhibit the classic symptoms, particularly Harry.'

'The baby, Doctor, what of the baby?'

'I don't know, Ben. Young children run these temperatures for quite long periods.' He shook his head. 'I just can't say.' He rose to go. 'If you wish, I will drop in again tomorrow.'

Ben accepted his offer gratefully. 'Thank you Doctor. I expect - I hope we will know the best or the worst in the next few days.'

Closing the front door, he turned to find his wife standing in the hall. She looked frightened.

'What did he say, what did Dr. Coburn say?'

He thought - how unjust this is, how could it happen?

'Ben?'

He could now bring himself to answer.

She whispered. 'Is it that bad? Tell me Ben.'

He slipped his arms around her. 'I think - I don't know, Francie. The next few days will tell.'

She clung to him. The telephone shrilled in the surgery. He returned carrying his bag. 'Must you go? You've had nothing to eat.'

Ben spoke grimly. 'Hansen has cut his throat.'

'Dear God!' Frances was on the verge of collapse.

Ben hastily poured brandy into a glass. 'Drink this Francie. Come on now, you have the children to look after. Ethel will be here tomorrow.' He tried to soothe her. 'So many are suffering darling. Now take care of them until I get back.'

A week passed. Gerald recovered completely, Harry hovered on the brink, his tenacious laboured breathing audible with each gasp. Gradually his fever subsided.

Dr. Coburn folded his stethoscope. 'Your son will survive Ben. You must accept that he will be a cripple you understand.'

'Thank you Doctor, for all you have done. Yes, I do understand. We must be thankful he is still alive.' At the door he confronted his mentor. 'I'm concerned for Frances, Doctor. She has never left the baby. Matron Jones and Miss Halsey have sat with the other children.' He frowned shaking his head. 'I know she loves him dearly, I just don't understand.'

The older man took his arm. 'Walk to the gate with me Ben.' He turned to face him. 'I'm going to say what you must already know. The infant is dying, forty eight hours at the most, perhaps sooner.'

Ben put his hand to his head. 'How in God's name will she take it? And my mother, she knows nothing of this.'

'My dear boy, I am deeply sorry. Perhaps you will permit me to talk to your mother?'

'Thank you, I would be most grateful. I feel utterly helpless in matters concerning my own family. I feel I can't cope with it.'

'I know, but you will. Believe me, you will.' He let himself through the gate. 'Goodnight, call on me any time I may be of use.'

Ben was thankful for a busy surgery. The last patient gone, he leaned back in his chair regarding the broad back of Ethel Jones, busy at the sterilizer. 'Ethel.'

She turned after closing the lid. 'Yes Ben.'

'Thank you.'

'For what?'

'For everything. You know what I mean, staying on.'

She sat down facing him. 'You look worn out. Get some sleep while you can. I'll look after things here. If anything urgent turns up I'll ring Dave.'

'How can I every thank you?'

'You don't.' She smiled briefly. 'We've been through bad times before remember.'

He nodded. 'I can't get the sight of that poor devil, Hansen, out of my mind. His brothers wouldn't let him near the front of the shop. He got a boneing knife somewhere.'

'Dave told me. The wife has been under heavy sedation apparently.'

'To tell the truth, I wouldn't mind sedating myself, whiskey for preference.'

'Come on my boy, bed for you. I'll wake you if I need you.'

In the hall a dim light was burning, the house so quiet he could hear his own breathing. Suddenly a terrible wailing cry broke the stillness. His heart froze. Standing in the doorway to the baby's room, he saw his wife, the infant in her arms. Ethel came quickly, switching on the main lights. Ronnie lay limp in her arms, his head back, the long dark lashes now even darker against the pallor of his skin. The golden curls she had so lovingly brushed now wet with the sweat of his struggle, lay clustered thick on his head.

Ronnie was dead. Dead forever. This joyous, small life wrenched from their hands, leaving only grief that nothing could console.

'Sweet Jesus, Ethel take the child.' He took his fainting wife in his arms, half lifting, half dragging her to the bedroom.

Ethel Jones, who had never in her life lost her head, quickly took the child away and returned with the merciful hypodermic. Ben held his wife close as the drug was injected. Her eyes closing, Frances whispered the name of her dead child over and over again.

Through the night while Ethel kept her solitary vigil, Ben sat by his sleeping wife, his face buried in his hands. Perhaps he slept himself, he couldn't tell. He roused as morning light filtered through the window. Lifting the sash he caught the sweet fragrance of verbena, recapturing the previous moments he had walked with his little boy along those paths. In a cluster of tall Citronellas, magpies were scolding.

Frances was still sleeping. He watched as the effects of the drug slowly wore off. Occasionally a low moan escaped her lips. As she turned slight tremors shook her body. His hand to the stubble on his chin, he made his way to the kitchen. Matron Jones, professional in her starched white uniform, met him at the door. She took his arm. 'Sit down.' It was like an order. Meekly he obeyed. The blessed aroma of coffee filled the air. A platter of bacon and eggs was set before him. Gratefully he sipped.

'I must shave, Ethel. Surgery.'

'Not today, Ben. Not for you anyway, I have already spoken to Dr. Coburn.'

He put his cup down. 'Damn it, Ethel, we can't do that. He has retired, you know.'

She smiled wryly. 'That man will never retire, he actually sounded grateful. You wife and children need you, Ben.'

He nodded. 'Perhaps you're right. There is so much to do.'

'I've done everything that's necessary. Will you phone Cawley?'

'Yes, I'd better do that right away. He will be buried at *Monaro* - this could kill my mother!'

'I think you underestimate your mother, Ben. Dr. Coburn is with her now. He is coming straight from there to the surgery.'

Bathed and clean shave, he looked into the bedroom. Frances was lying back amongst the pillows, her eyes blank staring straight ahead. He took her hands, strangely cold. 'Francie, Francie, look at me. How are you, my dearest?'

He eyes turned to him accusingly, almost hostile. 'My baby is dead. I told you, I told you, you did nothing!' Her voice rose. 'I told you he was sick. You didn't care.'

He held her tightly to him. 'Shush, shush. There was nothing anyone could do. Please believe me, please Francie.'

Terrible sobs shook her body. He held her close. 'There now, that's better, let it out.'

Ethel appeared in the doorway, a small glass in her hand, he shook his head. Suddenly Frances turned her head away, he bent low to hear her whisper. 'I want Dan. Please tell Dan to come.'

The ceremony was simple. They stood silent before the freshly dug grave next to the child's grandfather. As he listened to the priest's comforting words, Ben's eyes strayed to the little Chapel. Through the open door the mother of pearl font glowed like fire in the shafts of refracted light filtering through the stained glass window. The font where his infant son had so lately been christened. 'Here is where my bones will lie. Mine and those dearest to me.'

A sense of normality returned to the big house in town. The housekeeper returned, the surgery resumed busier than ever. Dave Aitken announced his intention to take a year off. 'Might as well, Ben. I'm still young. See the world, catch up a bit.'

'Don't blame you, Dave. Good luck to you. Don't know what the hell I'll do though, too much for one man.'

'What about Tom Coburn? Ethel reckons he will never retire.'

'Well, if it comes to that, if I can't get a locum, I'll ask him.'

The young man studied his colleague. 'May I ask you something?'

'Of course, fire away.'

'Why in Hell do you do it? I understand you are a very wealthy man. What is it? Noblesse Oblige, or something like that?'

Ben laughed. 'Nobless Oblige? No, Dave, nothing like that. My home is here, my heart is here. I think the war made me realize I have certain obligations.' He looked up. 'If that's an explanation.'

'Well, there are not many like you, more's the pity.'

'Thanks for the compliment. When do you intend leaving?'

'I thought after Christmas, if that suits you.'

'Of course. Gives me time to sort things out.'

The year wore on, the seasons changed, storms rolled across the land. It seemed as if memories of the tragic epidemic faded as the Christmas season drew near. Faded for those who had not been touched, ever present with those families affected. Frances went about her duties as before, meticulously caring for Harry, his twisted body now confined to a wheelchair. Gareth and Gerald now completely recovered, were back at school She would not speak to Ben of the baby's death. At night she wept, he would take her in his arms desperately trying to find words of comfort. She would lay limp turning her face to the wall.

Ben confided in the only one he could turn to. 'Sorry Ethel, I've got to talk to somebody.'

'Well, if it will help.'

'Francie blames me Ethel. Nothing I say or do makes any difference. I've failed her.'

'You know better than that, Ben Wakefield. You haven't failed her. Give her time.'

He sighed. 'Thank God for Dan and my mother. Francie packs Harry in the car and goes up there every other day.' He shook his head. 'She won't have that Anglican priest in the house. What's his name, Father Lomas - Logan or something. Prissy self important little bugger. Anyhow that's how it stands.'

Ethel sat down. 'Look here, Ben, I understand Frances' grief. I feel as if I have lost someone of my own, but life goes on. We both know that. Just give her time. She has spirit, she will come round.' She stood, began fussing with history cards. 'You are my worry, you look terrible. You are obviously not sleeping. Just remember, a lot of people are relying on you.'

He grinned weakly. 'Thanks Ethel, I needed that.'

The weeks dragged out interminably. Ben used the spare bedroom, no longer sure he was welcome in the common bed.

On a burning afternoon, out on calls, he turned the car towards *Monaro*, his first visit since the epidemic. His mother was sitting in her favourite chair, knitting. His heart jumped as he saw how thin she had become. He pulled a chair close beside her. 'Hello Mum, how you are?'

'I'm fine, dear. Why haven't you been to see me?'

'You know what's been going on, I haven't had a minute to myself.' He put his arm around her. 'I've thought of you every day.'

They sat silent for a moment. 'Frances has been to see you, hasn't she?'

'Yes.' The needles clicked. 'Why do you ask?'

'Oh Mum!' He rested his head on her shoulder and began to weep, tears of a man not given to crying.

Her thin arms folded around him. 'There, there, my darling. It's all right, it's all right.'

He struggled to control himself. 'Haven't done that since a small boy, have I?'

'I'm glad you did, my dear. I had so little of you as a child, now I'm your mother again.'

Anguished, he asked. 'Why won't she talk to me, Mum? I love her, she treats me like a stranger.'

'Give her time, Ben, you must give her time.' Tears sprang to here eyes. 'I do grieve for her. Frances is such a giving woman and I know she loves you dearly.'

He nodded. 'That's what Ethel says, but it's hard. So damn unjust. Christmas is almost here again, perhaps things will be better then. Christmas!' He stood staring moodily out over the garden. 'Not much to celebrate this year.'

'Ben,' he detected a note of urgency in her voice, 'please dear, it's all the more reason.'

He bent low, tenderly kissing her. 'And what about you? You know I worry about you being here alone.'

'Please Ben, we've been all over this before. You have no cause to worry. Mrs. Ellis comes every day and Bob Martin three days a week. Just look at the garden, he is such a hard worker. I do appreciate him.' She smiled. 'Asks me before he touches a plant.'

'Yes I know, worth their weight in gold.'

They both fell silent, then - 'What does she talk about, Mum, can you tell me?'

The needles stopped clicking. 'Just talk, darling. Frances misses her mother and has turned to me. I pray I don't fail her.'

'Does she go to the chapel, you know, the grave?'

'Yes sometimes. She takes flowers.'

'It's dangerous along that track, snakes are bad this time of year.'

'Don't worry dear, Bob goes with her as far as the gates.'

'I don't understand Mum, she has three other children, one hopelessly crippled. Surely she thinks of them.'

His mother looked at him, her old veined hands resting on her lap. 'He was her baby, Ben.'

He had to be satisfied with that.

'Would you like some tea?'

'No thanks, too damn hot. Something cold would be good.'

As if on cue, Mrs. Ellis appeared with a tray. 'I heard your car, Doctor.'

A jug of homemade lemonade nestled in a bucket of ice. 'You read my mind, Mrs. Ellis. Thank you very much.'

He sipped the cool drink. 'Dan tells me he sees you and Muriel, and most of the old gang visit.' He smiled. 'You are a very popular lady.'

'I love to see them. They are all very dear to me.'

'What about Father Lomas, the Anglican priest?'

'He is welcome to call dear. I wish him no disrespect but no one can take the place of Martin Trendel and his wife. They were part of our lives.'

'I'm tiring you, Mother.' He looked at his watch. 'Promise I'll come more often from now on.' He held her hand, surreptitiously feeling her pulse.

'Be patient with Frances dear, be patient.'

Ben drove away with mixed feelings. Thankful that his wife was finding some comfort in her grief, and a sinking feeling the evidence of his finger tips had revealed.

Along the curving driveway to the gates, memories flooded back. Days of his childhood. How he loved this place. Trees formed a cool canopy overhead.

Abraham's old stone cottage was now almost hidden from view. He sighed - if only life was all so simple again. In his mind's eye he saw his mother long ago, cool in her long white dress. Only dimly could he remember his father, always busy at his easel. The years had flown. He must speak to Dr. Coburn again about his mother, for all the good that would do. And Frances, pray God, that will come right soon. He muttered, 'it's damn unfair. Doesn't she realize I have suffered too, am suffering? What was that Dan said about a soul surviving? The joy of meeting our loved ones again.' He shook his head. 'I wonder if he believes that stuff himself. The corpses I saw in France didn't look like they were going anywhere.'

CHAPTER XV

Mid December. Christmas 1928 was almost upon them. The town never more prosperous. Leafy saplings were cut and lashed to the verandah posts along the main street. The pubs were crowded and a general feeling of well being prevailed.

Cards from Frank announced his return by Easter. Ethel Jones took Ben into her confidence, swearing him to secrecy. Muriel had come to live with her. 'Turned up early one morning Ben, utterly confused.'

'Can't imagine Muriel falling out with those other women. What happened?'

'The poor girl still doesn't understand. Apparently they came home late after a night out and got into bed with her.'

'For God's sake, a couple of lesbians! I though those two got about with those young blokes with the Service cars!'

Ethel smiled briefly. 'They do but they still prefer women.'

'Poor Muriel, she must have got one hell of a shock.'

'Apparently, but she still doesn't know what it's all about.'

'Funny isn't it? You can never tell. The human race never ceases to amaze me. People who move amongst us and we never suspect what simmers under the surface.' He grinned. 'Anyway, all's well that ends well.'

'I'm glad of her company Ben. It's nice to have someone to talk to.'

'By the way, will your daughter be up at Christmas with the girls?'

'Only Christine, you remember the youngest.'

'Of course. What about, you know the one with the biblical name, Ruth?'

'Oh Ruth is quite the socialite. She was always close to her father.'

'No talk of divorce I suppose.'

'Good heavens no. It would ruin his prospects.' She added. 'They have what you would call, a civilized arrangement.'

Ben murmured. 'Something like Frances and myself.'

'Ben Wakefield, stop wallowing in self pity. For heaven's sake, be patient, give her time.'

'You're a hard woman Ethel. I'm sure she thinks I failed her, somehow I could have done more.'

'You didn't fail her. She will come to realize that, in fact I think she already has.'

'Thanks old girl, you keep me going. Merry Christmas in advance.'

The pre Christmas gathering of old friends was more subdued this year. Some had lost well-loved children, others were left with shadows of what had been their hopes for the future.

'Good to see you Dave, thank God your boy is all right.'

Ben's childhood friend wrung his hand. 'I don't know what to say Ben.'

'Don't say anything Dave. Just help me keep everyone talking.'

They moved mingling with the guests. 'You know Ben, they are sending a young bloke to assist me next month. I can certainly use him.'

'About time, you've carried this town too long, by yourself. Hey look, there's Pieter cracking the nine gallon. That should get them started.'

'Your friend is a popular man.'

'Yes, a little gin punch for the ladies too, should loosen things up. Keep it going Dave. There's Mr. Wardrop and his wife talking to my mother I should pay my respects.'

Dusk fell, warm and purple, magic lanterns glowed along the driveway. The air redolent with the fragrance of frangipani and jasmine. Most seemed reluctant to leave, lingering on as if an unknown, mysterious sense of foreboding hovered in the air. Cabs and sulkys, fewer now, left later than usual. Rose no longer stood to farewell those she held so dear. She sat at the gate taking leave of each as they passed by.

'Leave the lanterns on for the night, Mum. I love them, they bring back such happy memories.' Ben kissed her gently. 'Before dinner I am going to the tower, you don't mind do you?'

'Don't be long Ben, everyone will be expecting you.'

Having climbed the stairs, he sank into the captain's chair, staring out at the moonlight-blanketed landscape, all the way to the ocean. 'Why, why in God's name? I know others have suffered, but why must I go on? I think she hates me.' His eyes filled with tears. 'Too bloody much to drink, bugger it, why should I care? I've done my best.' Time passed, the moon sailed along, clear and white against the great orb of the sky. He hardly heard the soft footsteps behind him. Swivelling around, he saw her standing in the doorway. Her voice came in a whisper-'May I come in?'

'Francie, oh Francie!' She came to his outstretched arms.

'Oh Ben, dear Ben.' She clung to him sobbing. 'Will you ever want me again?'

Ben smoothed her hair, holding her close. 'Hush, hush. I've never ceased to want you, never.'

She looked up through her tears. 'How can you forgive me? I've hurt you so but I love you with all my heart.'

'No more now, no more. Just be thankful we have found each other again.' A surge of happiness and relief flooded his being.

She stood taking his hand. 'Dear forgiving Ben.'

Feeling light hearted from the events of the last half hour, Ben took his place at the head of the table. Smiling, he held his glass aloft. 'Forgive me for keeping you. Please, before we begin, allow me to propose a toast to those who could not be with us tonight. Dave, my able colleague, although I understand he is having dinner with Ethel,' he added with a smile.

'Don't forget the beauteous Christine!' broke in Pieter. A ripple of laughter swirled round the table.

'And my good friend and brother in law Frank, I'm happy to say, home again this Easter.' Ben glanced at Muriel who had blushed deeply at the mention of Frank. 'Also dear friends, while I am on my feet, and with your indulgence may I add, on behalf of my mother, Frances and myself, how glad we are to have you here.' He smiled in turn at each of them, Dr. and Mrs. Coburn, Pieter and Ellen, Professor and Mrs. Brelat and Muriel. He wiped his forehead. 'Good Lord, I have rattled on. I meant to leave that little speech to later in the evening.'

A burst of clapping erupted round the table. Ben glanced at his mother, so small and frail at the far end.

'Ben dear, that was charming. Now please attend to the wine.'

An air of delicious well being pervaded the little company. Without a word being spoken, all knew husband and wife had found each other again.

'So Frank has not forgotten his Christmas donation this year, Ben.' The fragrance of fine cigars drifted over the men lounging on the verandah.

'Arrived a couple of days ago, Doctor. Posted from somewhere in America. Thankfully well packed, fresh as a daisy.'

'Yes, yes, a thoughtful fellow, your brother in law. What does he intend to do on his return?'

'Architecture still, I suppose. Should be plenty of openings.'

'Hmm, I trust so, From what I hear from one of my sons in law, things are starting to slow a little.'

'But surely nothing to worry about, Doctor?' Pieter broke in. 'I had occasion to visit Sydney recently, business seemed to be fairly humming.'

'Well, perhaps you are right, Mr. DeVries. Let us hope you are.'

Ben stood, decanter in hand. 'Allow me to replenish your glasses, gentlemen. I'm positive this brandy improves with age.' He leaned against the rail, facing them. 'And may I propose a toast to fair sailing through 1929.'

Dr. Coburn joined him, gazing out along the lighted driveway. 'My wife and I have spent many happy times here, Ben. It seems so long ago since your mother first found those lanterns. How they have lasted. I never cease to be charmed by the beauty of this place.'

'You have seen many changes, Sir.'

'Indeed. Even the great trees seem larger. Of course the place was a wilderness when your parents found it. Look at it now! So ordered, yet one has the feeling that it would revert back to the bush given half a chance.'

'I have the same feelings, perhaps that's why I am so attached to the place. I only hope our children feel the same.'

'I am sure they will, Ben. Ah, here is the coffee.' He smiled. 'These are the few pleasures age cannot diminish.'

In the depths of sleep, Ben was conscious of a constant tapping noise. His dream sensor made a dozen explanations. His eyes opened slowly. Someone was at the bedroom door. Switching on the bedside light, he saw the clock displayed 3 am. Finding his slippers, he opened the door to find Alice Coburn with torch in hand. She whispered. 'Tom wants you to come. It's your mother.'

He fumbled for his dressing gown, switching off the light. Frances lay, one arm outstretched, breathing gently.

Dr. Coburn was standing by Rose's bed. 'How bad, Doctor?'

'Pretty bad this time, Ben. She is responding. Angina can be frightening.'

'Thank God you were here. How did you know?'

'Fortunately Alice heard her, she is a light sleeper. Don't worry my boy, I've given digitalis. Sorry I didn't call you sooner, she insisted I was not to tell you.'

Ben looked down at his sleeping mother. 'I understand, Doctor, she still thinks of me as her little boy.'

'Dave has put off his trip til May, Francie. It's damn good of him. Gives us a chance to straighten things out here. Mrs. Ellis has agreed to stay permanently now. Her married daughter comes up weekends to give her a hand.'

'I'm glad, Ben. Truly, I'm happy to get away from the town for a while. Please be honest with me, how is your mother?'

'Francie, with care she has quite a few years left. Really you know, she's no age.'

'I know, but Dr. Coburn says age doesn't come into it.'

Ben nodded. 'She is so damned self willed. Refuses to believe anything is seriously wrong with her.'

Frances smiled. 'She has always been like that. The phone hasn't stopped ringing, Muriel is with her now.'

Ben found his mother fully dressed seated in her comfortable armchair with Muriel carefully brushing and arranging the once luxuriant brownish red hair, now thinning and streaked with grey. He tenderly kissed her. 'How is my patient today?'

Rose held his hand, smiling up at him. 'I thought I was Tom's patient'

'You are, my love, you are. He has put me in charge until he comes up again.' He spoke with mock severity. 'And I can be very severe with patients who don't obey my instructions.'

'Oh you two, anyone would think I was an invalid.'

He laughed. 'You, an invalid? Nobody would believe that. But Mum, you must rest for a few days. Now,' he picked up the bottle of white tablets by her chair, 'you know if the pain gets bad you must put one of these under your tongue. You know that, don't you?'

'Ben for Heavens sake, Tom told me all that.'

'I know, I just want to be sure.'

Rose's armchair was moved so that she might look out over her beloved garden. In the afternoon when the sun came around, the blinds were drawn, leaving her room in cool shade. The days passed noisily, the children trouping into her room proudly displaying the day's catches of silver perch and mullet. Their friends stood shyly at the open doorway, Gareth gravely introduced them. 'This is Dave Palmer and Hal Wynter, Grandma and Dorothy caught a big eel but it got away.'

Dorothy, who was staying over the school holidays, came and stood close to Rose. 'I thought it was going to bite me, Grandma.'

Rose felt a great surge of love for this beautiful child who claimed her as her own. 'I do hope you are careful, Gareth, taking Dorothy down to the creek. You must remember she is just a little girl.'

'You don't have to worry about Dutchy, Grandma.' Gerald and the others were laughing. 'She's tough. She puts the worms on herself!'

'Gerald, why on earth do you call Dorothy that name?'

'That's what everyone calls her, Grandma.'

'Do they now, well I hope her mother doesn't hear you.' She felt shocked but let it rest there. 'Where is Harry?'

Gareth wheeled his brother in, sitting lopsided in his wheelchair. Rose fought back tears. 'Wheel him over here to me, please.' She took his withered hand. 'I'm so glad you came to see me, dear. What have you been doing?'

'Fishing, Grandma.'

'Fishing? With the others?'

'Harry comes everywhere with us, Grandma. We push his chair everywhere. He's a good fisherman, too.'

Mistily Rose looked at the perfect head with it's infectious smile and the poor crippled body. She felt very tired. 'Well, I think you should run along now, children. Mrs. Ellis will have lemonade and cakes, I am sure.'

They were gone. She lay back closing her eyes. 'If only Harry could have seen this.'

Tom Coburn made his examination the following day. 'I think we should confine visits to just a few close friends, Ben. The children obviously tire her.'

'I agree, Doctor. Emma, she insists on seeing. You recall Mrs. Wardrop.'

Dr. Coburn smiled. 'A remarkable woman I hold in great affection. A most capable lady.'

'And Frances of course, and Ellen and Muriel.'

'Yes, if it can be arranged, have one sleep in her room. To be on the safe side you understand.'

Frances, Ellen and Muriel took turns keeping a vigil with the failing woman so dear to them.

Rose was indignant. 'I don't know what all the fuss is about. You make me feel like a hopeless case and I really am very well!'

Ben humoured her. 'It's only for a short time, Mum. Just until you are stronger.'

'Well I think it's foolish. I had a long talk with Emma yesterday, we laughed and joked over old times. Now does that sound like a sick person?'

Ben smiled. 'Of course not. Next week you can get up and walk around a bit. Anyway, the holidays will be over soon and you will only have Mrs. Ellis to worry you.'

Rose woke early the next morning, Frances woke with her and pushed the armchair to the window. Rose leaned back taking her daughter in law's hand. 'Frances, isn't it beautiful? Harry and I used to go walking on mornings like this. Please dear, I would like to stay here all day.'

After she was forced to eat a little, washed and changed, she sat, knitting on her lap, overwhelmed with a strange happiness. The window commanded a wide expanse from the tree-lined driveway to the tower on her left. As the sun rose higher she could see the gleam reflected off the burnished brass of the captain's telescope. The day passed slowly, a perfect day. One or other of the young women came in to talk a while. Frances brought in tea, setting the tray on the table beside her chair. She poured, leaving the cup close to where it could be easily reached. Rose smiled at her. 'Thank you, dear. Now don't fuss, I am perfectly all right. Please go and leave me for a while, I love this time of day.' She knitted for a few minutes-such a strange fluttering in her chest! What did Tom say? A touch of angina. They do fuss! Suddenly the room flooded with light. Drat Frances must have opened the blinds. She looked up. Harry, her Harry was standing in the doorway in his white suit, a grin on his face, his hat as always swinging by the brim. He held out his hand. 'Come on Rosie old girl, you've kept me waiting too long.'

Frances' cry brought Ben rushing to the room. Hot tears flooded his eyes as he bent over the frail body. 'It's all right Francie, it's all right. She knew nothing, she just went to sleep.'

Rose was buried the next day, close to the only man she ever loved. Their tiny grandson between them.

The days following seemed endless. Only those she had known from former times had come to the brief ceremony. Long before she had confided to Ben that when her time came she wanted Dan, not the Anglican priest. No, she had not embraced the Catholic faith, she just wanted the man she had known as a shy little boy, one her heart had gone out to.

Ben spoke earnestly to his wife. 'Help me Francie. We could retire here, now. I could easily give up the practice. We need never go down there again.'

'You know you don't mean a word of it, Ben Wakefield. Your sense of duty would never allow you.'

'How well you know me, old girl.' He smiled at the thought. 'In any case, I would be bored to death.'

Arrangements were made with Mrs. Ellis, she would live in. Those parts of the house not closed up to be kept in perfect order. Bob Martin would tend the grounds and garden as before. 'My wife will telephone before we come up, Mrs. Ellis, so you can air the rooms. I'm sure we won't give you too much trouble.'

'I will be glad to do it, Doctor. I was so fond of your mother, she was a wonderful lady.'

The children reluctantly returned to the big house in town, mollified by the fact they would be able to see their friends more often.

Ben talked long and earnestly to his wife, lying together in the great bed. A bond of heartache and grief held them closer than ever. 'Don't let us talk of the past, Francie, we have been luckier than many others. Our life begins anew each day we wake.'

She moved closer to him. 'Sometimes I hate myself. I wonder you should want me again.'

'Shh, no more of that, darling. We agreed you know.'

Frances felt warm and secure beside him.

'Before I become the 'World's Greatest Lover' again, I want to talk a while.'

She giggled - the sweetest sound he had heard in a long time.

'All right dear, talk to me.'

'I must go down to Melbourne, darling, before Dave leaves. I must see my grandmother. She doesn't know about Mother and it's ages since I saw her. Must be at least three years.' He kissed her yielding lips. 'Do you mind?'

She murmured holding him close. 'Yes darling, of course you must go. Please stop talking.'

CHAPTER XVI

Melbourne. With mixed feelings Ben approached the familiar front door. The great polished brass knocker gleamed like soft gold. While he waited he glanced over the well remembered grounds, the neat hedges and flower beds, the ordered trees flanking the driveway. He turned as the door opened. An elegantly tailored young woman regarded him curiously. 'Good morning Sir, can I help you?'

'I am Dr. Wakefield, is my grandmother in?'

Her inquiring look gave way to a welcoming smile. 'Of course Doctor. Please forgive me, I did not recognize you.'

Ben smiled. 'Well that's hardly surprising, we haven't met before. May I ask your name?'

'Anne Holley, Doctor. I am the housekeeper.'

'I see. Well Miss Holley, I am anxious to see my grandmother, where is she?'

'In the drawing room Sir. She spends most of the day there.'

His heart beat faster entering the familiar room. On the satin couch, now faded, sat a tiny birdlike creature, all in black, white hair crowned with a cap of similar material. He thought - God help me, she is still in mourning for him. She must be ninety if she is a day.

She lifted her head as he approached. 'Benjamin Mon Cher! Where have you been?' Her voice was peculiar to old people, yet unmistakably still carrying the accent of her forebears.

Ben sat, taking the blue veined hands in his. 'Dear Grandma, forgive me, it's been so long, so much has happened.'

She nodded. 'Harry always said you would be a great man. I have no right to expect you to be always visiting me. You have your wife and Rose dear Rose, she writes me such wonderful letters.'

He looked up as the door opened. Miss Holley wheeled in a tea trolley. 'Tea Doctor? Madame always takes tea this time of day.' She poured the fragrant liquid, carefully placing the cup and saucer in his grandmother's hands.

'Thank you Miss Holley, do you mind leaving us alone?'

The housekeeper smiled, closing the door behind her.

'Grandma,' he stopped short as the cup rattled in it's saucer. Terminal tremor, he wondered? Her eyes were fixed straight ahead. He leaned closer examining the loved face then moving his hand in an arc close to her eyes. He suppressed the groan that welled up in him - dear God, she's blind!

A faint smile hovered about her lips. 'You know, Benjamin, don't you?'

He cursed himself for having neglected, so long, this woman who had been his surrogate mother, who had loved him as her own. He took the cup, holding both her hands in his. 'Yes dear Grandma. I'm so sorry. How did you know it was me?'

She spoke in the tones so well remembered, firm, practical, loving. 'I know your step my dear, so like your grandfather's'

He smiled. 'Is it so distinctive?'

She nodded. 'Yes my dear. Now I cannot see, I remember everything. Now please give me my tea.'

They both smiled. He wondered, should he tell her about Rose? He laid his hand on her arm. 'Are you all right? I mean, are you being well looked after?'

'Of course I am, little one.' She used the endearing expression she had used when he was a child. 'Anne looks after me like a daughter.'

'She seems very nice. Who engaged her, is she a nurse?'

'Of course not, dear. The nurse comes every day.' She made a little impatient gesture. 'Now stop worrying about me. Young Mr. Scully manages everything.'

'Of course Grandma, I'm sorry.' Ben made a mental note to see the solicitor and to have a long talk with Anne Holley.

'You have come all this way to see me.' She patted the sofa. 'Now sit down and talk to me.'

Ben agonized, should he tell her? The decision was swiftly made, he would say nothing. They talked of old times, it seemed her mind dwelt mainly in the past. She spoke of his grandfather in the present tense, of Ben's school days, of the trips overseas. She tired quickly, he noted her breathing, she was so old, he knew in that dear breast the coronary arteries were narrow and hardening.

'I would like to rest now, dear. Will you ring for Anne?'

Anne Holley came into the room with a rug and pillows. 'Madam rests this time of the afternoon, Doctor.' She carefully arranged Madelaine on the couch.

'See that Dr. Wakefield's room is prepared, Anne.'

Ben kissed her. 'Rest now Grandma. I will still be here when you wake.' As she settled down he ushered the housekeeper to the door.

Pushing the tea trolley before her, she stopped, facing him at the entrance to the kitchen.

Ben spoke gently. 'Now Miss Holley, perhaps you will tell me the situation in the house.' Adding apologetically, 'it's so long since I have visited. I've left everything in the hands of the solicitor.' He smiled as he spoke, looking the young woman over without appearing to do so. He judged her to be in her mid twenties, slim, of medium height, her dark brown hair pulled back severely from her forehead. With her blue eyes and frank expression he felt comfortable with her.

'I take my instructions from Mr. Scully, Doctor. We have Mrs. Herbert to do the cooking and housework. She comes in daily. There is not a great deal to do as most of the house is closed up.'

'I understand.'

'The nurse comes each day. Father Martin, three or four times a week and the doctor, Dr. Croft, every Monday.'

'I am very relieved to hear this, Miss Holley. Obviously my grandmother is in capable hands.'

'Thank you, Doctor.' She smiled slightly. 'I'll have Mrs. Herbert air your room.'

The following day Ben made his way through familiar streets to the office of James Scully, Solicitor. 'How good to see you, Ben.' They shook hands warmly. 'Sit down, please.'

Facing the younger man across the big maple desk, Ben thought - nothing changes, he looks just the same.

'Pieter has kept me informed, my sincere sympathy, Ben.'

'Thank you. I intended telling my grandmother, I've seen her, you know. Changed my mind, it would be too much for her.'

'I understand. You will call on me won't you, if I can be of any assistance.'

'You can, James, I need your advice on a number of matters.'

'Of course, if I can help. You understand I act as Pieter's agent, Ben. Instructions should come through him.'

'I know that, but there are certain local matters where your expertise would be invaluable. Firstly I must congratulate you on the running of the old house. The charming Miss Holley seems most efficient.'

'Yes, Anne is a charming girl, delightful in every way.'

'Hmm, yes I noticed she mentioned your name with a hint of reverence.'

The lawyer smiled broadly, then fumbled in the bottom drawer of his desk, producing a bottle of Scotch and two glasses. 'The finest malt, Ben. Here, try this.' He held his glass high. 'You are the first to know - we are engaged!' He smiled. 'I know, I know, I reckoned I would be a bachelor, but a man needs companionship.' He assumed a wry expression. 'Especially when the bloom of youth has departed.'

Ben laughed. 'The best move you ever made, I would say. Every man needs a good wife.' He added, 'I think you have found one.'

James leaned back in his chair. 'Well now that's settled, how can I be of service?'

'My grandmother, James, she won't live much longer, that was obvious to me yesterday.'

The lawyer nodded.

'Unfortunately, I must return home. I am booked on tomorrow's train. I trust I can leave arrangements in your hands. The plot is reserved next to my grandfather. Telegraph me, I will come immediately.'

'And the house?'

Ben shook his head. 'No, I don't want to sell it but I do want it kept in good order and condition.'

James looked thoughtful. 'I can't say with any certainty, Ben, but things are beginning to look a little queer. Mind you, I can't be specific, but the smart heads are getting out of property.' He opened a manilla folder tied with pink tapes. 'And your holdings are considerable.'

'Do you think the boom is coming to an end?'

'I don't know, the coming year should tell.'

'That property was left me by my grandfather, James. I'll hang onto it, I can afford to.'

'Please discuss this with Pieter when you get back, he'll write me accordingly.'

Ben rose with a sigh. 'You certainly have a wonderful view of old Collins Street from here. Brings back pleasant memories.'

'Well, get your hat old man, I'm taking you to my club for lunch.'

Ben's train from Sydney pulled into Lambruk station about 3 am, the morning not yet born. He stood stretching, sniffing the cool night air, not moving until the glow of the departing engine disappeared. So quiet, the sky like black velvet, great stars seemed almost within reach. The crunch of his shoes on the gravel was all that broke the stillness. He mused as he made his way to the dim light in the Station Master's office - in all the world could there be another place like this?

Jim Smart, the night porter, came out to meet him. 'Why it's Dr. Wakefield, didn't expect you on the night train, Doctor.'

'I know Jim, terrible time to arrive. Fortunately I've only a half hours walk.'

Somewhere in the office a bell clanged, the porter hurried off. 'Goodnight, Doctor.'

'Goodnight Jim.' Ben left the station walking swiftly along darkened streets. A dog barked a long way off, another answered. He felt a little shiver of pleasure - how good to be home again! He hoped Dr. Coburn would not be put out this time of morning.

Little did Ben expect the summons to return to Melbourne so soon. A fortnight later to the day, the telegram arrived. 'I don't think I could face the train again, Francie. I'll take the steamer from Brisbane, the service cars run almost every day now.' He wired James that he would be arriving in Melbourne three days later.

The plot had been reserved next to his grandfather's. 'Will you handle the headstone for me James? Just her name, status, you know the rest.' He felt a difficulty in speaking. 'And the maintenance of the sites, of course.' He looked once more at the fresh mound. 'Believe me, she was a great old lady, they were a great couple. Too damn good for what passes as society now.'

Later after dinner, they talked. 'I give you carte blanche to act for me here, James. I've spoken to Pieter, he agrees.'

'I have prepared a list of properties held in your name Ben, all within the city. You remember last time you were here, I advised selling.'

'I know, thank you James. I have decided not to sell, not yet anyway.'

'Things are rather queer here at the moment but naturally I will carry out your wishes.' He paused, pulling on his cigar. 'What about the house?' He smiled. 'Mansion, I should say.'

Ben shook his head. 'I don't know. I simply couldn't sell it. Damned if I know what to do.'

'Sorry I can't advise you there.'

'That's another burden I must lay on you James. I would like it kept in it's present condition.' He leaned forward. 'That old place is filled with fine furniture and valuable art works. I couldn't bear some upjumped grocer or crooked share manipulator to rampage through those rooms. That house has a place in my heart.'

'Well, what are your instructions?'

Ben sighed. 'Just do what you are doing now, I suppose. By the way, when do you and Miss Holley intend tying the knot?'

'Oh that.' James grinned. 'Sometime between now and Christmas. I am taking in a partner, soon as he settles in, we plan a honeymoon overseas.'

'Sounds very pleasant. Congratulations. Where do you intend living?'

'No idea, my bachelor quarters are very comfortable but hardly suitable for married life.'

'May I make a suggestion?'

'Go ahead.'

'Would you consider the old house? As a temporary home of course, until I make up my mind what to do with it.'

James smiled with pleasure. 'What a wonderful idea! I could cut a grand figure indeed.'

'Peppercorn rent, of course.'

'Done!' They shook hands. 'Wait until I tell Anne!'

They stood. 'Now let's go and have a brandy in the reading room.'

'So, how is life at Myuna?'

'Apart from the troubles we have had, very satisfying.'

'How is your brother in law, Frank? Remarkable fellow. Still interested in politics?'

'Due back next Easter. Yes, I believe he still intends forming a new party, he is still enthusiastic. God knows what support he will get.'

'Frankly Ben, I am sympathetic to his views. He can count on me. This country will never be worth a tinker's curse until it finds itself.'

'As my dear old grandfather used to say. Anyway, Frank is sincere. I am positive he will find a following.'

'Agreed, but you can be sure he will find bloody stiff opposition as well. Really Ben, I don't see any great changes happening in my time.'

'No perhaps not. We're a poor lot when it comes to patriotism, for our own country.'

'Well, we are an isolated community. The average man in the street has been well brainwashed. England is the be all and end all. While there is beer, racing and football, he is not likely to change.'

'And the others? I mean the wealthy and middle classes.'

'You know as much about them as I do, Ben. Worship all things English refer to England as 'home'.' He motioned to the waiter. 'Two more brandies, please.' He continued. 'Mind you, I am not saying the average native-born Australian isn't the best of fellows, he is, but we are cursed with unimaginative leaders with their eyes firmly fixed on the main chance.'

'You mean money?'

'Yes, I would say that. Money, power, knighthoods. God, I know it's been said before but some would sell the country down the drain so that their vapid spouses may style themselves, Lady.' He grinned sardonically. 'Even though that could be a contradiction in terms.'

Ben rose, stretching himself. 'Well old friend, you have painted a rather gloomy picture. I'm sure though there are others out there who think as we do.'

'Don't misunderstand me Ben, there are, it will just take a long time.'

CHAPTER XV11

Christmas, 1929

'Mrs. Ellis has done a first rate job, Francie. I believe you have been up giving her a hand.'

Frances smiled with pleasure. 'I am so looking forward to it Ben. Now the holidays have started, Muriel has been coming up with me.'

'Hmm.' Ben grinned. 'Now there's a lady waiting in keen anticipation.'

'What a shame it could not have been this Christmas.'

'Never mind old girl, all good things come to those who wait.'

She gave him a little push. 'Oh men are so unromantic!'

The pre Christmas get together of old friends seemed quieter, less boisterous than former years. 'Sugar is down Ben. They are laying off men at the mill. Did you hear anything in the city?'

'Nothing more than you read in the papers. These down turns come and go, I wouldn't worry too much.'

'Trouble is, most of us owe money to the bank. Crops are good, seems prices are tumbling.'

Ben nodded. 'We will just have to leave things in the hands of the politicians, such as they are.'

'Small comfort there.'

'I agree, Jack.' He clasped his old friend's shoulder. 'But today is the one day we get together, don't let's waste it. Come on, the ladies, as usual are watching us.'

Dinner that night was a sober gathering. The house blazed with lights. The magic lanterns, with their attendant swarms of moths, turned the long drive into it's usual fairyland.

Dr. Coburn led the conversation. 'From what I hear from a son in law, things do look serious, Ben.'

'Yes, I think the boom has ended.'

'What are the consequences for Australia, do you suppose?'

'I've no idea, apparently share markets have crashed overseas. How it will affect us, only time will tell.'

Dinner over, the men retired to the verandah for cigars and brandy.

'Your younger brother married, I hear, Mr. DeVries.'

'Yes, Doctor. They are presently overseas.'

'Fine young man, of course we have only met on a couple of occasions. Impressed me as most competent in his profession.'

Pieter smiled. 'Yes, I'm very fond of James. Sadly we don't get to see each other often enough.'

The doctor turned to Ben. 'Meaning to mention this, Ben, but hardly suitable for the dinner table. I saw one of your patients a couple of weeks ago.'

Ben smiled. 'The time I've spent away Doctor, I am surprised you haven't seen more.'

'That has nothing to do with it I'm afraid. Poor man came to see me asking for work. Lives along the main road, has a brood of children, married his dead wife's sister, I believe.'

'You must mean Mick Flannery. I heard he lost his job at the mill, must be damn hard on them.'

'Well the upshot was I found a few days gardening for him. Knew something was wrong though, he wouldn't sit down during the day. I asked what was troubling him, although, frankly I had already guessed. Poor devil said he couldn't do a - well, you know what, said they hung out like a bunch of grapes. His words of course. Anyway, I had a look at him, one of the worst I've seen. To cut it short, I put him in hospital, did the job last Friday.'

'Thank you for that Doctor, but you know, I don't understand, he has never hesitated to see me when he has had troubles.'

'Don't concern yourself, Ben, I asked him the same thing. Had to drag it out of him. Apparently he is embarrassed, hasn't been able to pay his bill since his wife died.'

'Well I'll be damned.' Ben stood, pacing the verandah. 'So this is how we treat our returned men, badly wounded as he was. God help this country if that's our attitude.'

The older man spoke calmly. 'Come Ben, sit down. I think a little more brandy is called for before coffee arrives. In any case, Alice has been to the family. They won't want for food for quite a while. The young woman there seems very capable, so there is no immediate cause for alarm.'

'The trouble is, Doctor, Mick and his family is only one case of many. What is to become of the others?'

Dr. Coburn drew on his cigar. 'This town, no doubt like many others will have to face those problems as they arrive.'

The first months of the New Year brought extreme heat and disquiet in the town. Men who thought their employment would last their lifetime, suddenly found themselves out of work, eagerly picking up any casual job that came along. The bountiful river's fish and oysters, the numerous home vegetable gardens that suddenly appeared, saved many a family from starvation.

Ben, who felt a special responsibility for his old patient, put Mick Flannery to work assisting Bob Martin around the grounds. 'Keep the wolf from the door, Mick.'

'Don't know how to thank you Doc.'

'Don't try. You and Bob know each other, don't you?'

'Yeah, Bob's one of the best.' He grinned. 'He's the boss, I do what he tells me.'

'Good. Like I told you now, no heavy lifting. I've spoke to Bob, he'll keep an eye on you. And thank you Mick, for that pup. He and Gerald are inseparable.'

Ben smiled to himself as he drove down the road to the town below. At least one problem solved, wonder where that name came from, Carlo, funny name for a dog, must remember to ask Mick.

A couple of weeks later, Frances confronted her husband. 'Ben we must have a talk about the children.'

He looked up, amused, from his paper. 'I thought that was your department old girl.'

'Oh Ben, please be serious.'

'I'm sorry my love, I will be.' He sat back, puffing gently on his pipe. 'What is worrying you?'

'Gareth is twelve now, the nearest high school is Lambruk. He will have to go there next year.'

'That is taken care of Francie. I've written to the Anglican Grammar School in Sydney. They will take him as a boarder next year.'

Frances was indignant. 'Why didn't you tell me?'

'I was going to my dear. I've only had confirmation back this week.'

'Have you spoke to him?'

'Of course, he is looking forward to going. You know what a serious character Gareth is. He is bored here Francie, he needs a challenge.'

'I will miss him terribly.'

'We all will. What of the other villains?'

'Gerald is wild, Ben. They get around in a group, you know Dave Truman, Hal Wynter, Jack Rayward and that Greek boy, George Donatos.'

'What's so terrible about that?'

'They get into all sorts of mischief, and they take Harry with them.'

Ben signed. 'I'll talk to him, Francie. Any other sins I should know about?'

'Well, he takes Dorothy to school on the cross bar of his bike.'

'Good God, does Pieter know?'

'Yes.' She sounded cross. 'Typical of you men, he finds it funny.'

'What about Ellen?'

'I don't think she knows.'

'Well it seems harmless enough to me.'

'Harmless! Ben don't you understand? I have to face the ladies of this town. That's my duty, as you pointed out to me long ago.'

He looked at his wife with rueful amusement. 'Don't tell me they find the actions of children scandalous!'

'Oh Ben, you know who I mean.'

'Ah yes, our fair Society Matrons, the bank manager's wife, the shopkeepers' wives, our power station manager's wife. He's not a bad bloke actually, she's got delusions of grandeur. Of course being English, a sort of Noblesse Oblige towards the Colonials.' He burst out laughing.

Frances laughed in spite of herself. 'But it's true. And you know something Ellen told me - although they would never say it to me - they feel affronted they are not invited to *Monaro*.'

'Well my mother was loyal to the old friends she and my father made when they first came here, Francie. In any case most of them are patients and that rules out personal relationships.'

'But you look after your old friends and they are invited whenever we go up there.'

'That's different. I knew all of them as a child and spent all my holidays with them. Besides, I feel comfortable with them.'

'Well, I know all that, but they don't.'

'Don't worry about it Francie. In any case, they appear well occupied at the moment.'

'You mean the Revue?'

'Yes, Henri Brelat told me about it.' He chuckled. 'The thought of our wealthy matrons kicking up their legs to the tune of 'Forty Thousand Frenchmen Can't be Wrong' boggles the mind!'

'Don't be horrid Ben, Muriel is in it too. It's going to be a big concert to raise funds. I am on the Committee, remember.'

'Sorry old girl. The town can use every penny raised. What pensions the Government is paying the disabled wouldn't keep a bird in seed.'

After the concert the whole town buzzed with gossip and praise for the Brelats who had handled the whole affair. The following day Ben gave a lift to Gerald who was forever running late for school. 'What did you think of the concert son? I noticed all your friends were there.'

'Gee, great Dad. Hasn't Miss Halsey got nice legs?'

'Nice legs!' Ben's voice sounded strangled. 'I didn't think boys of your age noticed such things.'

Gerald regarded his father gravely. 'That's all right isn't it Dad? All the blokes thought it was great. You know, their short dresses and jazz garters and things.'

Ben dropped his son off at the school gates - Good God, nice legs! My children are growing up and I haven't noticed.'

That night he related the conversation to Frances. They buried their faces in their pillows to suppress their hilarious giggling. Finally composing himself, Ben dried his streaming eyes. 'Gawd strike me hurray, as Mick would say. They will be bringing their wives home next!' Again they broke into paroxysms of mirth.

CHAPTER XVIII

A few days later Ben had occasion to confront his son again. Surgery over, Gerald was summoned to his father's presence. 'What is this I hear, you and your friends fighting with other boys?'

Gerald stood silent, facing his father.

'Well out with it. I haven't all day.'

'They called Buddy a cripple, said he couldn't walk.'

Ben sat studying his son's face. 'That was a pretty rotten thing to say. Who were they?'

'Oh you know Dad. The mob from the south side.'

Ben felt a surge of pride but kept his voice under control. 'You must avoid this sort of thing, Gerald. You are old enough now to understand my position in this town. You must set an example.'

'I'm sorry, Dad.'

'All right, well run along now and keep out of trouble.'

Gerald stood fidgeting with his hands.

'Well, what is it?'

'It was the Hagan boy, Dad. You know, the big one. Anyway, Gareth belted shit out of him at school yesterday.'

'Gerald!' Ben fought to control the smile threatening to overwhelm him. 'Mr. Hagan is a very decent man, they are a fine family. I don't want any more of this. Now buzz off and mind your language.'

Hands behind his head, the humour of the situation forgotten, Ben sighed deeply. 'God, children can be cruel.'

Outside, Gerald joined his friends waiting behind the hedge.

'What did your old man say, Gerry?'

'Bugger all. We've got to keep away from the Hagan mob, Dad being a doctor and all that. And I can't take Carlo to school anymore.'

At that moment Matron Jones appeared around the corner. They stood stock still under her stern gaze. 'I won't ask which boys left those five live crabs in my kitchen. They gave Miss Halsey a bad fright.'

No one spoke.

'All right,' she opened her purse, 'here's two shillings, go buy yourselves some soft drink. The crabs were delicious.'

They didn't move until she disappeared through the surgery gate.

'Bloody old dragon.'

'She's not bad though Gerry, she gave us two bob.'

'Yeah, Jonesy's not bad, she'd never split on ya. Come on round to Harries' shop, then down to the river for prawns.'

They raced to the little shop, pushing Harry's chair in a shower of gravel. Creaming Soda, Cherry Fizz, Orangeade. 'Jeez I'll bet sweet Miss Halsey got a fright.'

'Wet her bloomers I'll bet.' They hooted with mirth.

'When's yer Uncle Frank comin' back Gerry?'

'Easter I think.'

'Is he and Miss Halsey goin' t'get married?'

'Yeah I think so. I heard Mum talkin' to her. Come on finish that piss Hal, your turn t'push Buddy.'

They stood suddenly still as a young girl approached, a basket on her arm. 'Here's yer girlfriend Dave.'

'Wish she was. She's the nicest girl in school, prettiest too.'

They chorused together. 'Hullo Beryl, how's yer Dad?'

Beryl Caroll was an only child, her father, a returned man, lay dying of Consumption. Just ten years old, she had the serious look of one who knew poverty too early in life.

'We'll bring up some oysters for your Dad, Beryl, will that be all right?'

'Thank you Dave. Mum will be pleased.' She disappeared into the shop.'

'Jeez, wish I was rich, I'd buy Beryl anything she wanted.'

After surgery that night, Gerald asked his father about the stricken man.

'Mr. Carroll is very ill, I see him every other day. Why do you ask?'

'We got some oysters for him today. Dad, will he get better?'

Ben hesitated. 'Perhaps, you can never tell in cases like this. It was good of your and your friends to think of him. I'm sure it was appreciated.'

'We don't mind. Dave likes Beryl, he'd like her to be his girlfriend.'

'I see, what about you?'

His son coloured slightly. 'Everybody likes Beryl, Dad, but I like Dutchy best.'

'I beg your pardon?'

'Sorry, I mean Dorothy. You know who I meant.'

'I certainly do and I would appreciate your using her name correctly.' Ben returned to his newspaper. 'All right, run along now, and don't forget to clean your teeth. And one more thing young man, that dog is not to sleep on your bed.'

In the cozy darkness of their bedroom, Ben recounted the day's happenings. 'Good God, Francie, I don't think I was cut out to be a father. I just don't know how to handle children.'

'Of course you do. They love and respect you. They aren't babies any more, darling, they are growing up.'

'They certainly are, girlfriends at that age. I can't believe it.'

'Didn't you have girlfriends?'

'Only one, I married her.'

'I don't believe a word of it.'

He stretched out, her head on his chest. 'Do you know the Carrol child? Beryl I think her name is.'

'Yes, she is a dear little thing. Her mother is very nice but Ben, they are bone poor.'

'I know. Gerald asked me about the husband today. Poor devil will be dead by Easter.'

'What will she do?'

'I don't know, there are so many in the same boat. Do what we can to help, that's all we can do.'

In the stillness of the early morning, the bell rang. Ben struggled into his dressing gown. At the door stood a small figure, he peered at her in the dim light. 'Why Beryl, what is it child?'

'Mother said can you come Doctor, dad is badly.'

Bag in hand, he entered the cottage. The skeleton-like figure of Martin Carrol lay propped up on pillows, a blood stained towel to his lips. Ben bent over the dying man gently taking the fluttering pulse in the wrist. The rasping, laboured respiration seemed thunderous in the tiny room. He folded the man's hands across his chest, turning to the stricken wife standing in the doorway. 'Come with me Mrs. Carrol. There is nothing you can do here, there is nothing anyone can do.' He guided her gently into the next room, speaking quietly. 'I won't tell you there is any hope, there isn't.' She began to cry. 'Now dear lady, you must be brave, you have a little girl to look after.

I am going to give Martin an injection to make him sleep now. You go to bed, I'll be back at eight in the morning.' The man's eyes were fixed on Ben as he prepared the merciful syringe. With practiced skill he found the vein in the emaciated arm. 'Don't worry old man, I'll see to it that your wife and little girl are all right.' He watched as a faint smile played around the dying man's lips as the tired eyes slowly closed.

Ben arranged and paid for Martin Carrol's funeral. Beside the wife and child, he and Frances and Ethel Jones were the only mourners.

Over dinner, Frances broached the subject. 'How will she live Ben, has she anything?'

'She will get a few shillings a week as Carrol was a returned man. Not enough to live on.'

'What on earth will she do?'

'Ethel has managed to get her a few days a week cleaning at the hospital.'

'Thank Heaven for that. She is still a young woman, quite good looking, she might marry again.'

'God knows. This bloody depression is getting worse. She would find it hard to find anyone willing to take on a woman and child.'

Gerald and his friends rose to the occasion. They plied Mrs. Carrol with fruit and eggs, anything they could lay their hands on. 'We got some good perch down at the creek, Mrs. Carrol. Would you like some?'

'Thank you Dave, that would be very nice.'

The youngsters politely took their leave, stopping briefly at the point where they usually separated before making their way home. 'Beryl thinks you're all right Dave. Bet you get a fat when you see her.'

Dave raised his fist. 'Take that back, you asshole!'

Ben had brought the expression back from his association with his American friends during the war and now through Gerald, it was common usage.

'Yeah, cut it out Hal. Listen I've got something to tell you blokes.' They gathered round. 'You've got to keep it a dead secret though. You've gotta shut your gobs. Buddy can't come, but we can see into Dad's surgery from under the house.'

'Shit, what if we get caught?'

'We won't, just keep quiet. You can see everything. There's a big crack at the bottom of the wall. Only one at a time though.'

'What if Buddy splits?'

'He won't, we'll tell him what we see.'

'What about Gareth?'

'Don't be bloody mad! You know him, he'd stop us.'

'Jeez, if we get caught my old man'd kill me.'

'Mine too.'

'Don't worry, I'll let you know a good time to come. You can say you are coming round to our place to play ping pong or something.'

Jack looked at the setting sun. 'I better get going. Mum goes crook if I'm late. You blokes coming?'

About to separate, Dave asked. 'Going up to *Monaro* this weekend Gerry?'

'Yeah, of course we are. Why?'

'What about we go fishing up the North Arm? Gareth might let us use the canoe.'

'Pigs he will. The bastard won't let anyone touch it.'

'Doesn't matter, we can fish off the bank. Will that priest, Father Whatshisname, be there?'

'Only Saturday, that's when he comes up.'

'Didn't know your old man was a Tyke.'

'He isn't, ya silly bugger. They are old mates, been friends since they were kids.'

'He's not a bad bloke though, even if he is a Tyke.'

'Jimmy Murray's mother thinks so anyway.'

'What d'ya mean?'

'Dead secret. Jimmy told me not to breathe a word.'

'Come on Hal, out with it.'

'Well, he's always there.'

'That's all right isn't it? They're Tykes.'

'Yeah, but he comes late at night and Jimmy saw his pyjamas in the wardrobe.'

They stood silent, digesting this choice item of news. Gerald, hands deep in the pockets of his knickerbockers, kicked a stone in the dust. 'Jimmy's a good bloke. His old man was killed in the war. We should shut our traps and forget what Hal told us.'

'Yeah, we should.'

Hal turned on his heel. 'I'm off, you blokes coming?'

The next few weeks with Easter coming on, were filled with preparations for Frank's return.

'Ben, I wish you could take time off. You look so tired, you need a rest.'

'Not much chance of that, old girl. With Dave away, well you know what it's like. Without Doc Coburn I would be lost.'

'He is a wonderful man, isn't he?'

Ben shook his head. 'Francie, you have no idea. He works like a young man. Did you know he takes a swim in the creek every morning?'

'Yes, Alice told me.'

'Alice?'

Frances laughed. 'Oh Ben, she is so much younger than he is. She told me to, only in private though. She is always Mrs. Coburn, at committee meetings.'

Ben leaned back in his chair. 'I enjoyed my lunch today, Francie.' He looked at his watch. 'I've got half an hour to spare, fill me in with the town gossip.'

'You should know by this time, I don't listen to gossip, Ben Wakefield.'

'Francie, I don't mean scandal, no doubt there is plenty of that. I mean anything new.'

'Only the talk of a High School for Myuna. Old Mr. Wardrop is leading a delegation to the State Government.'

'We need it all right. Too late for Gerald though. I guess he will have to go Lambruk. Well, duty calls, but I will tell you something which may surprise you.'

She helped him into his coat. 'Tell me quick, you know I can't stand surprises.'

He kissed her lightly. 'Francie, I firmly believe the old boy would like to come back to his house again.'

'Are you serious?'

'It's just a feeling my dear. You know, after morning tea he slips out into the garden and just walks around examining every rose and shrub. Take a look sometime.'

'That doesn't mean anything, they have lived there for so long.'

'Yes, perhaps you are right. Just crossed my mind, that's all.' He called to the dog. 'Here Carlo, if you want a ride, get going.'

In the grounds of the little overcrowded school, children stood around or played in groups. The boys keeping to the open spaces, the girls clustered around the three wooden classrooms. Space had become crucial, two of the lower classes were held in the Presbyterian Church Hall near the centre of town.

The little band of conspirators stayed close together. 'Did you know we're getting a High School?'

'Who said, Hal?'

'My old man, Mr. Wardrop told him.'

'When?'

'Don't know. Soon I think.'

'Won't be in time for us though. We'll have to go up to Lambruk.'

'Good fun though, going up in the bus.'

'Except for me.'

'What d'ya mean Dave, except for you?'

'Going down to Sydney to school. It's all arranged.'

'Didn't know your old man was rich.'

'He's not. Policemen, even sergeants, don't get much. It's me Mum's people, my grandfather.'

'Jeez Dave, we'll miss you. When do you have to go?'

'After Christmas. Come on, there's the bell, we've got all year yet.'

After school, Gerald drew the group together. 'Listen, not a word remember. Mum will be out tomorrow night, I've pulled a bit of lattice away behind some bushes, we can get under the house there.'

'Where will Gareth be?'

'Reading of course. Buddy's got a new Meccano. You'll be all right, won't you Bud?'

'Course I will. You've got to tell me though if I mind Carlo.'

'You know we will. Come on, Buddy wants to do a hundred miles an hour.'

They met the following night, nervous, twitching with excitement. Gerald led the way crawling on hands and knees, the others following close behind. A dim light filtered through a gap between skirting board and floor. Gerald fixed his eyes to the crack, peering up to the examination table. His voice came in a hoarse whisper. 'Jesus, take a look at that!' Mrs. Gladys Simpson, a large lady who suffered from haemorrhoids, lay on her side, her generous naked posterior shining white under the overhead light. 'Dad's got his finger up Mrs. Simpson's bum!'

Each took his turn, finding the discomfort of the unfortunate woman hilariously funny. Stuffing handkerchiefs into their mouths, they emerged from the little opening, running at full speed to the safe grass of the orchard behind the house. They rolled around shrieking with mirth, tears streaming down their cheeks.

George found his voice. He gasped, falling back again. 'Did you see Mrs. Simpson's face? I thought her eyes would pop out!' Howls of mirth greeted this observation.

'Hope your old man washes his hands before he eats his dinner.' This led to further fits of helpless laughter.

Gerald struggled to his feet. 'Look you blokes, I have to go in now, Mum will be home soon - not a word remember.'

A few days before Easter, Ben arrived hot and tired from hospital rounds. He worried over the persistent depression. Times were hard, people were suffering. Pieter recently back from Sydney, painted a dismal picture.

'Seems bloody hopeless, Ben. People are walking out or being thrown out of their homes. God knows what's to be done, I don't.'

'What about this bridge they are building down there?'

'The Harbour Bridge? Yes, a great project. Hardly dents the labour force though.' He shook his head. 'There is so much we could do, so much needs to be done, but as you well know there is no money. Every farthing is controlled from London now. Ever since they sent that gentleman from the Bank of England out here to discipline the Colonials.'

With Pieter's words still ringing in his ears, he parked and entered the surgery. 'Just go through the calls before lunch, Ethel. Anything specific?'

'Dave Truman wants you to call at the station, he sounded serious.'

'Some poor devil with pneumonia or worse, I would guess.' He fanned through the message slips. 'Dave is the softest-hearted fellow you would ever meet, Ethel. He hates sending them on but he is obliged to.'

'He is allowed to give them a hand out, isn't he?'

'Six bob for a single man, about eight for a family. Not enough to feed a dog for a week.'

'It's hard.'

'It's disgraceful but that's the government allowance. Even worse, many would like to stay, the river teeming with fish and oysters for the taking but as I said, Dave has his orders to keep them moving.'

Dave Palmer stood waiting at the entrance to the solid brick building, Police Station and Courthouse combined. 'Thanks for coming, Ben. A sad business. Two youngsters, both parents dead, came in this morning.' He led the way into the Charge Room. A boy and girl sat close together on a long wooden bench. They were thin, hollow cheeked, verging on emaciation. Ben guessed their age to be about eleven or twelve. Both showed signs of sand fly and mosquito bite infection. The girl held tightly to an old well worn rag doll.

'This is Dr. Wakefield, children. And this is Judy and Peter, Doctor. They are twins.' He smiled kindly. 'Now just wait here, we will be back directly.' He led the way into his office. 'This is a hard one, Ben. The father was a shearer, came from up Queensland way. They have been travelling for three months. Never seen the sea before, camped up the coast last night. The father went fishing, they had nothing to eat, caught a big flathead and a couple of pufferfish.'

'Good God!'

'Yes. The kids had the flathead and the parents ate the pufferfish.'

'Christ Almighty, they must have died in agony.'

'Apparently. The kids found them dead this morning. The horse was buggered, I've given it a feed, but what do I do now?'

'How did the youngsters get them here?'

'Put them in the luggage tray of the sulky, how I'll never know.'

'You need a certificate I suppose. What about the children?'

'Send them down to a home in Sydney, I guess.'

'They'll separate them you know. Those places are bloody inhuman.'

Dave nodded. 'So I've heard. What else can I do?'

'Well for a start, I'm hospitalizing both of them. They are simply not well enough to go anywhere yet.'

Over dinner that night he told his wife of the tragedy. 'You know I hate to bother you with my troubles Francie, but those poor little kids worry me. When they are fit to travel they will be sent to Sydney. They are a heartless bunch of bastards down there, they will separate them all right - the boy to labour on some farm and the girl to domestic drudgery.'

'May I go to see them?'

'Of course. Muriel has been already. They are polite but just won't say much. Can you blame them?' He stood, throwing his napkin on the table. 'Talk about a quandary! Damned if I know what's best to do.'

Gerald and his friends huddled in serious conversation. The topic was the newly arrived teacher. As the school was overcrowded and understaffed parents welcomed the arrival of Charles Cummings, a small dapper man who brooked no nonsense.

'Seen that cane he's got? Must be over three feet long!'

'Ask George, he's copped it already.'

'Little bastard, gave me two on each hand this morning, just because I forgot me books.'

'Yeah, he looks like a Cupie doll - with a bloody walloper.'

'Good name that. Let's call him Cupie, Cupie Cummings.'

'Tell ya what, we'll go round back of his house one night and yell out - how ya goin' Cupie!'

'Might be risky Gerry. Where does he live?'

'Mrs. Golding's boarding house. You know the joint, the girl friends of the service car drivers live there, and old Mr. Henry.'

'He's a good bloke, Mr. Henry. Knows where the perch are.'

'Yeah. Ya don't think Cupie's a friend of Ray the poof, do ya?'

'Hell no. I've heard Mum talking about him, he likes the ladies. Plays the goanna for the Glee Club.'

'Struth, must be a pants man.'

'Could be. Come on, there's the bell.'

In the quiet of their room, Frances told her husband about her day. 'I've seen the children, Ben. It's heartbreaking, they don't seem to understand their parents are dead.'

'It's natural Francie, it will take time.' He sighed. 'Anyway, I have seen to it they had a decent burial.'

'You are a good man, Ben Wakefield, that's why I love you so.'

He laughed. 'I'll bet you say that to all your admirers.' She laughed back at him. 'There is something else we must talk about.'

'Oh no, not tonight. I'm not in the mood for bad news.'

'It won't wait Ben, it's Gerald, he's running wild.'

'For God's sake, what's he done now?'

'It's nothing specific - it's, well it's what I hear.'

'And what do you hear, old girl?'

'I hear so much gossip at the Committee meetings. I just don't know what to believe.'

'Who is saying what?'

'Mrs. Bidwell says she heard a gang of young boys using bad language and making rude remarks. She didn't mention Gerald but it was plain he was included.'

'Forget it Francie, she's a mischief making old bat, that one.'

'That's what Grace Rayward says. I'm very fond of Grace. Will she be all right?'

'I don't know. I warned her of a second pregnancy. Kidney trouble is a doctor's nightmare.'

'Is there nothing you can do?'

'Nothing. Perhaps in Gareth's time there will be. Now we wait and hope.'

For a few minutes they lay, lost in thought. Down in the hallway the grandfather clock softly tolled midnight. Ben took his wife's hand. 'Time for sleep my dear. Don't worry about Gerald, I've had a good talk to him. At least I've put a stop to him doubling Dutchy - oh my God, I'm saying it now - I mean Dorothy, on his bike.'

Frances giggled in spite of herself. 'At least Mr. Cummings is instilling some discipline into the older boys.'

'So I heard. I understand our wayward son has incurred his displeasure.'

'Four cuts with the cane. I think it's really too severe. Gerald's hands were all red and swollen.'

'What did he do?'

'I don't know, couldn't have been much. Gerald is a good boy really, I'll have to speak to Mr. Cummings.'

'Good boy! He's a little bugger, Francie and you know it. Don't you dare interfere. Boys of his age would get away with murder, if they could.'

'All right, but promise you will make him do his half hour piano practice and not miss Professor Brelat on Wednesday.'

Ben turned on his side, his voice seemed to come from far away. 'Without fail old girl, without fail.' Soon only his regular breathing broke the silence of the room.

Sleep escaped Frances. She lay eyes unblinking, into the darkness. So much she hadn't told him. So much she wanted to know. What was to happen to the orphans in the hospital - how glad she would be to see her brother. Like a mist, sleep finally descended and she was lost in the world of dreams.

Frank Chapman arrived early in the morning on the day school was to break up for Easter. The big Buick Tourer, like the driver, was covered in dust.

Bathed and shaved, he sat facing his sister and brother in law. 'Best coffee I've had since I left here Francie.' He sat back sighing with satisfaction. 'Yes, I've seen the world, Europe and America and I'm damn glad to be home. I've a lot to tell you but I want to see Muriel first. Is she still at school?'

'At the Presbyterian Church Hall, Frank. They have had to put Fifth class down there, the school is hopelessly overcrowded.'

'Wasn't there some talk of a new High School?'

'Well under way. They awarded the contract to a Sydney builder, name of Wells. I've met him and his wife, very decent people.'

'When does he start?'

'Next month I believe. They've rented that big house on the road to *Monaro.* Nice little family, two girls and a boy.'

'I was terribly sorry to hear about your mother, Ben. When I received Muriel's letter I was on the point of returning.'

'Thanks old son, glad you didn't. Yes, it was a shock. We had known about her condition for a long time, so it wasn't entirely unexpected.'

Frank cuddled the bowl of his pipe. 'You two have certainly had your share of trouble. That accursed Polio thing is a blight on the human race.'

'We have been luckier than some, brother dear.' Frances put her arms around him. 'It's good to have you here again, promise you will stay.'

He smiled at her. 'Only a few weeks Francie, then I have to go back to Sydney for a while.'

'Oh Frank, what for?'

He held up his hand. 'Now Francie, no questions. I'm here to see Muriel.' He fondly kissed his sister's upturned face. 'And you two and the kids of course. But Muriel and I have much to talk about.'

'She loves, I know she does.'

Ben pulled her down beside him. 'Stop matchmaking Francie.' He groaned. 'God, women are incurable romantics.'

Frank roared with laughter. 'I'm going to pick her up after school. We will tell you all the news later.'

At lunchtime in the noisy school grounds, Gerald and his friends huddled together. 'Thank Christ, only a couple of hours and then we break up.'

'Yeah, watch yer step, Cupie's watchin' us. Give the prick half a chance and he'll keep us in.'

'Hey look, there's your girlfriend Dutchy, over there Gerry. And there's Beryl.'

'Don't look, don't look, if ya wave or call out, he'll be on ya.'

They sauntered away, out of the watchful eye of Master Cummings.

'Did I tell you my Uncle Frank arrived early this morning? Got a new Buick!'

'Jeez, he must be rich.'

'Ain't married, not yet anyway.'

'Is he goin' to marry Miss Halsey?'

'I dunno. Tell you what though, after school we'll look around for his car. Sure to be down town somewhere. He's always good for a few bob.'

The school bell rang early and an eager, boisterous, shouting mass of children made for the gates.

'We gonna wait for the girls?'

'Not t'day Dave. Let's find Uncle Frank, he'll give us ten bob I'll bet. Hal, your turn t'push Buddy.'

They wandered the town till Jack pulled them up short. 'Hey, we're wasting our time, he'll be round t'see Miss Halsey, won't he?'

'Jack you're a bloody genius, course he will. Come on, round to the Presbo church.'

'The bloody hall's locked up.'

'What'll we do, knock at the door?'

'Don't be bloody silly, course not, he might be proposing.'

'What's that?'

'Forget it. Tell ya what, y'know the trap door near the desk where they signal anyone on stage who forgets what to do?'

'I've never seen it.'

'I have. If you open it real quiet you can see the stage at the other end. Dave and I opened it once. We could see right up Miss Halsey's dress. She had blue bloomers on.'

This was greeted with hilarious mirth. 'Ya dirty buggers, lucky she didn't see ya.'

'Listen you mugs, we'll leave Buddy here behind the fence and have a look. Don't mind do ya, Bud?'

'All right, don't be long, Mum'll be looking for us.'

Crawling under the elevated floor of the hall, cum church playhouse, they located the trap door. 'Quiet, don't make a sound. Here Dave, give us a hand, get that bit of wood.'

Slowly the lid of the opening in the floor used for signalling instructions to the players on stage, opened inch by inch. 'Chree-ist, look at that, Uncle Frank is eating Miss Halsey!' Frank and Muriel were locked in a passionate embrace.

Gerald's voice came in a low whisper. 'He's got his hand on her bum, he's lifting up her dress!'

'Looks like she likes it.'

'Shh, quiet for Christ's sake, ya want t'get us killed?'

'Ohhh Uncle Frank, you naughty old man - he's pulling her bloomers down!'

'Jeez, she's got nice silk bloomers.'

'And silk stockings with blue jazz garters, yer Uncle Frank likes that.'

'She's making funny noises.'

'Shut up Gawd, he's pulling the stage curtain down.'

'Jeez, I'm gettin' a fat.'

'Shut up will ya, who isn't?'

'Gawd look, he's got her down on the curtain now.'

'What's that he's got?'

'A French Letter, ya silly bugger. A pink one, what a beauty!'

Muriel's eyes were closed in ecstasy, her arms locked around her lover's neck. She uttered a sharp cry of pain and pleasure as her body was penetrated for the first time.

The little group watched in growing fascination as the lovemaking grew in intensity. Her legs, first wide open, now slid around his body. Frank found her half opened lips as they writhed and moved in their passion. Suddenly, she seemed to hold him closer to her, a gasp then a stifled scream as they climaxed in unison. Their bodies grew limp. Muriel lay, eyes closed as Frank caressed her hair, whispering endearments. The trap door closed quietly, they inched their way from under the building and raced at breakneck speed to where Buddy sat waiting patiently behind the fence.

'What did you see, anything interesting?'

'Nothing much Bud, tell ya later. Quick, we've gotta get out of here. Down Main Street to the river. Quick!'

They ran, rolling their eyes, exchanging meaningful glances, not knowing whether to shriek with mirth or quake with fear at what they had seen. 'Phew, this is good enough Jack. Let's sit down here, nobody comes this way.'

'Yeah, Buddy's hard to push that fast.'

They lolled back on the park bench, breathing heavily, hardly exchanging a word.

Jack broke the silence. 'Say Gerry, how do you know about those French Letter things your uncle had?'

'Of course I know. Got a chair and looked on top of the wardrobe in me mother's bedroom.' He fished in his pocket. 'Here look at this, I pinched one out of a little packet.' He blew vigorously, the device inflated, the small teat on the end stuck out like a little finger. They gathered around smirking.

'Jeez, can ya get any more?'

'Don't be bloody silly, I took a big risk getting this.'

Hal look up suddenly. 'Thought you said nobody comes this way, Gerry?'

They stood gaping, transfixed with terror as Frank's buff Buick pulled up beside them. Muriel Halsey was sitting close beside him. Frank beamed down at them. 'There you are boys, Miss Halsey said we might run into you.' He looked at them closely. 'Whatever is the matter with you fellows, are you all right? Looks like you've seen a ghost.'

Gerald's voice quavered. 'We had to push Buddy fast Uncle Frank. A horse bolted.'

Frank grinned. 'Well, all's well that ends well.' He climbed down from the car. 'Here's ten shillings, go and buy Eskimo pies or whatever it is you like these days.' He moved around to the wheelchair, his voice grew gentle as he bent over the little hunched figure. 'I'm glad to see you Harry. You are a brave little man.' He pressed a note into the withered hand he held between his own. 'This is just for you mind, remember, just for you.'

Harry smiled up at him 'Thanks Uncle. I promise. I think I'll buy Mum a present.'

Frank looked around. 'Well, I hope you fellows don't look so glum when next we meet.'

The boys clustered together as the car disappeared in a cloud of dust. 'Holy bloody Moses, I though we were gone. Jeez you were quick Gerry. A bolting horse. Honest to God, I thought he knew.'

Gerald's courage was slowly returning. 'Not on yer life, mate.' He took hold of the wheelchair. 'Come on, we'll go round to Harries' shop and calm down. Ten bob goes a long way.'

'Yeah we need it. See how close Miss Halsey was sittin' next to your uncle?'

'Yeah, bet she had his dick in her hand.'

'Yeah, reckon she thought it was the gear stick.' Hooting with ribald mirth they made their way along the dusty road.

CHAPTER XIX

Easter at Monaro 1929

The house looks splendid Mrs. Ellis. Thank you for the trouble you have taken.'

'It's a pleasure Doctor. When will you and Mrs. Wakefield be arriving?'

'Tomorrow morning. You will be able to stay?'

'Of course. May I ask you something, Doctor?'

'If I can answer, what is it?'

'I heard about those two poor children in the hospital, are they all right?'

'Doing very well. They will be up and about in a week or two.'

'What is to become of them?'

'That I don't know Mrs. Ellis. We will just have to wait and see.' He smiled at her. 'I really must be going.'

He found Mick in the garden. 'How are you Mick?'

'Pretty good Doc. Thanks for the ham, Bob got his too.'

'Well a few day's break will do you both good. How's the wife and kids?'

'Couldn't be better, thanks to you.' He leaned on the spade. 'That sulky you gave me was a godsend. The old gelding's still pretty good, goes like a charm.'

Ben clapped him on the shoulder. 'Well, don't waste time here. Harness up and get on your way.' He pressed a ten pound note into the man's hand. 'See you have a good Easter.' Mick watched him disappear down the driveway. 'Jesus, he's a good bloke. There ain't many like him.'

The topic of conversation at dinner the following night was Muriel and Frank's engagement. Earlier the women had all admired the sapphire and diamond engagement ring Frank had brought with him from Sydney. Their admiration and pleasure were genuine.

Dr. Coburn, sitting at the head of the table, raised his glass. 'Well my dear Miss Halsey, I know I speak for all of us. Great happiness, a long life and all you wish to yourselves.' He looked at Frank. 'In your future husband, who I have had the honour to know for some years now you have a man of great integrity. You will make a handsome couple.'

'Hear, hear doctor, I second that.' Ben raised his glass, the others followed.

Frank squeezed Muriel's hand under cover of the table. 'Thank you, thank you all very much.' He smiled at his fiancee. 'No one could ask for dearer friends.'

Dr. Coburn rose. 'Your Mrs. Ellis did us proud tonight, Frances my dear.' He sighed. 'I'm afraid as I grow older my appetite for good food and wine does not diminish.'

Pieter DeVries patted his abdomen. 'I'm afraid we all suffer from the same complaint, Doctor.'

Frances stood, surveying her guests. 'Now if the gentlemen will retire to the verandah for cigars, we ladies will attend to the coffee.'

With a sigh, Dr. Coburn settled himself into his favourite chair. 'Never tire of this sight Ben, it is beautiful. I'm surprised the lanterns have survived all these years.'

'Mick takes care of them now, most meticulous. He hung them yesterday and after Easter he will clean and pack them away again until the next occasion.'

'Poor chap, how is he?'

'Well as far as I can see, the leg still bothers him. We make sure he does only light work.'

'Hmm, yes, few survive a compound fracture, he was one of the lucky ones.' He puffed with pleasure on the long Havana. 'Believe you brought these back from America Captain. How are things over there?'

'Chaotic when I left about six weeks ago sir. Absolute panic on Wall Street. I'm afraid we are in for a hard time.'

'And Europe?'

'Appalling, unemployment rising. Particularly bad in eastern Europe, people are literally starving.'

'Not much prospect of the good times returning eh?'

'I doubt it. Germany has a rising star, a firebrand named Hitler, Adolph Hitler. Seems to be getting things done. One hears ugly rumours but then the whole place is alive with rumour.'

The door opened to the delightfully satisfying aroma of coffee. Pieter held the door. 'Mmm, coffee here tastes as good as it smells Frances.'

She smiled. 'You can thank Mrs. Ellis for that, she is the magician.'

Cigar finished, cup drained, Dr. Coburn stood buttoning his coat. 'We must be getting along Ben. A delightful evening as usual Frances.'

'As must we.' Pieter pushed back his chair. 'Long past Dorothy's bed time.'

'Of course Pieter.' Ben smiled. 'I believe Gareth has been teaching them to play chess.'

'Excellent idea. I must say the finer points of the game are beyond my patience.'

Dr. Coburn laughed. 'It can be a great comfort at times. Ah, here are the ladies, ready and waiting.'

Ben took the old man's arm. 'Thank you for taking over for the weekend Doctor.'

'Nonsense my boy, Alice and I are delighted to be back in the old house.' He lowered his voice. 'Hope you don't mind Ben, Alice is busy in the garden. You know, pruning back, all that sort of thing.'

He looked so serious, Ben laughed in spite of himself. 'For heaven's sake Dr. Coburn, it is your house, you do whatever you wish.'

At the gate leading to the drive, hurried goodbyes and wishes for a happy Easter were exchanged. Ben with his wife and Frank with Muriel, stood watching until the headlights of the cars disappeared around the bend. Frances shivered. 'It's always cool at night this time of the year. Muriel and I are going in, will you be in soon? We'll make some more coffee.'

'Good Francie. Frank and I will put the lanterns out. Be about twenty minutes.'

The two men strolled along the drive towards the entrance gates. 'Well you certainly popped it on us suddenly Frank. Arrived yesterday, engaged today. Frankly, I think you're a damn lucky man.'

Frank was silent for a few moments, snuffing each lantern as they passed. 'Think I'm doing the right thing?'

'I said I thought you were lucky. She is a wonderful girl. Never seen her look so radiant.'

'Yeah, I suppose you're right.'

'Don't tell me you are having second thoughts.'

'No, no of course not. We've straightened out our differences - but you know I was never the marrying kind.'

'I think you will both thrive. I'm glad you've cleared the decks of any differences between you.'

'I told Muriel she can go to her church if she wants to. But - I tell you Ben, I made it very plain, there will be no suffering Jesus or bleeding hearts in our house.'

'How did she take that?'

'It's agreed. She wants Dan to marry us and I've no objection to that.'

'What about children?'

'Buggered if I know! I'll leave that to the future. Far as I'm concerned there won't be any.' He stopped suddenly, taking Ben's arm. 'Listen, this is between us, there is something I've never told a soul.'

'Sure you should tell me?'

'Got to get it off my chest.' They walked slowly towards the house, the gravel crunching beneath their feet. 'Remember that last hospital, you know where we met Jonesy?'

'Of course I do, that was my lucky day.'

'Remember a nurses aide, tall, beautiful blonde girl - well, reddish blonde, I suppose?'

'Can't say I can place her, there were so many. Why?'

'You would have remember Virginia.'

'I probably saw her - what about it?'

Frank snuffed the last lantern. 'We were lovers, God she was lovely.'

'For God's sake! What happened, why didn't you marry her?'

'Marry her? For Christ's sake I wanted to, desperately. She was already married, and titled - what a combination!'

'That's a secret you must keep to yourself forever, old friend, if you don't mind my advice.'

The foursome sat talking over fresh coffee. 'Would you mind if Muriel and I took a stroll to the tower Ben? The moon is up, should be beautiful up there tonight.'

'The house is at your disposal. Take a bottle of champagne, special occasions call for good wine.' He stood smiling. 'Time for old married couples to be in bed, come on Francie. Remember Frank, you are to tell us all about your trip tomorrow. Goodnight to you both, see you at breakfast.'

'You will have to be up early old man. Muriel and I plan to go riding first thing.'

'Plenty of time. I've got three whole days.' Ben yawned, stretching himself. 'Three days and I intend to rest, rest, rest.'

In their bedroom, Frances mildly scolded her husband. 'Ben, you really shouldn't have encouraged Frank to take champagne with them.'

'I noticed he didn't refuse.'

'That's not what I meant. What if Muriel has too much to drink?'

'Don't worry on that score, she only sips her wine.'

'I know, but Frank doesn't.'

'Francie will you stop worrying over things that don't concern us?'

She snuggled up to him. 'Muriel looks radiant doesn't she?'

'That she does. It wouldn't surprise me if she looked even more so tomorrow.'

Good Friday morning, Ben woke to a silent house. He found his brother in law in riding breeches and leggings taking the sun on the lower verandah. 'Where is everybody Frank? Apart from you and Mrs. Ellis, there is not a soul in sight.'

'Morning Ben, you're a late riser. Tell the truth, I'm happy to loaf here for a couple of hours.'

'Sounds like a late night.'

'It was. I finished that bloody bottle of champagne - got a head like a melon.'

'My sympathies, but where are they all?'

'Well, the kids and the dog have gone down to the creek, reckon the fish are biting. Gareth's with them so they are safe enough. Frances has taken Muriel to mass then later to the DeVries.'

'To give Muriel some sound advice, no doubt.'

'I imagine - whatever women talk about.'

'A mystery to me too, but it's a good opportunity to have a bit of a yarn.'

'Yes, I've been wanting to talk to you about a few things, especially the Movement. That's why I am going back to Sydney.'

'Muriel understand?'

'About the Party? No, I've told her I have some contractual obligations to fulfil. She accepted quite happily.'

'Has the date been set? Women like to know about these things.'

'New Year's Day.' He grinned. 'That should give her plenty of time.' He tapped his knee with his riding crop. 'There are some bloody good men in the Party, Ben. The type of men who should be running this country.'

'Any prospects of running a candidate? What electorate do you have in mind?'

'No, times not right, the depression has everybody nervous.'

'I'd have thought you couldn't pick a better moment to move.'

'Not for the men we have in mind. They can't afford to express their views in the present climate of uncertainty.'

'Understandable I suppose.'

'And there's this new crowd, call themselves the New Guard, extreme right wing reactionaries, armed too so I'm told, although I'm cautious of rumours - like to see for myself.'

'For God's sake, in this country?'

Frank gave a short laugh. 'They talk of a communist plot but I suspect their avowed purpose is to put the working man in his place.'

'That includes the unions, no doubt.'

'Naturally. Tell me, what in Hell is the matter with this country? If the average Australian can't be made to realize he is nothing more than a wood and water joey for his English overlords, well dammit, there's no hope for us.'

'I don't know Frank, I really don't know. Apathy I guess. Feed the ordinary bloke his beer and sport, you've got him. You know I've sometimes thought of pulling up stakes and going to America.' He shook his head. 'But there is so much here I simply couldn't leave.'

'Know what you mean, I've felt the same way, but while I live I will strive to give this country a sense of identity.'

Ben touched his arm. 'Leave it alone Frank. Take my advice, leave it alone. If the people are too bloody stupid or too uncaring to see they are being led by the nose, so be it. A faint hope I know but one day they may wake up.'

They sat in silence, enveloped in the pleasant aroma of pipe tobacco. Mrs. Ellis appeared with a tray. 'Tea gentlemen. I thought you might appreciate a cup.'

Ben placed a small table between them. 'Thank you Mrs. Ellis, yes indeed, much appreciated.'

'Splendid woman, Ben, you were lucky to find her.'

'She's a widow you know, husband killed in the war.'

'Wonder she hasn't been snapped up before this.'

'She has had offers, that I know. Thank God she is not interested. Funny thing isn't it, he was like thousands of others, bored with married life and its responsibilities. Just joined up and left.'

Frank nodded. 'As you say, there were plenty like him.' He bit into a buttered scone. 'Hmm, great cook.'

'Isn't she? To get back to the subject of identity. What the Hell does it mean?'

'It means being ourselves, being an independent nation. Republic if necessary.'

'Can't see it Frank. Without the British market we would collapse. We are in fact a captive economic state. Besides that, there is a hard core of Anglomaniacs here, imitate everything English, refer to England as 'home'. They would regard the Party as traitorous Republicans, rabid insurrectionists, mutinous. Upset their comfortable illusions. You know the saying, 'Hell hath no fury.'

Frank gave a short laugh. 'I've met them, Ben. They crowd the best hotels in Sydney, it's pitiful really. I know it has been said before but it's true, so help me, they would sell their children for a Knighthood.'

'Make no mistake Frank, the same feelings exist in the middle classes. Take this town for example. Fortunately you weren't here in '27, you know, the Royal Visit, the Duke and Duchess of York. We were the last stop on their tour by train. The two carriages must have cost a fortune to outfit. The Council even painted the station! The crowd went wild, nothing like it had ever happened before yet you know if Tom Mix had turned up it would have been the same.'

'We are so bloody isolated, Ben. People are hungry for diversion - anything to break the monotony of their lives.' He grinned. 'As a leading light of the town, I suppose you were on the welcoming committee?'

'That, old man, I would rather forget. I've never been over popular with the society matrons of this town but since then I've become a virtual leper.'

'They still see you though.'

'Oh they see young Dave Aitken or the new man who has opened up. Fellow named Charley Hawkes, nice young bloke, charm the birds out of the trees. Tell the truth, I'm glad, I don't have to put up with them. Flatter myself Frank, I've still got the real people, thank God.'

'That I can believe but tell me what happened, I'm all agog.'

'I was on the committee to choose ten, ten only, who would be there to bow and generally make fools of themselves - with a few exceptions of course. I was given the dubious honour of nominating ten. The phone never stopped ringing - I must include this one, that one. It was a nightmare. I picked old Mr. Emery, the chemist, and his wife, Tom and Mrs. Coburn of course, Pieter and Ellen, Dave Truman the Police Sergeant, a couple of others and an old bloke you wouldn't know, Jack Chlohessy.'

'Can't say I've heard of him.'

'Old miner from Cessnock, badly dusted, lungs ruined. He came up here to live, I should say die, with his daughter and her husband. One of natures true gentlemen.'

'Obviously not one of the town's Social Set.'

'Hardly. They live in a little place down by the river. Jack sits on the verandah all day, smoking his vile old pipe. I drop in to see him every few days. Get Mr. Emery to send round a bottle of mixture every Friday, heavily laced with opium of course, Jack thinks it's curing him.'

'So you included Jack in the welcoming committee.'

'You should have heard the commotion - the man's an illiterate labourer, what possessed me to ask such a person?' Ben poured more tea. 'Well, to continue the story - the daughter had fits. She fished out his ancient serge suit, must have worn it on his wedding day, hung it on the line, brushed and ironed it, bathed him, trimmed his handlebar moustache, blacked and polished his boots until you could see your face in them.' He chuckled. 'Jack was the Perfect Gentleman. He stood at the back, I told him beforehand - Jack don't smoke that bloody pipe of yours - it must have been an effort, seldom out of his mouth.'

'All went well?'

'Oh yes. They only stayed twenty minutes or so. She is the stronger of the two, he looked very tired. Not robust, I should think.'

'So Jack had his day.'

'He did indeed. The Duke stayed talking to him longer than most.'

'How did he take that?'

'Honestly Frank, as natural as if he was talking to any other man. I think the young Duke sensed that.'

'Good for him. I trust the ladies were duly impressed.'

'To say the least. Amongst the more genteel ladies, I suspect a little incontinence, my olfactory nerves detected the faint odour of urine.'

Frank roared with laughter. 'Well I'll be damned! You've still got your sense of humour Ben. Listen, I think I hear the return of the fishing party.'

Along the driveway the children came laughing and joshing, Gareth leading the way, a string of silver perch slung over his shoulder, Carlo at Gerald's heels.

'So Gareth finished primary school Ben. I know he goes to Sydney after Christmas. What has he been doing?'

'A bit of private coaching. Cummings takes him for Latin and Maths, the Brelats for French and Muriel helps. He will be all right. Hopefully he will go straight into Second Year.'

'I see. Well here they are. By George, Pieter's daughter is with them and another little girl, who is she?'

'That's Beryl, Beryl Carrol. Lovely child, her father died last month desperately poor. Her mother's a fine looking woman, does some cleaning at the hospital.'

'She shouldn't have much trouble finding someone. Bloody awful I know but women in her position have little choice.'

'There is someone hanging around. Small, fat character, cashier at the local store.'

'She could do worse I should think. At least the child would have a father.'

'Not so sure, heavy drinker, can't say I take to the man.' Ben stood. 'All right people, wash your hands, Mrs. Ellis will see to lunch. Gareth make sure those fish are cleaned before you take them to the kitchen. Gerald, see the dog is dried off.'

Easter and the following two weeks passed uneventfully. Dan came to dinner on the last day of the holidays. Dressed in civilian clothes, his bubbling good humour and wit made for an enjoyable evening.

Over a late drink Frank confided to Ben. 'I like him, always have, great company.'

'Yes, a tragedy really, should never have entered the priesthood. He has made himself known to the various Protestant ministers in town.' Ben laughed. 'They must have just about keeled over, the old priest would never have countenanced such a thing.'

'Bloody ridiculous isn't it, never able to marry, to enjoy a woman. He's still a vigorous, healthy man.'

'I wouldn't worry on that score Frank. Between you and I, Dan looks after himself all right, he receives more than tea and sympathy from a few accommodating ladies around here.'

'Good luck to him, but what about the excommunication they threaten them with?'

'Dan laughs at that, he knows damn well the humblest man knows as much about the hereafter as all the churches put together.'

'How true. Wish to Christ all the faithful felt the same way.'

'That will never change old friend but I tell you, if they ever try to discipline or shift him, they will never see him again.'

'Oh well, such is life. We're a strange lot, we humans.'

Ben nodded. 'So you're off tomorrow. A long drive.'

'Bloody rough one too. Might come up by train Christmas time. By the way Ben, when are you going to change that old car of yours? Bit old fashioned isn't it?'

'I've been thinking about it for some time, one for Francie too. The new models are coming out about the end of the year, I believe. Have to go up to Brisbane to look them over.'

Frank looked at his watch. 'Thank Heaven it's not too late, I promised to take Muriel to the tower again tonight.' He grinned. 'I'll swear that captain looks at me each time we pass by.'

Ben smilingly clapped him on the shoulder. 'Perhaps he knows something.'

The holidays over, Ben resumed the demanding life of a country practitioner. 'You're a brick Ethel, I needed that rest. Everything went well I hope.'

'No real problems. The Glenning children are up and about. What are you going to do with them?'

'I don't know, damned if I do. I must go and see them and talk to Dave and Pieter, see what the position is. Anything else?'

'Tom Coburn has hospitalized that nun you saw about a month ago.'

'Cervical cancer. Sadly it appears to have spread throughout her body. What is he doing for her?'

'Nothing, she refuses anything to alleviate the pain.'

'Sometimes martyrs change their minds, I'll talk to Dan.'

The next day on hospital rounds, he found the children in the garden, quite recovered. 'I must say you look very well.' He smiled. 'Peter and Judy, isn't it?'

'Yes Doctor.' The little girl seemed protective of her brother. 'What is to become of us now Mum and Dad are gone?'

Ben steered them to a garden bench. 'Come and sit down. Now, first I will have to talk to some people then we shall see. But I promise you, you will not be parted. Believe me, we will work something out that will keep you together.'

Deep in thought, he continued his rounds. Matron Truman met him in her office. 'I can't keep them here much longer, Ben. The staff love them but you know the rules.'

'Leave that to me Faith. Now what about Sister Beatrice?'

'Poor thing is in terrible pain, she needs morphine but won't have it. I've tried to tell her, she simply refuses.'

'So I hear, the Christ on the Cross complex.'

'She should be in a Catholic Hospice but it's too late to move her now. Trouble is Ben, her moaning is causing distress amongst other patients.'

'It's a problem, I'll see what I can do.'

'I've put her out on the verandah, you know the covered section. She seems happier there.'

'A wise decision Faith, gives her privacy when the Sisters visit.'

That night Ben told Frances. 'Beautiful children Francie, fraternal twins. The girl is a beauty, I've never seen such green eyes. The boy is a solid, good looking lad, intelligent too. What to do with them beats me. I've foolishly promised they will not be separated but from what Dave tells me, that is highly unlikely.' He told her of the suffering nun. 'God help me, she suffers terribly but won't hear of morphine.'

'Isn't there anything you can do?'

'I don't know. I'll talk to Dan, she may listen to him. Anyway, I'm completely fagged out old girl. Sleep well.' He kissed her goodnight.

In the hallway below the Grandfather clock ticked with a soft comforting regularity. The night closed in with the deep stillness only the country knows. As the clock chimed one o'clock Ben was awakened by his wife's gentle shaking. 'Ben, Ben wake up, I want to talk to you.'

Mumbling, trying hard to believe he was not dreaming, he sat upright reaching for the bedside lamp. 'Good God woman, what is it? It's after one in the morning, you frightened the daylights out of me.'

'I'm sorry darling, I can't sleep. I keep thinking about those poor children.'

He groaned. 'What do you expect me to do? I've told you the situation. It is up to Dave and the authorities.'

'Couldn't we take them? You know, until things are settled.'

He switched off the light, settling back into the pillows, silent for a moment. 'I've even though of it myself. Could we manage? I'll have a talk to Dave and Pieter tomorrow.'

Wide awake now, they talked long and earnestly.

'Gareth and Gerald will be at school next year. Yes, the more I think about it the more the idea appeals.'

'Do you think the children would like to come to us?'

'I think so darling, I hope so. We can give them a home at least.'

Frances snuggled up to him. 'You're a kind hearted, sweet man.'

'Sweet enough for a little comfort now I'm wide awake?'

She kissed him. 'Need you ask?'

Ben discussed the matter with Pieter DeVries. 'Taking into account that Dave's inquiries have found no relatives and the children can give no information, I would say there is nothing to stop you taking them in.' 'Strange though, don't you think, they must have seen grandparents at some time or other.'

'I don't know Ben. He was a shearer, they moved from place to place. If there were any living relatives surely they would have turned up by now.'

'One would think so.'

'Anyway, the Department would raise no objection, they are desperate for foster parents.'

'Does that mean if somebody turned up to claim them, or at the Department's whim, they could be taken from us?'

'Yes, I'm afraid that is the position, unless you adopt them of course.'

'That's a little premature I think. Have to wait and see how things turn out. Will you make the necessary arrangements?'

'Leave it to me. I'm sure the kids will be happy, poor little tykes, all alone at that age.'

Frances took a keen delight in outfitting the children with new clothes. 'Oh Ben, I've longed for a little girl. She is the sweetest child. It's given me a new interest, buying her pretty things.'

'What about the boy?'

'The children like him. He has attached himself to Gareth, they are just about the same age and you know Judy has taken such a fancy to Harry. She insists on wheeling his chair.'

'I imagine Gerald and his mates won't object to that. What about schooling, have they any education at all?'

'Muriel has talked to them. Very little formal education apparently but the mother must have been literate because she thinks they are good enough for sixth class.'

'I suppose you haven't found out anymore about their background?'

'No, you told me not to press them. I am sure they will tell me when they are ready.'

Ben nodded. 'Wisest course, just let nature have it's way.'

Peter joined up with Gerald and his friends in the school playground.

'How d'ya like it here Pete? Sorry about your Mum and Dad.'

'Thanks. We're going up to the cemetery on Sunday, would you like to come?'

'Yeah, we'll come and bring some flowers. How does your sister like it over in the girls section?'

'Real good. She's made friends with those two girls you introduced her to.'

'That's Dorothy and Beryl. Nicest girls in the school.'

'She says some of the others are nice too.'

'Suppose so but there's some rough heads. Hey watch it, here comes Cupie, we're supposed to walk around and exercise.'

They strolled around, keeping as far away from the dreaded teacher as possible. 'Bastard gave me the cuts yesterday, just because I spoke to Jack in lines.' Gerald displayed his hands bearing two well defined weals. 'How do you get on with him Pete?'

'All right, he gave me stacks of homework. Reckons I've got to catch up for high school next year.'

Dave chimed in. 'What was that your sister called you this morning Pete? Sounded like Punch.'

Peter smiled. 'Yes that's right. Dad always called me Punch, 'cause my sister's name's Judy.'

They stopped in a bunch, regarding their new comrade. 'Gee, that's good, mind if we call you Punch?'

'Hope you will, makes me feel better.'

The following month two events occurred, one of which cast a shadow of sorrow over those who knew her. Grace Rayward died of kidney complications due to her pregnancy. The other was the marriage of Beryl's mother to Darby Moss.

'She can't possibly love him, Ben.'

'Times are desperate my dear. She has nothing and he has a secure job.'

'Well I think it's awful. I only hope he treats her well.'

'Time will tell Francie. Just remember, it was her decision.'

A few days later, Gerald met his mates by Harries' shop. 'Look, don't say anything to Punch but tomorrow night we can take a look under the house again.'

'Well, Punch hangs about with Gareth anyway, they're always out fishing in that old canoe.'

'Tell yer mother we're goin' to play ping pong. I'll meet ya at eight o'clock sharp. Mum will be out at her committee meeting.'

The arrangements proceeded smoothly. 'Hope there's no bloody snakes under here.'

'Only trouser snakes. Shut up will ya George?Here, quiet now, here's the crack. Gawd, take a gander!'

Lying face down on the couch, was the quivering figure of one of the districts toughest characters, his trousers pulled to his ankles. The fascinated watchers gaped at a huge carbuncle rising like a small red mountain on his right buttock. Ken Murphy was a bullocky, afraid of neither man nor beast but here, his courage wilted. He quavered 'Won't hurt much, will it Doc?'

'Very little, Mr. Murphy. Matron, swab the area will you? Scalpel please.'

Dave nudged Gerald. 'What an ass! Like one of his bloody bullocks.'

Gerald clapped his hand over his mates mouth. 'Quiet will ya, quiet!'

Ken Murphy seemed to shrink at the doctor's approach. Ethel stood ready with gauze and a small enamel bowl. Ben swabbed and made a quick incision through the angry head of the shining protuberance. Through the bullocky's clenched teeth came the throaty cry of a wounded steer. 'Christ Doc, that was murder.'

'You will feel better for it, Mr. Murphy. Matron will clean it up now. You'll be right as rain in a few days.'

Quickly the boys made their way to the open air, running to the safety of the orchard, they rolled and rocked, hands over mouths suppressing shrieks of mirth pent up inside them. 'Jeez, never seen anything like it. Looked like a big red apple on his bum!' Again they dissolved into mirth.

As they separated for the night, Gerald held up a warning hand. 'Remember you blokes, not a word to anyone. We could get into real trouble, besides my old man would kill me, for sure.'

'Mine too. Don't worry Gerry, our little Secret Society never blabs.'

School next day brought unexpected dismay. Gerald and Dave were summoned to Master Cummings office. Reluctantly they made their way, with other pupils gazing with fascinated anticipation at the luckless twosome.

'Jeez, what's he want? We've done nothin'.'

'Nothin' the bastard knows about.'

Charles Cummings stood waiting, hands behind his back, the dreaded lawyer cane conspicuous on the desk. 'Ah Wakefield and Truman, you have excelled yourselves this time, haven't you? I intend to show you obscenity will not be tolerated while I am in charge. Also, I intend to speak to your parents but first you must be punished.'

Dave was the first to speak. 'Punished! What for Sir? We've done nothing wrong.'

'So you say. What of you Wakefield?'

'I don't know Sir. Same as Dave. What have we done?' He stammered, his mind flashing over the nightly excursions under the house.

'I have been well informed. I do not intend caning you on the hands so you will have no excuse for not taking mid term exams. Fortunately the offensive writing has been cleared from the school fence but that does not lessen the crime. All right, you first Wakefield, bend over that chair.'

The flexible cane swished six times across the seat of Gerald's tightly stretched knickerbockers. He bit hard on his lip to suppress the howls that escaped through clenched teeth.

'You next Truman.' The exercise was repeated, the wack of the cane on serge pants echoed like pistol shots. Charles Cummings resumed his seat. 'You may go now but you have not heard the last of this matter.'

The two emerged from the office red faced and desperately trying not to show the indignity they had suffered.

School out, the boys met at Harries' shop. 'Christ, I won't be able to sit down for a month. The rotten little bastard, what did we do?'

'Jeez Gerry, we're all with you. Haven't you heard?'

'Heard what?'

'What was written on the fence.'

'Of course I haven't, what was it?'

'Cupie Cummings is a turd. Big letters in whitewash.'

'Well Dave and I didn't bloody well do it. Why did the little bastard pick on us?'

'He got a note, someone said they saw you and Dave do it.'

'It's a bloody lie, you know we didn't. Anyway, how do you know about it?'

'Gareth told us. He thinks he knows who did though.'

'Does he, is he sure? Who is it?'

'Bully Hagam, you remember Gareth beat him up that time.'

'That bastard! That's his form all right. Gawd, my ass feels it all right. How's yours Dave?'

'Bloody awful. I'm going to tell my father.'

'Better wait, see what Gareth finds out. Where'd he go, d'ya know?'

'Dunno. Finish yer drink an' we'll go lookin' for him.'

They found Gareth with Peter in one of the narrow leafy lanes that ran between the streets. They had cornered Bully Hagam and his mate Bernard Shey, a big boy known to the group as Fatty Shey. Accusations led to a fist fight. Bully Hagam, nose bleeding profusely, backed up against a paling fence, drew his sleeve across his bloodied face. 'Fuck you Wakefield, you'll get nothing out of me. Hope Cummings breaks your bloody neck.'

Gareth held him fast where he stood. On the ground nearby, Peter held the other boy face down in the dust with his knee in the victim's back and the boy's arm twisted up behind. 'Cut it out will ya? You'll break me bloody arm. I never did nuthin'

'I'll break it all right.' He gave another twist. 'You and Hagam did it, didn't you?'

This was greeted with a howl of pain. 'I bloody told ya I didn't.'

'Don't tell him Bernie, don't say nuthin'.'

The arm was twisted higher. 'Gawd, no more! All right, I know who did but it wasn't me.'

'Get your paper and pencil Gerry. Write down-I confess to writing, Cupie Cummings is a turd, on the school fence. All right Hagam, you won't sign it but your mate will, unless he wants a broken arm.' The paper and pencil were thrust under the moaning victim's nose.

'Don't sign it Bernie.'

'Shut your mouth Hagam or I'll finish you off good and proper.'

The luckless boy's eyes filled with tears. 'I ain't signin' for somethin' I didn't do.'

Gerald folded the paper and put it in his pocket. 'All right, I believe you at least, now you two ratbags piss off.'

At the end of the lane Josh Hagam turned. 'I'll get you Wakefield, you bastard. You and yer greasy brother and his mate. You wait.'

Gareth ignored him. 'Come on you blokes, time we were off.'

After surgery that night, Gareth told his father of the day's events.

'You mean he caned Gerald and Dave without any proof they had actually written on the fence?'

'Someone sent him a note Dad, naming Gerry and Dave.'

'I see. Well, did they do it?'

'No.'

'And how do you know, may I ask?'

Gareth stood silent, looking intently into the far corner of the room.

'I see, yes I think I understand. Cummings is a bit too free with that cane of his. I'll have a word with him tomorrow.'

Gareth continued to stand silently by his father's desk.

'Is there something more Gareth?'

'No Dad, not really. Mr. Cummings is a good teacher though I know he has a quick temper. But you know Dad, some of the big kids get out of hand sometimes.'

Ben sat back looking at his son. 'Thanks my boy, I understand what you are trying to say. Leave it to me, I'll think about it.'

Ben's meeting with the schoolmaster was brief. 'Perhaps you should have waited Mr. Cummings, until you were sure Gerald and Dave were the culprits.'

'I am truly sorry Doctor, but please understand my position. I received a note implicating your son and his friend, how was I to know it was not genuine?'

Ben felt a sudden sympathy for the man. It was his first visit to the overcrowded school in over a year, the three wooden buildings were crammed beyond capacity. 'I don't envy you your task Mr. Cummings. Consider the incident closed. I'll explain to my son, I'm sure Sergeant Truman will do the same.'

'Thank you Doctor. I'm relieved to see work on the new high school is progressing well.'

'Yes indeed. The contractor tells me it will be ready to take it's first pupils in the new year.'

Gerald and his mates were far from mollified. 'He told Dad he was sorry. Bloody nice, isn't it, didn't tell us though. Should see my ass, looked at it in Mum's wardrobe mirror, black and blue. Bloody Hagam was right for once, he is a turd all right. Wish we could get back at him.'

They stood with their soft drinks outside Harries' shop. 'Money's hard, Gerry. The old man says we're in a depression, where'd ya get the dough?'

'Got it from Buddy, some that Uncle Frank gave him.'

'Hey, how come we don't bring him anymore, what's happened?'

'Punch's sister has taken over. They get on real well t'gether. Buddy reckons he'd rather be with her than us.'

'Nice bloke, Punch, so's his sister. What about Cupie, anyone got any ideas?'

'George reckons he has.'

'Yeah? Tell us George, what's the big idea?'

'Listen, it's risky but it could work.' They crowded close together.'

'You know the boarding house where Cupie lives, only him and old Mr. Henry and those girls live there.'

'Yeah, we know. What about it?'

'All those houses back onto the lane that runs behind them and all the dunnies are right against the fence so the dunny man can empty the pans.'

'Jesus George. What've ya got in mind?'

'I'll get a pineapple from our orchard, a big green one, put it on a long stick-'

'Oh George, you bloody genius. How could we do it?'

'Easy, I've watched. Cupie goes to the dunny straight after tea. We'll let him get comfortable, open the little door at the back and give him the rough end - right up the ring-a-ding-ding!'

'Christ, what if he sees us?'

'No way Gerry, it's dark when he comes down.'

They dissolved into laughter until the enormity of the proposed indignity suddenly occurred to them. 'What if we get caught, we'd be killed. We wouldn't be let back into school again.'

'You're right Jack, it's bloody risky.'

George broke in. 'It's not risky if we do it right. Blacken our faces with burnt cork, it's so dark there we can give Cupie the rough end then run like hell down the lane.'

The mental picture of the dapper teacher again brought on fits of mirth until Gerald spoke up. 'All right, it's agreed. When do we do it?'

'Friday night mate. The bastard goes out Fridays and we don't have to go to school the next day. And listen Gerry, tie up Carlo, he would be a dead give away.'

For the rest of the week the conspirators made their plans. George produced a large pineapple firmly fixed to a stick about two feet long, the rough leafy part of the succulent fruit up front.

'Tell your mothers we're playing ping pong at the School of Arts. I've got the cork and matches. Meet ya here near the shop.'

In the inky blackness of a moonless Friday night, the boys positioned themselves against a high fence opposite the boarding house lavatory. Faces blackened, they kept a silent vigil, watching as neighbours made their way to the small houses to relieve themselves.

'Christ, he's taking a long time. Thought you said he was regular.'

'Shhh, quiet. He'll be down don't worry.'

Their patience was rewarded. Footsteps were heard coming from the boarding house. The door of the outhouse creaked open then the sound of a match scratching to light the candle attached to the wall and finally the bang of the seat cover thrown open.

Quietly they moved forward. 'Bloody beauty, our birdie's on the nest!'

'Real careful now, open the door Dave.'

In the flickering light of the candle, the victim's buttocks glowed, dimly visible. George with a twisting motion thrust the coarse leaves of the luscious fruit upwards into the well defined crease.

A bellow like that of an outraged steer rent the night. The door crashed open. 'Gawd strike me bloody purple, a man can't have a shit in peace!'

Mr. Henry, his pants around his ankles, stood in a small circle of light from the candle, peering into the darkness. 'You little buggers. I know who you are. S'help me I'll kill yer when I get yer!'

'Run,' George hissed. 'run, fur Chrissake!' They ran until they felt their lungs would burst, breaking at last by the river. There they lay panting until suddenly one of them broke into howls of mirth.

'Oh Gawd, poor old Mr. Henry, oh Gawd my sides are hurting!' They rolled on the grass, laughing uncontrollably. 'Jeez, I think I've pissed meself!' This brought on further fits.

Hal Wynter was the first to sense it might not be so funny if Mr. Henry did suspect who had so outrageously assaulted him.

'Not on your life Hal. How could he? It was dark an' we pissed off too quick.'

'Well even if he didn't, it was terrible getting him instead of Cupie.'

Now sobered up, there were murmurs of agreement. 'He's such a decent old bloke. Always knows where the fish are.'

'Yes, and always tells us first.'

'What can we do? We can't go up and apologize.'

'No, yer right. Gerry, what d'you think?'

'Well he's pretty poor, I know that. How about we get him some tobacco?'

'Maybe a new pipe, if we can raise the dough.'

'Yeah, good idea, but we can't buy tobacco, they won't sell it to us.'

'I know, but there is someone who will do it for us.'

'Who?'

'Mick. He's a great bloke. Get him to give it to Mr. Henry too. Tell Mick to say he can't say where it comes from. You blokes get what money ya can, Dave and I will ride our bikes up to *Monaro* on Monday.'

'Well, we better get back to the School of Arts, we can always say we were there.'

'What about the black on our faces?'

'Thought of that mate, got some soap and a piece of rag in me pocket.'

'Great, the park tap's just over there. How's yer pants Jack?'

'All right, managed t'get it out just in time.'

After school on Monday, Dave and Gerald pedalled their way along the leafy driveway to *Monaro* and found Mick busily raking the gravel surface. He stopped as they approached.

'G'day Mick, how ya goin'?'

'Good, how're you blokes?'

'All right Mick, wondering if ya'd do us a favour?'

'Depends what it is.' He leaned on his rake, a broad smile on his face. 'Want me t'mind yer dawg again?'

'Not this time Mick. You know old Mr. Henry?'

'Course I do, good mate of mine.'

'We'd like to give him a present, but you know we can't buy tobacco.'

Mick's smile broadened. 'That's mighty generous of you. What's the occasion?'

'Oh just something that happened, bit of a mistake. We want t'make it up to him.'

Mick slowly rolled a cigarette. 'You mean gettin' the wrong man Friday night?'

Gerald felt the hair on the back of his scalp rise. 'Jesus Mick, how'd you know? We'll get bloody killed!'

Mick slowly exhaled. 'Don't get yourselves in a knot, old Charlie told me, no one else. It won't go any further.'

'Jeez, we're real sorry, Mick. Is he all right?'

'Yeah, he's okay, had to sit in a dish of Condy's Crystals over the weekend, reckons he's got a purple ring now.'

'Gawd, that's a relief. How did he know it was us?'

'Ya left the pineapple behind. George's father is the only one with 'pines. Anyway, how much ya got?'

'Eight bob altogether.'

'That should do the trick. I'll get the 'baccy and call in on me way home. I'll tell him you're real sorry, it was all a mistake.'

'You're a bloody beaut, Mick. Hope we can do something for you someday.'

Mick resumed his raking. 'Better get goin' boys, ride easy on yer way home.'

The following week Frances had a long discussion with her husband.

'I've really had enough of the Committee, Ben. There is so much bickering, I would rather stay home and look after my family.'

'You do that very well Francie. What's the trouble?'

'Oh some of the women think that by helping people you only encourage laziness.'

'You will always get that, particularly from those who have never wanted for anything.'

'It's only from a few, really it's the gossip I can't stand.'

'What sort of gossip?'

'Well, it's Gerald again-I hear it second hand of course, mainly Mrs. Bidwell and her little group.'

'She's a damn busybody. What have you heard this time?'

'The usual thing-how disgraceful, a doctor's son mixing with the riffraff of the town.'

Ben lit his pipe. 'Ignore her. I'd rather Gerald mixed with the so-called riffraff than with some I can think of. In any case, the fathers' of the boys he mixes with are old friends of mine. To hell with her. You know Francie, George Donatos' grandfather never believed in banks. After the crash of '93, the old man had ready money, that's why he could buy and sell the lot of them. That's why they resent him.'

'It's because they are Greek. She says they are nothing but peasants.'

'My love, the Greeks were civilized when her forbears still lived in thatched huts.'

'She wouldn't believe it. But Ben, that's not the worst of it.'

'God help us, don't tell me there's more?'

'She says Peter and Judy should be handed over to the proper authorities. I'm worried Ben.' Tears glistened in her eyes.

'Does she, the old bitch. Just leave that to me. Get hold of Peter and Judy after school, if they would like us to adopt them, we will.'

That evening after surgery, the twins sat gravely listening as Ben outlined his plan for them. 'We can never take the place of your parents, my wife and I know that, but you will always have a home and as I promised you, you will not be separated.' He smiled, 'please tell me how you feel about becoming part of our family.?'

Peter stood holding his sister's hand. 'If you want us Doctor.' He turned to Judy who had begun to cry, a rare smile lit his face, 'I think Judy would too.'

Ben felt a pain in his heart-taking out his handkerchief, he wiped the child's face. 'There, there my dear. Only smiles now, no more tears.' He took her hand. 'Come now, we will tell the rest of the family.'

The next day he put the matter of adoption into Pieter DeVries hands.

'Not a problem Ben. I'll expedite the application. I'd say you'd have two permanent additions to your family within the month.'

They sat talking for a while. 'This bloody depression is ruining the country Ben. Poor devils are just walking out of their homes, others living on credit. God knows if they will ever be able to meet their debts. I do what I can but it is precious little.'

Ben sighed deeply. 'Yes I know. What do you hear from Melbourne by the way?'

'Well, as per your instructions, I've given James carte blanche re your properties. Afraid there may not be any rents from them before long.'

'I still intend to hold them Pieter. What of the old house?'

'As you asked, he has taken up residence there, keeping the place in shape as you instructed.'

'What of the delectable Miss Holley? Married her, no doubt.'

'We've heard nothing, you know James, a secretive bugger. All will be revealed in due course.'

Ben laughed. 'I must be off. I'm going down to Sydney next month, want to see Frank and see about the boys' schooling.'

'I thought Gareth was the only one going down.'

'That's what I meant. What are you doing about Dorothy?'

'Presbyterian Ladies College, try and make a lady out of her.'

'Good idea. Must go. Let me know when you hear anything.'

At school Gerald and his friends were distinctly nervous. 'Think he knows anything? The prick keeps looking at us.'

'No way, Mick said Mr. Henry didn't say anything. Why would he think it was us?'

'Quick, there's the bell!'

After school as usual, they clustered round Harries' shop. 'Haven't got the price of a drink, that money for Mick cleaned me out.' Hal thrust his hands deep in his pockets.

'She's right.' Gerald held up a silver coin. 'Got it from Buddy, he knows all about it by the way.'

'Good old Buddy. Jeez he's a good one. Judy still looking after him?'

'Yeah, she's great. Did ya know they're part of the family now?'

'Ya mean they're your brother and sister?'

'Jesus, don't be silly George, they're adopted. It's great, Mum and Dad treat them just like us.'

'Oh shit! Look who's coming.'

'Christ, it's Mr. Henry!'

They stood transfixed, soft drink bottles in hand.

The old gentleman approached. 'How are you, boys? Thought you might like to know, the mullet are running up North Arm, catch them on a bit of bread.'

'Thanks Mr. Henry, thanks a lot. We'll cut down there tomorrow.'

'Good idea boys.' He waved a brand new Briar, 'you can't miss.'

About to enter the shop, he turned, a smile crinkling his face. 'How are your father's pineapples doing, George?'

Quietly they made their way to the nearest lane. 'Gawd, what a bloody great old bloke. He could have had us expelled.'

'Mr. Henry's the greatest!' They raised their bottles. 'Let's drink to that, as Uncle Frank says.'

CHAPTER XX

With the seasons slowly changing, rain set in. Ben pulled the side curtains of his trusty old tourer down, glad to return each night to the dry warmth of the house. After dinner with surgery over, he would sit late making meticulous notes of each and every case that came to his attention. Often the clock chimed midnight before he closed his case book. Frances brought hot tea and toast, lingered a few minutes before kissing him goodnight. She knew he silently grieved over the seemingly simple infections that took a child's life or left a once healthy man bubbling for breath, the vital spark finally extinguished. That very day he had amputated a mill worker's leg-compound fracture of the tibia. The spectre of septicaemia haunted him. Some day they would be able to change all that. He prayed he would still be alive to see it.

On such a night, the rain softly drumming on the roof, he packed his pipe, stretched his feet to the glowing fireplace and mulled over the last few weeks. Pieter had been as good as his word, the adoption papers were finalized. He smiled to himself-what do they call us now? Dad, Mum, Uncle, Aunt? A chuckle escaped him, no doubt that would work itself out, no worry there.

A faint tinkle of the outside bell interrupted his reverie. A quick glance at the mantle clock showed ten minutes to one a.m. 'For God's sake at this hour?' With slippered feet he moved silently along the hall. Opening the door a few inches, the faint white of a clerical collar glowed in the dim light. 'Dan, is that you?'

'None other, old friend. May I come in?' He grasped Ben's hand and was ushered into the warm surgery. He unbuttoned his greatcoat and stood, back to the fire, a faint haze rising from the legs of his damp trousers.

'You need a scotch, my lad.'

'No, not yet, Ben. I need one all right but not yet.'

'This sounds serious. Sit down, you look tired out.' He lit his tamped pipe. 'Sit down, have a cigarette at least.'

Dan continued to stand. 'You are the only one I can turn to Ben. I've just come from the hospital, Matron Truman called me.'

'Sister Beatrice?'

'I hope I never live to see again such torment. Dear God, she is no longer human. She has received Extreme Unction. Ben, how much longer? She holds her cross out, screaming to Jesus that she is coming!'

'I know, I'm reminded every day. She refuses help in any form. The whole hospital is in a state of upset.'

'Would you let an animal suffer like that?'

'Not if I could help.'

'I beg you Ben, help her. Do what you have to do. She lapses into unconsciousness so often, she doesn't know.'

Ben puffed on his pipe. 'I begin to understand you. You are quite sure?'

'As a priest, as a human being, I truly believe allowing suffering like that is sinful, wicked in the extreme.'

'I wish more thought like you Dan. Here,' he held out the damp coat, 'perhaps some day, in more enlightened times, things may change.'

Ben let his friend from the house, returning quietly for his bag and rain gear.

Matron Truman sat in the dim light of her office, she looked up with tired eyes, a smile of welcome on her face. 'I hoped you might come.'

The rain cleared, the morning soft and fine, the leaves of the vast cane field shone and rustled in the breeze smelling faintly of the sea. The Church claimed it's own. The Sisters, silent in their grief, the Blessed Virgin had heard their prayers. Almighty and Merciful God had taken her in the night. Sister Beatrice, peaceful at last, her suffering ended.

Weekends at *Monaro* acted as a renewal. Often when Frances and Muriel were busy with plans for the coming wedding and the children, five now, were roaming the countryside, Ben sought solace in the tower. From the captain's chair he could see the distant glittering ocean, the wooded slopes leading down to the flat canefields and the town. Here was peace, a retreat from the world below.

Passing through the gallery to the spiral staircase, he would pause, gazing as he had so often before, at the portraits of the handsome seafarer and his hauntingly beautiful wife. He felt compelled to linger, to wonder at the skill of the unknown artist. The piercing blue eyes of the Captain stared at him-Jesus, no wonder Frank felt uneasy. Turning he made his way to the high tower, there to give himself up to blissful solitude, dozing until a knock at the door announced dinner was ready.

At night, when the house was silent, they talked quietly. 'Francie, I've made up my mind. I want to move up here permanently after Christmas if possible. How do you feel about it?'

'I have always wanted to, especially since your mother died.'

He turned to face her. 'It's how it should be darling. It's not just a feeling I have, it's obvious in every way. Tom and Alice would love to have their house back.'

'How do you know, what about the house at Lambruk?'

'I think they would sell it tomorrow. Just look at the way they love to have the place to themselves when we come up here. Alice can't wait to get into the garden and Tom sits in the surgery as if he had never left it.'

'They are getting on in years.'

'All the more reason for them to return to what they know so well. Don't worry about the old boy, Francie, he's remarkable and remember, she is ten years younger than he is.'

'Will you speak to Dr. Coburn?'

'I intend to, I've been planning to for a long time.'

On Monday morning Ben kept his word. Before leaving for the hospital he approached his older colleague. 'Could you spare me a moment Doctor?'

'Of course Ben, sit down.'

Ben outlined the conversation he had had with Frances.

Dr. Coburn looked at him. 'Tell me Ben, have I said or indicated in any way that we would like to return to this house?'

'Certainly not Sir. It was just a thought. I sincerely hope I haven't offended you?'

'Offended me? My dear Ben, it's a wonderful idea. Alice will be ecstatic. It will be like coming home again.'

Ben sighed with relief. 'Does the time suit you? After Christmas, I mean.'

'Perfectly, gives us a chance to put things in order at Lambruk. I think we will manage very well.'

'Well, *Monaro* is only a short trip away now and Dave Aitken will be back in a couple of months.' He glanced at his watch. 'I should be on my way. I'm so glad that is settled.'

They shook hands warmly. 'And so am I, my boy. By the way,' he took Ben's arm, 'I haven't mentioned before, that matter at the hospital. Poor thing, she suffered too long, far too long.'

It was late when Ben returned from his rounds. 'All settled Francie. Honestly, he was delighted. Said it would be like coming home for them. I'm a damn fool, should have seen it long ago. They make the trip down here three times a week, then take over for the weekend, now.'

Frances took his arm. 'I am happy if you are, darling. It seems the sensible thing to do. They are such a wonderful couple. Will he retire then?'

Ben laughed. 'Not while there's breath in his body, my girl.'

Dave Aitken returned in August to a heartfelt welcome. He was brimming over with tales of his tour but most of them had to wait. Within a week Ben left for Sydney taking Gareth with him. Frank met them at Central Station, and drove them firstly to their hotel and then after lunch on a tour of the suburbs.

He smiled at the boy's wonderment. 'They call it the city of red roofs, Gareth. What do you think of it so far?'

'Bit different to Myuna, Uncle. Why is everybody rushing around so much?'

Frank chuckled. 'All cities are the same, Gareth. Think you will like going to school here?'

'I think so. Dad is taking me to the Grammar School tomorrow. I'm going home for holidays you know.'

'Don't blame you. After your visit tomorrow we'll have a good look round, go to the theatre, things like that.'

'Gee, that would be great!'

The next day, with his son's enrolment for the following year completed and after leaving Gareth in Frank's care, Ben took a taxi to a famous Catholic school for boys. The doorbell was answered by a pleasant middle aged woman who ushered him into the Headmaster's office. The wide windows overlooked well kept lawns and gardens down to a tree lined river. A thin soutaned priest sat at a polished maple desk. On the wall behind hung a simple crucifix.

Brother McSweeney looked up, an expression of surprised delight creased his face. 'Before I ask what brings you to the city, let me say how glad I am to see you. Come sit down. Now I insist you take afternoon tea with me Ben, or is it coffee?'

'Tea will be fine Sean. I must say you don't look a day older. How long is it now? What's your secret?'

'Hard work Ben and don't flatter me. I know my face resembles an old prune more and more as the years roll by.'

They both laughed. A knock at the door announced the arrival of the tea tray, complete with elegant silver service. The same woman that had answered the door, carefully placed the tray on the desk. Sean smiled. 'Thank you Mrs. Clements, you anticipated me.'

'I saw the gentleman in Father, please ring if you need more.'

The door closed behind her. 'My housekeeper, an absolute gem.' He poured the tea into fine Bone China cups. 'Now,' he sat back regarding his visitor with obvious enjoyment, 'you must tell me what you have been doing Ben, all the news from *Monaro*.' He sighed. 'How I miss those wonderful days when we were young. Such peace, such tranquillity.' He grew serious. 'Your mother's death grieved me greatly.'

'She was not well for a long time Sean, it was not unexpected but one is never prepared. And your own mother Sean, I know from Dan and Ellen.'

Sean nodded. 'It's sad isn't it? The first time the three of us had been together in years. I am deeply troubled Ben, I should not worry you with my problems but you are one of my dearest friends.'

'What is it Sean, can I help?'

'Thank you but I doubt it.' He leaned forward. 'In strictest confidence Ben, Dan is trying to be released from his vows.'

'Is that possible?'

'In some cases, yes, but it is a very long complicated process. It could take years for his application to be considered.' He sat back. 'But enough of the serious side of life. Tell me all about *Monaro*. And please forgive me for burdening you with my troubles.'

Ben smiled. 'I'm you friend Sean and always there if I can help.' He related all he thought the priest would like to know, leaving out that which he knew would upset him. They talked of old times, of old friends.

'So you have enrolled your eldest at the Grammar School. Fine school, excellent reputation.'

'So I believe, which brings me to the main purpose of my visit today. You see Sean, our second eldest, Gerald, is a fine boy but on the wild side. I don't want him at the same school as Gareth.'

'May I ask why?'

'Gareth has always fought Gerald's battles for him. Time he stood on his own two feet.'

'I see.'

'The point is, do you take pupils other than of the Catholic faith?'

'Of course we do. We have Jewish boys, boys from Protestant families, mostly from the country. There are no problems, they simply do not take religious instruction.'

'Would you consider taking Gerald. For the new term next year, I mean.'

'Of course. And I promise to keep an eye on him. The Brothers are pretty strict you know, but I am prepared to guarantee he will receive a sound education. We have quite a sporting reputation too, would that appeal to him?'

Ben laughed with relief. 'Appeal? Apart from a few diversions, it's the love of his life!'

An hour later, Ben took leave of his old friend, promising to meet again in the New Year.

That night, with Gareth sleeping the healthy sleep of exhaustion, he discussed his visit with Frank.

'You mean enrol Gerald in a Catholic school? How will he take that?'

'Not too well, I should think. In any case nothing definite decided yet. To tell the truth Frank, it was a spur of the moment impulse. I was going to visit Sean anyway, then after talking to him and a tour of the college-well, I was very impressed.'

'You could do worse I guess. I think I've only met your friend a couple of times-seems the genuine article-damned if I know though why men choose to become priests.'

'It's in the blood, my friend, in the blood. Of course there are many misfits, there are in every calling, we know that.' Ben picked up the phone for room service. 'I'm ordering up a bottle of Malt and soda, any objection?'

Frank leaned back, a serene smile on his face. 'You took a bloody long time!'

The waiter set the tray down. 'Shall I pour sir?'

Ben pressed a note into the man's hand. 'No thank you that will be all.

'So here I am all the way down from the bush, tell me what is happening.'

Frank held his glass to the light. 'What's happening? If this is Australia 1929, I wish to Christ I had done what you once suggested and gone to America long ago.'

'Cut it out, it can't be that bad.'

'You have seen the evidence. The country has come to a standstill.'

'It's the same all over the world Frank. What of your group, any plans?'

'As I told you last time-wrong time to show our hand, but we are planning believe me.'

'What of this New Guard crowd?'

'Must be taken seriously Ben.' Frank lowered his voice, opened the door, looking up and down the passageway before returning to his seat. 'This is strictly confidential, almost unbelievable. I have seen a list of names, significant figures from both city and the squattocracy, early days yet but obviously, from what I can learn, planning to form a sort of paramilitary force.'

'For what purpose?'

'To maintain the status quo, to put down any riots or revolution that might take place. They take themselves seriously and if my information is right, they are slowly accumulating arms, you know-guns, ammunition.'

'If your information is right, this could divide the country. Who have they got in their sights?'

'Labour and the Unions of course. Although, from what I hear, it's early days yet, but careful planning is under way. I've no reason to doubt my informant.'

'God help Australia, even if it doesn't deserve help. We suffer from an acute deficiency of patriotism. Come on old chap, pass the bottle. I feel bloody depressed.'

They settled back in their chairs. 'You said patriotism. To an extent that is true enough but I've always felt we need a leader, a man of vision, someone to galvanize us to change. Don't you think that is possible?'

'Perhaps. Frankly, I'm not sure of anything anymore. Must be this damn depression.'

'It's bloody hard all right. By the way, you leave tomorrow don't you?'

'Yes, we're booked on the sleeper.'

'There is someone I'd like you to meet. English bloke, Alistair Pryce, Philosophy department at the University. A brilliant mind. How about lunch? A lady friend of mine can take Gareth to the zoo for the day.'

'Do I hear right, you say this man is English?'

'He is, and absolutely committed to the movement.' Frank grinned. 'Didn't you tell me your grandfather once said, any great movement in this country would be led by an Englishman?'

'Hmm, I believe he did say something like that.' Ben smiled in return. 'Of course I would like to meet him. Lunch here is very good, say about twelve thirty?'

Frank stretched, yawning. 'Excellent old boy, see you tomorrow.'

Sitting in the hotel lobby awaiting the arrival of his guests, Ben gave the headlines in the Herald a cursory glance. 'Things are bad all right, damn bad. Must talk to Pieter again. Good old Frank, always the fighter. Wonder what this fellow is like that he has in tow. Queer the picture you conjure up of someone you have never met, is invariably surprising in reality. Some fussy little superior knowall, I shouldn't wonder.'

'You look far away old man, dreaming of home I'll bet.'

'Good Lord, I didn't see you come in.'

Frank, accompanied by a tall bespectacled young man clad in a well cut tweed suit, stood looking down at him. 'Ben, meet Alistair Pryce. Alistair, my brother in law, Ben Wakefield.'

'Pleased to meet you, Doctor.' He gave a firm handshake. 'From what I hear, your *Monaro* must be a veritable Utopia.'

'Hardly that Alistair, we have our problems. Please use my christian name.'

'Thank you, I'm finding it hard to come to terms with Australian egalitarianism but I must say I find it refreshing.'

'Well, let's not stand here, we have a table by the window, quite private with a good view of the park.

'So, I believe you are interested in Frank's brand of politics, Alistair.'

'To a degree yes. I haven't been here long enough to form any firm opinion but from what little I have seen, the time seems hardly propitious. You can appreciate, as a new chum I'm just feeling my way.'

'Yes of course. I believe you and Frank met in London.'

'It was a spur of the moment decision to come out here. I was seriously considering an offer from America, one of the western universities.'

'Philosophy eh, I'm afraid such profound esotery escapes me.'

'He undersells himself Alistair. How are the oysters?' 'Delicious, finest I've tasted.'

'Port Jackson oysters are considered the best in the world. Here try this wine, thoroughly recommended. Goes down well with the fish too.'

Lunch over, the young man leaned back with a sigh of contentment. 'Thank you for a delicious meal. Mind if I smoke?'

Ben rose. 'Not at all, I'll join you. I suggest we retire to the lounge for coffee.'

Settled comfortably, Ben regarded the young Englishman with interest. 'Granted you have been here for only a short time, Alistair, surely you have gained some impressions of this country?'

'Well I have, somewhat superficial I admit. Perhaps it's the people I have met so far, certainly not a broad section.' He paused, appearing to be weighing his words carefully. 'Perhaps it's a lack of patriotism. Australians do not appear to understand or even want to know, who they are. Even the poorest European and certainly the Americans are fiercely proud of their identity.'

'Perhaps we don't express our feelings so openly.'

'If you will forgive me Ben, it seems something deeper than that. I've read as much as I can find of Australian history. The terrible early hardship and cruelty have left their mark. From what I can see there are almost insurmountable divisions, including sectarianism. How can I put it? A, Them and Us, mentality flourishes.'

'Alistair is right Ben, we know that. But I believe, in fact I'm absolutely convinced, people will respond to the right leadership, which has been lacking so far.'

'The people associated with the Movement are exceptional people Frank but so few, and as we know this would be the worst possible time to show our hand.'

Ben motioned to the hovering waiter. 'Brandy gentlemen?'

'Thank you.' The young philosopher leaned forward sharply, and in a lowered voice. 'You know, I live in constant amazement at the people I meet. I'm often asked to little do's-soirees, if you like. The conversation is invariably England. I've never experienced anything quite like it. I suppose you would call these people upper middle class, or what passes for 'Society'. Damn, they refer to England as 'home', wear English clothes, read English magazines-more English than the English! They have no empathy with Australia.' He took a long pull at his cigar. 'My accent gives me away of course-they assume I must be titled at least. Every gushing matron buttonholes me, eager for news of 'home'.' He smiled sardonically, 'the number of times I've felt like saying-you are at home you silly woman!'

Frank fished out his cigar clippers. 'Yes, I think that was the sort of thing that first persuaded me something had to be done. It's pitiful really, would even be amusing but it's sad and serious because husbands of these women make the decisions that affect us all. They determine the future of the country, god help us!'

'What do you suggest Alistair, migration?'

'I think that is absolutely necessary, but you must not be selective.'

'How do you mean?'

'Bring in more Europeans. Don't worry too much about their backgrounds, they will soon adapt. Their children will be the beneficiaries and Australia will be the richer for them.'

'We do get British migrants, unfortunately not many like you. Some of them size up the situation pretty quickly and take full advantage of it.'

'I don't doubt it Ben. The best go to the United States or Canada. What you get here, how can I put it, except for a handful, are the poorest types. They, in their ignorance, imagine the streets are paved with gold. From what I can see, they end up homesick, unhappy and disillusioned. It's the terrible feeling of isolation, the vast distance from anywhere that frightens people.' A faint smile crossed the young man's face. 'Transportation all over again!'

'You draw a pretty dismal picture. But don't forget there are third and fourth generation Australians who are the backbone of this country.'

'That is your hope of salvation Ben. They are the type of people Frank has introduced me to. But seriously, I wouldn't say all in that category would share his sentiments.'

'You mean this dogged devotion to King and Country, England, Home and Beauty?'

Alistair Pryce nodded. 'Precisely, and the British, my own countrymen will exploit that misplaced loyalty when and if it suits their purpose.' He rose, pushing back his chair. 'It has been a pleasure to meet you Ben. With men like you and Frank, this country may one day be a great nation.' He shook hands. 'I can offer little, but Frank knows he can rely on me for whatever small support I can offer. Goodbye for now, I sincerely hope we meet again.'

'So, what do you think of him?'

'I like him. He's genuine, pity there aren't more like him.'

'There are. We met them during the war, but as he said, they don't come here. Most go to America.'

'He is right you know. Our isolation, lack of contact with the world is our greatest enemy. But you know as well as I do, we are always glad to get back home from overseas.'

'Why wouldn't we be-a country the size of the United States populated by a few million people-food for the taking.'

'Tell that to the half starved women and kids you see in the back streets of the city, Frank.'

Frank saw his brother in law and nephew off on the night train to the north.

'Take care old man, you have a good friend in Pryce, just don't rush things!'

'You can rely on that Ben. Give my love to Frances.' He pressed an envelope into Gareth's hand. 'Something here for you and the gang, young man, equal shares remember. See you at Christmas.' He stood waving as the long train huffed it's way from the brightly lit station into the darkness of the night.

Their bunks made up, Ben lay sleepless, listening to the clicking of the rails, the mournful whistle of the engine passing through some lonely hamlet. The muffled noises, the swaying carriage wove their hypnotic spell. It seemed he no sooner closed his eyes when a gentle tap on the door announced the conductor with two steaming cups of tea. Sunlight streamed through the partially closed blinds, they would soon be home.

'How was the trip darling? Oh it is so good to have you home again!'

Ben chuckled. 'We've scarcely been away a week Francie-but it certainly is good to be back again.'

'The school is terrific Mum. I spent a whole day there. The Headmaster read the reports from Mr. Cummings. He said I would be ready for Second Year all right.'

'I'm glad you like it dear, but I wish you weren't going down there. The new high school will be finished before Christmas.'

'It's all settled my girl. Come on, we're starving, you can tell us all the news over lunch.'

Ben sat back with a sigh of contentment. 'It's good to eat home food again.' He looked at his son. 'Where are you off to, Gareth?'

'I want to get the canoe in good order Dad. Can I bring it up to the shelter, you know, behind Abraham's old house?'

'Certainly, but may I ask, why?'

'Be right for when I come home for holidays.'

'Off you go. Don't forget you've got a lot of study to do between now and next year.'

Gareth gone, Ben turned to Frances. 'How are the others?'

'Just the same as when you left. Now you can tell me about Frank.'

'Nothing much to tell my love. He seems busy enough, although things are really bad down there, building almost at a standstill. We had dinner and lunch together, sends his love and is looking forward to Christmas.'

'Oh you men are all the same-never remember anything interesting!'

Ben laughed. 'Leave that to the women. Now, if there is anything new here, I promise to listen,' he looked at his watch 'before I go in to see Dave.'

'Please Ben, stay a little longer, have some more coffee.'

'All right, seeing you're bursting to tell me something.'

'Mrs. Wells and her daughters have arrived at last. I've met them, she is very nice and the girls are lovely.'

'That must be a relief to Wells. What kept them?'

'I didn't ask. After the school is finished, she said he has tendered for the new library.'

'That's good news, Wells is a solid citizen. What are the daughters like?'

'Enid is the eldest. They have three, Enid is twelve, then there is Julie and the youngest, Virginia.'

'Hmm, well I hope they enjoy their stay.' He kissed his wife. 'I must go Francie, see how Dave is coping.'

'Ben.'

'Yes my dear?'

'I've asked them to *Monaro* for Sunday. Do you mind?'

'You are the lady of the house my girl. Look forward to meeting them.'

'Yer old man and Gareth's been away, where'd they go'?

'Down to Sydney t'see Gareth's new school. Same one you're goin' to, isn't it Dave?'

'Yeah, wish I was stayin' here. Hey, any of ya seen Beryl? She hasn't been t'school all week.'

'Must be sick. We can go down this arvo, take some flowers, what d'ya say Dave?'

'Yeah sure. I missed Beryl, she's nice. No smartass cracks from you mugs either. I do like her, she's the best.'

'All right Dave, take it easy. We'll come with ya.'

Later that day the little troupe, grasping flowers from whatever source available, arrived at the little cottage by the river. After a period of heavy knocking Mrs. Carrol, now Mrs. Moss, opened the door. They stood staring in amazement, this pleasant faced woman they knew so well, stood holding the door jam for support. Her hair was dishevelled, one eye badly blackened, a great bruise across her right cheek.

They goggled, Dave found his voice. 'Are you all right Mrs. Carrol, I mean Mrs. Moss, did you have an accident?' He rushed on. 'We came to see why Beryl hasn't been to school.'

She spoke in a whisper. 'Please go away boys. It's all right, Beryl will be back next week.' She closed the door. They stood looking at each other then slowly walked on. 'Gawd, did you ever see anything like it, what could've happened to her?'

'I'll bet it's that bastard she married. I heard Dad say something about him.'

'Jesus, if he's hurt Beryl, I'll kill him, I bloody will!'

'Take it easy Dave, wait till she comes back, we'll ask her.'

Dave confronted them. 'I mean it-if he's hurt Beryl, I'll kick the bastard to death.'

Gerald spoke up, 'Listen, I'll tell Dad. He'll find out and see your dad, Dave. Maybe it's not as bad as it looks.'

After surgery Gerald told his father of the day's events.

'Afraid there's not much I can do son. I simply cannot interfere in domestic problems.'

'But what about Beryl, Dad, she might be hurt.'

Ben glanced at his appointment pad. 'Mrs. Moss is bringing her daughter to see me tonight, she has a bad cold. I'm sure there's nothing to worry about. People do have accidents you know.'

His son gone, Ben sat thinking-that drunken little bastard, I suspected something like this. I'll see what Dave can do.

After leaving his father Gerald ran all the way to the Station House. He found his friend sitting dejectedly on the stone steps of the Court House. 'Dave listen, she's bringing Beryl to the surgery tonight, we can get under the house and hear what happened.'

Dave looked up, tears glistened in his eyes.

'What's the matter mate?'

'I dunno-thinking of Beryl, she could be hurt.'

'Cut it will ya? I told ya, we can find out tonight. Tell yer mother we're doin' special homework at my place.'

'What time?'

'Not sure, we'll get under there early. I think they will be the last in.'

'All right, see ya about seven, don't tell the others though.'

The two boys lay in the warm dust just below the crack in the skirting board, the figures in the surgery clearly visible. Dave whispered in his mate's ear. 'I don't want to look, makes me sick. Wait 'til they come.'

'Yeah, me too. Buggered if I want to be a doctor. Gareth does though, all he talks about.'

After what seemed an endless succession of patients, Matron Jones ushered in Beryl and her mother. Gerald nudged his companion. 'Here they are now.'

They strained to hear the conversation, only a faint murmur filtered through. Ben stood carefully examining the woman's eyes and forehead, then held her left hand closer to the desk lamp, it was swollen to almost twice it's normal size. He talked earnestly to her as she sat nodding dully. Finally he went to Beryl taking her by the hand, smiling and talking quietly beyond their hearing. Matron Jones slipped the girl's dress off, her slender body bare to her bloomers. Gerald felt Dave's vicelike grip on his arm tighten. The child's back from neck to waist was covered with angry red weals. Where they crossed the bony protuberance of her shoulder, blood had oozed, now dried to thin scabs. The doctor's voice raised in anger, was now audible to the watchers below. 'This must not go on Mrs. Moss. You and your daughter must not be subjected to this brutality. How long has this been going on?'

They could not hear her subdued answer. Matron helped the girl into her clothes again. She cried out as the cotton garment touched the raw flesh of her shoulders. Dave was crying. 'I'll kill the bastard-I will, I will, I swear I will!'

Gerald clamped his hand over his mate's mouth as Matron Jones glanced curiously down at the skirting board. 'For Chrissake shut up! It'll be all right, Dad'll fix it.'

Ben was speaking to Beryl's mother again. 'Will you wait outside Mrs. Moss? I must speak to Matron for a moment.' When they had gone, he looked at her. 'They can't go back there Ethel, he's dangerous. Contemptible little bastard, I'll never know why she married him.'

'Loneliness Ben. Can anything be done, I mean can he be restrained?'

'I don't know. I'll see Dave Truman tomorrow. He is a drunk you know, frankly I doubt if anything can be done to stop him.'

'He will end up killing them. He has certainly hurt the child.'

'Ethel, can you put them up for the night? Just until I can see what can be done, if anything.'

'Of course I can. Look, I'll see Frances about some tea for them. I'll be back to help you in a few minutes.'

Hastily making arrangements with Frances, Matron fended off her inquiring glance. 'Tell you about it later dear. I must hurry back.' She left by the back door, walking swiftly around the side of the house, arriving at the broken lattice just as Gerald's head emerged. Her strong fingers grasped his thick thatch yanking him to his feet. 'All right you little begger, who else is there?'

Dave slowly emerged, his tear streaked face faintly visible in the dim light from the sitting room window.

'Quickly now, anymore under there?'

Gerald's legs turned to jelly. He quavered, 'No Matron, only Dave and me. Honest, we didn't mean to hear.'

'Hear what?' She looked closely at Dave. 'Young Truman, what's the matter with you?'

'It's Beryl, Matron. Dave likes her, he's sorry for her.'

Ethel Jones was in a hurry, she quickly summed up the situation. 'I don't want to hear anymore, you have done a very wicked thing, both of you.' She gave Gerald a shake. 'I won't mention this to your father but let me tell you young man, if you ever do such a thing again, I will. He would skin you alive. And you, young Truman, if your father ever got to hear of this, you know what would happen to you.' She turned to go. 'You can stop your blubbering, Beryl and her mother are coming home with me tonight.'

Wordlessly the two boys made their way to the safety of the orchard.

'Never mind Dave, your Dad'll fix him, put him in jail, I bet.'

'I don't care, I'm going t'get him.' Tears welled in his eyes again. 'Beryl's done nothing, the rotten mongrel!'

'Cut it out mate, just wait and see what happens. He'll get his, sooner or later.' Gerald put an arm around his friend's shoulder. 'We'd better get goin' now. Remember, not a word to the others.'

'All right, see ya tomorrow. See what you can find out Gerry. I still feel sick thinkin' about it.'

'So do I, bloody terrible. We were damn lucky Dave, Matron coulda got us killed. She's real good, old Jonesy.'

Dave nodded. 'She's a beaut, she'll help Beryl.'

The next morning Ben found the sergeant in his office. The door closed, they discussed the situation.

'There is absolutely nothing I can do Ben. It has been going on since they were married. He beats her up regularly, Friday nights especially. That's when he gets a proper skinful.' Dave sighed, shaking his head. 'Had no idea he touched the girl. Is she all right?'

'Ethel took them both home with her last night. She called me at four this morning, the daughter is running a temperature. I've hospitalized her, could be pneumonia, she is certainly anaemic.'

Dave whistled softly. 'Bad as that? I'll have a word with him. Truth is, I can barely bring myself to talk to the man.'

'You are sure there is nothing you can charge him with?'

'Not a thing. A married woman has no rights really, he can damn near do what he likes, apart from murder.'

'It's bloody disgraceful!'

'I agree, and mind you, she is not the only one in this town on the receiving end.'

'I know, I see them. Such pitiful excuses, fell down the stairs, walked into a door. No doubt you have heard them all.' Ben rose to go.

'Thanks anyway Dave. I will keep you informed on the little girl.'

'I'd appreciate that. If it's any comfort, I'll send to Sydney to see if he is known to the police, never know what might turn up.'

Returning to the surgery, Ben was surprised to find Ethel supervising the carpenter they used for odd jobs, removing the skirting board.

'What's the trouble Ethel? Hello there Clem. What have we got, white ants?'

'Bit of shrinkage Doc, just this bit. Matron found a couple of cockroaches.'

'Good work Ethel, disgusting things.'

'I've asked Clem to fix a piece of lattice around the side of the house too, is that all right?'

'Certainly, it's our responsibility, we must keep the place in perfect condition.' He motioned her outside. 'I've seen Dave Truman, not much there. He is going to have a word with Moss.'

'What is to become of them, especially the child?'

'I don't know Ethel. If anything happens to the little girl, that would be different but from what Dave says, he would probably get off. Children have no rights apparently.'

'Ben, somehow that child has to be protected. Faith rang, her temperature hasn't changed.'

'I'll look in before lunch. How is the mother?'

'She is terrified. Really Ben, I don't know what to do-he might come looking for them.'

'Good God yes. Well, there is nothing more we can do. He might behave after Dave speaks to him. How long before Clem finishes? It's almost time for surgery.'

At school the friends huddled in earnest discussion. 'Don't say a word-Beryl's in hospital. Matron told me this morning. Take it easy Dave, Dad's looking after her.'

Dave, hands deep in his pockets, had turned away.

'Maybe the girls can find out how she is. Let's ask Dutchy and Judy to go up after school.'

'Better not mate. Wait 'til Matron says it's okay. Nobody's supposed to know but Dave and me.'

'Why don't we get him?'

'Get him, how d'ya mean, Hal?'

'Let's think about it, there must be a way. There's the bell, we'll talk down at the shop later.'

School over they gathered away from others crowding the counter.

'Thought of anything?'

Hal Wynter motioned them close to him. 'Listen, this might work. The mongrel needs a lesson he won't forget. He needs a flogging.'

'Yeah, how ya goin' t'do that? He's a nuggetty little bastard, anyway he'd know who did it.'

'What d'ya reckon Gerry?'

'Dunno, unless we trap him somehow.'

They moved off discussing how their plan could work.

'I heard Dad say, Friday nights he's worse, staggers home along the river by that little park.'

'If we could get a bag over his head, then hold him down.'

'How could we do that?'

'Dunno, must be some way.'

Jack Rayward stopped suddenly. 'I've got it! Make a net like a big butterfly net. You know, get some strong fencin' wire, make a loop, thread a chaff bag onto it and lash it to a pole.'

They all stopped. 'What a beauty, you're a bloody genius Jack!'

'Just a minute,' Hal cut in, 'chaff bag's no good, too thin. We'll need a corn bag.'

'Yer right Hal. What about tomorra, it's Saturday. You're right Gerry, we can work on it then.'

'Course I am. Where we gonna make it?'

'What about the old shed down by the wharves, the old fisho's shed? Nobody goes there anymore.'

'All right. I'll call for Dave, meet cha there after lunch. Got a few jobs t'do at home first. Can ya get the stuff, Hal?'

'No trouble. See ya all tomorrer.'

Dave and Gerald left, their friends walking in the opposite direction.'Don't take it so hard Dave, I told ya Dad's lookin' after her.'

'Can ya ask him?'

'I'll ask Matron, she'll know. See ya later, I've gotta practice the bloody piano.'

In the privacy of their bedroom, Ben related the events of the past few days. Frances shuddered. 'I've heard about it, most of the women know. It's awful, that poor woman and little Beryl. Will she be all right?'

Ben slipped a comforting arm around her. 'Take it easy darling. The next few days will tell. There is nothing to her, the poor little mite. Ethel has been talking to the mother, apparently this has been going on almost from the time they were married. He is a sadistic little swine-forced the child to stand in the corner for hours, twisted her hair and used his belt on her. Doesn't bear thinking about.' By the little night light he could see tears on her cheeks.

'Come on, no more Francie. Bad as this is, she is not the only child, or woman for that matter, mistreated in this town. Believe me, I see plenty of it. Yes, amongst our wouldbe town society too.'

'It's a rotten world isn't it?'

'It is darling, especially the part we try to hide.' He kissed her. 'Time we got some sleep my girl. We can't change things, do our best that's all.'

Progress on the corn bag net developed by trial and error. They cut the blade from an old oar and lashed the loop to the thicker end.

'We'll have to cut the sides of the bag about six inches then sew it to the wire with this bit of cord fishing line.'

'Gotta packin' needle?'

'Yeah, everything's right Gerry.'

'How's Beryl, you find out anything?'

'Not much. Matron said, about the same, can't tell yet. Dr. Coburn's up there now. I'll tell ya anything I find out.'

'Where'll we hide this?'

'Under the shed, nobody'll see it there. Ready for next Friday night. Hope the bastard comes home through the park as usual.'

'That little path through the trees'd be the best place. He cuts through there, I've watched 'im.'

'Beauty, not a soul about. What'll we do after we got him trapped?'

'Tie the bastard's hands, pull his duds down and get inta 'im with a lawyer cane. You can get some can't ya Gerry?'

'Yeah, goin' up to *Monaro* tomorrow, cut some outta the bush.'

'I'd like t'bash him with the bloody oar.'

'Cut it out Dave. We're just gonna beat shit outta him, not murder for Chrissake!'

'Okay it's finished.' Hal swished the device through the air. 'Not bad mates, not bad. Come on we'll hide it under the shed.'

Gerald warned them. 'Remember we've gotta be careful about this. He could have us up, so don't forget the old burnt cork and wear anything black y've got, we can't let him see us. Buddy will mind Carlo.'

Sunday morning at *Monaro*, Ben and Frances met the Wells family.

'We've met before Mr. Wells, this is my wife Frances and you must be Mrs. Wells.'

'I think we are just about ready for morning tea.' Frances took Mrs. Wells by the arm. 'We usually use the lower verandah, so shady and cool.'

John Wells stood critically viewing the house. 'I must say Doctor, I find this place remarkable. I know there are some grand homes in this country, but this place is unique. Such symmetry of line, such balance. The man who designed this, knew his business.'

Ben smiled. 'I'm no expert on architecture Mr. Wells but yes, I agree it is pleasant to the eye. My parents certainly thought so.'

'They obviously recognized a masterpiece.'

'You must look through before you go. How is the school coming along, by the way?'

'Right on schedule Doctor, ready for the new year.'

'Any plans for the future here?'

'Well, of course money is tight but I believe funds are available for a new Municipal Library. I have quoted and I believe my figure has been favourably received.'

'I certainly hope so. Ah there, I see Frances waving. Time for morning tea.'

Conversation flowed smoothly, Frances warmed to Emily Wells. They were on christian name terms by the time the men arrived.

'Your place is so lovely Doctor, so restful. Did you plan the gardens?'

'I leave the gardening to my wife. I'm afraid I haven't much talent in that direction Mrs. Wells. Of course, much of the landscaping was done by the original owners.'

Further talk was interrupted by the arrival of the children, Judy trailing slightly behind stopping every few yards to pick flowers from the borders that graced the driveway. She pushed Harry before her, placing each new bloom in his hands, Frances introduced them. Shy and reserved, typical of children, they muttered acknowledgments, then sat silently eating, eyes averted.

Gareth, who normally showed little interest in girls, surreptitiously lifted his head to gaze at Enid. She was tall for her age, slender, blue eyed with two thick blonde plaits tied with blue ribbon, hanging to her waist. She coloured slightly when she met his gaze.

'Would you like to see round Enid?' Judy took the girl's hand. 'We'll take Harry with us, he loves to come.'

Enid eagerly accepted, glad to escape the company of grown ups, Frances was surprised to see her eldest son join the girls.

'Mind if I come with you? I know all the best places.'

Frances watched Enid look up through her long lashes, a little smile on her face. She sighed, her son was growing up.

The younger girls were content to stay chasing each other across the lawn.

Gerald approached his father. 'Mind if I go into the bush Dad? Promised Miss Halsey I'd look for some orchids for her.'

Ben nodded. 'Be careful, take a good stick with you and watch out for snakes.'

Safely out of sight, Gerald found a long, well formed lawyer vine threaded amongst the great trees. Using his sharp fishing knife, he carefully measured and cut six canes, each about three feet long.

The week seemed to drag. Each day the little band of conspirators went over their plans, checking every detail.'Surprise, that's the main thing. Do we need gloves?'

'Forget it. We haven't got any anyway. What about rope to tie his hands?'

George got some greenhide strips.'He won't get outa them in a hurry.'

'Jeez, it gives ya the wind up just thinkin about it.'

'Yeah but we agreed-anybody wanta get out of it?'

'Not on yer life, it's scary but sure excitin'!'

The battered woman stayed in hiding with Ethel Jones. Beryl's condition remained unchanged. She was moved into Matron Truman's private room where Friar's Balsam fumed over a small spirit stove. The doctors discussed her case in low tones. 'Dr. Coburn, what do you think?'

The old man shook his head. 'If she showed a spark, I would feel better. Pulse is weak. Gentlemen, I don't know. I have seen cases like this, sometimes one is surprised. The prognosis is not good, I'm afraid.'

Moss, who had sulkily accepted his wife's absence for a few days, came home one night much the worse for strong liquor. Frustrated, he broke the front windows of the house, smashed any crockery he could lay his hands on, before falling into a drunken sleep.

Ben told his wife. 'Thank God she wasn't there. Dave tells me there is still nothing he can do.'

'But it's her house, her husband left it in her name. Pieter told me.'

'Well my dear, that's the position, unfortunately. You know the strange thing is, he goes on these dreadful benders but he is always at work on time, deferential as usual. The men dislike him, drinks alone at the pub, so I'm told.'

'Have you been to see her? Beryl's mother I mean. I can't bring myself to call her, Mrs. Moss.'

'You must not become too involved old girl, but yes, she is improving. Ethel takes her up to the hospital so she can sit with Beryl.' He sat down with a groan. 'Damned if I know, even old Tom Coburn doesn't know what to do, apart from what we are doing already. Let's have some tea, I'm beat.'

Frances waited until he sat back relaxed, filling his pipe. 'Will she have to go back to him, Ben? Doesn't she have any right to protection?' He shook his head. 'Not according to Dave. Pieter says the same. Domestic violence is something in which no one wants to become involved.'

'It's cruel, it's wicked women should be treated like that.'

'I know, I know.' He took her hand. 'Perhaps if women made enough fuss, something would be done. What is needed,' he smiled at his wife, 'is for women to stand for Parliament.'

'Do you think we could?'

'With women like you and Muriel and Ethel, plus others I could name, I am positive.'

Friday morning it rained, soft warm rain. The branches of the trees hung low, heavy with moisture. After lunch it stopped, leaving the sky overcast with promise of more to come.

'All my friends are going to the pictures tonight Mum, there's a great 'Tom Mix' on, can I go?'

'Yes, but see you come straight home and take your raincoat.'

Gerald ran all the way to Ethel Jones' house, catching her before she set out for the surgery. She loved all the children and Gerald, in his cocky way, appealed to her. 'I'm sorry dear, there is no change. Don't worry, I'll let you know. Tell your friend, young Truman, your father is doing everything he can to help her.'

'Thanks Matron, Dave is real upset, I'll tell him.'

By the light of a candle in the old shack, they made their final plans. 'The ground's wet, when he comes through the trees he won't hear a thing.'

'What time is it now?'

'About twenty past six, the pub's closed but he gets a bottle of wine I've watched him, he comes through the park about half past six.'

'Well let's get a move on. Who's got the net?'

'Hal, he's the strongest.'

'I've got the greenhide. Hurry with the burnt cork, we don't want t'miss him. You got the lawyer cane, Gerry?'

'You bet. It's in the bushes. Come on. let's get goin', we'll be there a few seconds before him.'

Secreted in the dense thicket of trees, they stood waiting, straining their ears for the sound of approaching footsteps.

'He's coming!' Dave's voice came in a hoarse whisper. 'Listen to the pig, he's cursing and swearing.'

Shortly the swaying figure of Moss appeared on the path through the trees. Stepping silently behind him, Hal brought the corn bag net heavily over the man's head and shoulders. With a muffled howl of terror, he fell to the ground, the wine bottle flying from his hand. With a bound Dave landed on his back, twisting Moss' arms behind and rapidly tying them together with the greenhide strips. Quickly his pants were pulled down to his boots, his fat white buttocks visible in the dim light.

He began to plead. 'Don't hurt me, ya can have me money, don't hurt me. I'll give ya more come payday. I swear!'

Jack and George held his legs while Dave and Gerald fished out the lawyer canes from where they had lay hidden all week. They set to with a will, the flexible canes made a cracking noise as they flailed the quivering flesh. As the first strike landed, a shriek came from the corn bag. The victim writhed, arching his body in a vain attempt to escape the searing pain. Dave was beside himself, he flogged until, even in the darkness, they could see the great welts, raised and purple, some beginning to bleed.'This is for Beryl, you bastard!' Dave raised both his arms.

Gerald, with sanity returning, grabbed his arm. 'Enough,' he hissed, 'untie his arms, let's get out of here!'

The shrieks from the bag had given way to moaning sobs. 'Yer killin' me! No more please, no more. I'm dying, I tell ya. Oh God, I'm dying'.'

They left him, heading for the river. 'The bag, get the bloody bag!'

'Jesus! Hang on.' Dave ran back to where Moss was writhing and tugged at the bag over his head. With a quick jerk the boy pulled the bag with it's heavy handle clear. Resisting the temptation to kick his victim, he rejoined the others. 'Quick, let's throw this in the river, the tide'll take it out. What about the canes Gerry?'

'Gottem, they can go in the drink too. Hurry up, we'll have to clean up and get to the pictures. Cripes, what a night! That should fix the mongrel.'

For the first time, they laughed. 'Squealed like a bloody pig!'

'That's because he is one. Come on get a move on.'

It was Tuesday before Ben received a visit from the Police Sergeant.

'Hear you had a late call Friday night.'

'Friday night?' Ben smiled. 'Oh, you must mean our Mr. Moss. Actually I got the call from Faith at the hospital. Terrible business, set upon by half a dozen big men, thugs, he called them.'

Dave Truman tried to keep a straight face. 'Yes, I knew nothing about it until Faith told me.'

'Mmm, whoever attacked him did a good job. To tell the truth Dave, I've never seen anything like his backside.'

'Good heavens, poor devil. He must have suffered.'

'Yes, my heart bleeds. Anyway, I patched him up, gave him a tetnus shot and let him go. I'm afraid he will be sore and sorry for quite a while.'

Dave pulled a piece of message pad from his pocket. 'This came over the wire this morning, wait until you hear it - wanted for bigamy both in NSW and Victoria. Marries a woman, takes her for all she's worth then shoots through. Record for violence too, against the weaker sex of course but has never been charged.'

'I'll be damned! That explains what he is doing up here, out of sight out of mind. You going to charge him?'

'Too late. He was seen getting on the milk train Sunday night. I've wired ahead. He will be making for Sydney for sure. He doesn't know but there will be a reception committee waiting for him down there.'

'Marvellous! That poor woman can breathe easy again, get back to her house.'

'He's done a fair bit of damage there, broken windows etc.'

'So I hear. I'll get Clem to fix things up, poor thing she needs all the help she can get.'

'How is the little girl?'

'I think her chances are reasonable. Faith is getting some food into her now. Her mother never leaves her side. I will say, I am cautiously optimistic.'

'I'm very glad to hear it Ben, believe me. The wife goes up there but there is nothing she can do.'

'It's the thought that counts old friend.'

They stood looking at each other, a slight smile hovering round their lips. 'Any clues, I mean, any idea who was reponsible?'

'Matter of fact, I have. No actual clues, you understand but a strong suspicion, a very strong suspicion.'

Ben smiled, shaking his head. 'Couldn't have been the same gang who assaulted Mr. Henry with the pineapple, surely?'

'Funny you should say that, yes it did cross my mind. You know, they still think we don't know about that, the little buggers.'

'Mr. Henry would never let on he recognized them. He's a grand old fellow.'

'Of course he wouldn't. If that woman whose fence they sat by, hadn't heard them talking, we would probably never have found out.'

'Yes, Cummings escaped a severe shock to his system that night.'

They began to laugh. 'Undeserved though Ben. He's a strict believer in discipline, which they never take kindly to.'

'You're right. The trouble is, he is a bit quick with the cane but a first class teacher. They might not know it now but they are lucky to have a man like that.'

'Well, Dave will be off to school in the new year, thanks to the wife's people. Any plans for Gerald?'

'Not at the moment, I'm still thinking about it. Trouble is Dave, the boys are becoming pretty wild, don't you think? A bit out of hand.'

'Too wild for their own good. I'll be glad to see Dave off to college. He's walking round very scared at the moment, I'll talk to him later on but for now I'll let him stew.' He stood to go. 'Faith tells me he is up there every afternoon with flowers and God knows what else. Rather touching in a way.'

'So I have heard. He's a fine lad. Perhaps it would be wise not to say anything for now. They are all scared out of their wits and we don't want heroes. They need their backsides tanned I'll admit, but somehow I admire them.'

Beryl continued to improve. On warm days she was moved to the sunny open verandah then wheeled back into her own room in the late afternoon. She was allowed visitors for short periods. Dorothy with Judy and other close friends came and sat gossiping until Matron shooed them out as her young patient showed fatigue. Her mother, never far away, sat knitting. The bruises on her face gradually faded. She wept when Dave Truman told her of the man she thought she had married. 'I was lonely, Sergeant, it was a terrible mistake. Are you sure I am free of him?'

'You are dear lady and as soon as Beryl is well enough, you may go home.'

'I will be so glad. I can't wait to tend my garden again. You have all been so kind. 'Tears rolled down her cheeks. 'I don't know what possessed me to marry him.'

'There, there, it's all over now. As you said, you were lonely and he came along, that's all. We all make mistakes. In any case, he was never your legal husband.'

The day came for Beryl to leave the hospital. Ben drove them to the house by the river. The grass was cut, the garden neat and tidy. Mrs. Carrol stared in amazement. 'It looks so lovely, who did this?'

'I think you can thank Sergeant Truman's son and his friends, Mrs. Carrol.'

Her face glowed at the sound of her old name. 'Will you come in for some tea Doctor? Oh dear, I don't think there will be anything in the house.'

Ben smiled at her.'I don't think you will have any difficulties there the ladies of the committee have tidied up and stocked your pantry. Now keep Beryl in bed today, she can get up tomorrow for a few hours. She must keep taking nourishing food, remember, I want some weight on those bones.' He took the girl's hand. 'I know you want to know how long before you can go back to school. We will see, perhaps a week. I'll call tomorrow. Now I must be off.' He glanced back as he turned the corner, mother and daughter were entering the house, hand in hand.

In the comfort of their bedroom, Ben and Frances lay talking quietly.

'So they are back home. I'm so relieved Ben. That poor woman, and Beryl, is she all right?'

'It will take a little time. The physical scars have healed but God knows how it will affect her.'

'I heard he is a bigamist and some men beat him half to death. Is that true?'

'He is a bigamist all right, I don't know much about the other business. He is gone now and she is free again.'

'How will she manage?'

'She gets a few shillings War Widows Pension and Faith has kept her job at the hospital open. The way things are she is lucky to have that.'

For a moment Frances was quiet, recent events turning over in her mind.

'Ben, what do you think of the Wells?'

'Nice family, I liked them.' He chuckled.'Isn't it funny, people tell things to doctors they would never dream of telling anyone else.'

'What do you mean?'

'He told me his life story. He was a brickie, a good one apparently. Anyway, she was a school teacher, with plenty of ambition. They decided to try their hand at building. She does all the calculations, all the costing and tendering. It has worked out very well, he says. They put in for the high school here because things were at a standstill in Sydney. Looks like they will get the library too. He says it's only a small job but they are enjoying the country.'

'Emily is very nice, I like her and Ben, aren't the girls lovely?'

'Only saw them briefly but they seem nice children.'

'Gareth is quite smitten with Enid, the eldest.'

'Rubbish! How do you know? Gareth hardly notices girls, not like his younger brother.'

'Women notice these things, especially mothers.'

'God preserve us, what next?'

'He wants me to ask Enid's mother if she can go riding with him.'

'You going to ask her?'

'Yes I think so. Apparently she has had riding lessons.'

'Well, if you and her mother agree, I suppose it's safe enough. One thing about Gareth, he is responsible.'

'Judy and Peter are going with them, they can both ride.'

'I'll bet they can. Francie, I've been wanting to talk to you about those two. It's odd, even though we have legally adopted them, Peter never calls me anything but Doctor or Sir. He seems happy, seems to have entered into the family. Why I wonder?'

'Perhaps he is still shy, not sure of himself.'

'I suppose, what about Judy?'

'Oh Mum slips out every now and then. I love her dearly Ben, and to see her with Harry, it's wonderful.'

'Do you think Peter might call me 'Uncle', maybe he would be more comfortable with that.'

'Why not speak to him? Tell him how you feel about it.'

'I have spoken to him, not about that but trying to find out more about their background. Without pressing too hard of course. But apart from the travelling from station to station, little else. According to the marriage certificate, their parents were married in Sale, Victoria. Dave has made pretty wide inquiries but nothing has turned up. Damn strange in a way. The certificate lists him as a shearer and her, a school teacher. Funny that, school teachers seem to marry men their intellectual inferiors. Anyway, that explains how the children are advanced for their age.'

'What if someone turned up one day, grandparents, aunts or uncles and claimed them?'

'I wouldn't worry old girl. In any case it would be the children's choice.'

Frances snuggled close to him. 'I wonder if other couples talk in bed like we do?'

'God knows, they've probably got more sense and go to sleep.'

'Christine is coming home for Christmas.'

'That's nice,' he mumbled, his eyes closing. 'Ethel will be happy.'

'They are going to announce their engagement, Dave and Christine.'

'What!' He was suddenly awake. 'Nobody told me. The next thing, he'll be off to Sydney to some fancy practice.'

'No darling, Christine loves it here and Dave would never leave. Ethel told me.'

He grumbled. 'Why the hell don't I know these things? I'm always the last to know.'

She comforted him. 'It's confidential for now, Ethel told me not to say anything until the announcement.'

'You told me.'

'You are my husband, darling.'

He settled down, punching his pillow. 'Goodnight Francie, I'm sure I am going to have nightmares.'

At breakfast, Ben regarded his wife through the steam of his teacup. 'Did I dream it or did you tell me last night that Dave and Christine are engaged or intending?'

'No dear, you did not dream it, it's true.'

'And when may we expect this momentous announcement?'

'Don't be sarcastic Ben.'

'I'm not. Francie, I'm delighted for them, really I am. It's just that I am thinking Dave may look for greener pastures now. There is not much money coming into the practice these days.'

'I'm sorry darling. Those patients Dave sees pay surely?'

'They do, thank heaven. The well to do matrons of the town naturally prefer a good looking, personable young feller like Dave to a cantankerous old cuss like me.' He grinned at her. 'Like Tom Coburn, I'm left with the hoi polloi, you know the ones who pay when they can or swear they will when things look up.'

Frances put her arm around his shoulders. 'Even if I was young again Ben Wakefield, I've never seen anyone I would change you for.'

He kissed her lightly. 'Dear loving Francie, what a woman you are.'

Matron Jones, starched and professional, was busy preparing for the first patient. Ben sat at his desk idly fingering through the history cards. 'How does it look, Ethel?'

'Busy, the waiting room is almost full. I've had to put out more chairs!'

He sighed, resting his chin on his hand. 'If only they knew how little I can do for them.'

'They like you and trust you, that is half the battle.'

'I'll see the baby with croup first.' He looked at his watch. 'Let's not rush, we've got five minutes yet.'

'That little boy bitten by the death adder, died'

'Tom Coburn told me. Took out six inches of vein. Pointless really. Bloody disgraceful Ethel, an eight year old boy rounding up cows for the dairy at four thirty in the morning. Got down off his horse and stepped right onto it.'

'All those dairy farms are the same. The children work almost as soon as they can walk.'

'I know and they barely scrape out a living.'

'It's a wretched business. Muriel tells me some of the young ones from outlying farms come to school fast asleep on their ponies.'

'That's why they leave the farm as soon as they are old enough. And the girls marry the first fellow that asks them.'

'I think I had better bring the first one in. The baby with croup I think you said?'

At school, Gerald and his mates were untypically well behaved. Charles Cummings thought his efforts were bearing fruit at last. He had little cause for complaint, behaviour was acceptable, homework faithfully presented. Unknown to him, there lingered a nagging unease in the minds of the band of conspirators that the truth regarding the assault on Moss might come out.

'The old man looks at me sometimes and says he hopes I am behaving myself.'

'Did yer old man talk to him Dave?'

'No I don't think so, he shot through. But Gerry's dad saw him, didn't he Gerry?'

'Buggered if I know, he hasn't said anything.'

'Let's forget it. You seen Beryl, Dave?'

'Only said hello, Dutchy and Judy were there. When she comin' back t'school?'

'Next week if Gerry's old man says so. Gee, she looked pretty, the girls were doin' her hair.'

'Hey, you seen the new girl yet? Enid Wells, you know, her old man is building the high school.'

'Yeah, not a bad sort, she gets around with Dutchy and Judy.'

'She was with Gareth the other day.'

'Yeah, old Gareth must be feelin' his dick. I thought he was only interested in football.'

They hooted with mirth. 'Shh, quiet for Chrissake! Cupie's over there, he'll wanta know what it's all about. Come on, the bloody bell's due any minute. See ya at Harrys' later.'

Ben called on his old friend Pieter DeVries, recently returned from a visit to the southern cities.

'I don't want to be an alarmist but I suggest you keep some cash on hand Ben.'

'What do you mean, the banks are sound aren't they?'

'Your bank is, but one can't be too careful.'

'Surely things aren't that bad?'

'Bad enough and getting worse from what I can see.'

'You saw your brother?'

'Oh yes, he and his wife or chatelaine, I didn't enquire which, are still living in the old mansion.'

'How did it look?'

'As usual, nothing has changed. I'd say it looks the same as you last saw it.'

'Well he has to keep his end of the arrangement.'

'And why not? It is very much to his advantage. With that address and his money, they are quite the social lions these days.'

Ben smiled. 'Good for him. What about the other properties?'

'You couldn't give them away Ben. Half are empty and rents for the others hardly meet expenses.'

'Nevertheless, I intend to hang on to them.'

'I think you are wise, this depression can't last forever. There is nothing being built in the city and you can well afford to hang on.'

Ben nodded. 'So I noticed when I went down to Sydney.'

'How is Frank?'

'Fine he's very much into politics these days. I am going to try to persuade him to stay up here after he and Muriel are married.'

'Best place on earth. I've never regretted leaving the city. Did you see Sean by the way?'

'Matter of fact, I did. Same old Sean, he is a remarkable man. A true Christian, if there is such a thing.'

'Dan's not the same mould.'

'No. Dan was never meant for the priesthood. I often wonder whether he will stay.'

'Has no option, has he?'

'No, but you know Dan.'

'Yes, it has crossed my mind several times. Confidentially, the old lady left quite a fortune. Either because of good luck or shrewd judgement, she sold everything long before the rot set in. She never left the old shop, wealth meant nothing to her.'

'It was not sold with the rest?'

'Oh yes, she sold it all right, then rented it back.' Pieter smiled. 'I told you she was a shrewd business woman.'

'I take it you were chosen executor?'

'Yes. After the usual costs, the money was equally divided. I've advised Ellen not to do anything yet. Probably invest in land once we see how things turn out.'

'I wonder what Sean and Dan will do with theirs.'

'God knows.'

'Well, I have calls to make.'

'Before you go.' Pieter tapped a folder on his desk. 'As your lawyer Ben, you know I have your interests at heart. Look I know you hate to be bothered with figures, but your practice is being run as a charitable institution!'

'Times are hard Pieter, I know most of my patients. Don't worry, they will settle when they can.'

'Hmm, I hope so. There wouldn't be many places where such a charity was available.'

'But it's not a charity old friend, it's my duty, and I enjoy helping them if I can. In any case, Dave's patients pay, which satisfies him and pays Ethel's salary.'

The lawyer closed the folder with a sigh. 'I know I waste my breath talking to you about these matters.' He rose, clasping his friends shoulder. 'I should know better but thank heaven for Ben Wakefield's of this world.'

CHAPTER XXI

Entering through his front gate, Ben came face to face with the second eldest. 'Where are you off to in such a hurry, young man?'

'Down to Stanley's place Dad, to see Mr. Stanley's new car.'

Edward Stanley was publisher and editor of the *'Myuna Daily'* which was delivered to the house every morning. A well spoken educated man, he had visited Ben privately complaining of persistent indigestion. After a careful examination, Ben folded his stethoscope then, 'please put your shirt and coat on Mr. Stanley.' He motioned to the chair opposite, 'sit down when you are ready.'

The man's usual composure was shaken. 'What is it Doctor?

'I won't go into the technical details Mr. Stanley - you have a certain heart condition which must be carefully watched.'

'Heart!' He was white around the lips. 'Good God Doctor, I'm only forty-two, are you certain?'

'The symptoms are unmistakable Mr. Stanley. Of course you are entitled to a second opinion. Perhaps a specialist in Sydney?'

'No, no Dr. Wakefield, I trust your opinion implicitly. What am I to do?' He laughed nervously. 'I have a wife and two children as you know and I have just ordered a new car. If only I had known.'

'Mr. Stanley,' Ben spoke firmly. 'Follow my instructions and I am certain you will have many more years ahead of you. Smoking is definitely out. You must lose some weight and exercise is essential. I mean gentle exercise, I suggest you walk to your office every day.'

Edward Stanley stood up. 'Is that all doctor, just give up smoking and do some walking?'

'For the moment Mr. Stanley. I want to see you in a fortnight. We will see how things are then.'

Later Ben confided to Frances. 'You know I don't usually talk about patients but I know you like his wife.'

'Sarah is one of my dearest friends. Is it serious?'

'Serious enough, he could go on for years or drop dead tomorrow.'

'That's terrible! Isn't there anything to be done?'

'Francie you have been a doctor's wife long enough to know there is nothing, apart from what I have advised him. We don't know a damn thing more than we did during the war. A compound fracture is still a death sentence unless we amputate. A simple surgical procedure can turn to septicaemia. Women come to me in tears with gynaecological problems for which there is no simple treatment. No, nothing has changed, it may in Gareth's time, I doubt it will in mine.'

'It all sounds so depressing.'

He put a comforting arm around her. 'Don't worry about it old girl, shouldn't have mentioned it.'

'I'm glad you did. Sarah is the only one who knows all the infighting that goes on in the Committee. She told me what these women are saying about Dan.'

'About Dan, what about Dan?'

'Darling, surely you know about Dan and that pretty little widow Mrs. Murray?'

For a moment he was stunned into silence. 'Mrs. Murray? Of course I know her, she is one of Dave's patients. How the hell do these mischief making biddies know anyway?'

'He leaves his clothes there. They have seen his pyjamas on the line.'

'Oh my God, how could he be so careless?'

'They are outraged. They've written to the Bishop.'

'I'll bet they have. I must have a word with Dan, warn him, put him on his guard. But how to do it, I'm not sure.'

'He probably knows.'

'Probably. I'll see if I can get him to come up to *Monaro* on Saturday.'

The Stanley's new car was the talk of the town. The big Silver Anniversary Buick, blue with black mudguards. Mrs. Stanley drove, Mr. Stanley walked.

Gerald and his friends ran an approving eye over the handsome vehicle.

'Terrific car Gerry! When's your old man gonna get a new one?'

'Buggered if I know. He says there's a 'recession' on and we shouldn't waste money. Anyway, what's a 'recession', you know Hal?'

'Dunno for sure but my mother says I can only have sixpence a week now.'

'Jeez, things are crook. If things get too bad we can always touch Buddy fer a coupla bob, can't we Gerry?'

'Yeah, try and get past Judy though, she watches him like a hawk.'

'Forget it. Let's run down t'the shop before the girls get there, they're always on the bite for a free drink.'

The invitation for the priest to visit *Monaro* proved unnecessary. After a late surgery, Ben answered a discreet knock at his front door. Dan stood in the dim light, smiling. 'I come as a thief in the night.'

'You come as a welcome stranger, you will-o-the-wisp. Come in, come in, I need an excuse to open a bottle of Malt.'

They sat comfortably facing one another. 'To what do I owe this unexpected but most welcome visit? Before you say anything, try this.'

Dan leaned back, savouring the golden fluid. 'You always did keep the best.'

'Thanks to the captain.'

'Ah yes, of course, the captain.' He raised his glass. 'To you, Captain Slocum, wherever you are.'

Ben chuckled. 'He must have been a remarkable character.'

For a few minutes they sat in silence, then, 'You have heard the gossip no doubt?'

'Only very recently. What is the situation?'

'They will shift me, there will be the usual appearance before my superiors.'

'What are you going to do, I mean, what can they do?'

'Make life very uncomfortable for me I imagine. But I'll be damned if I will let it come to that.' He held out his glass. 'Thanks Ben, I need a little courage tonight.'

'You know you can rely on me for whatever help I can be.'

'Thanks old friend, there is nothing you or anyone else can do. The die is cast. Ben, I am in love with Jean Murray. She has given me the only love I have ever known. I am telling you because you are one of the few people on this earth I can trust.'

'I don't know what to say, Dan.'

'We are leaving, Ben. You know I am independent financially.'

'Where will you go?'

'Overseas, where nobody knows me. Europe, America, I'm not sure.'

'She has a young son, hasn't she?'

'Yes, a fine boy. He has been living with his grandparents these last six months. Happily too, for all concerned, thank God.'

'Well Dan, I can only wish you all the best. When will you go?'

'Soon.' He paced the floor, hands behind his back. 'I do want to ask a favour of you, Ben.'

'What is it?'

'Would you mind driving us to Lambruk next Friday night? The Brisbane train makes a brief stop there about midnight. I've booked a sleeper-assumed name.' A slight smile creased his face. 'I'll be in civvies of course.'

'Have you told Ellen?'

'Not yet but I will. She understands, always has.'

'And Sean?'

'No, but you know dear old Sean, he will forgive me.'

'Will it affect him in any way?'

'No, absolutely not. He is one of the chosen.'

Ben clasped his friends hand. 'Rely on me. I will pick you up about eleven. My heart goes with you Dan. I admire the courage of your convictions. Just a card now and then to let us know you are safe and well. That's the only promise I ask.'

Ben sat deep in thought after his friends departure- Religion, the perfect method devised by man to manipulate his fellows. Fear of the unknown. Thank God there are men like you Dan with the courage to follow their own star.

Later, swearing Frances to secrecy, he told her of Dan's visit.

'You mean Jean Murray?'

'Of course. Remember, if you hadn't told me what Mrs. Stanley told you - I would never have been prepared.'

'Oh Ben, everyone knows. Surely you must have guessed.'

'Sorry old girl, I had no idea.' He smiled wryly. 'You don't disapprove, do you?'

'No I don't, I'm glad. She must love him very much. It's so romantic, but it's frightening. Will he get into trouble?'

'I wouldn't think so, they will be long gone.'

'Will they marry?'

'No idea. Let's just wait and see, Dan promised he would keep in touch.'

'I hope they will be happy. They will be, don't you think darling?'

Ben laughed. 'I'm sure they will be.' He grew serious. 'Remember, not a word to anyone. If Ellen wants to talk about it, she will. Knowing her she will confide in you sooner or later.'

The Sydney Morning Herald always arrived a day late. The *Myuna Daily*, confined itself mainly to local news, interspersed with snippets which came over the telephone from Sydney. The contortions of the financial world, which grew more ominous daily, culminated in October, later referred to as Black Friday, when the overheated money market crashed. Like a giant tidal wave, the Wall Street collapse rolled around the world. Great institutions were wiped out. Bankruptcies became common events. Men who had so recently lived like feudal lords chose suicide rather than penury.

Ben sought out his friend and adviser. 'It's unbelievable Pieter. How could this happen?'

'Been coming for a long time. I hope you took my advice and put some ready cash aside.'

'I did. But surely to God, you don't mean to say the banks will be affected.'

'Some will I have no doubt. Time will tell, but I doubt your bank will be. I don't hold myself out as a financial genius Ben, but I would reckon it is rock solid.'

'Marvellous isn't it, I thought we were only in a recession, that we could manage, come out of it in time. Now this looks like a real depression. God help us.'

'The trouble is, we are tied to sterling. If the English bankers think we have been living beyond our means, they will impose their will, make no mistake.'

The solicitor's pessimism proved only too true. Public Servants salaries were cut twenty five percent, jobs became virtually non existent. Men walked out of their homes. At times the whole country seemed mobile, the swaggy became a familiar sight trudging from town to town. Myuna, mainly through the efforts of it's committee of dedicated women suffered little. Acting on orders against his nature and natural kindness, Dave Truman sent the transients on their way with scant ceremony.

'Bloody terrible Ben, there are more of them than ever. They beg me to let them stay, just a week or two but it's more than my job is worth. They get their food coupons, that's all. Hardly enough to get to the next town.'

Father McSweeney's sudden departure and the disappearance of the widow Murray became the talk of the town. At Committee meetings Frances assiduously fended any questions regarding the 'scandal', as it was referred to. 'I understand your husband was a friend.' That was as far as it went. Frances would smile, pretending not to hear, turning her attention to more serious problems under discussion. They knew better than to ask Ellen, who as the solicitor's wife was held in some awe. Dan was replaced by a priest of the old school, a tartar, loyal to his faith who would brook no nonsense.

With Christmas fast approaching, the Women's Committee became busier than ever. With Alice Coburn in the Chair, business proceeded smoothly.

The majority of Ben's patients no longer muttered the pretence of 'pay you when I can Doc.' Payment in kind was invariably left on the verandah. Bags of potatoes, pumpkin, vegetables and fruit of the district lay in heaps along the wall. This proved a godsend to the Committee and to the hospital which, starved of funds, received any contribution with gratitude.

One lunch time, Ben met his young colleague stepping out of his car.

'Sorry to hold you up Ben. Time for a word?'

Ben groaned inwardly, this was what he had anticipated. Dave was dissatisfied, why would a bright young man bury himself in a practice like this? He felt suddenly tired, burdened down with troubles. 'Certainly Dave, what is it?'

The young man beamed. 'Christine and I are engaged.' He grinned. 'You probably know already.'

Ben kept silent.

'The thing is Ben, we want to marry this Christmas. Sooner than we planned but we reckoned, why wait?'

'Christine is a lovely girl Dave. Congratulations.'

Dave took him by the arm. 'Ben, I have no right to ask and you will probably think it damn cheek,' he hesitated for a moment. 'Would it be possible for us to have our Reception at *Monaro?*' He went on quickly. 'I would pay all expenses, naturally.'

Ben felt weak, he leaned against the car door, laughing. 'Dave, God help us, of course *Monaro*. How could you think of anywhere else? Frances and I would have been offended. I don't know, but I'm willing to bet, the women have plans underway at the moment.'

'Thank you Ben. You have been very good to me, believe me I am more than grateful.'

'Dave before you go, I must ask you, do you intend to stay in Myuna? I mean after you marry?'

'Stay?' The young man looked at him with a grin. 'Wild horses couldn't drive me away!'

With a lightness of heart he hadn't felt for a while, Ben went off to lunch.

CHAPTER XXII

The patronage of Harries' shop dropped considerably as the depression bit deeper. The close knit little band pooled their finances. 'Just enough for a drink. Watch out for the girls, funny thing, I know they've always got some money, yet they expect us to pay.'

'How d'you know Gerry? I mean about the money.'

'Buddy told me, Judy tells him everything.'

'I don't mind buying Beryl a drink but the rest stand around with their tongues hanging out.'

'Me neither. I'd buy Dutchy one but it's every man for himself now. Come on, let's go before they get here.'

They walked away. 'Seen the new High School Gerry?'

'Yeah, looks all right, pity Dave won't be there.'

'Yeah, that's crook, won't be the same anymore.'

'Aw, he'll be home on holidays, won't cha Dave?'

'Not the same though. I don't wanta go but it's all arranged. My grandad is paying, he's the one with the money. Anyway we've got holidays coming up, plenty of time yet.'

'Yeah, might as well enjoy ourselves. Anyone gotta smoke?'

Gerald fished in his pocket. 'Got Mick t'get me a packet of Woodbines, taste like crap but better'n nothin', five fer thripence.'

'Don't light up here fer Chrissake, somebody might put us inta Cupie!'

They moved into the shelter of the park trees. Gerry casually lit his cigarette. 'I've got news fer you blokes, heard Mum talking t'Miss Halsey. Guess whose gonna be deputy head at the new school?'

They stood stock still, Hal fond his voice. 'Ya don't mean bloody Cupie?'

'That's what Miss Halsey said. The Headmaster and a coupla new teachers are comin' up from Sydney.'

Gloom settled over them. 'Shit! I thought we'd get rid of the little bugger.'

'Not on yer life, Cupie likes it here, he's goin' out with one of the ladies from the choir.'

'Wonder if Cupie ever flips the elastic in her bloomers.'

'Ya never know, bet he's well slung though, little blokes are, they reckon.' Gerald puffed on his Woodbine. 'Tell ya somethin' else too. Dr. Dave is gettin' married at Christmas to Jonesy's grand daughter, Christine.'

'Jeez, is he? Seen her a few times, a real good sort. Bet they don't have any kids, doctors know how, I bet.'

'They will unless he wears a pink overcoat like Uncle Frank.'

This brought howls of mirth. 'Jeez, we were lucky that day, remember? We thought he'd caught us, nearly filled me duds, we were gonners fer sure.'

'Yeah, too bloody close fer comfort. Anyway, Uncle Frank's gettin' married at Christmas too-should be good fer a quid, I reckon.'

'Bet lovely Miss Halsey can't wait.'

'Bet yer Uncle Frank can't either. Where they goin' fer their honeymoon Gerry?'

'Dunno, Sydney I suppose. Time we got goin'.'

They reached their usual point of separation. 'Mrs. Carrol said I could take Beryl to the pictures Saturday night. Gotta go cut the grass at the Station fer me pocket money. What about you Gerry?'

'Yeah, I'll take Dutchy. Mum gives me two bob if I do me practice. What about you other blokes?'

'Aw, you know the girls at school, y'can always find one t'go with, don't ya reckon, Jack?'

'Yeah, don't want anyone special, not yet anyway, costs too much.'

During the week, Ben had occasion to drive the carpenter up to *Monaro* for some small repairs. He was an exquisite workman, a ship's 'chippy' before he got his land legs. He liked working for 'Doc' who paid well and gave him pills to relieve his rheumatism.

'I'll get Mick to drive you back Clem, and pick you up in the mornings until you finish.'

Later Ben sought out Mick, busy at the never ending job of weeding the driveway. Months before he assured the three people who worked for him that their jobs were safe as long as they wanted them.

'How are you Mick?'

Mick rested on his hoe. 'Pretty good Doc. Leg's not bad, bit of a twinge now and then.'

'See that you do as I tell you, sit down and take the weight off it whenever it starts to pain.'

'Sure Doc, always do.'

Ben looked at him closely. 'Hmm, I wonder. How's the family?'

'Good Doc, all doin' well.'

'No more on the way?'

'Not on yer life, got enough to last a man a bloody lifetime.'

Ben smiled. 'Met the new priest yet?'

Mick carefully rubbed tobacco between his palms, took the paper from his lips and slowly rolled a cigarette. 'Yeah, I met him. Came up to the house, wanted to know why I wasn't coming to church, me and the kids and Bridget.'

'Wasn't your eldest, young Michael, an altar boy?'

'He was when Father Dan was here. He was a real man, that one. Anyway, one thing lead to another, said he heard I'd been goin' to old Mr. Emery, the chemist, said what I was doin' was a Mortal Sin, I would burn in Hell.'

Ben felt deep sympathy for this battler. 'I'm sorry Mick, I'm sure he didn't mean it.'

'He meant it all right Doc. I've met types like him before, turn ya off religion. Him talkin' about Hell after what we've seen.'

'What will happen now then, you going down to talk it over with him?'

'Not on your life. I pissed him off, told him off, told him if he ever showed up again I'd sool the dogs on him.'

'I don't know what to say Mick, I hope things turn out all right.'

'Don't worry Doc. I told him Michael ain't goin' down there anymore and the kids will go to the new high school.'

'I wish you all the best Mick. I think it's time I was on my way.' About to leave, he turned suddenly. 'By the way, I passed your house the other day, looks very nice. Painted and a new fence, you've been busy.'

'Me and the boys and the Missus, I own 'er now, thanks to you.'

'Thanks to me, how do you mean?'

'This steady job helped me pay it off. It was a crown lease, you know. The old man took it out years ago. Permissive Occupancy, I think they call it. Three hundred acres there, a hundred and ten pounds was the price. Bridget and me. Well we scrimped and saved and now it's ours. Mr. DeVries did the paper work for me.'

Ben warmly shook his hand. 'Congratulations Mick, you deserve everything you've got.'

Mick stood watching as the car disappeared down the drive. 'Yeah, and without you Doc, I'd have bugger all.' He rolled another smoke.

'Look at this Francie, a letter from Caves Motors in Brisbane and look, a picture of the new Cadillac. Handsome looking vehicle, very handsome indeed. What do you think?'

She smiled. 'If I know you, Ben Wakefield, you made up your mind the minute you saw the picture.'

They sat at the breakfast table, late today as Dr. Coburn had insisted on taking morning surgery twice weekly now. 'Damned if I know how he does it. God, he must be old. I wouldn't dare ask his age, but he delivered me, you know.'

'Your mother told me the minister's wife and the housekeeper, Emma Wardrop, did. He came after the creek went down.'

'Well, he's ageless, so is his wife-wonder what the secret is.'

'Alice is much younger than he is.'

'I suppose that might have something to do with it. Anyway, I thought we were talking about motor cars.'

'You would have to go to Brisbane to pick it up, wouldn't you?'

'That's no trouble, the service cars run every day. Leave here at six, be in Brisbane early afternoon.'

'You could take Harry with you. He needs a new boot and splint for his bad leg. Judy has him standing now.'

'I hadn't thought of that. I'll ring Caves right away, there are only two in stock apparently.' He smiled as Frances poured more coffee. 'That girl has been a godsend, Harry worships her. Talk about a little mother, I've never seen anything like it.'

'He is growing too, have you noticed?'

He put his hand over hers. 'Francie, he won't grow very much, you know that don't you? Maybe four foot ten, five foot at the most. He will never walk unaided.'

'I don't care, we still have him, that's what matters.'

'You are right old girl. I suppose we are blessed in a way, everybody loves him.' A shadow crossed his face. 'Yes everybody loves him. Christ, life is unjust, he would have been a big man you know.' He stopped suddenly, she was looking at him, tears in her eyes. He took her hands. 'Oh my dear, I know, fool that I am, I swear I'll never mention it again.' He knew what she was thinking. Remembering the baby she still grieved for, little Ronnie. 'Come on, let's not dwell on the past, come and walk in the garden.'

His arm around her waist, they walked amongst the well-tendered flower beds to the shade of a spreading Lilli Pilli, it's red fruit carpeting the ground. Here on an old garden bench they sat close together. 'I'll miss it in a way, I guess we all will. I'm glad Tom and Alice are coming back here, glad for their sakes.' He stopped, realising there were too many ghosts, too many memories here to talk further. They sat silent, each lost in their own thoughts.

Frances spoke, without looking at him. 'Have you spoken to Peter and Judy? You said you would.'

'Yes, but somehow I think I should have left it to you. You know how to handle these things better than I do.'

'Everything is all right, isn't it?'

'Oh yes, Peter agreed it might be better to call me Uncle but dammit, he still calls me Doctor! Why do you think?'

'He is very sensitive, I don't think we will ever know what they have been through.'

'Do you think they are happy with us?'

'Trust a woman's intuition darling, I know they are.'

'I told Peter, or Punch as the kids call him, he could go to the Grammar School with Gareth. Wouldn't hear of it. Judy the same. I asked her if she would like to go to the Presbyterian Ladies College with young Dorothy.' He shook his head. 'I thought she was going to cry. No, she wants to stay here. How do you explain that?'

'I think they feel safe with us. I don't think Judy would leave Harry, she is devoted to him.'

He stood, pulling her to her feet. 'I could sit here all morning my dear.' He glanced at his watch. 'I was due at the hospital twenty minutes ago.' He kissed her. 'Please be happy for me Francie, without you I would be a lost soul.'

December came in hot and dry. The ladies Committee became a hive of activity. The big cooking range at *Monaro* was put to full use cooking Christmas puddings and cakes. 'So many have helped Ben, we have been promised vegetables and meat. Did you know Mick is donating a pig and he said his watermelons will be ready too.'

'Good old Mick, he would give you his coat.'

'Trouble is dear, we are short of money, people just don't have it.'

'What do you need money for?'

'The children, we must have some little present for them. There are so many families out of work, they just can't manage.'

'Will this help?' He opened his wallet and counted out twenty five pounds.

'Oh Ben, that will be such a help.' She looked at him curiously. 'You don't usually carry that much with you, where did it come from?'

He grinned. 'Promise you won't lecture me on the evils of gambling.'

'Gambling? I've never known you to gamble on anything. Surely there is no gambling in Myuna?'

'You might be surprised. The point is-I have had this in my wallet since November.'

'For heavens sake, Ben Wakefield, stop being mysterious!'

'You've heard of the Melbourne Cup? You must have, having come from Victoria.'

She answered tartly. 'Of course I have. Dad always went, he took me once-when I was a little girl, that is.' She added hastily.

'Thank heavens.' He teased. 'If you had been older you might have gambled the farm away.'

She pushed him into a chair. 'Now will you be serious?'

'I will, truly, if you will pour me some of that cold lemonade.'

She set the jug between them. 'Tell me all!'

'Ah. just what I needed. Well, Francie my love, the truth, the whole truth, in fact nothing but the truth. It all started with Pieter. I should say with James, I suppose. He is quite the racing man in Melbourne, I believe. He rang Pieter and said he had a sure thing for the Cup, a horse called Nightmarch. Apparently he is in the know and a pretty good judge of horseflesh. The upshot was, Pieter told me, James got the best price for us and we won. So there you are, twenty five quid, coin of the realm.'

'Well, if you put it like that, I suppose it's all right. Thank heaven we don't have racing in Myuna.'

'Don't forget the so called Picnic Races, and they have regular races at Lambruk.'

'But surely people can't afford to bet money now, it would be wicked.'

'My dear, Mick tells me there is a regular S.P. bookmaker at the Star Hotel. Men can't afford to feed their families will put their last sixpence on a horse. According to James, Melbourne went crazy for the big day. I suppose the bookies made their usual killing.'

'No doubt people lost all their money.'

'Most of them do, you can't beat the books. I've seen men, fellows I thought had more sense, pouring over form guides, never suspecting that most mid week races are lost or won before the horses leave the barrier.'

'I can't believe it.'

'You might as well my dear, because it's the truth. They call it the Sport of Kings, what a joke. My old grandfather was right when he said, booze and horse racing are the curse of this country.' He drained his glass. 'Duty calls, I must be off.' He smiled as he kissed her goodbye. 'Your husband is no gambler old girl but I won't promise I won't have a bet next Cup day-especially if James gives us the good oil.'

'The good oil - what's that?'

'Oh you wouldn't understand old girl, a promising horse named Phar Lap.'

A week before School broke up for the Christmas holidays, Ben made his trip to Brisbane. Judy shyly approached him - would it be all right if she came too, to keep Harry company? He told Frances. 'How could I refuse her? There is plenty of room in the service car.'

Three days later he proudly drove his new car home to Myuna. 'It's a beautiful machine Francie, a joy to drive. Has new type of gearbox, synchronised gears, the agent said,' he grinned delightedly. 'Even you could drive it without clashing gears!'

For a week the new Cadillac was the talk of the town. The gang gathered around admiringly. 'What a beauty Gerry, yer old man must be loaded.'

'Yeah, not bad eh?'

'What's he gonna do with the old one?'

'Dunno, it's up in the coach house at *Monaro,* Mick's cleanin' it up. Polishin' the brass an all that.'

'Guess he must be gonna keep it as a spare.'

'Yeah, use it when it rains.'

'Pigs bum! Ya know me old man never gets rid of anything.'

They sauntered off. 'Did ya know there's gonna be a sorta party or dance or somethin' when school breaks up?'

'Where d'ya hear that?'

'Heard the girl's talkin' about it. Gonna be at the new school, in the assembly hall.'

Dave whistled. 'Gee, that sounds good. Wonder if Mrs. Carrol will let me take Beryl.'

'Dunno mate, ya can only ask. It's not gonna be that great anyway.'

'What d'ya mean Gerry?'

'Well, Cupie's got the girls in the choir, they're gonna sing and Gareth's playin' the violin and all those other twerps're gonna perform. You know what I mean.'

'Yeah, enough to put ya off.'

'Hey, I see old Gareth and Punch are wearin' these crapcatchers.'

'Why don't we ask our mothers for long pants for Christmas, get em early, in time for the concert?'

That afternoon Gerald assiduously applied himself to piano practice, staying long after the allotted half hour. A thrill of anxiety ran through Frances as she glanced at the clock-what on earth was he up to now? 'You have done very well dear. Your scales are improving, I'm very proud of you.'

Gerald swung round on his stool. 'Mum, can I ask you something?'

'Of course dear, what is it?'

'Mum, can I have a pair of long trousers like Gareth?'

She laughed with relief. 'I'll take you down to the store tomorrow, I'm sure they will have a pair to suit you.'

'Gee, thanks Mum, you're a sport.'

Lunch time for Ben was the most relaxing time of the day. He could talk freely, over any private or intimate details of the day without the presence of children. He laughed over the incident of Gerald and his long trousers. 'Our children are growing up Francie.' He clasped her hand. 'Do you realise we will be moving to *Monaro* in a couple of weeks?'

'I've been packing all week. Oh Ben, I'm so happy I don't know whether to laugh or cry. Please promise me we will never leave there.'

'You have my word my love. *Monaro* is our last station, the last stop on the line.' He turned his attention to the mail, the morning delivery lay by his plate. 'Better look through this, I guess.' He handed all but one to his wife. 'You handle these Francie, usual bills, begging letters etc.'

She waited while he scanned the one he kept back.

'Well I'll be damned!'

'What is it?' she asked, alarmed.

'Frank's not coming, at least not for Christmas. Not until after the New Year.'

Frances was aghast. 'But what about the wedding? All the arrangements have been made. Why isn't he coming?'

'Read it, says he has to go down to Melbourne, some urgent business or other.'

'For heaven's sake, couldn't it wait?'

'Darling, I don't know any more than you do. The worst part is, he has asked us to explain to Muriel. Why the hell he couldn't have done that himself, I don't know.'

Frances read the letter. 'Dear lord, I don't know how I can face her. What can I say?'

'I'm sorry Francie, I truly am. I just don't understand Frank, it's not like him. Look, I'm sure she will understand. It will only be a matter of a few weeks.'

'But the arrangements! I've sent out the invitations.'

'Just phone or call and explain, then see the priest, tell him there has been a slight change of plans.' He paused and looked at her. 'Muriel should do that though, shouldn't she? An approach from us might not be diplomatic.'

Frances nodded. 'Yes, she will have to do that. Oh Ben, it's a rotten shame. Frank has no consideration.'

'Don't let it upset you my dear. Few things in life run smoothly. It will turn out all right in the end.'

Outside, he sat in the car, thinking-what the hell is he up to? Bloody politics, I'll bet! He started the car-poor Muriel, she is going to have her job cut out taming that one.

With school breaking for the holidays, last minute packing and the Committee at it's busiest, Frances felt thankful to be occupied.

Muriel had taken the news calmly. 'Of course I understand Frances. Frank is such a busy man. I think it was considerate of him, not writing to me directly. Professional men can never call their time their own. Really I am a little relieved, I'm not nearly ready with school and coaching Gareth, time has flown.'

'Oh Muriel, I am so relieved my dear. I will help you in any way I can. Have you spoken to the priest?'

'Father Kelly? Yes, he is really quite an old dear-told me just to let him know when we are ready.' She frowned thoughtfully. 'Do you think Frank will mind Father McSweeney not being here?'

'I'm positive it won't make any difference.'

'Have you heard any more?'

Frances shook her head. 'Not a word. Ellen may have but she hasn't said anything to us. Please don't worry Muriel, the time will pass so quickly you won't notice.'

Long trousers were much in evidence amongst the sixth class boys on breakup day. Skylarking and breaches of discipline which would ordinarily not be tolerated, Master Cummings chose not to see. Teachers as much as pupils were anxious to be finished with school for the year and when it was announced all could leave at lunchtime, loud cheering echoed round the grounds.'

Harries' shop had few customers, time was too precious to waste there except for the faithful few. They sat outside on an old bench made from a massive slab of red cedar. They sipped their fizzy drinks. 'Did you see Mrs. Carrol, Dave?'

'Yeah, no good though, she's goin' too.'

'Bad luck Dave, you'll never get your end in there.'

Dave stood up. 'Enough of that. I like Beryl, I'd never try a thing like that. You've got a dirty mind Hal.'

'All right, all right, I was only kidding. You'll just have to use Mrs. Palmer and her five daughters like the rest of us.'

Dave sat down. 'You're bloody disgusting, fair dinkum you are.'

'Cut it out you blokes, we're mates ain't we?'

'Sure, sorry Dave. What about you Gerry, you takin' Dutchy?'

'No such luck, she's goin' with her parents too.'

'Dutchy's a real good sort Gerry.'

'Bet yer life! I get a horn when I double her on me bike.'

'A horn's no good if ya can't use it.'

'Ran me hand up her leg once. Jeez, she started t'cry, shit scared I was, thought she'd tell her mother.'

'Yer lucky she didn't.'

'Yeah, me legs went weak whenever I saw Mrs. DeVries after that, thought I was a goner.'

This appealed to their sense of humour and they rolled around with mirth.

'Jeez, it'll be good when we grow up and get our end in when we want it.'

'Like dear Miss Halsey and yer Uncle Frank.'

'Hey, did ya see Miss Halsey at school t'day? That real short dress, when she walks it swishes from side t'side, y'can see her jazz garters.'

'Ooh, I wonder if she likes boys, I mean young gentlemen, that's what she called us t'day.'

Dave stood up. 'I'm goin' t'get me deposit back. Yer a dirty lotta buggers, all ya can think about are yer dicks. I'm goin' home t'mow the grass.'

'Hey, before y'go Dave.' Hal drew them close together. 'The concert'll be boring, let's have a little party of our own.'

'Whaddayah mean, what sort of party?'

'Ya know Curly McCoy, the useful down at the Star?'

'Yeah, what about him?'

'He'll slip us six bottles of beer for ten bob.'

'Jeez, what a beaut idea! Where could we go?'

'Down by the old boat shed. He'll leave the beer in a sugar bag, we can pick it up, leave it in the river to keep cool.'

'Terrific idea Hal but whose got ten bob? We wouldn't have that much between us, worst bloody luck.'

'What about you Gerry, any ideas?'

'Well I could borrow it off Buddy, if I can get past Judy that is. She knows he's a soft touch, got eyes in the back of 'er head.'

'She goes to choir practice though doesn't she?'

'Ya might have it there, mate. Good ole Buddy, never asks for it back.'

'Be pretty low not to repay 'im, wouldn't it?'

'I will mate, I will. Uncle Frank'll be good for a quid, anyway leave it to me. I'll be off now, see ya tomorrow.'

The Saturday night concert was considered a great success. Before they departed, Ben smilingly regarded his family. 'Sorry I can't be with you but I must stay. in case I'm needed.' The look he received from his wife told him she knew any excuse would be good enough for him to get out of going. He ushered them to the front door. 'Mrs. Stanley will be waiting in the car.' He sniffed the air delicately. 'Mmm my word, what a delightful odour.'

Gareth coloured slightly. 'It's California Poppy, Dad. Punch and I got it from the barber, it's the latest thing.'

'Of course I should have known, delightful perfume. Have a nice evening now.' He patted Gerald's back. 'See you behave yourself, young man.' Closing the door, he sighed contentedly. 'Glorious peace. Now for my slippers, a scotch and to hell with anyone who disturbs me tonight.'

The new Assembly Hall gleamed with light. It smelled new, freshly varnished wooden seats in neat rows. The far end of the hall taken up entirely by a raised stage complete with piano, a gift to the school from Mr. and Mrs. DeVries. The little group carefully manoeuvred until they occupied part of the back row nearest the door, except Jack Raywood who was firmly wedged between his mother and aunt.

'Jack's buggered, he can't get out.'

'Not so loud. You wait, old Jack will reckon he wants a piddle in a minute.'

'We can't leave yet.'

'I know, for Chrissake. Ooh look, there's dear Miss Halsey in that short green dress with all those little beads!'

'Yeah, and there's all the girls in white dresses in the choir.'

'Ssh, there's Mum and P and J and Punch and good old Buddy's there in his chair.'

'Who's P and bloody J?'

'Tell ya later. Look, things are moving, Professor Brelat is getting the girls ready t'sing.'

The lights dimmed, the inevitable shuffling ceased. On the stage, Muriel at the piano, struck the first chords of the National Anthem. In the noise and confusion of people standing and pushing back their chairs, the conspirators crept into the night. From the shadows, a broadly grinning figure joined them. 'What did I tell ya? Come on Jack let's go.'

In the fishing shed they sat laughing and congratulating themselves on how clever they had escaped the concert.

'Right, sit on these corn bags, don't wanta dirty the new duds.'

'How's the beer Hal?'

'Comin' mate, comin'.' He pulled steadily on a rope leading out to into the river.

'Shit, the tides out, watch for the oysters.'

'She's right, don't worry.' He lifted quickly, the sound of bottles clinking in the sodden bag.

'Light the lantern Gerry. Ohh, don't they look lovely? Six of the best. What about glasses?'

'Got 'em. Mum's packin' up for the shift to *Monaro*, they're a bit cracked but they'll do.'

'How do we open 'em?'

'The old scout knife mate, got a bottle opener on it.'

'What ya got in the bag George?'

'Pig's trotters, the old man makes 'em.'

'Pig's trotters? Never bloody heard of 'em.'

'Try this then.' George handed the delicious pig's foot around.

'Hey, these are good. Come on Gerry, open the beer.'

Cap off, the beer flowed, foaming over the bottle neck to be poured into eagerly held glasses.

'Gets in yer nose. Whoops, open some more Gerry.'

'Pass those trotters George. This is what I call a party!'

'Yer right mate. Hold out yer glass.'

They settled down, backs against the wall. Inhibitions vanished under the influence of the highly alcoholic beer. 'Gawd I feel good! This'll do me-bugger the concert.'

Hal turned to his friend. 'Sorry I said that about you and Beryl the other day Dave. I s'pose yer gonna marry her some day.'

'Sure mate, if she'll have me. Don't worry about it.'

'What about you Gerry, goin' t'marry Dutchy?'

'Buggered if I know. One of these days I reckon, she's real nice.'

'What the hell's the P and J business Gerry? I heard you say - 'here's old P and J'.' Hal asked his 'best' friend.

'That's what I call Gareth when he can't hear me. He's Dad's Pride and Joy.'

'Whaddaya mean, Pride and Joy?' He belched loudly which brought forth gales of mirth.

'Because Gareth's gonna be a bloody doctor, that's why. At least he reckons he is. Goes around with the old man on calls sometimes.'

'Bet he hasn't seen what we have.'

They fell about in helpless laughter. 'Ooh poor old Mrs. Simpson, remember? Gawd, what a way t'make a quid. Come on Gerry, fill'em up.'

'So old P and J's gonna be a doctor eh? Seen 'im with Enid Wells the other day, him and Punch.'

'Yeah, Punch's a bit sweet on the Stanley girl, what's 'er name?'

'Not sure, Lois or sumthin' like that.'

'Yeah, they all go ridin' every weekend. Very smoochie it looks.'

'Hope it's only the horses what gets rode.' More laughter.

'Ooh Gawd, I feel funny, any more steam Hal?'

'Just a bit-that's the end.'

The last bottle emptied and thrown into the water, they staggered out onto the grassy bank that merged into the riverside park. Dave fell down rolling onto his back, laughing hysterically. 'Jesus, I can't get up, I'm drunk!'

'Gimme yer hand mate.' Jack reached down. 'I'll pull ya up.'

'Not on yer life, I'm stayin' here.'

The others staggered around then fell in a heap beside him. Jack straightened up, tried to take a few steps forward then with arms flailing careered backwards, disappearing into the darkness.

Owl eyed, they looked at each other. 'Where's Jacko gone?' they roared in unison. 'Where are ya Jack, what the hell ya doin'?'

'I'm here ya bloody goats.' Jack crawled towards them on hands and knees. 'That bloody gully, fulla bloody water. Me new stides're soaked, so's me shirt.'

'Jeez mate, that's bad.'

'Bad? That's not half of it. Me old lady'll kill me.' The dunking had sobered him considerably. 'I'm pissin' off, try and get in without bein' caught.'

Gerald pushed himself upright. 'Yeah, time we all got goin', the concert'll be over an' we'll be missed. Come on Dave, get up ya silly bugger.'

Dave rolled over onto his knees. 'I'm not feelin' so good - think I'm gonna chunder.'

'Well chunder for Chrissake, ya'll feel better. Then a good walk home and you'll be all right.'

'Oh those bloody pig's feet!'

'Too much beer, you drank more'n the rest of us.'

To the sound of their friend noisily vomiting, they made their separate ways, Gerald staying long enough to haul his friend to his feet.

'Yer me best friend Gerry, best anyone ever had. Jeez I'm crook.'

'Come on, stow the bullshit. I'll walk with ya far as the Station.'

Reaching home, Gerald found the house in darkness. Carefully lifting the sash of his bedroom window, he painfully eased himself over the sill, falling noisily on the floor. He heard the door open and the room was suddenly flooded with light. His mother, in her dressing gown, stood looking at him.

'And where may I ask, have you been young man?' She only used that phrase when she was very angry.

'Just to a party Mum, just the blokes. We had a little school breakup party, me and Dave and the others.'

'Really? Just look at your new trousers and your shirt. Obviously, you have been drinking.'

'Not much Mum, honestly, not much. We were down at the park.'

'Everybody remarked that you and your friends were not at the concert. Now get into bed, your father will speak to you tomorrow.'

'Sorry Mum.' That was all he could mumble as the door closed behind her.

Frances sighed, making her way to the bedroom-Ben said they were growing up.

Gerald received his summons after morning surgery. 'Your father wants to see you. Better not keep him waiting.'

With leaden footsteps he made his way along the passageway. The surgery door was open, his father sitting at the desk, busily writing. For what seemed an eternity he waited as page after page was filled. 'Close the door will you?' He spoke without looking up. Turning round, he found his father looking at him, leaning back in his chair, hands behind his head.

'And what do you have to say for yourself this time?'

'Nothing Dad, we didn't mean any harm.'

'Not to others perhaps but certainly to yourselves. Your friend Dave was very ill last night. How you are not would probably baffle medical science.'

'Gee, I'm sorry Dad, I didn't think Dave was that crook.'

'That's your trouble Gerald, you don't think of the consequences of your actions. Sergeant Truman could jail that fool McCoy for selling you that beer. It's only because he is married and it's close to Christmas, he got off. I can assure you he won't do it again.'

Gerald shifted uneasily from foot to foot.

'I don't know how your other friends got on but Dave is confined to the house for the next week. As this is a busy time for your mother, packing and trying to do her Committee work, your job is to help her in every way. Do what she tells you, go where she tells you. Understand? No more disappearing on your own devices.'

Gerald felt relieved, he had got off better than he had imagined. 'Can I go now Dad?'

'In a minute, I have something to tell you. I have come to the conclusion that Myuna is too small a town for a gentleman with your talents for mischief, so you will be going to school in Sydney after Christmas.'

Gerald's face lit up.'With Gareth and Dave?That's great!'

Ben held up his hand. 'No, not with Gareth and Dave. To another school-St Peter's.'

'St. Peters? That's a tyke school Dad, I'm not a tyke.' His eyes started to fill with tears. 'I can't go there, I'm a Protestant.'

Ben softened at his son's distress. 'There are Protestant boys, Jewish boys, boys from other countries even. You don't have to take religious instruction, they won't try to change your religion. I think you will enjoy being there. They are great on sport and Father Dan's brother, one of my dearest friends is the Headmaster.' He smiled. 'Now dry your eyes. You will be home for all the holidays and I've no doubt you will be able to see Dave and Gareth if you want to, during weekends.'

Unconvinced, Gerald without another word, left the surgery. Ben sat for a long time, thinking-I wonder if I've done the right thing. God knows, I don't. He re-read, then signed the letter he had written to Brother McSweeney.

Gerald found his mother busy packing. 'Dad said I've gotta help you, Mum.'

'Well, I don't know anyone I'd rather have as a helper.' She smiled, she could never stay angry with this tousle haired son for long.

'Dad says I have to go to some tyke school after Christmas.'

Frances could see he was upset. 'I know dear. Come and sit down here by me. Your father told me about it, he is only doing what he thinks is best for you.'

'I'll hate it Mum, I know I will. I'm not a tyke.'

'You don't know what it will be like, wait until you have been there for a while.'

He sat glum and dispirited.

She continued. 'In any case, if you are not happy there, your father says you can leave at Easter and transfer to Gareth's school or perhaps, come back here.'

The boys face brightened. 'Gee, that's better. I feel a lot better already, that's great!'

Frances laughed. 'Well, you can start stacking these boxes in the corner. Just be careful, my best China is in there.'

On an errand to town, Gerald made sure he passed the Police Station. Sure enough there was Dave, carefully raking old seed pods from under two great spreading Poinciana trees. He rested his bike against the fence. 'How're ya goin' mate?'

'A bloody prisoner, that's what I am.' Dave grinned. 'How'd you get on?'

'Crook. I'm bein' sent to school in Sydney after Christmas.'

'Nothin' wrong with that, we'll be able to see each other. Same school as me and Gareth?'

'Ya won't believe it Dave. I'm goin' to a tyke school.'

'A tyke school?' He fairly goggled. 'You're not a bloody tyke!'

'Mate, it's a long story. I don't haveta become one, and best of all, I can leave at Easter and go to Grammar or come back home.'

Dave scratched his head. 'Beats me. I suppose yer old man knows what he's doin' though.'

'How'd the others get on, seen any of 'em?'

'Only Jack.' he laughed. 'Know what the cunnin' bugger did? Rolled his wet shirt and strides up next morning, told his mother he was goin' fishin' and took 'em up to my aunty at the hospital.'

'She fix 'em up for him?'

'Yeah, you know what a good old stick Aunty Faith is. She was a friend of his aunty-you know, the one that died. Anyway, she washed and ironed 'em good as new.'

'Good luck t'him. Seen anyone else?'

'Bunch of the girls came by yesterday. Beryl and Dorothy was with 'em. Jeez, I felt a bloody goat. One of those smart ass Buller girls called out,' he mimicked the girl's voice, 'working hard Dave? You can come up to our place when you finish, the grass needs mowing.' He spat in disgust. 'Anyway, Beryl smiled and waved at me.'

Gerald mounted his bike. 'Gotta get goin', haveta work for the old lady all week. Whatcha gettin' for Christmas by the way?'

'Dunno, maybe nuthin', or a kick up th'ass if I don't finish this. See ya later.'

The week before Christmas became a frantic race against time. Dave Aitken and Christine were to be married on the twenty third. After their reception they would spend two nights at their new home, have Christmas with Ethel then leave for a small village on the Queensland Coast, aptly named Surfers Paradise. Two weeks, Dave said, was long enough. His fiancee agreed. She secretly yearned for the new house built on a large block overlooking the river, financed largely by the groom's adoring parents.

'They make a handsome couple Francie.' Ben and Frances sat at breakfast. 'I know you are busy old girl but thankfully the surgery isn't. Funny thing, this time of year, few people get sick.' He held up his cup. 'Appreciate another cuppa. There are a few things I want to talk about.'

'Nothing serious?'

'No, not really. I've spoken to Tom Coburn about shifting the surgery into town. I said once they moved back, it would be encroaching on their privacy to have it here.'

'What did he say?'

'He just said not to worry, he would let me know if it got too much for him. He still works like a young man and there is not another man I would consult if I was in trouble. I've had a talk with Charlie Hawks, you know the young bloke who hung up his shingle and is doing quite well apparently. Funny thing, I never knew before, his father was a partner with Dr. Coburn in the old days.'

'What became of him?'

Ben shook his head. 'Anyway, what I was about to say, he has agreed to split time with us, so that gives me one full weekend in three.'

'Thank heaven for that, at last we will be able to have a restful weekend without the phone.'

'It should all work out quite well. By the way Francie, I've asked him up to our usual Christmas get together, is that all right with you?'

'Since when have you had to ask me who we ask, Ben Wakefield?' She grew curious. 'Is he married?'

'Not that I know of.' He grinned. 'I suppose that pretty receptionist he has may cater to his needs.'

She shoved him out. 'Men! You always think the worst.'

He kissed her fondly. 'You think so old girl? How awful of me. I promise I'll never tell you any more scandal I hear.'

Frances held him tight. 'Oh yes you will. I'd die if you didn't.'

He left the house smiling. 'Women's curiosity, their fatal flaw.'

The Committee's work of distributing largess began in earnest.

'For God's sake Francie, pick who makes the deliveries. A lot of those people may be down on their luck but they have their pride. Some of those old biddies you have down there, embarrass them.'

'I can't pick and choose Ben, you should speak to Alice.'

'I can't do that. Look just tell them to leave the hampers or whatever they are and wish the recipient a Merry Christmas.' He hesitated. 'I know you have done it before, it's just that I've heard a few things.'

'Well, you know how things are. I'll speak to Alice, but I can't be sure.'

'Do your best old girl. Sorry I put my spoke in. By the way, I was talking to an official who has been touring the Western District. >From what he says, it's pure hell out there. Myuna is a paradise compared with most other places.'

The last issue of the *Myuna Daily* for the year gave a glowing account of the wedding of Dr. Dave Aitken and Miss Christine Gray. Dr. Benjamin Wakefield gave the bride away and Mrs. Wakefield acted as Matron of Honour. The Rev. Father Tomlinson of St. Johns officiated. There followed a detailed account of the bride's dress, what the attendants wore etc. This honour had fallen to Judy, Dorothy and Beryl, the inseparable three. The Honorary Social Columnist for the *Daily* grew quite lyrical. 'A brilliant reception was held at *Monaro*, the Wakefield's magnificent home. Many friends attended including the groom's parents from Sydney who are presently staying with Dr. and Mrs. Wakefield. It is understood the newlyweds will enjoy a short honeymoon at Surfers Paradise in Queensland before returning to Myuna.'

With glass in hand, Ben exchanged greetings with friends old and new, slowly making his way, avoiding twirling parasols, to the cool shade of the verandah. At the farthest end he found Ethel Jones sitting by herself, dabbing at her eyes.

'Why Jonesy, you old sentimentalist. In all the years I've known you, you have never shed a tear.'

'Can't a woman cry if she wants to?' She snapped.

'Not today you can't.' He took her firmly by the arm. 'Come on, you and I are going to split a bottle of bubbly and face the crowd.'

Earlier that morning Ben had driven up to *Monaro.* He found Mrs. Ellis and her daughter putting finishing touches to a three tiered wedding cake.

'I am sorry to put you to so much trouble Mrs. Ellis. Everything looks quite marvellous.' He placed an envelope on the table. 'A little extra for your trouble, which I can assure you is very much appreciated.'

She coloured slightly. 'Thank you very much Doctor, but really it is not necessary, it's a pleasure, really it is. I do hope everything turns out all right.'

'I'm sure it will, thanks to your capable management.'

She wiped her hands on her apron. 'Dr. Wakefield I haven't had the opportunity to ask Mrs. Wakefield, how many will there be for Christmas dinner this year?'

'Ah yes, I meant to speak to you about that. Just the family and Miss Halsey. Things are a little hectic this year with moving to *Monaro* and my wife's work with the Ladies Committee. There will be little time for entertaining. In any case most of the people we know will be here this afternoon.'

'In that case Doctor I will just cook a turkey and a ham. The pudding just needs heating up. Will that be satisfactory?'

'Certainly, I trust your good taste implicitly Mrs. Ellis. Just leave the food in the refrigerator.'

She eyed the new fangled Westinghouse with it's funny looking evaporator on top. 'Will the food keep cold in there Doctor?'

'Absolutely Mrs. Ellis.' Ben hid a smile. 'They are the very latest thing, all the way from America.'

'Well, I ordered six blokes of ice, just in case Doctor. The ice chest is full.'

'Very wise. Now I must go, I wish you and Daphne the compliments of the season. Remember now, you must rest your legs. We will see you again in a couple of weeks.'

Ben sought out Mick, hanging the last of the magic lanterns. 'Time you knocked off, Mick. Bob left this morning.'

'Another ten minutes Doc, like to finish proper before I go. Anyway, Christmas ain't here yet.'

'Don't be too particular. I gave Bob his ham yesterday. Yours and a case of beer are in the coach house and don't forget to pick up ice on your way home. I didn't leave any beer for Bob because I know he is a non drinker.'

'Yeah Doc, thanks a million. No Bob don't touch it, he's a Methodist.'

Ben pressed the usual ten pound note into the man's hand. 'I don't want to see you again for at least two weeks Mick. The place will still be here when you get back.'

Mick rolled a cigarette. 'See the young Doc is gettin hisself hitched at last. Mrs. Ellis reckons they're goin' straight into their new house.'

'Just for a few days Mick, then they're off to a little place in Queensland, Surfers Paradise, for a couple of weeks.'

'Reckon the old bed'll get a poundin' t'night Doc.'

Ben turned his head to hide the smile on his face. 'Better get hitched up yourself Mick. Time you've had a couple at the pub, you will be late getting home. Have a good Christmas now, see you again in the New Year.'

'Same to you Doc, same't you and many of 'em.'

The afternoon wore on and as dusk spread across the countryside, most of the guests departed. A few lingered just long enough to enjoy the magic lanterns glowing like fire along the driveway. The Aitkens planned to leave on the early train the next day. Active in business, Aitken Senior was anxious to be back in Sydney for several important functions.

Ben fighting fatigue, steeled himself to be the gracious host.

'Of course Doctor, my wife and I had other plans for David. I offered to put him into a Macquarie Street practice. We also hoped he might marry someone of his own set, if you know what I mean.' Seeing Ben's steady gaze upon him, he added hastily. 'Of course we are very happy he has found the right partner. A charming girl, but I am sure you understand our position.'

'Perfectly, Mr. Aitken. A little more Brandy?'

The conversation grew desultory, Mr. Aitken drank more Brandy. Ben left him snoring noisily, sprawled on the leather couch.

Sleep evaded him so he climbed the spiral staircase to the tower and sat lost in thought in the captain's chair, until dawn broke over the distant ocean.

In the early morn at Lambruk station, the Aitkens had little to say as they climbed into their previously booked first class compartment, just a few words of thanks. Ben waited until the train departed in a train of steam.

It was pleasant driving back along familiar roads. Perhaps he had been too critical of Aitken, she was quite enough, still they were city people and probably felt lost in the country. His heart lifted as the gates of *Monaro* came into view. Along the driveway the magic lanterns, their lights doused, tinkled in a gentle breeze. We'll leave them there, Gareth can take them down after Christmas. He entered the house to the delicious aroma of frying bacon and fresh coffee.

Frances greeted him. 'Oh Ben, you look so tired.' She pushed him gently onto his chair. 'Now enjoy your breakfast, we have so much to talk about.'

He reached up, his arms encircling her waist. 'So how does it feel to be the Mistress of *Monaro*?'

Frances smiled happily. 'Wonderful!'

Sighing with satisfaction, he sat back holding his cup for more coffee. 'Where is everybody, are we the only souls in this old house?'

'They have all gone swimming at the big waterhole in Boondi Creek, Muriel has gone with them.'

'Well that's safe enough, Gareth is capable too. Lovely spot, I feel like going myself.'

Boondi Creek rose high in the hills behind *Monaro*, gathering springs along it's course and finally emptying into the North Arm of the river. The water was so pure, so crystal clear that in the deep pools the quartz pebbles and lurking Perch could be clearly seen. From this source, *Monaro* drew it's water, feeding by a gravity line into two immense stone cisterns.

The favourite swimming hole was in cleared country, overhung with trees along the banks. Many a child learned to dog paddle there. Gerald and his mates regarded it as their exclusive preserve.

'I think you should rest today dear. Tomorrow is Christmas Eve don't forget.'

'Frankly, I could do with a snooze. Thank God we have the place to ourselves this year. The reception took care of the usual get together and the Coburns will have both daughters and their families home for the holidays. Pieter feels it's time they spent Christmas together.' He smiled. 'I'll bet old Tom and Alice are as glad to be back in their old house as we are here. Wake me if anything untoward happens and Francie, tell Gareth not to light the lanterns tonight. Just check the oil, we don't want them going out on us tomorrow night.'

'Ben, I know I am being silly but do you believe in ghosts?'

'What on earth made you say that?'

'I don't know, I just wonder sometimes.'

'It's the house Francie, ghosts around here would only be friendly, I'm sure of that.'

'Before you go, Muriel is going to Midnight Mass tomorrow night, some friends are calling for her. You don't mind do you?'

He laughed at her. 'Why should I mind? I'm sure most of the churches will be well attended.'

'She is very devout, I hope Frank understands.'

'That my dear, will be up to them. Thank God my grandfather taught me to be a free thinker.'

'But you do believe in God?'

He put his arms around her. 'I don't know what I believe old girl. Funny thing, old Thommo pulled me up the other day. Asked me when we were coming to Communion. I told him I considered the Chalice, from which everyone sips, was a potential source of infection.' He smiled at the memory. 'The old boy was quite horrified. He said if my faith was strong I had nothing to fear.'

'He is such a nice man. He doesn't look at all well.'

'I doubt if they eat well. Ethel tells me he gives away half of his miserable stipend. One of the true Christians of this world. Not like some of the well fed Gentlemen of the Cloth we have had here. Most had private incomes. I really must take that nap now- a sure sign of old age creeping on.'

Christmas Day. The sun was barely up before the house echoed to excited voices. Ben had cut the top from a sapling, setting it firmly in a tub of sand. Decorated with coloured ribbons and tinsel, it stood glittering in the huge downstairs room. Muriel had fixed a little angel to the top most branch. The adults were still in pyjamas and dressing gowns.

'Look what I got Dad. A watch!'

'Me too!'

'Look, Judy's got one that goes on her wrist.'

'Hey, just look at these books.'

'What did you get Dad?'

'Slippers my boy, leather ones. Just what I wanted.'

'What about you Mum?'

'Oh some perfume and a nice box of soap.'

'What did Santa bring you Miss Halsey?'

Muriel carefully untied the blue ribbon from around a flat white box. Inside nestling in white tissue lay a silk Chinese dressing gown. The card read- Happy Christmas Muriel from Ben and Frances. Eyes averted, she ran the fine silk through her fingers. When she spoke her voice sounded very husky. 'Thank you both so very much. It's really beautiful.'

Ben turned pleading eyes on his wife. 'My dear, I know it's Christmas Day but I'd sell my soul for some coffee.'

Muriel stood quickly. 'Please let me, Frances.'

As the door closed behind them, Gareth stood beside his father. 'Is Miss Halsey all right Dad? She sounded sort of sad.'

'Of course she is, son. Christmas affects people like that you know.'

That night they lay talking quietly in the cool darkness. 'Well, here we are, in the captain's bunk, my dear.'

'Our bed, if you please. Ours for the rest of our lives.'

'I wonder if Tom and Alice are glad to be back in theirs.'

'Of course they would be. They should never have left in the first place.'

'I don't think they have sold their place in Lambruk yet. Wonder what they will do with it, for that matter, I'll never know what possessed them to move up there.'

'He did say he was going to retire.'

'Retire!' Ben snorted. 'The old cuss will never retire. How old would you say he is?'

'You would know better than I.'

'Mmm, let's see then. I was born in '87. He must have been about twenty six or seven, so that makes him at least seventy, or thereabouts.'

'That's not old Ben, lots of men are active at that age.'

'True enough, but I wish he would agree to shift the surgery from the house.'

'Have you asked him again?'

'I have but he wasn't too enthusiastic. I have got to find some way to change his mind. I haven't told you, haven't had the chance really, Charlie Hawks has approached me to put up a two storey brick building in Orama Street. Pieter and Dave are in it too. Have the surgeries on the ground floor, offices on the top. It makes good sense, puts everything under one roof and it's central, which is the main thing.'

'It sound perfect. When will you do it?'

'Actually, it's well under way. Pieter has formed a company, equal shares. We've bought the land and Wells is working on an estimate for us.'

'I hope he won't be offended. Dr. Coburn, I mean.'

'So do I. I'll just have to be diplomatic. Deep down, I've got the feeling he will be glad to get Dave and me out of the house. I'm sure Alice will.'

'I hope so.'

He yawned. 'Let's not worry about the future. Did you think our first Christmas here, our first as a family, went well?'

'Yes, I'm glad it wasn't extravagant, everything was perfect. Except for Muriel. It really is inconsiderate of Frank, not even a card let alone a present for her.'

'Darling, you know your brother is one of my closest friends but that is how he is. He will make it up to her when he gets here.'

'He could have phoned at least.'

'Stop worrying about it, they will work it out.'

'She is upset, I know that. He is my brother but he should be ashamed of himself.'

'For heavens sake, cut it out. What's she going to do until he gets here?'

'I asked her to stay but she is going back to Ethel. I think she feels more comfortable there.'

'Well, I'm exhausted my dear, let's leave things to work themselves out. It's not our business in any case.'

Never a sound sleeper, Ben woke in the half light before dawn. He glanced at his wife, her eyes closed, gently breathing. Slowly he drew back the covers and slipped quietly out of bed. He dressed quickly and let himself noiselessly out of the house. It was becoming lighter by the minute. He filled his lungs with the fragrant air-Glorious, best part of the day! He let himself out through the green gate in the stone wall surrounding the garden. Outside, leaning against a tree, was the supple stick he had cut and shaped years ago. The track was clear, Mick had even raked the leaves and fallen branches before he left for his break. Around a bend the Chapel came into view. Entering the walled enclosure, he stood gazing at the familiar headstones, his eyes wandering to the last one, that of his baby son-Dear Lord, flowers. They look so fresh, Francie must have put then there yesterday.

Opening the door of the Chapel, he sank heavily onto the front pew. The sun, now just above the horizon, sent light slanting through the leadlights above the little altar. Here stood two tall silver vases, each containing a single white rose. In the cathedral silence of the forest, broken only by the call of distant Wood Pigeons, he could hear the sound of his own heart. A slight rustle at the door broke his reverie, he turned his head. His wife stood there, her arms full of flowers. Wordlessly she came to him, taking his hand in hers.

Outside in the still air, they faced each other. Frances spoke softly. 'I knew you were here, your stick was gone.'

He was silent for a moment then, 'so you know I come, I wondered if you knew.'

'Yes my dear, I knew. Why didn't you ever ask me to come with you?'

He shook his head. 'I thought we agreed not to dwell on the past. We have other children to think of.'

Tears welled in her eyes, 'I don't love them any less, but he was our baby. I can never forget, never.'

He put his arm around her. 'Come on old girl, let's spread these flowers. Time we were back at the house.'

About to enter the front door, Frances glanced toward the driveway. Pointing towards the gate where there stood an attractive little roadster, blue with black mudguards and white wire spoke wheels. She grasped Ben's arm. 'We have visitors, somebody is here.' She grew excited. 'It might be Frank?'

He grinned. 'No, it's not Frank. It's your Christmas present. Quick, come have a look at it.'

'It's beautiful.' She ran her hand over the shining paintwork.

'It's the latest Chevrolet, darling. The first six cylinder model. Look a dicky seat in the back and roll down side curtains.'

The new car was a two hour wonder. The children admired it, sat in it, and pretended to drive it before the gathering heat of the day made the call of the swimming hole irresistible. Later in the day, Muriel sat rather nervously in the passenger seat. 'Will you be able to drive it all right, Frances?'

'Of course Muriel. The gears are the same. Ben took me for a little spin, it handles beautifully.'

Harry did not go with the others this time, propped up with cushions in the dicky seat with the wind tearing at his hair, he told them later, felt like flying through the air.

Back in harness, Ben waited an opportune moment to speak privately with his older colleague. 'We thought it better to be centrally located Doctor. There will be more room, especially now Dr. Hawks wishes to come in with us.' Then added hastily. 'And I am sure Mrs. Coburn would be glad not to have patients cluttering up your home.'

The old man smiled. 'What does young Aitken think of the idea?'

'He is quite enthusiastic.'

'Well then Ben, the decision seems unanimous. To be honest, I have given the matter a good deal of thought since you last spoke to me. It has been a great joy to both my wife and myself to move back into our old home. Why I ever contemplated retirement is a mystery to me. But there you are, the unexpected always seems to happen.'

'I am grateful Doctor, your advice and judgement have always been invaluable.'

'Thank you Ben, thank you, but I must tell you this. As you know, I have some loyal followers in the town and surrounding area. If you have no objections, I will see them here. I simply don't know what else I would do with myself. I would prefer not to use your rooms but I will always be available for whatever advice I can give.'

Ben felt an emotion he found hard to control. 'Thank you Doctor, thank you very much. I don't know what to say.'

'Don't say anything Ben, just do what you believe to be the right thing.'

The New Year came in with dry storms. The country needing rain, shimmered in a heat haze. The nights became oppressive. Unable to sleep, Ben would quietly slip out of bed and make his way to the high verandah. Comfortably sprawled in one of the deep cane chairs, with a drink by his side he would doze fitfully, gazing at the great stars just above, lulled by the love calls of the frogs and crickets. How pleasant it was, the world to himself, not a light to be seen. On such a night, into the second week of the new year, half awake, half asleep, he became aware of two pin points of lights moving upwards in the moonless blackness of the night. Steadily they moved on. Suddenly he was wide awake. They were coming up the hill towards *Monaro*. He stood gazing intently. It was a car, no mistake. Then suddenly he could hear the motor. The car stopped, he heard the handbrake applied. The gate in the wall opened and a tall figure came toward the house. 'By God, it's Frank!' He leaned over the railing. 'Frank, where the hell have you come from?'

'Long story my friend, come down and let me in.'

They stood in the entrance wringing hands. The lights above the staircase suddenly flooded the room and Frances stood looking down. She came running into the arms of her brother. 'Frank where have you been? Not a word or a letter, we have been worried sick. Muriel is so withdrawn, I'm sure she thinks you weren't coming back.'

Frank laughed, holding his sister at arms length. 'Calm down Francie, calm down. I've been busy. I am here now, that's all that matters isn't it? How about some coffee?'

'Right away. How did you know we were up here?'

'I didn't. I went to the old place and Dr. Coburn answered the door. He's a decent old stick, wanted me to come in but I thanked him and apologized of course, and told him you were expecting me.'

'I must remember to back up your story when I see him. Here have a drink.'

Frances brought the coffee. 'Well, tell us all the news Frank. What have you been doing, why were you so long coming back?'

He smiled at his sister. 'Not tonight old girl. I'm bushed and my leg hurts. The bloody road up here is atrocious-a gravelled track.'

'I thought your leg was in good shape now, what happened?'

'Bit of an accident on one of my jobs. Would you mind taking a quick look at it Ben?'

'Certainly. Francie,' He kissed his wife, 'go back to bed my dear. You will have all tomorrow to talk to Frank.'

Reluctantly she agreed. 'All right but do get a good night's sleep, what's left of it. Don't keep him up Ben.'

'Come on old chap, there's a room here where I keep a few things of convenience. This way.'

'This looks like a regular surgery-examination couch and all the other paraphernalia.'

'It was my mother's sewing room. It has come in handy at times I can tell you.'

Frank hoisted himself onto the couch, pulling his trousers down to his knees. Ben adjusting the examination light looked on in amazement.

'Yeah, some leg eh. It's my prick I want you to look at.'

Focusing the light on the affected area, Ben examined the small hard ulcer on his friend's penis. He drew in his breath sharply. 'Holy Jesus Christ! Do you know what you've got here?'

'Yeah, the bloke I went to in Sydney told me. A chancre. It's syphilis isn't it Ben?'

'It's syphilis all right. How in the name of God, did you get it?'

Frank stood adjusting his clothing. 'You know the old one about a stiff prick having no conscience. To cut it short, I went to a buck's party. They hired a few girls, reckoned they were clean, obviously the one I got wasn't.'

'Here, sit down, hold your glass out. We'll have to talk about this.'

'Thanks. I take it this means the marriage is off?'

'Out of the question. God, Frank what can I say?'

'Ben, is there a treatment?'

'There is a treatment, an arsenic compound, Salvarsan. I say a treatment, not a cure. You would have to go to Sydney. It's a notifiable disease you know.'

Frank's face was haggard as he sat looking at his brother in law. 'I'm buggered then. What the hell do I tell Muriel?'

'I don't know Frank, I just don't know. She has counted every minute waiting for you.'

'That's what hurts most. God, I'm sweating, pass the bottle.' He downed the Brandy at a gulp. 'You'll have to help me Ben, say my leg has gone bad on me, I have to go back to Sydney.'

Ben shook his head. 'It won't wash Frank, we'll have to think of something else. There is a great homecoming planned for you, you will have to go through with that at least.'

'What about this thing-can I kiss anybody? Christ, what about Frances, will she be all right?'

'You are not infectious at this stage, except for sexual intercourse, and I know you won't be indulging in that. So you can kiss who you like. When the chancre disappears and you are in the second stage, you will be very infectious.'

Frank paced the room. 'Christ, one bloody goddamned mistake and I'm ruined! Swear to me that you will never tell Muriel, Frances, anybody!'

'You know better than that. Only you and I and the Doctor in Sydney know, or ever will.'

Frank gave a short laugh. 'He won't, I gave a false name and address.'

'Perhaps just as well. Come on, have some more. I wouldn't dare give you a sedative-you wouldn't wake up.'

'That would suit me, my troubles would be over.'

'But not for me old son, you know that.'

After a late breakfast, Frances telephoned Muriel. 'He is here, arrived late last night. Oh Muriel, dress your best, I'll come and get you. Frank's leg has been bothering him, he's with Ben now.'

An hour later, trembling with excitement, Muriel stepped, fresh and lovely in her beige linen dress, from the little roadster. Frank swept her into his arms. 'Let me look at you. More beautiful than ever!' He told a long detailed story, how trouble on a new building had kept him, the accident which had exacerbated the injury to his leg. How sorry he was he hadn't written or sent a Christmas gift, he had bought it with him.

Muriel undid the wrapping-a leather case-she released the catch. Nestling in it's satin lining lay a beautifully crafted gold crucifix. Gently he took it from her and fastened the chain around her neck. He tingled at the feel of her soft hair.

Tears filled her eyes. 'Oh Frank, it's lovely!' She took his hand.

'Can you manage a walk for a while? Ben and Frances won't mind, will you?'

'Well, not too far. I've advised Frank to rest, Muriel. I'm sure you understand my dear.'

'Oh dear, how selfish of me. We will just go around the garden.' She looked with concern into her loved one's eyes. 'Can you manage dearest?'

Frank affecting a bad limp, leaned on his walking stick. He kept his anguish and grief well hidden, his voice under control. 'My dear, dear girl there is nothing I would like better.'

Frances turned to her husband. 'Ben, I never imagined Frank was so badly hurt. Will he be all right?'

'I don't know. We will just have to wait and see.' he shook his head. 'I'm not sure. It really needs to be x-rayed and that can only be done in Sydney.'

'Will he be all right for tonight? Everything is prepared. Mick is hanging out the lanterns now.'

'Oh that, yes of course. Frank insisted. Anyway, it's strictly a family affair, so that won't be too hard on him.'

'I'm glad. he can see everybody else later. Here they come, doesn't Muriel look radiant?'

'Yes, yes she does.'

Frances took him by the arm. 'Well, please sound a little more enthusiastic, come and see what Mrs. Ellis has prepared.'

Later, having Muriel to herself, Frances asked had plans for the wedding been discussed.

'I only mentioned it, Frances. He is in so much pain. He said he must rest for a few days, I'm sure he will like Father Kelly.' Her voice trembled. 'Oh Frances, he is so brave. He tries to hide it but I can see it in his eyes.'

'Muriel, few women would have been as patient as you. My brother is a very lucky man. Just give him a few days, I know he will be back to his old self again.'

In the cool of the evening the four sat in the semi darkness of the high verandah. Below a slight breeze stirred the leaves, the magic lanterns turned slowly on their swivels. They were silent, Muriel close to her lover on the cane lounge. 'Does your leg hurt Darling? You are so quiet.'

He kissed her hair, breathing in faint perfume. 'No my dear, I was lost in thought. Just thinking how lovely this place is tonight. Francie, could we have a little soft music, not the piano, a phonograph record. Something soft and soothing-something Viennese.'

Frances wondered, her brother had never asked such a thing before. 'Of course dear. Ben will help me with the Victrola. Tell me what you would like to hear.'

'My favourite, you know-Rosen Vom Suden, Roses of the South.' He laughed softly. 'Francie, remember London, the little shop that sold German records? Glad you got there before it became traitorous to buy anything German.'

The machine wound and steadied, the record revolved on the turntable. The night air filled with the intoxicating, lilting strains of the waltz.

Frank took his fiancee's hand. 'May I have this waltz my love?'

She held his arm. 'But your legs darling?'

'Tonight my dear, my leg does not exist. Ben's good brandy has given me strength. Come now while the music lasts.' Holding her close, they moved in perfect harmony.

The music stopped, he called from the far end of the verandah. 'Once more Francie, just once more.' Their bodies close together, her head buried in his shoulder, they swayed again to the strains of the music. Again the record came to an end, they stood for a moment locked together then slowly returned to the couch.

Muriel held tightly to his hand. 'Darling, that was heavenly.' She whispered, her head on his shoulder. 'Shall we go to the tower tonight?'

Ben frowned in the darkness. 'Forgive me, I overheard that Muriel my dear. As Frank's doctor and friend, I'm afraid I must insist he rest tonight. I know you would not want him to do further damage to his leg. Now it has been a truly wonderful evening, I'm sure you ladies must be tired. If you will excuse us, Frank and I will linger a while longer, we have much to talk about. Business matters, you understand.'

The women left reluctantly. There was a long silence. 'For God's sake, how could you even contemplate such a thing?'

'I didn't Ben, I had no intention. But how I was tempted, she is so loving, so sweet! I wish to God, she had found someone else.'

'I am truly sorry Frank. Pull your chair up close, even whispers carry in this place.'

'Remember London Ben? Remember the little house in Surrey? They were the good times. I can still see you the day you came to pick up Frances from that boarding house. Remember the Savoy and that song we all used to sing? 'Oh, oh Antonio, he's my sweetheart'?' He hummed a few bars. 'Something like that. Lately that tune keeps running through my mind. Thanks old man, a drop more would help. Yes, I remember all those good times and when I see all the hell we went through. It's not right Ben, it's not bloody right to survive all that and be laid low by this stinking disease.'

'Easy old man, easy. Yes, I know, I think about it too. How bloody futile the whole business was, but the main thing now is, what are you going to do?'

'Yes, what to do. I've agonized over this Ben and I'm not sure. I'll sleep on it-better still, I'll think on it.' He picked up the half empty Brandy bottle. 'I'd like to be by myself. Do you mind if I sit a while in the tower?' He gave a short laugh. 'Sitting up there in the captain's chair, concentrates the mind. Such a sense of peace. Would you mind?'

'I don't mind, if you think it might help. Tell me in the morning what you decide. Frank, promise me you will never listen to quacks, the arsenic treatment is your best hope. It's probably been greatly refined since last I read about it.'

Ben came down to breakfast later than usual, he pressed a hand to his forehead. 'Thank God, Charlie Hawks is standing in for me. Think I'll swear off late nights for a while.'

'Perhaps a little less to drink might help dear.'

He looked at his wife. 'Francie, don't say that. You know it was a special occasion.'

'I'm sorry darling. Here is your coffee, you will feel better after breakfast.'

He grinned. 'Thanks old girl. Has Frank come down yet?'

'I haven't seen him since last night. He must still be very tired. You could wake him when you are finished.'

Upstairs Ben knocked on his brother in law's door. Receiving no answer he looked inside. The bedclothes were thrown aside, spilling onto the floor. 'Now where the hell has he gone? Looks like he left in a hurry. Only one person might have seen him, Mick, he's always here early.'

He found Mick trimming branches along the drive. 'Morning Mick.'

'G'day Doc. Just took the lanterns down. Doin' a bit of trimmin'.'

'Good Mick. Have you seen Captain Chapman?'

Mick stopped sawing. 'Why yes Doc. Saw him first thing, he left pretty early, just as I got here. Got me t'help him give the car a push, battery was flat.'

'Did he by any chance say where he was going?'

'Down to Caves Motors t'have the car overhauled.' Mick lit up a roll your own. 'Dressed up in 'is ridin' gear, he was.'

'Riding gear?'

'You know Doc, breeches an' leggins, all that.'

Ben felt a strange sense of foreboding. 'Thanks Mick, you've been a big help.'

About to go, Mick's voice stopped him. 'Funny thing Doc, you know I've only seen the captain a couple o'times, he shook hands with me-said returned men should stick together.'

'That's typical of him Mick, he has always thought that way.'

'What I was goin' t'say Doc,' for a moment Mick seemed lost for words. 'He wished me compliments of the season and pressed this into me hand. Look, fifty quid, a bloody fortune! Fair dinkum Doc, I was flabbergasted. He must 'ave thought I was a bloody idiot or somethin', I didn't know what t'say. He just grinned an' gave me a wave.' Mick held the money out. 'You better give it back Doc, he probably didn't realise. I shouldn't have taken it anyway.'

'Of course you should Mick. My brother in law doesn't make mistakes like that. It's yours and good luck to you.'

Ben found his wife waiting in the doorway. 'Has Mick seen him?'

'He has just gone down to get the car fixed Francie. Where is Muriel?'

'She is getting dressed, Ellen is calling for her. You would have thought he would wait until she came down.'

'He's a busy man Francie, got things to do. Now stop worrying. I'm going down to meet him, he'll want a lift back. We won't be long, I promise you.'

Inside Caves Motors workshop he saw a familiar buff Buick. The foreman came to meet him. 'Morning Doc. Car all right?'

'No trouble Joe, thought I might see my brother in law here.'

'Left an hour or so ago Doc. Just left the car, told me to give her a complete overhaul, new tyres, the lot.'

'Will he be coming back later, did he say?'

'Not today Doc, this is a two day job.'

'I see. Did he say where he was going when he left here?'

'Matter of fact he did, asked me to drive him up to the stables, said you would be picking him up later.'

'Yes, yes of course. Thank you Joe.'

The police sergeant was busy with paper work when Ben walked into his office. He looked up. 'Well, this is a pleasant surprise Ben, what brings you down here?'

'Dave I need your help. Please don't ask me why now, but I've reason to think Frank has had an accident. He's gone riding somewhere and I'm worried about him.'

'You surprise me Ben, I've seen him ride, he's a good horseman.'

'Well I should tell you, it's his leg Dave, he is in a bad way. If he fell he would never be able to mount again.'

Dave eased himself from behind his desk. 'I've got young Ned, he's a good bush rider. Where do you reckon he'd go?'

'I'm not sure. We'll have to go to the stables first and pick up some horses.'

Ben questioned the stable hand. 'How long since Captain Chapman left?'

'Couple of hours Doctor. Will these do?' He led out three horses. 'All well shod and in pretty good nick. Keep a tight rein on the black.'

They headed into open country. 'Think we'll follow the creek Dave, Ned can do the hills, especially the timber.'

They rode in silence, inspecting every paddock and gully. Dave reined in. 'Buggered if I know Ben. I think we'd do better to follow up North Arm.'

The north arm of the river, more a big creek, ran deep and green. In the shallows by the steep creek, water lilies bloomed in profusion.

'About a mile before it hits the bush Ben. Pretty clear going up to the next bend.' They rode on. 'Hold it!' Dave pulled up sharply. 'Look up there. That must be his horse, bridles loose, he must have come off.' They cantered to where the chestnut mare barely looked up from it's grazing. 'Don't see anything do you?'

Ben dismounted and walked to the edge of the steep bank. His heart contracted-in the water just beyond the mauve lilies was the body of a man, half covered in weed. He found his voice. 'Dave for Christ's sake come over here!'

'Jesus is it him?'

'It's him all right. Better tell the young fellow to keep away Dave, I don't want him to see this.'

The sergeant cupped his hand to his mouth, the young constable was galloping toward them. 'Ned, go and get the nearest spring cart, quick as you can. There's been an accident.'

Reluctantly the young man turned back. 'Right Sarge, won't be long.'

'I'll have to strip off to get him Ben. Get the bridles off and hook them together. I'll need a hand getting up the bank with him.'

The body was brought to the water's edge, Dave emerged breathing heavily. 'Christ Almighty Ben, I could hardly shift him, had his fingers tangled in the weed. Poor devil was holding himself under.'

With the hooked bridles under the drowned man's arms, they dragged the body to the short grass above the bank. Dave began towelling himself with his discarded singlet. 'Why Ben, why for Christ's sake, would a man like him do such a thing?'

Ben knelt over the lifeless form. 'I don't know Dave. I suppose he had his own private hell. We'll never know. How am I going to tell the women?'

The big man finished drying himself and began putting on his uniform. 'Was he sick Ben, something fatal. That might explain it.'

Ben lied. 'If he was, he kept it from me. You know his leg was badly injured-he was in constant pain.'

'Surely not enough to do this Ben.'

'God knows Dave. As one of your oldest friends, I want a favour of you. It would make things a lot easier if we could forget the details.'

'How do you mean?'

'The way we found him. I know it's a pretty weak story, but let's say he went down to pick water lilies, his bad leg gave way, he fell in and got tangled in the weeds. Can you think of anything better?'

'No, sounds reasonable.' He looked up. 'Here comes Ned with the cart and Ed Gray is with him.'

'Good, I'll straighten the body out a bit.'

Frank's body was loaded onto the spring cart and carefully hidden from view with a horse blanket.

The old farmer puffed on his pipe. 'A bloody shame Doctor, a fine man like that-prime of life.'

'Yes, indeed Mr. Gray, a terrible accident.' Ben knew the man as a patient. 'I would appreciate keeping the matter confidential for the moment. He was my wife's brother you know.'

'Certainly Doctor, rely on me.' He shook his head. 'A shame though, a terrible shame.'

Ben took his friend aside. 'Take him straight to the hospital Dave. Tell Faith I will be there as soon as I can.'

'Nothing I can do? You know, help break the news?'

'I will have to do this myself Dave, God knows how. Frances is steady enough but I don't know how Muriel will take it.'

Both women ran to meet him as he pulled up at the gate. Muriel had decided to wait to be sure Frank was all right.

'Where is Frank? Did you find him?'

Ben took them each by the arm. 'Come inside with me.'

They sat staring with shocked eyes as he told them. 'His leg obviously gave way, that North Arm is deceptively deep, his heavy boots made it impossible, probably trying to pick water lilies.'

Frances was weeping quietly, Muriel sat motionless. Ben felt alarmed. She was in shock. 'Come my dear, come and lie down. I'll give you something, sleep for a while, then we can talk.'

She drew away sharply. 'No, I must go, I must go home.'

'Of course.' Ben spoke soothingly. 'I'll take you down to Ethel.'

'No Doctor.' She was strangely formal. 'I want to go home to my mother. Will you drive me to the station tonight? There are always seats on the train.'

Ben moved toward her, she drew back. 'Muriel my dear, you are in no state to travel. Please rest a few days.'

She shook her head. 'No, I must go. Please drive me down so I may pack.'

Ben took a deep breath, he knew it was pointless to argue. 'I'll see to the train, book you a seat and wire your parents.' He motioned to his wife. 'Come with us Francie, you will be able to help Muriel.'

He stopped at the post office and carefully worded a telegram-Muriel arriving Brisbane Express 6 a.m. tomorrow. Has suffered great shock, no danger, needs complete rest. Signed, Wakefield Doctor.

Ethel came with them to the station, she had Muriel by the arm, talking in low tones. The train's giant headlight cut the blackness of the night. It hissed to a stop, the guard hastily pushed her case through the open door. She stepped inside, turned briefly as the train began to move. 'Goodbye.' They barely caught the sound above the noise of the engine.

Driving back to the sleeping town, Frances began to weep, her head on Ethel's shoulder. The older woman spoke gently. 'There, there my dear. You have Ben and the children you know, it's Muriel that worries me. How do you think she will handle it Ben?'

'Well, she is in shock at the moment, retreated into herself. I'll write to her parents tomorrow. I really can't say, I'd have felt better if she had given way.'

'You don't think, in her present state, she would do away with herself?'

'No chance of that Ethel, her religion forbids it.'

Frances' voice interrupted. 'It's so wrong, so unjust. Yesterday they were happy and loving and now -.'

Ethel comforted her. 'We have all been through so much together, be brave, life must go on.'

Frank was buried in the Myuna town cemetery. The *Daily* carried a large column-Captain Frank Chapman, M.M., victim of a tragic accident. All the more tragic because of the impending marriage of Captain Chapman and Miss Muriel Halsey, one of our most popular teachers-then followed details supplied by Sergeant Truman who was one of the first on the scene.

A guard of honour comprised of returned men, including Mick, bore the coffin from the church and stood reverently in silence as the Rev. Tomlinson conducted the service.

Ben felt an ache in his heart at the familiar words-the Lord giveth and the Lord taketh away. Blessed be the name of the Lord. He felt faint, swaying slightly, he whispered quietly to his wife, then hoping no one was watching, made his way slowly back to the car. Thankfully, he sank into the cushions, his head back, eyes closed.

Someone touched his arm. 'You all right Doc? Had me worried a bit.'

'No trouble Mick, bit too much sun. Just need a rest.' He smiled at Mick's anxious expression. 'Can we give you a lift back later Mick?'

'Got the sulky Doc, thanks just the same. Me and the boys are goin' t'the pub.'

Ben tendered a pound note. 'Will you have one on me?'

Mick shook his head. 'No thanks Doc, we're right.' He blew his nose. 'Jeez he was a man. Wish I'd been in his unit, I'd have followed him to hell and back.'

'I think he would have known that Mick. Take care now.'

It was a sombre group that gathered at Harry's shop. 'God Gerry, yer Uncle Frank! Can't believe it. Him a war hero too.'

'Dad was there with your father Gerry. Never saw Dad so upset-couldn't eat his dinner.'

'He was always a good sport to us whenever he was up here. What about poor Miss Halsey? Jeez, I feel sorry for her.'

'She's gone back to Sydney-to her home I think.'

Gerald kicked at a stone. 'No use thinking about it. Come on, it's my shout, he gave me a quid for Christmas.'

'Thanks Gerry. Won't be long before we'll all be goin' different ways.'

At *Monaro*, as his wife tended the children, Ben poured himself a stiff drink and retired to the peace of his study. He sank wearily into his chair, leaned back and closed his eyes. He went back too far and the chair sprung forward spilling whisky onto his sleeve. 'Bugger it!' He reached for his handkerchief and then stopped suddenly, his gaze resting on a large white envelope. Frank's bold script leapt out at him. 'Private-Dr. Benjamin Wakefield.' Carefully Ben slit the flap.

Dear Ben,

As I don't know how to begin, I won't worry. I know you will give me a decent burial and keep my confidence. In case you find this before you find me-the North Arm, just before the bush starts.

My will is with Bryson and Cahill, Pitt Street Sydney. I have empowered you to enact as my agent and co-executor. Frances is my sole beneficiary. I had never made a will before but after seeing the medico in Sydney I knew it was essential to do so.

A few loose ends my friend. The house I just finished in Mosman was to be our home. There are some finishing touches inside yet to be completed. Prime position overlooking the harbour. My heart went into that house Ben, don't sell unless you decide necessary. Also I invested in six semidetached houses in Woollahra, which I intended doing up in time. They are run down and rat infested. The poor devils can hardly meet a few shillings rent. Please don't turn anyone out, they would have nowhere to go. Sorry to ask so much but you are the only one in whom I can put my trust.

My foreman, Les Haines, has been with me since I started building again, my right hand man, always gets a good gang together before we start a job. He is still working inside the house-I paid him a month in advance before coming up here. He is married with a couple of youngsters, trying to pay off a cottage in Mowbray Road, Willoughby. I request you pay off his mortgage Ben, he deserves it, a returned man and a battler.

I am writing this in the tower by the way, drinking your good brandy and slightly drunk. I'm full of resolve now-pray it doesn't disappear by morning.

Anyway, one more request. I leave the old Buick to Mick. I have left it at Caves to be overhauled and have paid the quote, if any more please settle the account. How I wish I could see his face when he hears this.

No doubt you are wondering why I have not mentioned Muriel. She told me, and she is incapable of lying, that should anything happen to me, she would enter the church. Her passionate devotion to her religion did worry me Ben, so much so, I doubt our marriage would have worked out. In Vino Veritos, eh?

Good night and good bye old friend. Frank.

Ben read and reread the letter, making a few notes in his pocket book. Filling his glass, he drank a silent toast to his brother in law, then putting a lighted match to the edge of the letter, threw it in the grate where it flared briefly, curling into fragile ash.

CHAPTER XXIII

School holidays over, Frank's death and the approaching new term, cast an unaccustomed melancholy over the household. Ben found his wife alone, he sat beside her, keeping his voice steady, told her-'Frank spoke to me privately some time ago, Francie. He was always worried driving up here and gave me the names of his solicitors. I will drop in and see them when I take the boys down to school.'

'Will you be gone long? I can't bear being alone anymore.'

'About a week my dear.'

She looked at him, her eyes deeply shadowed. 'Why Ben, why must it be us? We are an unlucky family.'

He put his arm around her. 'Hush, never say that. We must help each other.' She was silent, her head resting on his shoulder.

Time came for the journey to Sydney. Gareth relaxed, reading, scarcely taking his eyes from his book. Gerald sulked, rarely speaking, even to his best friend Dave Truman. Out of his father's hearing, he whispered. 'I'll only stay till bloody Easter then I'm coming to your school.'

Two days later, standing bewildered amidst a crowd of equally bewildered newcomers, he felt a tap on his shoulder. His old enemy, Fatty Shey, was standing there. A big boy, it was obvious he had been crying.

'Jeez Gerry, I never expected to see you here. I thought you were a Proto, bloody glad to see you though.' He added with a ghost of a grin. 'Looks like we're the only two from up North.'

'I am a Proto and I'm only here 'til Easter. Anyway, when did ya come down, didn't see ya on the train?'

'Last week, me aunty lives here.'

'Might as well stick t'gether Fatty, while I'm here anyway.'

'Gerry, fer Chrissake don't call me Fatty. Me name's Bernard-call me Bernie.'

'Okay. Do they have a tuckshop here?'

'Yeah, but I'm broke at the moment.'

'On me. Come on, lead the way.'

They munched cream buns, washed down with lemonade.

'Still don't know how yer come here Gerry. I mean a Catholic school?'

'The old man's a mate of the Headmaster.'

'Christ, the Boss Brother? You'll be right. Shit, there's the bell. We've gotta go to the assembly hall.'

Mr Bryson, the senior partner, welcomed Ben to his office. He was a man who wasted little time. 'Ah Dr. Wakefield. Delighted to meet you sir. Yes, I have Captain Chapman's will here. I see you are named co-executor. We are at your service Doctor, we will be glad of any assistance we can give. Your wife, no doubt you know, is the sole beneficiary.'

'I understand. Some time ago, my brother in law charged me with certain responsibilities in the event of his death, which will require some expenditure.'

'Of course Doctor, be assured of our co-operation.'

Ben had booked in at the Wentworth Hotel. After dinner he took the ferry to North Sydney, then a taxi to Mowbray Road, Willoughby. A pleasant young woman, with two small boys peering around her skirts, answered the door.'Is Mr Haines in please?'

'Oh yes sir, of course. Won't you come in?'

Les Haines, a tall wiry man, rose to meet him.

'Good evening, I am Dr. Wakefield, Captain Chapman's brother in law.'

'Pleased to meet you Doctor. We just can't believe it, he was the best boss a man ever had. Please, will you take a seat?'

'Mr. Haines, I am here to put Captain Chapman's affairs in order.'

'Please call me Les, Doctor, I'm not used to being called Mister.'

Ben smiled. 'Of course, thank you. Now there are a few matters I must discuss with you. Firstly, I understand you are still working on the interior of the house at Mosman.'

'That's right Doctor. The boss paid me a month in advance before he left.'

'So I understand from his solicitors. Perhaps I could meet you there tomorrow?'

'I'm there by seven Doctor, whatever time you say.'

'Well, it won't be that early. Now, I have another matter that concerns you.'

An hour later he left the house to his waiting taxi, leaving behind man and wife staring at each other in unbelieving joy.

Next morning, in a quiet street in Mosman, Ben stepped from a taxi. 'No. 17, this is it. Wait for me will you? I may be some time.'

The driver was more than willing. Fares like this were rare indeed.

Ben walked along the unmade driveway, it's position marked by pegged timber. Two fine old Liquid Ambers almost hid the house, obviously a cottage had once stood here. He stopped suddenly, curiously moved. So this was the house that Frank built. The land was flat and even from the road, falling away sharply to a strip of bush and the expanse of the harbour below. Built of red textured brick, the house stood poised, just above the decline. the glazed tile roof shone in the morning sun.

Picking his way through the builder's rubbish, he pushed open the heavy oak door. A torn canvas runner protected white Italian marble running the length of the panelled hallway. The sound of a saw guided him to where Les Haines worked at his bench. 'Good morning Les.'

The carpenter looked up with a start, wiping his hands on his apron. 'Morning Doctor, been expecting you. For a moment I thought -.' He looked down at his hands. 'But I guess I'm still dreaming. The wife and I still can't believe-I mean, owning your own home! Just like winning the lottery.'

Ben smiled. 'Rest assured, it's quite true Les. You will receive the Title Deeds in due course.' He looked at his watch. 'Now, there are a few matters I want to discuss with you but first please show me around.'

Upstairs and down, glass had been used to take full advantage of the position. To the left the towering cliffs of the heads loomed clearly visible. To the right two great arches of the Harbour Bridge appeared to hang suspended against the clear blue of the sky. The harbour, alive with scurrying craft glittered in the brilliant sunshine.

'It's a great sight Doctor, even better at night.'

Ben nodded. 'I'm sure it is. A magnificent position.'

Together they returned to the carpenter's workbench. 'How long before you finish here Les?'

'Just the architraves, here and upstairs, about three weeks, maybe less.'

'Then what will you do?'

'Try for another job somewhere. Not much about these days.'

'But the house is not finished, there is more to be done.'

'There certainly is Doctor. Bathrooms to be tiled, the plumbers haven't finished yet and then there's the painters and the landscaping.'

'Good Lord.' Ben put his hand to his head. 'Where would I find people to do all these things?'

'It's right here Doctor, in this notebook. All the quotes. The boss always used the same contractors.'

Ben made a rapid decision. 'I will take these names Les but I will leave you to contact them. Do you have a telephone?'

'Yes Doctor, the boss had it put on so he could ring me.'

'This is working out better than I had hoped Les. Now, would you be willing to overseer the whole job for me?'

For a moment the carpenter was speechless. 'Just like before Doctor? The boss always left it to me.'

'That's settled then. I'll see the solicitors tomorrow. Accounts will be settled when submitted and your salary will be paid each week.' He scribbled his home telephone number in the notebook. 'You phone me if any problems come up, reverse the charges. Now before I go are there any questions I can answer?' Les shook his head. 'You can rely on me Doctor.' He hesitated a moment. 'Will you be selling once the house is finished?'

'I've no idea at the moment Les. My brother in law wanted me to keep it. We shall see.' He shook hands. 'Goodbye for now. Just keep me informed if any problems arise. Oh, I almost forgot, what is happening to those cottages in Woollahra?'

Les shook his head. 'No idea. We did up two, the rest are not bad. All rented as far as I know.'

Ben nodded. 'I'll look into it.'

Three days later he was back in familiar surroundings. After an initial embrace, he held his wife at arms length, examining her critically. She looked tired. 'Well, how are you old girl?'

Frances smiled wanly. 'I'm glad you're home Ben. Did everything go all right?'

'No questions, not before I've had a drink, a bath and a good dinner. We can talk then.'

'I'm glad you came by day train.'

'It's damn dark when it leaves Sydney, Francie. Ideal time to arrive though, just the two of us.'

They sat at a late dinner. 'Come on, a little more wine - put roses in your cheeks. Tell me all.'

'Dr. Hawks will be glad to see you back.'

'To hell with that Francie. How did school go?'

'They all seem happy there. Dorothy has gone to the Presbyterian Ladies College.'

'So I heard, what about the others?'

'Judy pushes Harry all the way.'

'She would, she is an exceptional child.'

'Was Gerald very unhappy?'

He took her hand. 'Let us wait until Easter. Have you heard from Muriel?'

She shook her head. 'Not a word.'

'Well I suppose that's understandable. I saw the solicitors by the way. You are the sole beneficiary under Frank's will.'

She seemed disinterested. 'What does that mean?'

'Well, he has left everything to you, including the house he was building at Mosman.' He hesitated, unsure how to proceed. 'Francie, I've seen the house. It's beautiful, really it is. Right on the harbour. If you like my dear, we can leave here, live in Sydney.'

She raised her eyes, filled with long past pain. 'Leave here? I could never leave here.'

'But you will come and see it, when things settle down?'
'Perhaps, one day.'

Easter, 1930

Lambruk station seemed a little more crowded than usual. Most stood gazing along the tracks as a long whistle heralded the approaching train.

'Stand back, stand back please.' The station guard waved away those too close to the edge of the platform. Brakes clanged, steam hissed, doors flew open disgorging impatient occupants.

'Mum, Dad!' There they were. Frances gathered her sons to her.

'Well, let's not stand here all day. Your father asked me to look out for you Dave.'

Gerald pushed his nose to the car window. 'Gee, it's good to be home, can't wait t'get t'the swimming hole! Coming Dave?'

'I'll say, can't wait.'

'You haven't said much Gareth.'

'Just glad to be home Dad.'

Ben smiled. 'Of course, best place. By the way Gerald, who was that boy that got off with you?'

'Oh that's Bernie, Dad. Bernie Shey.'

'Not that boy you were always fighting with?'

'That was when we were kids. Bernies' one of my best mates now.'

Under his breath Ben murmured. 'Good God, wonders will never cease!'

'Is Dut - Dorothy home, Mum?'

'Yes dear, she came home last week. Her school breaks up earlier than yours.'

'Have you seen Beryl, Mrs. Wakefield?'

'Yes Dave. Beryl is very well, she and Judy and Enid Wells are inseparable.'

'Didn't Enid go away to school Mum?'

'No dear, her mother wanted her to stay here. The family will be leaving once Mr. Wells finishes his contracts.'

Dave safely deposited and the children reunited, Ben sank into his favourite chair. He looked affectionately at his wife pouring tea. 'Well, altogether again my dear. Thank you.' He sipped from his steaming cup. 'Gerald was held up by a flat tyre on his bike, Mick helped him fix it. Francie, I never knew a boy that age used such language.'

Frances smiled. 'Sometimes I think I know more about young boys than you do!'

'My dear,' He shook his head ruefully. 'I don't doubt you do.'

That night he sought out his youngest son. 'Well, what's the verdict, are you going back or do we change schools?'

Gerald had always been open and candid with his father who seldom asked embarrassing questions. 'I like it there all right dad. There's about five or six Proto boys as well as me. We don't have to go to Mass or anything like that-except poor old Bernie, but he's a tyke.'

'I see. So you are happy there?'

'I don't want to leave now Dad, everybody treats me well. They all think you're a friend of the Boss Brother.'

'You mean Brother McSweeney, the Headmaster?'

'Yeah, but he doesn't give me any favours. He's a real good bloke but he can be a bas-he can be tough too.'

Ben smiled in spite of himself. 'Well then, time for bed by the look of you.'

His son hesitated. 'Dad, what's a Jew?'

'A Jew? Why just a person like you. Why do you ask?'

'There are some at the school. Lots of the boys don't like them, they call them names.'

'What about you?'

'They're all right. One of them's a mate of mine. Funny name Dad. Isaacs, Solomon Isaacs. We call him Solly for short.'

'I see. I'm glad you are not one of those who call people names.'

'Not on yer life! He invited me and Bernie out to his place one weekend, out at Bellevue Hill.'

'That was very friendly of him. Did you enjoy yourself?'

'Yeah, it was great. Mr. Isaacs is rich I guess, his mother was real nice too.' He grinned at the recollection. 'Gosh the food was good, a change from the grub we get at school. The best cakes I've ever seen, all chocolate and cream.'

Ben laughed. 'I'm sure it was very nice, now I think you had better get into bed.'

'Yeah, I'm sure tired. Dad, just one thing. Why do they wear those little caps at home? Bernie and I had one too, we thought it was terrific fun.'

'That's just a Jewish custom. Now, off you go and see that dog sleeps on the mat and not on your bed!'

The next morning after the house had settled down, Ben phoned his partners to apologise for being a little late at the surgery, or clinic as they liked to call it.

'Take your time Ben, no rush. Everybody appears to be fishing or swimming, great weather for it.'

He was surprised to find Mick in the garden, 'You are supposed to be taking a few days off Mick. What on earth are you doing here?'

'Had to drive the wife and four of the kids to the beach Doc. Michael and Kerry rode their bikes down. Bridget can't manage old Blackie, the old bugger knows it too-won't budge when she holds the reins.'

Ben laughed. 'And they say horses are dumb! I've something to talk to you about Mick.'

Mick rolled a cigarette, he was curious but not worried, his job was safe, that he knew.

'You know I was down in Sydney sometime ago attending to my brother in law's affairs-his will, all that sort of thing. You happen to be a beneficiary Mick. Frank left you his car, you know the Buick. It's still down at Caves Motors.'

The lighted match fell to the ground, Mick stammered. 'Me? He left me his car. The Captain left me his car?'

'Yes Mick, it's yours to collect whenever you want to.'

'But,' he quavered, 'but Doc, I can't drive. I've never driven a car. And why me Doc, fer God's sake, why me?'

'Don't think about it Mick. My brother in law liked you. He made a will because he was worried about the dangerous roads on the way up here. Anyway, the boys at Caves Motors will teach you to drive, simple as ABC. You will find it handy with that family of yours.' He left Mick, utterly bewildered, sitting on his barrow, drawing deeply on his cigarette.

During May, Ben made another trip to Sydney. The house was completed. He made arrangements to meet Les Haines on the job. His taxi dove along the newly gravelled driveway to where the carpenter was waiting at the front entrance.

They shook hands. 'Good to see you Les. All finished?'

'Yes Doctor, nothing left to do.'

'The landscaper's have done a first rate job.'

Les nodded. 'Going to take a look through Doctor?'

An hour later they again stood at the wide enclosed entrance. 'I am most impressed Les. You have done a splendid job. Those floors-wonderful colour, what is it?'

That's Tallow, Doctor, invisibly nailed. The boss always used Tallow.'

'I see. Before I leave there are a few other matters I want to discuss with you.'

'First I've got to tell you, I owe you money Doctor. I've been receiving my wages after the job was finished.'

'I know that Les, that's what I want to discuss with you.'

Les waited.

'I want you to maintain this place in proper condition, I think I told you, my brother in law stated specifically in his will, it was his wish, it was not to be sold.'

'What do you want me to do Doctor?'

'Just as I explained, keep it in perfect condition. Your wages as now, will be paid regularly and I want you to hire a gardener to come in, say weekly.'

'You mean just to look after the place? It's almost money for nothing Doctor.'

'It is what I want Les, and by the way, you are at liberty to take on any other jobs you wish. Now, when you hire the gardener and any other expenses incurred in maintaining the house, phone this number. It's Bryson and Cahill's clerk, Mr. Fisk. He is under instructions to pay out any expenses submitted by you.' He smiled. 'Goodbye for now, keep in touch.' Ben left the carpenter speechless.

The taxi driver held open the door. 'That's a beautiful house sir. Must be one of the best positions in Sydney and I've seen most of 'em.'

'Yes indeed, I think you are right. Back to the ferry now, please.'

Ben rang the University inquiring for Alistair Pryce-Dr. Pryce had left the faculty and returned overseas. No, there was no forwarding address.

He made a brief visit to the cottages in Woollahra, coming away shaken and disturbed-was this Australia, land of milk and honey? Strict instructions were left with the agent-no family to be turned out, any necessary repairs to be attended to. He left Les Haines' phone number.

Ben considered it wise to avoid visiting the schools and took the first available train home.

There was a letter from Muriel. He didn't ask to read it, Frances told him the details.

'The poor girl apologizes Ben, she said she hopes she hasn't caused us worry. She considered entering a closed order but the Mother Superior felt she was not ready for that life and suggested a teaching order. She seems happy enough, accepting I suppose, and look, this came this morning by registered post. Her engagement ring. She said it might help me to think of her sometimes.'

'Well my dear, perhaps she will find solace there.' He held her to him. 'It's time we put all this behind us Francie, we have our own lives to live.'

She nodded. 'I know. How is the house?'

He told her all that had happened. 'We will have to furnish it one day.' He kissed her lightly. 'Soon as I can persuade you to come down with me.'

The year wore on, the depression showed no sign of lifting. Weary dispirited itinerants passed through the town thinking for the moment they had found a small paradise. Dave Truman reluctantly kept them moving. No, they could not stay, those were his orders. Some rations, but they must be kept moving. Many town people who went through their meagre savings, were forced to face the disgrace of the dole. Some older children left school to the despair of Charles Cummings, many had shown promise. He confided his unhappiness to Ben. 'A damn shame Doctor. Once they leave that's the end. Even if they wanted to, they could never pick up again.'

Ben fumed, he told his wife. 'A bloody disgrace, so many of our best and brightest lost forever. Let's have some tea Francie, I feel down today. You know, there are sick people in this town who won't come to me because they haven't the money. Good God, I would never turn anyone away.'

'Perhaps they don't know that Ben.'

'Well I certainly can't advertise the fact.'

'You could put a small ad in the *Daily*.'

He gave a crooked smile. 'Francie my dear innocent, I would be struck off, or worse.'

He finished his tea. 'Dave tells me it's worse out west. People are simply walking off their farms. Goddammit, it's a bloody disgrace in a country like this.'

An event occurred during the winter of that year -

The chemist had employed a girl from a large family to work in his pharmacy. A plump, rather plain girl, she had learnt quickly and become quite competent as a shop assistant. Tom Coburn spoke to Ben in strictest confidence.'That girl, Dora McQuire, the one who works in Connors' Pharmacy, is pregnant. She came to me, she is desperate, wants an abortion. Even if I would consider such a thing, it's too late, she is over three months.'

'Poor child, who is the father?'

'I had to wring it out of her-Connors is, the bastard.'

Ben had never heard the old man swear before.

'Apparently he will admit nothing. Told her it's not his but said he will have it sent to a home in the city.'

Ben nodded. 'That's the sort of hypocritical creature he is. Is she still working?'

'No, and the family have rejected her. Staunch Catholics.'

'Where is she living then?'

'I've no idea, doesn't want to talk about it.'

Ben groaned.'God help us! It's a wonder they don't stone her.'

On his way home, Ben was surprised to find Mick standing by the side of the road. 'Bin waitin' for ya Doc.' Mick's horse, still hitched to the sulky was grazing in the short grass.

'I see you are still using that rig Mick, where's the Buick?'

Mick grinned. 'T'tell the truth Doc, I couldn't get the hang of it. Bridget drives, took to it like a duck t'water.'

Ben smiled. 'Glad to hear it, she is a capable woman, your wife.'

Mick rolled the inevitable cigarette.'Need your advice Doc.'

Ben waited.

'Y'know that girl, Dora McQuire? Worked in Connors' shop.'

'Yes, I believe I do.'

'She's livin' up with us now.'

'I didn't know that Mick.'

'She's in the family way. Family kicked 'er out.'

'Did they now?'

'In a bad way too, terrible crook in the mornin's. Bridget's known 'er a long time, that's why she came to us.'

'That was very decent of you Mick.'

'Doc, Dora don't tell lies, that bastard Connors is the father.'

'She told you that?'

'She told Bridget. Been goin' on for some time. Told 'er he'd tell the police she'd bin stealin' if she didn't come across.'

Ben muttered an oath under his breath. 'What can I do to help Mick?'

'Dunno, jus' thought I'd tell ya.'

'Glad you did Mick, keep me informed.' He drove away, deep in thought- 'Thank God for the Mick's of this world.'

That night he told Frances, she was shocked. 'That poor girl, what can be done?'

'My dear girl, what can I do? What can anyone do? Confront him? He would deny everything, his word against hers. In any case, you know the general attitude-it would be her fault. Women have no rights, especially a poor girl like Dora. It's different of course for the well to do. Little affairs, wife swapping. Why do you imagine so many go up to Southport for weekends.'

'I can't believe it! I feel ill even thinking about it.'

'Being the person you are my love, that's understandable.'

Frances looked at him. 'Ben, have you ever -.'

He laughed, putting his arms around her. 'You goose, how could you think such a thing?' He kissed her tenderly. 'We are still lovers aren't we?'

Ben missed his sons more than he would admit. He became increasingly fond of his adopted children. The bond between Harry and Judy grew ever stronger. She had him standing now and with a calliper on his left leg he could walk short distances. The three religiously visited the town cemetery each Sunday, taking flowers, keeping the twin's parents and Frank's grave lovingly tendered.

Ben chuckled when Peter told him how many of the farm children reacted to the septic system at the school. 'They reckon the cisterns are little wells.' He grinned as he told the story. 'Tell the truth Doctors, before we came here we had never seen one either!'

During this time Gerald's Carlo had grown to full size. Black with white feet and a white tipped tail held like a flag, he accompanied Ben everywhere. The moment the car door opened he was in the front seat, his head turned to the breeze. Ben told Dave Aitken. 'Never leaves the car, just curls up waiting for me. Actually, I believe he is waiting for Gerald. Every knock at the door, every car that comes up the drive, he is out like a flash. I don't know if dogs experience disappointment but he just comes back and lies on his rug, his head between his paws.'

Dave laughed. 'Dogs are a damn lot smarter than we give them credit for Ben.'

In the first heat of the summer Ben received an urgent call from Dr. Coburn. Dora's time had come, would he assist? They set Bridget to boiling water, the time honoured method of keeping anxious people out of the way. The birth proved difficult and the old man used chloroform liberally to ease the girl's agony. Finally, it was over, the cord cut and tied, the baby wrapped in a blanket. 'There is a little repair work there Ben. When you finish, I will see you outside.'

Ben met his colleague on the verandah. 'Thank heaven that's over. She had a hard time but she is sleeping now.'

'Yes, thank you Ben. The girl will be all right-did you notice the child?'

'You mean the colour? I have never seen one so blue before.'

'In my time, I have seen very few. A few cases appear in the Journals from time to time. Blue babies-cause unknown.'

'What's the prognosis?'

The old man shook his head. 'In my experience, a few weeks, a month at the most.'

In the privacy of their bedroom, Ben related the days happenings. 'A little girl, poor little thing. Perhaps it's all for the best.'

A month went by. Ben being the only surgeon in the group was kept busy. The matter of Dora and her baby completely slipped his mind. Leaving the hospital after a particularly trying morning, he stood on the steps adjusting his hat. The air felt heavy, a storm was brewing. He found Mick waiting by his car. He sensed trouble.

'Sorry to bother you Doc. Dora's gone missin'.'

'Missing? When Mick?'

'Baby died this mornin', she put it in the old pram and said she would take it down to Dr. Coburn.'

'But that's six miles Mick. When did she leave?'

'About six I reckon. Wouldn't hear of Bridget drivin' her. Said she wanted t'think.'

'Wait here Mick, I'll phone Dr. Coburn.'

Dr. Coburn was concerned. No, he hadn't seen her but in her state of mind, better start a search party.

'Mick, I'm going for Sergeant. Truman. We'll meet you up at your place in about an hour. Better take the old sulky.'

Along the road between Myuna and Lambruk, numerous timber cutters tracks led off into deep bush. They followed many to where they ended in stumps and smashed trees. With thunder threatening, they found her. She sat sleeping in a little clearing, under a giant Iron Bark, the pram covered with mosquito netting beside her. Mick pointed his whip. 'By God, there she is, sound asleep!'

Ben gently lifted the girl's head. There was a slight acrid smell, a trickle of dark liquid oozed from the corner of her mouth. Dora was quite dead.

She was buried with her baby in the Catholic section of the cemetery.

Details of the tragedy were kept discreetly quiet. Mick shivered with cold fury. 'The bastard! The bastard, I'll kill 'im, so help me!'

Dave Truman was fond of the game little digger. 'Take it easy Mick. Why put yourself and your family in jeopardy for a creature like that?'

The usual pre Christmas get together of friends had ceased after the death of his mother. Ben was secretly relieved. Pieter and Ellen DeVries were the only constant visitors of the old group. Dr. Coburn and Alice had their children and grandchildren to celebrate the season. Mick religiously hung out the magic lanterns. 'Ain't like it used t'be Doc!'

'Still, wouldn't be without them Mick. Wouldn't feel like Christmas.'

Out of numerous spares in the basement, Mick had carefully assembled four lanterns which glowed proudly on his front verandah. 'Bridget thinks they're extra grouse Doc. Y'can see them comin' home in the dark. Michael looks after them, he's a real good kid is Mike.'

Gerald with Dave, Dorothy and Beryl spent their days in the swimming hole or fishing the deep pools for perch.

Dorothy sighed. 'Oh, this is wonderful. At school we have to wear stockings and gloves. I hate going back there.'

Judy came with Harry, she seldom went in the water being content to sit by the wheelchair and watch.

Peter spent his days with Lois Stanley. They were inseparable at school, both reserved and shy they found pleasure in each others company. Gareth and Enid Wells roamed the countryside on their horses.

Ben looked forward to seeing the DeVries. Pieter was a good friend, one in whom he could confide.

'The partners, except old Tom of course, he only comes in two days a week, want a younger woman as receptionist.'

'They want to get rid of Ethel?'

'Hell no, they couldn't get on without her. She knows the business and they must have her for the women patients.'

'What does she think?'

'Haven't spoken to her yet but frankly, I think she will be pleased. She has too much to do as it is. However, enough of my problems, how is that young brother of yours?'

'In the pink, far as I can make out. Seems to be handling your interests faithfully. When are you going down again?'

'God knows. Here let me freshen your glass.'

Pieter settled back with a sigh. 'Glorious here at night. The women should be here with the coffee any minute.'

'Any news from Dan?'

'Just a card from California, no doubt Ellen will tell Frances all about it.'

'Poor devil, do you think he will ever be released from his vows?'

'God knows.' Pieter rose to open the door. 'Ah that aroma, let me help you, ladies.'

Monaro, 1932.

'Francie, no arguments please! I've booked into the Wentworth Hotel months ago. We can't miss the opening of the Sydney Harbour Bridge. Mrs. Ellis will look after the house and Mick will take care of Carlo. Now, what other objections have you?'

'What of the children?'

'We are taking them with us my dear. I've made all the arrangements-I didn't tell you before in case you found some reason not to go. And something else, Pieter and Ellen are going. They will have a few days with Dorothy and then go on to Melbourne.'

On the long train journey he called to his wife in the lower bunk of their sleeper. 'Glad we're on our way now?'

She smiled up at him in the dim light. 'Ben, I feel excited. I think I needed this-to get away for a while, but just for a little while!'

Sydney surged with people for the greatest event in it's history. Through contacts they obtained favourable positions, smiled at the pomp and ceremony then gasped at the sight of an absurd little man in uniform dashing forward on horseback to slash the ceremonial ribbon before the astonished gathering. He was handled roughly and quickly bundled away by the police and the official opening went ahead.

Ben hired a car and with his excited family was one of the first few hundred to travel from south to north without the aid of a ferry.

The house overlooking the harbour captivated Frances. Ben had seldom seen his wife so happy and excited as she tastefully furnished the empty rooms. She stood critically examining her handiwork. 'But what are we going to do with it? We can't just leave it standing here.'

'It was Frank's wish my dear. In any case I've hired Les Haines' wife to air it regularly and do what needs to be done. She is a fine young woman and glad of the money. There is a regular gardener too, so you see it's in safe keeping.'

'I still can't see the point of it Ben, a beautiful house like this and so many people homeless.'

'I know but there is nothing we can do about it Francie. Having wealth and property is a bit like religion, an accident at birth.'

Frances entered into the gaiety and excitement of the occasion. With Ellen she explored big stores. 'I never realised how dowdy I'd become, I felt terribly provincial that first night at dinner.'

Ellen laughed. 'You have always managed to look elegant Frances.' She ran her eye over her friend's new costume. 'And rather stunning now, I'd say.' Laughing they strolled on, arm in arm.

The days passed too quickly. By the weekend after fond farewells, they were on the train back to Myuna. 'Good Lord, how they've grown, isn't Dorothy a lovely girl?'

Ben smiled at his wife. 'Quite a young lady!'

'Perhaps it's just as well her Mistresses can't see her when she is on holidays.'

The Cadillac was waiting where they had left it, by the station.

'Glad to be home?' Ben asked Harry and the twins in the back.

'It was nice.' Judy spoke for the three. 'And it was good to see Gareth and Gerald and Dorothy, but Myuna is best.'

Late in the year Ben brought, what he thought was startling news.

'Strictly confidential Francie, please don't discuss it with your friends on the Committee, not until it becomes public anyway. Promise me?'

Frances nodded, a faint smile on her face.

'Charles Cummings has been seeing Beryl's mother. It's quite serious, I believe.'

'Oh that. Everybody knows that, they are going to marry this Christmas.'

He looked at her, slowly shaking his head. 'Is there anything you women don't know?'

She laughed, the soft laugh he loved so much. 'Of course not, it's our business to know these things.'

'Well, I'm glad. He's a solid fellow, Cummings. Used to be hard on Gerald and his mates but from what I've heard, it was richly deserved.'

'I'm glad too, they appear very fond of each other. He is like a father to Beryl, she has blossomed after that terrible business.'

The new surgery, The Clinic, as the young partners termed it, functioned smoothly. Dr. Coburn still made an appearance two days each week, his vast experience called on when all else failed. Even though the depression still held the country in a vice-like grip, Myuna expanded. The doctors were kept busy, Ben confined himself almost entirely to surgery.

Dave Aitken asked if he could have a minute of Ben's time.

Ben motioned him into his surgery. 'Sit down Dave, I've only hospital rounds, nothing urgent.'

'Thanks Ben. Had an odd case today, you may be interested. Remember that chemist, Connors, the one associated with that well hushed up scandal?'

Ben nodded. 'Not likely to forget that matter.'

'I saw him today. Complained of back pain, been consulting some Naturopath in Brisbane.'

'Those fellows make more money than legitimate practitioners.'

'So I've heard. Anyway, I put him on the table, palpated the abdomen-large mass in the lower right quadrant, size of a small melon.'

Ben looked interested. 'Really?'

'Yes. Fortunately Dr. Coburn was here, went over him carefully. Reckons the liver is involved as well.'

'What are you going to do, did you tell him his chances?'

'No, not really-you know how it is. Told him surgery is his only hope. Referred him to Dr. King in Sydney.'

'How did he take it?'

'Badly. Went to pieces, I had to help him to his car.'

That night Ben told Frances. 'I'm a doctor Francie, I've sworn to help and succour the sick but if ever there was a case of poetic justice!'

She shuddered. 'How long will he live?'

'Two months, three at the most. Personally, I would never operate in cases like this. King will though, he's a quick man with a scalpel. Even quicker with his fee.'

Monaro, 1935

Christmas Eve, the night calm and still, the magic lanterns casting their spell. Ben stood with his oldest friend, Pieter DeVries. 'Lord. I feel ancient. Where has it gone Pieter. Yesterday we had children, now we have young men and women. I just can't get used to it.'

'You had better my friend. For better or for worse, we have grown older-they have grown up.'

'So Dorothy is going to do law?'

'Well, she starts next year. I can only hope she stays with it. What of Gerald, any plans?'

'He is talking Architecture. One of his friends, the Shey boy, is doing it so hopefully he will stick it out.'

'Gareth coping with medicine all right?'

'Too early Pieter, they should not take them so young. They know nothing of life at that age.'

'I doubt if it will be a problem with Gareth, he was made for it.'

'I hope so. I tried to talk young Judy into giving it a go, she has the intellect.'

'Not interested?'

'Wants to do nursing, against my advice but promised she would think about medicine later.'

'She has to go to the city I suppose?'

'No, thankfully Faith will take her on. I tried to tell her what a bastard of a job it is, actually not in those words of course. Emptying bedpans, lifting heavy bodies, incontinent patients, ingratitude, long hours.'

'And she still wants to do it? Bless her generous heart.'

'Yes. She has become very dear to us. I don't think she wants to leave Harry. It's quite strange in a way, I have never seen such a bonding between two people.'

Ben refilled their glasses from the crusted old brandy bottle, holding the golden liquor to the dim light. 'Gets better with age. We must think of ourselves in those terms old man.'

They were laughing when their wives appeared, the fragrant odour of coffee on the air. They sat talking until the early hours.

'I wish Tom and Alice were with us.'

'They have their own interests now.'

Frances looked at her friend. 'You will always come, won't you Ellen?'

'As long as we can breathe. It's a second home. Just imagine trying to tell Dorothy we are going home tonight!'

'Where are they all?'

'Playing the gramophone and dancing by the sound of it. The girls will be agonising over what to wear for the wedding.'

'Ah, so we can sit here in peace and watch Christmas Day dawn.'

'Francie, I know I will be fragile tomorrow, in fact not fit for human company, but let's have some champagne-to celebrate our offsprings' launch into the cruel world.'

She laughed. 'I have anticipated you, Ben Wakefield. Shall we get it Ellen?'

'So Mick's boy, Michael, has been accepted into Duntroon.'

'And doesn't he deserve to be-Dux of the school, a finer specimen of young manhood would be hard to find.'

'Mick must be very proud.'

'In his own quiet way. They have done miracles with that land, been running prime vealers for years up there.'

'Surely the old boy must be able to retire now and take it easy.'

'Not Mick. I've told Bob to keep an eye on him but Mick's his own man. He has a proprietal attachment to this place. Yes, that's our Mick, a shortened leg, chronic bronchitis, the old hand gnarled with arthritis. I would miss him Pieter. Mick can stay until he is ready to go.'

At that moment Frances and Ellen appeared with four slender necked bottles of Champagne in their bucket of ice.

CHAPTER XXIV

Monaro 1937

Christmas time again, the two men sat as always on the top verandah. Ben ran his hand through his hair. 'Grey as a badger. Youth I'm afraid has gone.'

'You have little to complain of, at least you have hair! My barber should be charged for clipping my few remaining strands.'

Ben laughed. 'You old war horse-you're still sound as the proverbial bell.'

'So you keep telling me.' He sniffed delicately at his brandy balloon. 'How many years have we sat here drinking the captain's magnificent brandy? It must be practically finished by now.'

'You have seen the cellar Pieter, there are racks left.'

'Lord bless his providential soul, a man of impeccable taste!'

'True. I wish I knew more about him.'

'Do you think things are improving Ben, to talk of more practical things.'

'I think the worst may be over. As you know, we go down to Sydney every Easter now. Frances has made Frank's house very comfortable. Gives me a chance to catch up on whatever is new.'

'We should do the same, although nothing changes as far as the law is concerned. Only the well heeled can afford litigation.'

'You might say the same about medical high flyers, although there are some big names in Macquarie Street I wouldn't trust to lance a boil.'

A few moments silence then-'Our offspring are back with us again Ben.'

'Yes. I try not to show it but it's sheer joy to see them. Of course, Frances makes no effort to conceal her emotions.'

Pieter laughed. 'Nor does Ellen. They are rewarding but sometimes I feel they regard us as fossils. They may be right of course, fossils pickled in good brandy.'

'Had an unexpected visitor a couple of weeks ago, meant to tell you.'

'Anyone I know?'

'No, a ghost from the past really. An English bloke, Allistair Pryce, friend of Frank's from the days of the Movement.'

'Must have been quite a shock.'

'It was. Didn't recognise him at first, couldn't recall the name.'

'What has he been doing?'

'Left Australia after Frank's death and now teaches at some university in America. -Philosophy- quite a profound thinker. He has taken a years Sabbatical, just travelling. Doesn't think anything has changed here, disgusted with the sacking of Lang. Reckons the country lacks a soul.'

'Hardly charitable.'

'I'm not so sure Pieter. Here safe in our little cocoon, we are insulated from the political passions of the cities.'

'I suppose so but what did he reckon Lang could have done?'

'Marched that pompous little man to the nearest boat and packed him off home.'

'Good God! Can you imagine the Conservatives countenancing that?'

'Frankly no. He says Australians individually are the finest people he has ever met but our tragedy is we never had a Thomas Paine or an Abraham Lincoln.'

'What do you think?'

'He could be right. Anyway, he has gone again, only stayed a couple of days.'

'Back to America?'

'I imagine. He did make some disturbing comments about the situation in Europe, swears there will be a war.'

'God forbid!'

'Amen to that, but apparently this German, Hitler, has them all bluffed. Makes outlandish demands and gets his own way.'

'What of the League of Nations?'

'Hopeless according to Pryce, toothless, moribund. America pulled out, disgusted with the insincerity of the Europeans.'

Pieter sighed, rolling his balloon between his hands. 'I just can't bring myself to think about it.'

'Well, this is no time to be morbid. The ladies have promised Champagne to toast the day in. I trust you are still capable of a little bubbly?'

'Really Ben, you do me an injustice. I may be somewhat fragile tomorrow but,' he drained his brandy, 'it is Christmas after all.'

Joined by their wives, they gossiped until dawn lit the eastern sky.

'Dorothy has grown into such a beautiful young woman Ellen, you must feel very proud.'

'I look at her and try to remember my little girl in plaits. Sometimes I wish she had never gone down to University. Such strange talk. Spain, war, really there are times I feel I am talking to a stranger.'

'All young people are the same, it's a state we all went through.'

'Do you think so Ben? She only seems normal when she comes home to Myuna.'

'That's understandable, she is with her oldest friends.'

'All the girls are lovely, especially Judy. Those green eyes and dark lashes. She must have plenty of admirers.'

Pieter drew on his cigar. 'I'll never understand how she took on nursing, Ben.'

'That is all she wanted. I think her attachment to Harry had something to do with it. Believe me, I had it out with her. Reminded her of her promise to consider Medicine, perhaps she will later on.'

'She still likes the work?'

'Best Theatre Sister I've ever had. Knows what I want before I ask. Everybody loves her. Faith says she couldn't do without her.'

'Faith must be getting on.'

'She is. Same mold as Ethel, work until they drop.'

'Ethel is a great grandmother now, I hear.'

'Twin boys. Dave comes in for some ribbing, proud as Punch though.'

'Gareth still keen on the Wells girl?'

'Seems so, they are out riding every day he is home. Although with Gareth it's hard to tell. There is a bit of Frank in Gareth.'

'Not a serious relationship then?'

'Lord knows, only time will tell.'

The lazy weeks of the holidays passed quickly. The old gang were seldom apart. Dave and Beryl had decided to become engaged once he qualified and she finished Teacher's College. Hal Wynter and Jack Raywood had teamed with two pretty girls from their school days. They both attended Hawkesbury Agricultural College, although a year junior to Peter. George Donates was in Greece. His parents, loyal to the country that had brought them comfortable prosperity, felt he should know the land of his ancestors and secretly hoped he would marry a Greek girl.

Since the previous Christmas when he and Dorothy had first kissed, Gerald had yearned for more. Times they were locked in each others arms when he felt he could scarcely breathe, he was gently rebuffed. She told him, straightening her clothes. 'No Gerry not yet, I'm not ready.'

When the young bloods got together the talk was almost exclusively sex. 'Got between Dutchy's legs yet Gerry?'

'Don't be a turd Jack, I've got too much respect for her.'

'Oh yeah. What about you and Beryl, Dave. Got in yet?'

'God, you've got a dirty mind Jack. What about you and Hal, anyway?'

'I'm doing all right mate, fair dinkum. Don't know about Hal.'

'You're full of bullshit Jacko. Stop talking about sex anyway, I'm getting a fat. Come on you horny bastards. I know where we can get a drink.'

'We can't it's after six.'

'Yeah, and we're travellers. Old Bob'll let us in the back.'

'First sensible bloody thing you've said all day.'

On the last weekend of the holidays, Gareth called for Enid. 'Our last canter for a while. I'm going to miss it.'

'Oh Gareth, Dad wants to know if he can come with us, just as far as Johnson's paddock.'

'Why not?' He grinned. 'Is that nice old gelding his?'

'Yes, he hired it this morning. Wait just a minute, I'll tell him.'

They trotted through the town into open country. Enid's little mare, head pulling to one side, stepped daintily beside the bigger horses.

'How are your studies coming along Gareth?'

'Fine thank you sir, they keep us at it.'

'You like the idea of medical practice?'

'Very much Mr. Wells, hope to work with Dad one day.'

They came to a broken down gate lying between two huge posts, grey with age, one end still supported by rusted hinges.

'This is Mr. Johnson's property isn't it?'

'Yes Dad, he lets us ride through here whenever we like.'

'Well my dear, this is as far as I go. Be careful now.'

By the left hand post stood the rotting stump of a vast Tallowwood, long taken by the timber millers. On it's top, a green tree snake lay coiled, basking in the warm sun. At the sounds of the horses it whipped into action, disappearing with a hiss-like escaping steam, into the sword grass below. The little mare reared, plunged forward in fright then backed quickly, rearing high on it's hind legs. The light surcingle snapped. Unable to hold the reins, Enid was thrown, her head hitting the massive gatepost with a crack like a pistol shot. Gareth gathered her in his arms. Her eyes were closed, blood oozed from her ears, her skull was fractured. His stricken face turned to her father. 'Go quickly, get my father and the ambulance!'

Ben met them where the track joined the town road. In Gareth's arms, Enid lay like a rag doll, her long hair brushing the ground. Inside the speeding vehicle Ben folding his stethoscope, looked steadily at his son. 'There is no need for me to tell you, is there?'

Monaro, September 1939.

'Ethel look at this, just picked up the paper with the full gist of Menzies' speech-'England Declares War on Germany'.'

'It's been coming a long time Ben.'

'Christ, don't they ever learn?'

'I doubt it, mankind being what it is.'

'I suppose we will be fed the usual rubbish-all over in six months.'

She looked at him. 'God preserve the young ones. Your friend Mr. Pryce was right.'

'He told me things I couldn't believe. Inhuman treatment of Jews and other minorities, I'm not sure I believed all he said.'

Ethel became her usual practical self. 'Let us not worry until we have to Ben. For now it's work as usual. You have surgery scheduled for this afternoon, remember?'

He smiled at her. 'Yes Matron.'

Towards the end of the year, Ben received a phone call from the manager of Caves Motors. There were two Cadillac sedans in Brisbane. As a doctor Ben would have priority if he was interested.

'But my car is perfectly serviceable, it's in excellent condition, why should I want to change?'

'Because there won't be anymore coming in Doctor, The war you know.'

'Well, if you think so Mr. Summers. Would you be able to arrange delivery for me?'

'No trouble Doctor. I'll phone Brisbane right away.'

'Do you know the colours by the way?'

'Both dark blue, Midnight Blue, they call it.'

'Thank you Mr. Summers, let me know when I can expect delivery.'

Ben replaced the phone and leaned back in his chair. 'Smart man, Summers, knows his business.' He picked up the phone again. 'Get me Caves Motors please-Mr. Summers, it's Dr. Wakefield here. My wife's old bus is showing it's age, can you do anything about a new Chevrolet?'

'I think so Doctor, leave it to me, a few still available I believe.'

Monaro, December 1940

Meeting the train at Lambruk, Ben's heart leapt at the sight of his youngest son in the blue uniform of the R.A.A.F. He had driven over alone as Gerald had phoned and asked if he would mind giving a lift to Dave and Bernie Shey. Petrol was already rationed so it seemed the sensible thing to do.

'So you have all enlisted. I think you might have let us know Gerald.'

'We all went down together Dad. Lot of other blokes from the old school and Uni were there too. We're out at a place called Bradfield Park, just doing drill and having lectures.'

'And having injections?'

'Yeah that's right. Few of the blokes keeled over.'

Ben smiled. 'It's more the anticipation than the injection Bernie. Do you know where you go after this initial training?'

'Don't know, nobody does until we go before the selection Committee. Anyway, that's three months off.'

'I see. How long is your leave?'

'Only a week Dad but we get two extra days travelling time.'

'At least you will be home for Christmas. Do your parents know you have enlisted Bernard?'

'Not yet Doctor, probably be a bit of a fuss but they will soon get used to it. Gosh I'm looking forward to some good food!'

'Aren't we all?' Gerald leaned back in his seat. 'Gee, this is a beaut car Dad, you can hardly hear a sound.'

'Glad you like it. Well, there is Myuna, almost home again.'

'Is Peter home Dad?'

'Not yet, I'm sure if he will be. He, with Hal and Jack have enlisted in the A.I.F.'

'Phew! Soldiers eh? What about Gareth?'

'Gareth has been rostered to work at the hospital over Christmas. One of the other joys of being an intern.'

'Is Judy back?'

'No, she is still in Sydney. Should be home before long.'

'And Dorothy?'

'She is here and to put your mind at rest Dave, Beryl is home too.'

Frances fought back tears as she embraced her son.

'Aren't you glad to see me Mum?'

'Of course I'm glad to see you. It's just that I hoped I would never see my boys in uniform.'

Gerald hugged his mother. 'Don't worry Mum, nothing to worry about. Probably all over before I get to fly an aeroplane. Where's Buddy, I want to tell him all about it.'

The two old friends sat enjoying their brandy as they had for so many years. 'No magic lanterns this year Ben.'

'No, all lights banned. How do things look to you Pieter?'

'Can only go by the papers, this bloody Hitler seems unstoppable. Frankly I don't like the look of things. The Japanese worry me.'

'I saw some photographs when I was in Sydney last of the atrocities committed in China. Photos of Chinese sitting with their hands tied to a peg in the ground, a Jap officer, sword above his head, ready to bring it down. The next photo showed the head on the ground blood spurting three feet in the air. Bloody revolting! Put your mind at rest old friend, if the worst comes, no one here will suffer, I will personally see to that.'

'Apparently the Americans tried to talk some sense to both Germany and Italy without much success. Their mission was doomed from the start. Hitler doesn't want peace, he wants Europe.'

'Looks like he had already conquered most of it.'

'Yes, but I see the Japanese as our great worry.'

'There is Singapore of course, they should stop them.'

'They say an impregnable fortress. Thank heaven for that.'

'The boys have joined up I see, Gerald and his friends.'

'Doesn't give me any joy I can tell you but they are men now, they make their own decisions. Nothing I can say or do will change them.'

'We had a hell of a scene with Dorothy, wants to join the W.A.A.F.'s, I think that's what they call them. Anyway, after much persuasion, she has promised to stay with the firm that took her on for one more year only. Ben, that's what she actually said - one year only! Made it quite clear she is her own woman.'

Ben sighed. 'Don't know how we are going to manage at the clinic. Both Dave and Charlie are leaving. Apparently the army wants every medico it can get. Fortunately Judy is coming back after Christmas. Without Ethel and Faith, God knows how I would manage. They have so much experience.'

'Ethel left rather suddenly didn't she? I was surprised.'

'Yes, something to do with the divorced daughter. Back soon thank the Lord, can't manage without her.'

'Mick's eldest daughter started nursing last year I believe.'

'Mary, yes. She is coming along very well, another Judy.'

'Ah,' Pieter smiled, 'the ladies with the coffee.'

The holidays ended too soon, Gerald and his friends departed in high spirits which was not shared by their parents.

'Alone at last!' Ben stretched luxuriously. 'I'm bushed, I need a rest. There is so much happening I swear I'll make the most of every free moment we have.'

'What did the Government man want with you today?'

Ben groaned. 'My God, what didn't they want. We are to grow beans and peas, even Mick has a directive. Thank God his son is not old enough to join up. Apparently we are going to have an army of Land Girls to work the land and harvest the crop. Can you imagine it?'

'Why not? Women are capable. Where will they be housed?'

'Tents I suppose, I don't know. Leave that to the authorities. Where is Harry by the way?'

'Where he usually is, sitting in his chair by the gate, waiting for Judy.'

'By the way, that's something I'd like to discuss with you. She went to Sydney to do a Tresillian Course, almost twelve months ago. Why isn't she back yet?'

Frances seemed a little flustered. 'Would you like another drink dear? You usually have a brandy after dinner.'

'You know I've already had a drink, I could be called out seeing I am the only one available. Except for old, Tom and I certainly won't have him worried.'

'Could we talk for a while?'

'Nothing has stopped us before has it?'

'It's Judy, Ben.'

'What is there to talk about?'

'I don't know where to start.'

'For God's sake Frances, stop going on. What about Judy?'

When he used her proper name she knew she must be wary. 'She has had a baby.'

'What!' He stood up fixing his wife with an amazed stare. 'What the hell are you talking about?'

She kept her nerve. 'Judy had a baby three months ago.'

'Three months ago?'

'It's true Ben. She will be home next week.'

His voice took on an icy edge. 'Really, how charming. May I inquire the name of the father?'

She started to cry.

'Stop blubbering for Christ's sake woman! You have obviously known about this and never told me. Kept me in the dark.'

'Judy made me swear not to tell you. She thought you would disown her.'

'What sort of a man do you think I am?'

She whispered, holding back the tears. 'The kindest, most loving man I've ever known.'

He put his arms around her. 'Sorry darling, I'm acting like a bastard. It can't be all that bad. She must have known someone we didn't know about.'

She held him close. 'Ben, Ben darling-it's Harry. Judy has been sleeping with him, they love each other.'

'My God!' He held her at arms length. 'Well I'll be damned.' He fell back into his chair. 'I will have that drink now old girl.' Frances brought him his glass. 'Thank you, I need this. Now, tell me all, right from the beginning please.'

'When she knew she went to Dr. Coburn. She wanted to have it terminated.'

'Abortion you mean, don't mince words. As if old Tom would countenance such a thing.'

'He was wonderful to her. It was his suggestion she go to Sydney. One of his daughters arranged a flat and befriended her.'

'And Ethel knew all this was going on, I take it. That's why she disappeared for four months.'

'She stayed with Judy for a month before the baby was born, then looked after them both until Judy could cope.'

'For God's sake Francie, why didn't she come to me? I don't understand.'

'Ben she loves you. She was terrified you would hate her.'

He shook his head. 'Damned if I know, must be something about me.'

She sat on the arm of the chair, her arm around him. 'Ben, it's a boy. Ethel tells me he is beautiful. Judy has called him Tom, after Dr. Coburn. You don't mind do you?'

'Mind? Of course I don't mind. They will have to be married of course. Or has that little ceremony already taken place without the groom's father being invited?'

'Ben please, it's been hard on me too.'

'Yes I know, forgive me. It will all work out.' He smiled at her. 'Most of our troubles have, haven't they? Anyway, it will be a relief to have her back again.'

'I don't think it will be for long dear, Judy has enlisted as an army nurse.'

For a moment he sat speechless. 'Pass me that bottle Francie and if anyone rings tonight don't call me unless they are dying!'

Ben had a long talk with his son. 'It's a wonderful thing Harry. You and Judy have always been, how can I put it-there has always been something rare and, to me, very beautiful between you.'

'You are not angry, Dad?'

'Harry, my dear son, I could never be angry with you. Happy would be a better way to describe how I feel. Fate dealt you a cruel blow, but my boy you have gained more than most men could hope for in a life time.' He held his son's withered left hand, smiling fondly. 'And don't forget you have made me a grandfather!'

Judy stepped from the train, a neat trim figure in the uniform of an Australian Army Nursing Sister, followed by Ethel holding a tiny bundle close in her arms. Frances rushed forward. 'Judy, oh Judy my dear welcome home!'

In the flurry of excitement Ben took her arm. 'Welcome home daughter, we are very proud of you.'

In the car, Frances took the child from Ethel and pushing back the blanket exclaimed, 'look, he's sleeping and so beautiful.'

Judy took her hand. 'Will you look after him for me Mum? When I come home Harry and I are going to have our own little house. I will be able to care for both of them then.'

On the day after her arrival, Judy and Harry were married in a private ceremony, by the Rev. Tomlinson. Harry stood throughout, holding his father's arm. Earlier Ben had said to Judy. 'Please wear this, your mother's wedding ring. We have kept it all these years thinking you might wear it one day.'

The girl's eyes filled with tears, gazing at the thin gold band. 'For the rest of my life I will keep it on, no matter where I go or what I do.'

The few days she was with them melted away. It seemed she was no sooner home than she was waving goodbye as the train for Sydney pulled out from the station. On the way, Harry had sat holding her hand as they whispered to each other.

With his younger colleague gone Ben expected to be overwhelmed but to his surprise the surgery was remarkably quiet. 'It's odd Ethel, people seem to forget their aches and pains in time of trouble.'

'Just as well, we could never cope, even when Tom Coburn comes down.'

'Glad to have you back by the way.'

She busied herself at the steriliser. 'Sorry I was away so long.'

He waited.

'Aren't you going to ask me why I didn't tell you?'

He nodded. 'It crossed my mind. Damnation Ethel, why? She need never have gone away.'

'Of course she had to. Can you honestly say you would have understood?'

He leaned back, hands behind his head. 'I don't know. I've asked myself that same question a hundred times. I simply don't know. Anyway, it's all over and done with now. Judy has gone, our poor little Harry grieves and dammit, I'm a grandfather. And this bloody war, I don't like the look of it. If the Americans don't come in, well there is no doubt about it, we are done for.'

Ethel stood drying her hands. 'We have seen it all before Ben. Yes, I'm worried too but no use loosing heart, just hope and pray for the best.'

The following day, Ben sought out Mick. 'Just have to let things go here Mick. You can't be doing this and the farm as well. How many Land Girls have you got up there?'

'Just three Doc. Young Kerry does the bulk of the work but, by cripes, they're keen.'

'Kerry is still going to school, isn't he?'

'My oath. I've told him, without an education he'll end up like his old man.'

'If he did I would be proud to know him. Heard from Michael lately?'

'Just a note. He's gone overseas. He's a captain now, Doc.'

Ben smiled. 'He is a credit to you and Bridget.'

Mick rolled the inevitable cigarette. 'Things don't look good Doc.'

'No they don't Mick. God knows what will happen. The Japanese worry me.'

'Yeah, we're like a shag on a rock here. If they ever do come, me old Winchester'll take a few.'

'Let's hope it never comes to that. Now, the matter we were discussing before. Bob has gone and you can't do all this yourself.'

'I'm only doing the grass Doc, nothin' else. Yer missus, beg pardon, yer wife does the work of two men. Grows vegies only, reckons flowers are a waste of space, a time like this.'

'Well all right, the grass only. Remember, that's our bargain. Do I have your word?'

'Fair dinkum Doc, you know me.'

'That's the trouble. And, if you don't mind telling me, what's this I hear about you being on the coast patrol at night?'

Mick exhaled slowly. 'Yeah, just keepin' an eye on things Doc.'

'You're a bit long in the tooth for taking on so much. Just see you don't overdo it.'

'Know what they told us to do Doc? Bung holes in every boat along the river. Reckon the Japs might use then if they come. The bastards are mad.' He grinned. 'They won't get Gareth's though. Put it up in the bush under some roofing iron. Yeah, gave it a good coat of sulky varnish first though.'

Over the evening meal Ben told his wife of the day's happenings. He tried to avoid discussing war news but Harry dwelt on the subject.

'Things look bad Dad, according to the paper. Do you think Judy is in any danger?'

'Not in the least, nurses are kept well away from the firing line. Right back at the base.'

'You got injured though.'

'That was different Harry. I was in a forward dressing station. Nurses are never in places like that. In any case, Judy is still in Australia isn't she? What did she say in her last letter?'

'That was weeks ago dad. She said she would be having some leave. I haven't heard anything since.'

Ben looked at the handsome face of his crippled son, now drawn with anxiety. 'I wouldn't worry old son, she will just turn up out of the blue. See if I'm not right.'

That night Ben confided his fears to his wife. 'I'm worried Francie, far as I can see, the war is lost. If he attacks England that's the end.'

'What will happen to us?'

'I don't know, leave us to the Japanese I imagine.'

'But Singapore is there to stop them, isn't it?'

'That's our only hope. It's an impregnable fortress. Frankly my dear, I think that is where Judy may have been sent but for heaven's sake, say nothing to Harry.'

'It's so sad Ben, to see him sitting there every day, just waiting.'

'Well I'm damned if I'm going to worry any more until I have to.' He looked over at the crib. 'How is our grandson?'

'He is beautiful. Takes his food, never cries just gurgles and kicks. Ben he has filled an ache in my heart I thought I would never lose.'

'Listen my dear, don't become too attached. When all this is over and Judy comes home-just remember you are only his grandmother.'

'I can love him can't I? Nothing can stop me doing that.'

He sighed. 'No, you are free to love him, as I do. Just remember what I said.'

By the end of March the country still shimmered under a hot sun.

'Need rain Doc, but the creeks are still running. I've put in an application for a pump. They want the crops but they don't tell us how the hell to water 'em.'

'It will come Mick, as usual we'll probably have a flood.'

'Yeah, that's how she goes. Anyway, looks like I'll get me pump.'

A late night telephone call toward the end of the month, from Gerald, excitedly told his parents that he, Dave and Bernie had been selected for pilot training and would Ben please pick them up at the station. They had seven days leave before being sent to Elementary Flying Training School. Lucky for them, their leave came right on Easter, Dorothy and Beryl would both be home.
Frances worried, 'at least we will see Gerald but not a word from Peter or Judy.' She sat mending a sock. 'I've spoken to Jack's and Hal's mothers, they have heard nothing either.'

'That's the army my dear. Don't worry, they will turn up.'

She seemed unconvinced. 'I hope you are right.'

The weather remained hot and dry. A dance at the School of Arts Hall swarmed with Land Army Girls hungry for male company. Gerald whispered to his friend. 'Jesus mate, I'm dying of heat, I'm a lather of sweat. Let's get the girls and slip out of here before the bloody sheilas eat us alive. By careful manoeuvring the foursome, during the supper break, slipped out of the hall.

Both girls look relieved. 'It's so good to get out of there, some of those older men walked all over me.'

'Come on.' Gerald grasped Dorothy's hand. 'Let's get while the goings good.'

'Where are we going?' Beryl stood with her arm around Dave.

'I know, come on, the old waterhole!'

'But Gerry, we don't have swimsuits.'

'Who needs them? It's dark as pitch.'

The girls seemed hesitant.

'Come on, it's safe. Not a soul to see us.'

'You will behave yourselves.'

'It's only a swim Dutchy. You two stay together and Dave and I will stay together.'

The water was warm, like silk on their bodies. The girls stayed close, talking, laughing quietly. Gerald and Dave floated on their backs.

'Glad there's no moon. Don't the stars look close?'

'Yeah, just about touch them, great isn't it?'

'Gradually they moved towards the girls, just a touch at first then they were standing locked in each other's arms.

Gerald phoned his friend early. 'See you down by the river, mate. By the old boat shed. Can you get a couple of bottles of cold beer?'

They sat secure from public gaze, the comforting sound of water lapping the ancient piles of the shed. They drank without speaking until Dave broke the silence. 'Jesus, I'm between shit and a shiver. I don't know if Beryl will ever speak to me again. I want to get engaged before we go back.'

'What happened?'

Dave shook his head. 'What happened to you first, I don't know how to begin.'

'What happened? Christ mate, I thought the end of the world had come.'

'You mean-I mean you actually-?'

'Yeah, what happened-we were standing up to our knees - Dorothy took my prick and started playing with it. I'm telling you mate it was so hard you could break finger nails on it!'

'Gawd, what happened then?'

'She took it in her hand and guided it in. God, I was in up to my balls. She hung on like a limpet, put her legs around me. When I came I thought I was going to die.'

'Jesus!'

'That's not the end of it either. We went and lay on the bank. I was limp, she kept playing with it.' He groaned at the memory. 'I thought the first time was beautiful but the second-it lasted so long. I tell you Dave, it was the greatest thing ever happened to me.' He took another drink. 'And you know what? While we were kissing, she put her tongue in my mouth, God that was lovely.'

They sat silent, slowly sipping their beer.

'So that's it mate. I'm going to ask Dorothy to get engaged to me. I've always wanted to you know.'

'Yeah, you two were always pretty close. It's only natural. I rang my grandmother this morning, she's giving me the money for an engagement ring. I sure love Beryl, Gerry.'

'What happened between you two last night?:'

'We were kissing like you and Dorothy, you know tongue in mouth. I don't know where girls learn these things but I tell you Gerry, honestly I thought I'd faint! God, she had my prick in her hand-her skin is so soft. She put my hand between her legs and told me to rub gently. Then she put her tits, nipples isn't it, up to me and told me to suck.' He stood up. 'Open the other bottle mate, I'm getting a terrific hard just thinking about it.'

Gerald opened the bottle, a weary grin on his face. 'We'd better go for a long swim after this.'

'I begged her, bloody near cried, to let me do it. She just kept rubbing. I had my finger in her fanny going in and out like my prick should have been. Didn't you hear us? We must have come together. God, she had it so tight, it still hurts. I couldn't believe anything could be that beautiful.'

'Just as well you didn't put it in mate, I'm starting to worry I might have, you know, put Dutchy in the family way.'

Dave shook his head. 'Not the first time mate, I've heard that it's all right the first time. I wouldn't worry.'

'Jeez I hope you're right. So it was good with Beryl eh?'

'Good? It was marvellous. She did me again later, just gently. Just wanted me to keep kissing her while she did it.'

'Gawd, stop talking about it. Let's shoot up to the waterhole, cool our balls off. We can go in bare ass, there'll be nobody about.'

'Yeah, just keep an eye open for those Land Girls, one of them felt me up last night.'

'You're kidding.'

'Be buggered I am!'

'Any good?'

'No oil painting. Come on let's go. Here, come on Carlo, thank God he can't talk.'

On the last day of their leave, news of their engagements appeared in the *Myuna Daily*. Desperately short of newsprint the paper now appeared only on Mondays and Fridays.

To celebrate the occasion, the families gathered for dinner in the private dining room of the Star Hotel. Talk of the war was studiously avoided. The management went out of it's way to provide an excellent meal. Toasts were drunk, the girls compared rings. 'It's beautiful Beryl, I love rubies.'

'Dave's grandmother told him to spend as much as he liked. I do love it. And yours is gorgeous.'

Dorothy glanced around to make sure no one could hear. 'It was Miss Halsey's. Gerry's mother said she would have wanted me to have it.'

There was no chance for lingering goodnight's, the hour was late. Gerald called to his friend as they departed. 'See you at the station mate.'

Because of increasingly severe rationing, it was decided that Ben would take the four young lovers to Lambruk. He diplomatically waited in the car, first shaking hands with his son and his son's best friend, advising them to take care-wondering as they entered the station, what else he could have said. It sounded fatuous but what the hell could you say at a time like this?

On the hard station seats the couples sat, holding hands. The sound of the approaching train broke the spell. The guard wasted little time, mail bags and boxes were rapidly unloaded, mail and baggage taken aboard. Smoke belching the train was on the move again, the girls running along the platform grasping at outstretched fingers.

Dave and Gerald lounged back in their seats. 'Going to be a long night, bloody hate to leave. But I'm excited just the same.'

'Yeah, Mum made a packet of sandwiches and a thermos of coffee.'

'So did Mum, and take a gander at this.'

'Shit! A bottle of Scotch.'

'Yeah, only medium size but it'll help.'

Gerald lit a cigarette.

Thought we weren't going to smoke, they reckon it's no good if you're flying.'

'Just this one mate, I need it-promise.'

Dave sighed deeply. 'What a week, what a bloody gorgeous week!'

'Yeah, and we're both engaged. Can you beat it?'

'God I love Beryl. Can't wait for this bloody war to finish.'

'Me too. How about a little drink? Get those water glasses up there. I'll pour down low where nobody can see, they'll all want a bloody swig.'

'Let's have a sandwich, should eat with liquor, doesn't go to your head so much, so the old man reckons.'

'Right. By the way where's Bernie, don't see him anywhere.'

'Left yesterday, had a big blue with his old lady.'

'What about?'

'He's sweet on Mick's daughter Mary, you know, the nurse.'

'How do you know?'

'He told me. Mick's left the church, so she's ratshit with his family for a start.'

'I'll be buggered. Now you mention it, I saw them at the dance. She looks a good sort-Bernie was all over her.'

'Yeah, poor old Bernie. Can't believe it can you, we used to be deadly enemies.'

'Is he a good tyke?'

'Don't think so, he told one of the Brothers to prove there is a God, one day, and got paraded to the Boss but nothing much happened, far as I know.'

'They never made a tyke out of you?'

'I told you before mate, they don't try. There was even a Jewish bloke there, he and Bernie and I got around together. Clever bugger too, he's doing Medicine like Gareth. About a year behind him I think.'

'Well, let's knock the rest of this stuff off, we'll need some shuteye. Wonder where we're going-you know, where they'll send us.'

'No idea, we'll soon find out though. Canada they reckon.'

'Wonder what it's like over there.'

'Yeah, should be good. Jeez, you can't see a thing through these windows.'

'Blackout mate, you know, no lights.'

'Yeah. Wasn't a bad little party last night, whadaya reckon?'

'It was great but they spoilt it by taking the girls home with them.'

'I was dying to see Dorothy.' He grinned. 'Might have had a quick knee trembler!'

'Don't be bloody disgusting Gerry. You know you promised to be careful from now on.'

'Only kidding mate, only kidding. Say, wasn't old Cupie great? Shook hands, said he was proud of us.'

'His memory must be fading. Did you notice how Beryl's mother looks at him? Thinks he's the greatest thing that walks on two legs.'

'Didn't waste much time sinking the sausage, Mrs. Cummings is well and truly up the duff.'

'Good old Cupie, he knows it's not just to pee through now.'

The empty whisky bottle on the floor beneath them, the two young service men slept the rattling night through.

The hot dry weather continued, rain was desperately needed. Violent electrical storms lit the night sky. Cracks appeared in the thirsty soil, old pumps that had seen better days, were overhauled and repaired by the few men still maintaining the slipway. Reticulated water to the town was strictly monitored, hand watering of gardens was limited to one hour each day.

Arriving home Ben mopped his moist brow. 'Thank heaven our spring always runs. You know, we must have twenty thousand gallons in these cisterns of ours.' He sat back contentedly. 'I might as well not go into the Clinic some days, hardly any patients. Oh yes, a new girl from Sydney is down with measles.'

'I hope it doesn't spread.'

'Shouldn't think so, Ethel ran her up to the hospital and Faith has her in isolation.'

Frances brought a jug of cold lemonade.

'Thanks old girl, just what I need.'

She sat smiling at him. 'About those Army girls- wonderful, so healthy in their shorts. I never thought I would live to see the day girls would be so free and independent.'

'You were always one for the emancipation of women. This may be the beginning.'

'I certainly hope so. Most women are nothing but drudges, dependent on their husbands for a few shillings when the mood takes them.'

'Not all Francie, but I know what you mean. God knows I see enough of them.'

'I hope they keep their independence when the war is over.'

He grinned. 'What about women for Parliament?'

'Why not? Women are just as intelligent as men, you have said so yourself.'

'I know but how can you convince a hide bound ultra conservative electorate? Especially in the country. It would be considered presumptive. Female presumptuousness.'

Frances changed the subject. 'Ben, why hasn't Gareth come home for a visit? You said he would get some time off. It's been months.'

'He will my dear, he will. Times are not normal, you know that.' He had kept to himself his son's passionate avowal that he would never come back to *Monaro*. Enid's death had broken him. His grief, he kept from his mother. In the privacy of his study, Ben had seen tears, tears his son only revealed to him. He sighed heavily. 'How is our grandson?'

She was nursing the baby. 'You don't mind do you Ben? He is the only thing I have left to cling to.'

'Just don't leave Harry and me out, my dear.'

'I could never do that, you know I couldn't.' She pulled the blanket from the sleeping babies face. 'Isn't he beautiful?'

CHAPTER XXV

Monaro, July 1941

'Well I'll be damned.' Ben waved a page from a notepad at his wife. Only the second letter from Gerald. 'They have finished their Elementary Flying Training, now they are in Embarkation Depot. Says he thinks they are going to Canada for further training. Two days leave, not even time to come home.'

'That means we won't see him.'

He took her gently by the arm. 'It might be some time before we see any of them Francie. Just keep our spirits up. They will be all right, have faith my dear, just have faith.' In his heart Ben felt a deep foreboding. His fears were shared by Pieter DeVries.

'Don't like the look of things Ben. Just between us, I believe the war is lost. The British are damn lucky to get as many as they did off Dunkirk. You can forget any help from them.'

'You mean the Japanese?'

'Yes, we're bloody helpless.'

'There's Singapore.'

'Thank God for that. Our only hope, far as I can see.'

'How was your trip to Sydney?'

'Nothing changes, still the same crowd of wealthy half-wits thronging the 'Australia', spending their time between there and Romanos. Still get a good meal there by the way. Yes, women mostly, the Vaucluse set and like suburbs,. Haven't the slightest idea there is a war on. Honest to God, Ben it made me cringe. They regard anything Australian as vulgar and worship everything English. Read only English magazines, buy only products made in England and, God help us, most of them have never been out of the country. I can appreciate now, more than ever, how your brother in law felt.'

'It doesn't go for the average man in the street though, the average poor devil trying to make ends meet.'

Pieter opened a box of cigars. 'Lucky to get these. Went to Frank's old tobacconist in Pitt Street. You were saying the average man in the street? I don't know Ben, wasn't it your grandfather who said-give him enough grog and racing and he will believe in anything?'

Ben sighed. 'It seems so. We're a pretty apathetic lot when it comes to politics. I know most of the men around here who have joined up, have done so for the adventure or to relieve the monotony of married life.' He drew on his cigar. 'I pray to God they are not disillusioned as we were. Damned if I know though, they are a pretty gutsy lot.'

'To the point of foolhardiness at times. As shock troops I truly believe they have no equal.'

They sat silent for a few minutes, each lost in his own thoughts.

'I see Ethel is back. Rather sudden trip wasn't it?'

'Yes, naturally I don't question her movements. The divorced daughter again I think.'

'She is one in a million.'

Ben laughed. 'She is a warrior all right. Damn glad to see her back though.'

Surgery began around ten each morning. Ben sat at his desk waiting for Ethel to announce the first patient. He was mildly surprised to see her close the door and sit facing him. 'Nothing doing? I thought we were seeing a couple of Land Girls.'

'We are but I have something to talk about first.'

'I hope everything is all right in Sydney.'

'Just sit back and listen, Ben.'

'Good Lord old girl, you sound serious.'

'Depends on how you take it.'

'Take it? What on earth do you mean? You make me nervous!'

'I went to Sydney to see Dorothy, she wrote me. Ben, she is a little over three months.'

'What?' It was a long drawn out 'what'. 'Pregnant? For Christ's sake, who?' He put his hand to his forehead. 'Oh no, you don't have to tell me, I know Ethel. For God's sake, how am I going to tell Pieter and Ellen?'

'Ben, please wait until you hear the rest of it.'

'The rest of it?' He shook his head. 'I blame myself Ethel, I've never talked to him, never advised him of the risks.'

'Nature is not interested in advice?'

'How bloody true. Where is she, is she all right?'

'She is at my place, I brought her back with me. Now please, listen to what I have to say.'

'Sorry old girl, go on.'

'She wanted my advice, how and where to have an abortion.'

'God, no!'

'I told her to do nothing until I got there. That's why I left so suddenly.'

'Thank God you were here, she would have gone to some bloody butcher. It makes me sweat just to think of it.'

'I put that out of her mind very quickly. Poor girl, she was in a distressed state.'

'So she has agreed to have it. Where, who is handling it?'

'Yes thankfully. Looks like the honour of the delivery will fall to you.'

'What a rotten shame they hadn't married. They could have, you know.'

'I'm coming to that.'

'Coming to what? I don't follow you.'

Dorothy and Gerald are now married.'

He stared incredulously. 'Married? How could they be married?'

'If you would stop interrupting me, you would know by now.'

'I'm sorry Ethel, forgive me, I've had enough shocks the last year or two to last me a life time.'

'Well, I've still got contacts you know, back from the old days. Those that are still alive and back in uniform in chair jobs.'

He nodded without speaking.

'To cut the cackle, I managed an interview with the C.O. at Bradfield Park. Gerald and his group were still there in the Embarkation Depot. Managed weekend leave for him and they were married at the Registry Office.'

'Well I'll be damned!'

'Yes, the C.O. was a decent type. Dave and Bernie were there and Gareth as well. I don't know if you know but Gareth is going straight into the Army after Christmas.'

'As usual, I'm the last to know any bloody thing. So what now?'

'Dorothy wants you and me and Frances to come along when she tells her parents.'

'When is that to be?'

'Tonight if you can arrange it. I think the sooner it's done the better.'

He groaned. 'I'll ring Pieter. You will have to stand by me Ethel, I feel guilty somehow.'

'Don't be ridiculous Ben, for heavens sake.'

Ben waited until the evening meal was over. 'Delicious fish Francie.'

'We are lucky your older fishing patients still appreciate you.' She looked serious. 'Ben, did you know some of the men, those they won't take because they are needed here, have received white feathers?'

'No, I didn't know. Those that send them are moral cowards, I thought that disgusting practice disappeared with the last war.'

'Mick got one. He wears it in his hat band.'

Ben lay back in his chair, tears of mirth rolled down his cheeks. 'Oh Lord, isn't that Mick? He is giving those creatures the message they deserve.' He wiped his eyes. 'Anyway I have some news for you.' He looked at his son, his food scarcely touched. 'No news of Judy, old chap?'

'Nothing Dad, surely she has had time to write.'

'Believe me Harry, she will. Look, we haven't heard from Peter and Jack's and Hal's parents have heard nothing. It's typical of Wartime Harry don't worry, we'll hear before long.'

'I wish I could be with them. I'm just a blasted cripple!'

Ben tried to control the huskiness in his voice. 'I know you do old son, but you are the only ones we have left, you and Tom.'

Harry excused himself. 'I'm going to my room to read and write letters I'll keep them until I know where to send them.'

When they were alone Ben told Frances the news. 'I don't know how I am going to face Pieter and Ellen, they will be devastated.'

For a moment she looked at her husband. 'Perhaps they won't be. They might even be happy.'

'Francie I feel responsible, I should have advised the boy.'

'You are not responsible, how could you be? Gerald is a man now.'

'That's what Ethel says. I think I need a drink.'

'Do you think you should? I think it's best we pick up Ethel and Dorothy and get it over with. Dorothy needs her mother now.'

'I still think I need that drink. Just one, I promise.'

The following morning Ben was surprised to see his friend's Buick outside the surgery. Pieter wound down the car window.

'You're an early bird. Everything all right?'

Pieter nodded. 'Spare a minute?'

'Of course, come in.'

They sat facing each other. 'Phew, a bloody shock, I can tell you. I never dreamt!'

'Well, she is over the weeping stage. Fact is Ben, I think she is beginning to enjoy the whole thing.'

'How do you feel in the cold light of day?'

'Frankly, I'm delighted. Naturally the women would have preferred a big slap up wedding. You know, Mrs. Gerald Wakefield falls nicely on the ears.'

'I think it was always meant to be between those two, Pieter.'

'Yes, pray God all goes well with him.' He stopped, his hand to his head. 'Sorry Ben, that was best unsaid.'

'The risk is always there Pieter, we both know that.'

'I know, but I'm damned if I will even think about it. Incidentally, I would like to reimburse Ethel, she must have incurred considerable expense.'

'Don't try old friend, you would only offend her.'

'What a wonderful old girl, they certainly know who to turn to when there is trouble.'

Ben smiled. 'I can attest to that. What else is news? I know you have something else on your mind.'

'Couldn't talk to you last night, but truth is Ben, I need a change.'

'What have you in mind?'

'When I was in Sydney last, an old friend asked it I would be interested in the Legal Department of the Army.'

'Lucky devil, what did you say?'

'I've accepted and leave in a couple of weeks.'

'What of the practice?'

'No worry there, old Emerson up at Lambruk will handle anything that comes up. I'm restless Ben, feel so bloody useless.'

'I know, war does that to all of us. I feel the same. Have you told Ellen?'

'Not yet but she is so well occupied now I don't anticipate any objections.'

With Pieter, now Major DeVries, in Sydney Ben was at a loss to find anyone with whom he could discuss the progress of the war rationally. He confided his innermost fears to his wife. 'I honestly believe the war in Europe is lost, Francie. God knows what will happen. England is helpless and we will probably end up an occupied country.'

She seemed not to hear him, she had shut it out of her mind.

'Harry got a letter today.'

'At last, from Judy I hope.'

'Yes, she and other nurses are doing special training in Melbourne. She doesn't know when or if she can get leave.'

'At least we know she is safe. Still no word from Peter?'

'Not a line and nothing from Jack or Hal, I was speaking to their mothers today.'

'Typical war censorship Francie, we will hear sooner or later. By the way, how is the coffee holding out? I could do with a cup.'

'Almost gone, we will just have to do with tea and what I have tasted so far is not very good.'

About the only patients Ben saw over the following months were the usual long term regulars and a sprinkling of Land Army girls. It was all so easy. This day he felt faintly annoyed when Ethel ushered in the last patient. He didn't bother to look up as she sat next to him.

'Lieutenant Landon, Doctor.'

He closed his pad, looked up and stared. She was beautiful. Brown curly hair cut short, hazel eyes, a dazzling smile showing perfect teeth.

'Oh, I am sorry Lieutenant, please forgive me. Afraid I was miles away.'

'Jane, Doctor. Jane Landon.'

'I see, and what brings you here?'

She smiled at his confusion. 'I'm afraid I have a tick.'

'A tick? Where, are you ill? I mean have you felt ill in any way?'

'No, but I thought you should take it out for me.'

Ben stood up. 'Certainly, where is this little creature?'

'I really will have to get up on the table to show you.'

'I see, well please do.'

She lay on the couch, removing her skirt first, she pulled her slip up to her hips. 'Here Doctor, on my hip.'

He gazed at her long slim legs, browned by the sun, her brief pink panties, the ivory sheen of her skin. His hand trembled as he gently slid the elastic from her hips. The tick well burrowed in, clearly visible. 'They can be dangerous. I will just swab the area and cut the body close to the skin.'

He felt strange. The girl was looking at him, smiling. His hands felt moist. Composing himself, he opened the lid of the steriliser, dropping in the scissors and forceps. She was straightening her skirt. Ben assumed as professional an air as he could muster. 'I'll give you something for the itch Lieutenant, then see me about the end of the week and I'll remove the head.'

Ethel looked up as he ushered the young woman out. 'Last for the day Ben,'

'Well, we are not exactly overworked are we?'

'Pretty girl, Jane Landon. Her husband is overseas.'

'Really? She doesn't look old enough to be married let alone an Army Officer.'

'She is older than you think. I was talking to her while she waited for you.'

'She will be back Friday I think, to have the head removed. Goodnight old girl, see you tomorrow.'

Driving home, the vision of the girl's long slender legs, her firm healthy skin, sank through his mind. He felt sensations he thought long cooled. Aloud he muttered, 'no fool like an old fool.'

Jane Landon presented again the following Friday. She lay on the examining table in only her slip and panties. Ben busied himself at the steriliser, conscious she was watching him, that smile on her face. Completely relaxed, her knees drawn up, slightly parted, she watched him approach with forceps and basin of antiseptic solution. He felt slightly faint. 'Miss Landon, please straighten your legs and slip your underwear down so I may see the area.'

'Jane, Doctor. Please don't be so formal.'

He hesitated. 'If you wish. Just let me see the area so I can remove the head.'

Five minutes later he was seated at his desk. As she was leaving she fixed him with that dazzling smile. 'Thank you Doctor for being so good to me.'

The door closed behind her, he wiped his moist brow - Good to her? Now what the hell does that mean?

Surgery finished for the day, he took a bottle of brandy and two glasses from his desk and called to Ethel. 'Can you spare a minute?' She opened the door. 'Please have a spot with me old girl.'

She eyed him curiously. 'Looks like you need one.'

They talked until he could bring himself around to it. 'Ethel, when that young woman-if that young woman ever comes again, for Christ's sake come in with her!'

She eyed him with a faint smile. 'Bad as that eh?'

August, the last month of winter, rough rain sweeping in from the sea. Steady soaking rain driven by a cold wind.

Ben looked up from his paper. 'Good to be inside on a night like this Francie.' He stretched luxuriously before the glowing log in the fire place, Carlo at his feet. 'I've been meaning to talk to you, by the way. You look tired- you are overdoing it.'

'The committee is just doing what we have always done Ben. We are making up food parcels and knitting and things that have to be done.' She sighed. 'But I miss Ellen, she can only come two days a week now. I couldn't bear it if Alice wasn't there with me.'

'Bloody marvellous isn't it? Not so long ago you were helping the local poor, now everybody who wants work has a job. As a matter of fact, I'm told it's almost impossible to get help of any kind.' He turned to his son. 'Any news old chap?'

'Nothing more Dad. I'm not worrying though, Judy will write again soon.'

Ben smiled. 'And how is our grandson?'

'He is beautiful. Just sleeps, eats and plays.'

The strident bell of the telephone jarred the peaceful atmosphere. Ben strode towards the instrument. 'For God's sake, who could ring this time of night?'

It was the hospital, one of the Land Girls had fallen in the shower, suspected broken arm, some abrasions. 'You're sure Faith? Hell of a night.' He listened intently. 'Yes, sounds like it, I had better come. Just keep her quiet. I won't be long.'

'Be careful dear, terrible night for driving.'

'Don't worry Francie, I know the road blindfolded.' He kissed her lightly. 'Back soon as I can. Goodnight Harry.'

He found Jane Landon sitting in the hospital hallway.

'Sorry to bring you out Doctor, one of our girls.'

'So Matron said. Fell in the shower.'

She lowered her voice. 'No, I've already told Matron, she was attacked on her way to the lodgings.'

Ben hung his dripping macintosh on the coat rack. 'Nothing more serious? She wasn't molested in any way?'

'No, she is a strong girl, she managed to get away. He was drunk.'

'I see. How did you get up here?'

'Old Mr. Jefferies gave us a lift. He couldn't wait though, I thought you might drop me off later. I'll wait.'

The girl lay on the table uncomplaining. He set the broken bone, attended to the abrasions and sedated her for the night. 'I'll drop in first thing, Faith.

She will sleep the rest of the night, poor child. There is always some drunken fool hanging around.'

Jane was waiting for him.

'Well, I had better run you home now, your young charge is sleeping. I will keep her here a few days, she is badly shocked.'

In the big car with the heater running and the windscreen wipers keeping the glass just clear enough for him to see the side of the road, Ben drove slowly.

'Please stop Ben, please just for a minute.'

He pulled into a small clearing, turned off the lights leaving the motor and heater running.

'Please hold me.' He could just see the dim outline of her face. 'Please hold me tight.' She was crying. 'I'm so lonely, so miserable.'

'Jane please,' he protested. 'you know this is wrong, terribly wrong.' But he held her, yielding and soft against him - God, how long since he had kissed like this? Slowly he pulled away. 'I think we should stop Jane. You know my position. I love my wife, it could never come to anything.'

She clung to him. 'I know that. I'm sorry Ben, but I needed someone, I'm so lonely. I am responsible for all these girls and no one to lean on.'

'It's a natural reaction, my dear.' He smiled at her. 'Any man would give his right arm to know you like this. I think I had better take you home.'

She occupied the section of a house which had been made into a self contained flat. 'Won't you come in Ben? I'll make some coffee, coffee and chicory actually. I promise I won't make a fool of myself again.'

'Well, I shouldn't but just a few minutes.'

Next morning at breakfast he glanced at his wife, busy pouring tea. 'Busy day Francie?' He felt no sense of guilt, why should he? Nothing had happened. They had talked. She had been to University, gained her BA. and taught maths at a private school for girls. She had married young, her husband was in the Army, that was why she had joined up, to do her 'bit'. When he left they had shaken hands, perhaps he held hers a little longer than necessary.

'Today will be hectic, there is so much to do. I wish it could always be like this-the women so co operative.'

He smiled. 'Trouble brings out the best in most people.'

'I didn't even hear you come in last night, was it very bad?'

'Some drunken lout attacked one of the Land Girls. Broke her arm, knocked her about a bit.'

'Oh Ben, how terrible. She wasn't-I mean nothing else happened?'

'No, she got away. Dave is looking around, he is pretty sure he knows who it was.'

'I don't know what the town is coming to.'

'Worse things have happened. Anyway, the girl is being well looked after, be herself in a couple of weeks. Better be off, apart from the girl, we've got Mrs. Adams and Mrs. Roberts both close to term. Pray they both don't come good at the same time.'

For the balance of 1941, news of the war was sparse and confusing. Alone, he re-read the latest letter from Pieter, now Major DeVries, none of which was reassuring. In France the Petain Government had sued for an Armistice. The jackal Mussolini, fearing he might be left out of any peace settlement, had declared war on France and Britain. The unholy alliance struck between Russia and Germany, seemed to seal the fate of England and the rest of Europe. So where did that leave Australia he wondered. Exposed and undefended. He kept his fears to himself but if the worst came to pass, what of the people of this small town?

Frances noticed his long silences. 'Are things as bad as they say Ben? Does Pieter say anything in his letters?'

'Not much Francie. England is still there, saved by the channel again thank God, so let's not worry until we have to.'

It was by chance he ran into Jane Landon again. She was looking through the few books in the newsagency. 'Why Jane, you are quite a stranger, where have you been?'

'Busy as usual Doctor.' She was very proper under the ever watchful eye of the proprietor. 'Just looking around for something to read on the train.'

'I see, going on leave?'

'No, I applied for a compassionate posting to Sydney. My father is ill.'

'I am sorry. When do you leave?'

They left the shop together. 'Tomorrow. I was going to ring you at the surgery to say goodbye.' She looked up at him. 'And to say thank you.'

'I'm sorry to see you go.'

'If you come to Sydney you might look me up.' She took a pen from his coat pocket and scribbled a number on the book's fly leaf. 'There,' she tore the page from the cover. 'that's where I'll be Ben, if you come down.'

She was gone. He stood looking after her slim, boyish figure. 'Jesus, what temptation!'

Frances watched him with concern at the dinner table. 'Ben, I wish you wouldn't worry so, you hardly say a word.'

'I'm all right Francie. It does worry me though not hearing from Peter or Judy. The only one I can turn to is Pieter. He could probably find out what's going on but I can't use the phone. I could possibly slip down to Sydney for a few days, there is nothing Faith and Ethel couldn't handle.'

'I wish you would Dad.' Harry looked appealingly at his father. 'Only two letters and nothing from Peter.'

'I know old son, it's hard to take but be sure there is good reason. Judy will write.' His heart went out to this son he loved so well.

'You always make me feel better Dad, you never lose hope.'

Ben looked at his wife. 'If I have a tenth of your courage Harry, I never will.'

After what he considered a safe period, he announced to Ethel that he would be going to the city for a few days. Whether she suspected anything or not, he couldn't tell-perhaps, she was a wise old bird. 'You can hold the fort, there is nothing serious on the horizon. I'll only be gone a few days. Frankly, I've got to find out where Judy is, Harry is fretting. Peter I can understand, knowing the Army.'

She seemed persuaded to the idea. 'Just be careful Ben. Don't worry, you can leave things here to Faith and me. We can always call on Tom Coburn if needs be.'

He wondered what she meant by 'be careful', but did not press the matter.

The Wentworth was crowded but they knew the Doctor and a room was found. His first contact was Pieter. 'God, I envy you. A bloody Major, caught in the thick of things. I'd give my right arm to be back in it again.'

Pieter laughed. 'Someone has to hold the fort.'

'Don't give me that malarky Pieter, I haven't a soul to talk to. Anyway, see what you can find out for me.' He gave the details.

'Damned if I know Ben, I'll do the best I can. Where are you staying?'

'The usual, the old Wentworth. How about dinner tonight?'

'Sorry I can't, big meeting with the chief. How about tomorrow? I might have some news for you then.'

'I trust the 'Chief' doesn't wear skirts?'

'Ben, my best friend, how could you imagine such a thing?'

'Sorry old man, I feel humble in the presence of one so principled.'

Pieter chuckled. 'See you tomorrow night, you old sinner.'

In his room after dinner, Ben opened his wallet and took out the worn fly leaf with a telephone number smudged but still visible. For what seemed ages he sat looking at the telephone before reaching out to dial the number. 'Jane, is that you?'

'Ben!' She sounded breathless. 'Where are you?'

'At the Wentworth. How are you?'

'I'm fine Ben. It's wonderful to hear your voice.'

'I thought this was a military establishment.'

'It's not, it's my flat in Woollahra. I do have a private life you know.'

'Of course you do, I'm sorry to intrude.'

'Oh Ben, don't say that. I'm here all alone, can you come over?'

'Well, I really only rang to say hello and inquire about your father.'

'Dad is not very well, the Doctors say he must rest. It's his heart.'

'I understand. How is life treating you?'

'Ben please stop talking and come over. It's only ten minutes by taxi and this time I have real coffee!'

'All right, but only a short visit.'

For a few minutes he sat thinking-What the hell am I doing?

Fifteen minutes later, up two flights of stairs in what was once a fashionable address, he knocked gently at a solid green door. His heart raced as he heard the key turn in the lock. She was standing there smiling at him.

'Won't you come in?'

They sat facing each other. He tried not to notice she was wearing a black satin Chinese dressing gown, tied at the waist with a tasselled cord.

'Well, aren't you going to talk to me?'

He smiled self consciously. 'I don't know what to say.'

'I do. I'm so glad to see you Ben.'

'I'm glad to see you too Jane. You look lovely. I hope you weren't getting ready to go out.'

'Of course not, I just like to be comfortable.'

Through the slit in her gown he could see the sheen of her legs. He felt slightly dizzy.

She moved closer to him. 'Aren't you going to give me a welcome hug?'

She slipped his coat from his shoulders, untying his tie. He felt intoxicated by her perfume. 'Jane you mustn't, I'm not prepared.'

'Please Ben, I can't have babies, the doctor said I can't.' Her dressing gown slid to the floor, she wore only black silk panties and a brassiere. His hands explored her soft body, gently slipping her panties down as she unclipped her bra. In a dream, he was undressed lying in her arms. On the mantle, a little ivory radio played the popular music of the day.

The legal section was housed in a city building requisitioned by the Army. The Corporal at the desk looked up as Ben approached. 'Major DeVries please.'

'Yes Sir, who shall I say is calling?'

'Dr. Wakefield.'

'Please take a seat sir.'

Ben thought to himself-'Wonder what would have happened if I had said Jack Smith? That magical word, Doctor. Gods on Olympus! They bloody near bow, if the poor coots only knew.'

Pieter came from the inner office, with a welcoming smile, hand outstretched. 'Ben! Didn't expect to see you until dinner tonight.'

The floor had been partitioned off into sections, the walls of each cubicle barely four feet high. 'Is this private Pieter? I need to talk to you in confidence.'

'I don't imagine absolutely private, why don't we go out to lunch? The food at Romanos is excellent.'

'I'd rather not really. Somewhere more private.'

'I see. What about the Latin, not far from here, above one of the arcades.' He rolled his eyes to the ceiling. 'The spaghetti is magnificent take my word.'

They sat lingering over strong black coffee. 'You want my advice?'

'Not legal advice, a friend's advice. I had to talk to someone and you are the only one on earth I can.'

'She sounds very attractive.'

Ben rested his head on his hand. 'God damn it Pieter, I feel I'm in love with her! I felt like a young man again. God, what an erection, she drained me dry. Twice Pieter, twice in one night, at my age.'

'And it's on again tonight?'

'Yes. In a way I feel reborn. Guilt ridden but young again.'

'And you want my advice?'

'I suppose so, talk it over anyway.'

Pieter DeVries regarded his old friend gravely. 'You want me to be frank?'

Ben nodded then smiled. 'Yes, even if you leave me feeling a bloody old fool.'

'You are not that old friend. But love? No, I don't think so. It won't last Ben but,' he smiled in spite of himself, 'you will have some wonderful moments. Look, it's the war. Our normal lives have been thrown into turmoil- even for your oldest friend. I'm currently a regular visitor to the home of a ship's officer. Wives do get lonely you know.'

It was Ben's turn to smile, somewhat incredulously. 'No guilty conscience?'

'I've put it out of my mind. You of all people should know, sex is a normal function. Marriage merely legitimises the act. Nothing has changed since Adam.'

'But dammit Pieter, I'm old enough to be her father.'

'Some women are like that, they are attracted to an older man.'

'You think so?'

'I know so. I trust you are being careful, but you of all people should know about that.'

'She's infertile.'

'She told you that?'

'Of course.'

The lawyer eyed his friend narrowly. 'I hope for your sake, she is telling the truth.'

Dinner with Jane that night, his last in Sydney, was to stay in his memory. They ate by candlelight and talked until late. He questioned her about her infertility. It was true, she and her husband, Paul, had wanted children.

'And why me, my darling Jane? Any young man would sell his soul to be with you.'

'I don't know. Only Paul and you have ever attracted me in that way.'

Later as he snuffed the candles, she came naked from the bedroom and took his hand, he followed in a dream. In the big double bed he entered her as she clung to him, until the early light, they lay sleeping in each others arms.

December 7, 1941.

'Ben!' Ethel burst into his surgery. 'My daughter has just rung from Sydney. The Japanese have attacked the American fleet at Pearl Harbour. It came over the wireless.'

He stood quickly, scattering papers on his desk. 'It's true Ethel, are you sure it's true?'

'It is, it's official.'

'Thank God! I know it's a terrible thing to say, but thank God, now we have a chance. I'll ring Pieter. Please see if you can get him for me, I'm shaking like a leaf.'

Half an hour later she came in shaking her head. 'Hopeless at the moment Ben, the lines are full. It's true all right though, the *Daily* is rushing out a special edition.

He could hardly wait to get home. His wife met him, the infant in her arms. She smiled at his excitement. 'I heard darling, everybody is talking about it.'

He kissed her tenderly. 'I could never bring myself to say it Francie but God forgive me, I had mentally given up. I thought we were done for.'

'I know Ben, I know you were worried. What will happen now?'

'I don't know. I tried to ring Pieter but couldn't get through. I'll try later tonight.' He sat down. 'Let's have a drink Francie, I need one.'

After the evening meal, they sat talking. 'Has Harry heard anything?'

'He had a letter from Judy. She is safe and well, still in Melbourne.'

'Nothing from Peter?'

'No.' She hesitated. 'Ben, it sounds silly but do you think Judy doesn't want to come home because of the baby?'

'I don't know. Perhaps, but Melbourne is a long way away Francie. I shouldn't worry.'

'We haven't heard a word from Gerald either. Surely mail from England is getting through.'

'You know Gerald, my love. He is probably having the time of his life.'

'And Gareth, why haven't we heard from him?'

'The medical Corps are kept busy and you know our son, never thinks to write.'

'Sometimes I wonder why we had children.'

'Because you love them. That's your nature, my dearest Francie.' He came round by the chair. 'We don't have many cross words do we?'

She looked up.

'My dear, don't be offended but you are becoming too possessive. Tom is not our child and you shouldn't be lugging him around at his age. Put him on the floor and let him crawl. It won't be long before he takes his first steps.'

Tears came to her eyes, she looked away.

He was shocked. 'Francie my dear, don't please, I was only thinking of you. You must know that.'

'I love him so Ben. You don't blame me for that do you?'

He bit back his reply. 'Of course I don't, forgive me Francie.'

Later he made his way to the tower to have a quiet brandy. He sat in the captain's chair, alone with his thoughts-It's Ronnie again, she has never let go. My poor dear, faithful Francie. What a bastard I am! Yet if anyone told her I have been unfaithful, she wouldn't believe it. He felt the golden comforting fluid flow through his veins-What happens when Judy comes back? He sighed, gazing over the starlit land to the distant sea-I'll just have to face that when the time comes.

They occupied separate bedrooms now, Frances taking the child into her room. 'You don't mind do you Ben? He wakes so often, I don't want to disturb you.'

His thoughts turned to Jane-I miss her, 'God forgive me but I do miss her. Must be almost three months now.' He slipped the calming fluid-'I'll go again next week.' There was never any question about his regular trips to Sydney. After all Pieter, his only contact, was there and there was property at Mosman. Any excuse would do. Ethel and Faith held the fort and if anything tricky came up there was always old Tom Coburn-What a man, at his age still swims every morning!

Sydney was a changed town, American servicemen everywhere. As always, Jane answered his call with that low thrilling voice that sent shivers down his spine.

He dutifully called on his old friend. 'I can only stay a few days Pieter. Couldn't even get a room.'

'I've no doubt you are comfortably accommodated though.'

Ben smiled. 'Very. Now have you any news for me?'

'Come on, take me to lunch. Can't talk here.'

They spoke in low voices, stopping whenever the waiter approached.

'Strictest confidence Ben. Peter's division, The Eighth, will be going or has already gone, to Singapore. It will be common knowledge before long.'

'Anything on Judy?'

'I'm not sure, but on the information you gave me, her group have already embarked.'

'Singapore?'

'Yes I think so. It will play a vital role. The Japanese are moving fast against the Dutch and British possessions in East Asia.'

'What of the attack on Pearl Harbour?'

'Devastating apparently. American losses were enormous but by some miracle the aircraft carriers were at sea. Whichever Admiral made that decision should go down in history. If the carriers had gone, I think the Japs would be in Darwin by now.'

'As bad as that?'

'As bad as that Ben. And from what I can gather the real struggle is yet to come.'

'They underestimated the Americans, the treacherous bastards!'

'Yes, but I still think we are in for some bad times.'

'Apparently. Let's forget the war while we eat. What's the news from Melbourne?'

'They had twins you know.'

'That should keep them busy for a while. Still in the old house?'

'Of course. Best address in Melbourne, strictly Establishment territory. What are you going to do with it eventually?'

'No idea Pieter, can't even think about it for the moment.'

'Your interests are being well cared for. One thing I can say about that young brother of mine, he is dependable.'

'That brings me to a matter giving some concern Pieter, the house in Mosman.'

'What about it? Your Sydney solicitors are responsible aren't they?'

'Yes of course. Frank's foreman, Les Haines, is doing essential work, he was maintaining the place, keeping an eye on it for me. His wife still cleans it every couple of weeks and the gardener still keeps the grounds in order. Now, from your letters, I gather accommodation is becoming critical, especially for the top brass. Frankly, I'm afraid the house may be requisitioned by the authorities.'

Pieter nodded. 'It's a possibility.'

'What I am asking Pieter is, would you mind making it your official address. You know a few nights there, your official car in the driveway occasionally.' He grinned. 'I'm sure your lady friend, pardon me, your companion, might find it- how can I put it - convenient?'

The lawyer eyed his friend, a broad smile on his face. 'I believe you have a tenant, Doctor.'

Whenever he ascended the flight of steps to the green door, Ben's heart beat wildly. He was sure if he found her pregnant, he would faint. But no, she stood there as always, the same slim boyish figure, the same dazzling smile of welcome.

They talked over the meal she had prepared like an old married couple. He lifted his cup, savouring the delicious aroma of pure coffee. 'Wonderful isn't it, real coffee again. Will these six cans be enough until next time Jane?'

She nodded. 'More than enough, there is only me when you are not here you know.'

He smiled at her across the candles. 'Thank you for taking me in. I promise I will be most discreet when I leave.'

'How long will you stay this time?'

'About three days. Now tell me what you have been doing.'

'The usual. We are awfully busy now the Americans are here.'

'Have you heard from your husband?'

'No, I worry terribly Ben. I honestly don't know what I would do if anything happened to Paul. I do love him you know, as I love you, with all my heart.'

'I often think it is very wrong of me -', he couldn't finish.

'Never say that Ben-you have kept me normal.'

'Will you ever tell Paul about us?'

'No, it will always be my secret, my secret love. You will always be in my heart.' She smiled. 'Women need a secret.'

She came to where he was sitting, cradling his head in her arms. 'Just love me Ben, just love me.'

He arrived back in Lambruk a week before Christmas, having stayed in Sydney longer than intended. His conscience regarding his duty as Area Medical Officer, was clear. Telephone calls to Ethel had kept him informed. Nothing requiring his skills had happened. The Cadillac refused to start, he had left the parking lights on. He groaned-a positive sign of advancing years!

'Saw it a bit late Doc, the battery had had it when I turned them off.' The station hand appeared apologetic.

'Thanks just the same Jack. A push will get it going.'

A couple of burly fettlers came to the rescue. A mighty shove and the motor came to life. Ben waved from the window. 'Thank you boys, a Merry Christmas to you.'

Yes a Merry Christmas and please God, a safe one for all those we hold dear. A warmth engulfed him, how good to be home again. Home to everything he held dear, except for one he could only be with for so little time. Then the gates, the sound of gravel flying from under the tyres, round the last bend, the sound of hanging boughs brushing against the hood.

She met him at the door. He held her close to him. 'Frances, my dearest Francie, home at last. Just to see you makes troubles melt away.' His arm around her, they went into the cool of the house. He sat in his favourite chair looking up at her.

She took his face in her hands. 'I've missed you so Ben. You look so tired. Must you go down to Sydney again?'

He fought the desire to say, no never again. 'The only way I can find out anything my dear. Pieter has so many contacts and look,' he got up and set his heavy suitcase on a chair. 'coffee, pure perfect coffee. A treasure more precious than gold, courtesy of America. It's amazing Francie, they seem to have everything.'

Dinner over, Ben relaxed with a sigh. 'Mind if I have a cigar Francie?' He moved the long dark cylinder under his nose, savouring the delicate aroma, 'another pleasure of American largesse.'

She smiled. 'I love the smell of cigars, reminds me of your grandfather.'

'Dear old Grandad. What a gent he was, bless his soul.'

He turned to his son, sitting beside him. 'Any news Harry?'

'A couple of letters. She doesn't say in so many words but I think she is going overseas. Tells me not to worry, just look after Tom. She reckons we will all be together again soon. What do you think Dad?'

'I think she is right son.' But in his heart were dark forebodings.

Monaro - Christmas Day 1943.

'Something like old times Pieter. How long can you stay?'

'Just a few days Ben. I've been seconded to Intelligence, God knows why.'

'Things are starting to look better though, don't you think?' 'Ben I am convinced those two great battles turned the tide, saved our skins in fact. I hope to God future generations will celebrate the Battle of the Coral sea as our day of deliverance.'

'Yes, it's been a dramatic period old friend but full of anguish for us.'

'You mean Singapore?'

'Tell me, how the hell could it happen? We have been told for years that it was impregnable.'

'We will know some day Ben. But if we have learned anything, it's never put our troops under British command, ever again.'

'I hope I will see that day. But my worry is Judy and Peter.'

'We don't know Ben. Our boys may have got away into the jungle but we don't have any reliable information.'

'Peter can look after himself, it's Judy that worries me.'

'I wouldn't worry Ben. I'm positive they would have got the nurses out, first priority.'

'I hope you are right. Here let me top up that glass.'

Pieter sat back in his chair. 'Strange isn't it, the times we have sat here, yarning? I miss the lanterns Ben, don't you?'

'They made Christmas, Hope to God they will again.'

They sat lost in thought, looking out over the darkened landscape.

'This new Prime Minister, Curtin, seems a remarkable man.'

'Yes, he and Macarthur hit it off famously apparently. The nearest we have ever had to an Abraham Lincoln. I tell you this though Ben, the Establishment will never forgive him for calling on America for help.'

'The fools don't realise how bloody lucky we are. We could expect nothing from the British, Churchill made that clear.'

'Well, to be generous to them, their own position was desperate.'

'What of the General himself, ever get to meet him?'

Pieter chuckled. 'Don't move in those circles Ben but I have seen him a couple of times. Looks an impressive man, imperious you might say.'

'Sounds like Frank's type of man.'

'Yes. Just as well he didn't live to see the carrying on of those moneyed half wits down there. Fawning on the Americans, only the officers of course. Macarthur put a few egos out of joint, has no time for social junketing. I think his initial impression of the Australians was not flattering, excluding our troops of course. By the way, I did pick up an item of interest to us who live up here. Apparently, when the General was flying in from Darwin, he studied the map of Australia and spotted the Pacific Highway. He remarked to an aide how convenient it would be to move men and material to the North. Wonder what they thought when they saw it, a rutted dirt track.'

'I imagine what the rest of the world thinks of us, if they think of us at all- a huge undeveloped island continent, a vacuum waiting for someone to fill it.'

'Yes I often think distance has been a mixed blessing. At least we are a long way from the squabbles and hatreds of Europe but at the same time we miss out on the great advances in science, arts etc.'

'Things may change when this war is over.'

'To change the subject-when are you coming down again?'

'After Christmas. I've told Frances.' He lowered his voice. 'This matter with Jane must end Pieter. It's going to hurt but if I'm not a realist at my age, I never will be.'

'As your friend, I would say a wise decision and a practical one at that. Why not come down with me when I go?'

'Well,' he hesitated, 'I would like to, let me just check what is happening, I'll let you know. Now we have put the war aside, what do you think of your granddaughter?'

'Ahh, now that is indeed another subject. But you know, I simply can't get used to being a grandfather!'

Ben chuckled. 'You will, you will hardly notice the difference. She is a beautiful infant.'

'Hmm, so I'm kept reminded. That young grandson of yours is a fine looking boy.'

Again Ben lowered his voice. 'The only thing that has kept Frances sane Pieter. And the only reason I can get away without question.' He sniffed the air. 'Turkey if I'm not mistaken. Dinner must be almost ready.'

'Turkey eh, a rare treat these days.'

'Courtesy of Mick, he breeds them. The old cuss is making a killing.'

Pieter held out his glass. 'To happier days Ben.'

Their glasses touched. 'To happier days old friend.'

Boxing day dawned, the air heavy with threatened storms. Ben glanced up from his breakfast smiling at his grandson in his high chair. 'My word you are a solemn fellow this morning, Tom.'

Frances was busy feeding the infant. 'He is always like this in the morning Ben but he really is a happy child.' She smiled. 'He takes his food seriously.'

'That I can see, he is the picture of health. Where is Harry by the way?'

'In his room, he isn't well Ben.'

'What is it? I've noticed he hasn't been about in his chair much lately.'

'He seems so depressed.'

'Don't worry, I'll look in on him. I'll be very careful, he can be very touchy about his health.'

'Did Pieter tell you anything last night? Surely he must hear things.'

'Nothing more than we already know. After I see how things are at the hospital I will probably go down with him. He says he will pull every string he knows.'

She looked downcast. 'I hoped you wouldn't be going down again Ben. It's so hard here without you.'

'Only for a few days my dear, really it's our only hope of any real news.'

'You won't stay long will you?'

'Not a day more than necessary, I promise. Now I must have a look at Harry.' He found his son sitting in his chair, wrapped in a blanket, a pad and pencil on his knee. 'Not feeling too well old son?'

Harry tried to suppress a hard dry cough, looking at his father with the smile that always caught at Ben's heart. 'Nothing Dad, bit of a cough. Got caught in that storm the other day.' He smiled again. 'Can't say you didn't warn me.'

'Well, I should have listened to your chest, may I?'

'No, Dad no. It's all right, don't worry.' He pulled the rug up higher.'

'You should have something lighter around you Harry, it's too hot for that thing.'

'I'll take it off later Dad. Just bring me back some medicine for my cough. You know, same as last time.'

Ben nodded, he knew the mixture, well laced with opium. His son must be experiencing some pain. 'All right, but you must promise to take some soup, I will ask Mrs. Ellis to make some for you. Do I have your word on that?'

'I promise dad.'

Ben turned to the door hiding the worried frown on his face.

'Dad,' his son called to him, 'did Mr. DeVries say anything last night?'

'Things are still confused Harry. I intend going down to Sydney myself, probably tomorrow. If I have to tear the place apart, I promise I'll find out what is going on.'

'Please don't be long.'

Ben paused outside the door, listening to his son's suppressed coughing. 'God bloody damn it, there is no justice in this world!'

Sydney was a noisy jostling crowd of servicemen, mostly American it seemed, most scarcely more than boys. They spilled out of bars onto the footpaths. Others, hanging onto girls, walked or lurched along every side street.

'Christ, what a mess! I thought we were supposed to be fighting a war.'

'Don't be too critical Ben. Half the poor little bastards will be cannon fodder before they are much older. The American Brass feeds and pays them well but when they use them they are utterly ruthless.'

'Yes, I suppose so. You know Pieter, I think it was a mistake coming down but I am determined to put an end to that other matter.'

'Wise move old friend.' Pieter stopped the taxi. 'I get out here, see you in the morning.' He looked in the window. 'Be careful now.'

Ben rang the number Jane had given him for Victoria Barracks, his heart fluttered at the sound of her voice. 'Down for a few days Jane, any room for a boarder?'

She seemed hesitant. 'Can we have lunch Ben?'

'Of course, the Latin. Pieter can get me a table. Twelve thirty all right?'

'Yes. Can't talk now, see you then.'

He heard the telephone hurriedly replaced.

He met her in the Arcade, trim and beautiful as ever, in her uniform.

'Just let me look at you. You look lovely.'

She seemed reserved. 'Thank you Ben, it's so nice to see you.'

'I'm glad you could come.' He took her arm. 'Our table is reserved.'

He sat looking at her, reaching for her hand. She quickly withdrew it a slight smile on her face.

'What is it Jane? Something has happened, please tell me.'

'Paul is home, he is out at Concord Military Hospital.'

'How is he?'

'He was wounded at El Alamein and has been in hospital in England.'

'Did you know?'

She looked down. 'Yes, I feel dishonest in a way.'

'Don't.' This time he took her hand. 'How serious is his injury?'

'His knee was shattered but they saved his leg. He will always have to use a walking stick.'

'Something to be thankful for.' This time he squeezed her hand. 'Dear Jane, I will always remember you. Always.'

'Will you forgive me if I don't ask you to come home with me?'

'Dearest girl, of course.'

The waiter appeared with the spaghetti and a bottle of Chianti. He smiled at her across the table and held up his glass. 'To our last lunch together.'

The meal over, she rose hurriedly. Coming round to where he sat, she bent and kissed him lightly on the cheek. 'Goodbye dear Ben.'

She was gone. He watched as the waiter closed the door behind her, then glanced surreptitiously round the restaurant. Many of the diners were looking at him with friendly smiles-Oh my God, of course, I know what they think-'How charming to see father and daughter lunching together.'

Pieter was late getting back. Ben waited impatiently, reading and re reading the herald. Nothing there, how could there be? He heard the door open.

'Ben!! Didn't expect to see you so soon. Come in.'

Pieter regarded him closely, across the desk. 'So, what has happened? You look odd.'

'I've been reminded of my age.' He related the details of lunch. 'But I feel a weight lifted from me. An infatuation that possessed me for too long. Thank God it's over. I feel free again.'

'Probably not my place to say it, but I'm glad for your sake.'

'But I must confess to a feeling of sadness, and guilt too, Pieter.'

'It will disappear in time.'

Ben stood and began pacing the floor. 'If you have any news let me have it Pieter, then use your influence to get me on a train tonight. I want to get the hell out of here.' He sat down again. 'So what do you know?'

'It's no secret Ben. The troops captured by the Japanese are being brutally treated, our intelligence is reliable, conditions are appalling.'

'What about the Geneva Convention regarding prisoners of war, for God's sake?'

'The Japs regard it with contempt. Troops who surrender are not fit to live.'

'I can't tell Frances that.'

'She must know our troops are prisoners, the papers are full of it.'

'Of course she does and probably thinks Peter is safe until the war is over. What of Judy, do you know anything there?'

'Only that they got the nurses away at the last minute. Where they are now, we haven't the slightest idea.'

'Surely the Americans must know something.'

'They could be anywhere, some say India or even Darwin, we just don't know.'

'Hell! I know about as much as I did yesterday. Have dinner with me Pieter and get me on that bloody train without fail.'

Pulling into the driveway, his heart stood still-Dr. Coburn's car, Alice must be there too, the old man never drove himself anymore. Frances met him in the hallway, she looked weary.

'You are home so soon Ben, I am thankful. It's Harry, Dr. Coburn is with him.'

He held her for a moment. 'Don't worry, I'm here now. I won't be going away again, Pieter is going to keep us informed.'

'Did you find out anything? Is Judy safe?'

'Later Francie, later. I had better speak to Dr. Coburn first.'

'Alice is helping Mrs. Ellis make some lunch. You look so tired.'

In the sickroom Dr. Coburn was closing his bag. 'Harry is feeling more comfortable now Ben. I suggest another injection before he is ready to sleep tonight.'

'Thank you Doctor, thank you for your trouble. I'm sorry I wasn't here.'

Harry looked at his father, his eyes with dilated pupils, dark against the pallor of his skin. His voice came in a whisper. 'Did you find out Dad, did you find out where Judy is?'

'Good news son. Judy and all the nurses are safe in India. Safe and well.' How easily the lie came to his lips.

'I'm glad, I knew you would find out.' Harry's voice seemed to come from far way. His head slipped to one side, eyes closing. Merciful morphine had begun it's magic.

'Come Ben.' Dr. Coburn took him by the arm. 'Come outside.'

Lunch was on the table. Alice kissed him fondly. 'You look tired Ben. Sit down and eat then you and Tom can take a stroll in the garden.'

Under the shade of a flowering Tulip tree, the old man spoke quietly. 'Pneumonia Ben. If it were only that-perhaps. But tell me, have you ever sounded him?'

'Not since he was a child. He is very sensitive about that sort of thing.'

'It's unmistakable Ben. I found it hard to believe. Tuberculosis, both lungs are involved.'

Ben stared at him in amazement. 'But how can that be? Harry, to my knowledge, has never been in contact with anyone infected.'

'Don't ask me that question Ben. I have been too long in medicine to know why. The longer you live the more you realise there are too few answers. Often the symptoms in the young pass unnoticed until it's too late. Sadly some people seem susceptible to the bacillus, even families as well you know.'

'Just like my father.'

'Yes, sadly it probably progressed the same way.' He took Ben's arms. 'It will be a bad time for you and Frances. You know the situation, call on me any time I can be of help. Nature will take it's course, it's inevitable. I can see Alice is coming, take my advice my dear boy, keep him comfortable, he deserves that.'

During the second week Harry's condition deteriorated rapidly. Cradled in his mother's arm, his withered hand clung to his father. It was the early hour of the morning before night gives way to day, the time when the first rooster crows, the time when life ebbs and flows.

'If I could only stand up Dad, I know I would be all right. I could breathe, my chest wouldn't feel so heavy. Please Dad, help me to stand up.'

'A little later old son. Have you any pain?'

Harry fell back, a cloth pressed to his lips.

'Just lie still for a moment. I'll give you another injection then later you will be able to stand up.'

The crowing of the roosters grew more strident, the sun rose slowly over the glassy sea. As the bedside clock softly ticked the minutes away, Harry took his last fluttering breaths.

Ben and Frances stayed together in the Chapel after the others left. Only the Rev. Tomlinson, Ellen, Dr. and Alice Coburn and Mick. The grave diggers had gone first, quietly thanking Ben for the notes he pressed into their hands. Their little grandson lay between them, fast asleep, his head resting on his grandmother's lap.

So silent and cool in the Chapel. Frances sat head bowed. Ben's heart ached with the sense of loss and grief for his son. For all the things that had happened, for his dear patient wife, for his guilt. He raised his eyes to the exquisite stained glass mosaic above the altar. A golden halo above the head of a forgiving Christ, bathed the Chapel in amber light. Yes, he had suffered too, the lot of all mankind.

High in the giant figs, Wood Pigeons called, soft notes of distant flutes. Rousing he took France's hand. 'Come Francie, time we left.' They walked without speaking, little Tom between them. Faithful Carlo, whose canine instinct told him his humans were sad, followed quietly behind.

Frances seemed to accept Harry's death, at least she showed no outer signs. With her Women's Committee, her vegetable garden and above all, her grandson, she was well occupied. Ben felt uneasy, she was smothering the child. He would have to have it out with her, but not yet, wait until some feeling of normality returned. He steeled himself against bad news. Germany and Japan were being reduced to rubble. Best not to think, certainly not of the future. He kept busy, still making calls, often to outlying farms. Carlo on the front seat, head lolling in the breeze from the open window, kept him company. Gerald's dog, man's best friend indeed.

It was a Friday he would always remember. Mick was smothering the grass with a razor sharp scythe, Ben opened the door calling for Carlo. Whenever the dog came, he came running and with one great leap was impatient to be on the way. Ben called several times-where the hell is that dog? He called to Mick? 'Never seen him late before.'

Mick barely paused. 'He won't be far Doc. Probably chasin' a goanna.'

'You're probably right, let me know if you see him.' Getting into the car, he muttered to himself. 'Bloody funny though, he loves the car. First time he hasn't come when I called.' He drove slowly, looking as he drove. 'Wonder where he's got to. Dammit, I miss the mutt.'

Next morning ready to go, he called again-no answering back. No doubt about it Carlo was missing. Ben went back into the house. 'Mrs. Ellis have you seen Carlo?'

No she hadn't seen him, nor had he eaten the food she had left out for him.

Did she know where Mick was working?

Yes, along the trail to the Chapel and he was due back for his usual cup of tea.

Mick was raking leaves into little fires, the pungent smoke hung like mist in the canopy above. He looked up at Ben's greeting. 'Yeah, I know Doc, this place has gotta be kept clear though. I like it here, a man can think in peace.'

'Nothing worrying you is there Mick?'

Mick leaned on his rake, slapping at the odd mosquito. 'Smoke makes the buggers dopey.'

Ben knew it was pointless to hurry him. He waited while Mick rolled his cigarette.

'Young Kerry joined up, got his Leaving Certificate last year y'know. Couldn't talk him out of it.'

'I'm sorry Mick.'

'No use worrying about it.'

Ben looked at his watch. 'I just wanted to know if you'd seen the dog?'

Mick shook his head. 'No funny though, if he's not with you he spends the day with me. I'll keep an eye out Doc.'

Penicillin became available to civilian practitioners. Ben discussed the importance of the miracle drug with Faith and Ethel at the hospital.

'Never dreamt I'd see the day. Good God, think what we could have done with this. All those poor devils we wrote off as hopeless.'

'We won a few though Ben.'

'Just good luck and their strong constitutions, Faith. I wonder what Tom Coburn thinks about it.'

'He hardly ever comes down these days, he looks so tired.'

'He's getting on now. By the way, how are you managing with your helpers from the Women's Committee?'

Both women smiled. 'Very well, considering. Just a few problems until they get used to things. Mostly bed pans and urine bottles.'

Ben smiled. 'Can't say I blame them, not the most pleasant of jobs.'

Faith nodded. 'Surprisingly a few more delicate ladies took to it without turning a hair. You can never tell.'

Ben stood up. 'Well, we had better do the rounds. When does Mary leave by the way?'

'Ben, where have you been? Mary has gone. I suppose you realise, we are now without a Theatre Sister?'

'Good Lord, of course! My memory must be going.' He turned to Ethel. 'Looks like you are back in harness again old girl.'

A week passed, still no sign of Carlo. Probably chasing a bitch in heat. Of course, why didn't he think of that before?

Letters from Pieter told him the tide was slowly but surely turning. Germany and Japan were being bombed incessantly. He felt easier in his mind, surely it couldn't last much longer. At times he thought of Jane with pangs of longing, then guilt consumed him - What a bloody old fool, but what memories, God what memories! At times he could imagine her young body in his arms. When sanity returned he wished it had never happened. But it had, oh yes it had.

These days surgery was quiet. He came early so he could read the journals. So much that was new, so many exciting developments. When the war was over he would do a refresher course, necessary really. But at his age. Well, wait and see.

The outside door bell rang, he went to answer it. The postman stood there. 'Early aren't you this morning, Jim? Mail doesn't get in until ten.' He stopped short, icy fingers clutching his heart. The man was handing him a telegram.

'Thought it best to bring it here Doctor.'

Blindly he stumbled into the surgery, clutching the buff envelope. He knew before he opened it. 'Regret to inform you Flying Officer Gerald Wakefield missing, believed killed in action.' He stared at the hated paper. Through his numbed mind he heard Ethel come in and the clatter of tea being made. Without knocking she opened the door, tray in hand. She paused, set down the tray and picked up the telegram.

Tears came to her eyes. 'Oh my God, Ben!' She put her arms around him.

His voice came in a hoarse whisper. 'He was only a boy Ethel. Dear God, he was only a boy.'

Gerald's name appeared in the *Myuna Daily*, together with the growing list of sons and loved ones.

It worried him. Frances couldn't cry, she seemed to retreat more into herself. Yet she had wept at the news of Jack Raywood's death at El Alamein. Tom was never out of her sight. She carried him when he could quite easily walk himself. He gently remonstrated with her. 'Frances, Tom walks perfectly well. He is too big and heavy for you.'

She smiled, seeming hardly to comprehend. 'He is not heavy, he's still a baby.'

He thought, 'this will have to end sooner or later. I'll give her time but it will have to be soon, just can't go on like this.'

Leaving one morning, he found Mick waiting for him.

'Found the dog, Doc.'

'Where Mick, is he all right?'

'Dug 'imself a hole up there behind the Chapel. Just about done for when I found 'im.'

'Poor little tyke. Is he injured?'

'Nothin' much I could see. No ticks, no cuts. Looks like he was tryin' t'starve 'imself.'

'Where is he now?'

'In the coach house. I forced some water down 'im and some meat soup from Mrs. Ellis.'

Carlo was stretched out on some corn sacks, his head between his paws. Ben knelt and stroked the dog's head. 'What have you done to yourself old boy?' Carlo lay still, only the slightest movement of his tail acknowledged the familiar voice.

'What d'ya think Doc?'

Ben rose slowly. 'I don't know Mick. Looks like he has given up.'

Mick rolled a smoke. 'Never told you how sorry I was about Gerry, Doc. Tell the truth, I didn't know how.'

'Thank you Mick.'

'Ya don't think-I mean Carlo?'

'Impossible Mick, absolutely impossible.'

Mick slowly exhaled. 'Lived with animals all me life Doc, seen some mighty strange things with dogs.'

Carlo recovered slowly. With much coaxing, Ben finally got him into the car again. He refused to challenge the world through the open window anymore, he was content to lie still on a blanket beside Ben. On the days Mick came he spent some times with him, ears cocked listening for someone who never came.

A few weeks before Christmas, Ben woke early to the jangle of the telephone. It was Alice. 'I wanted to ring last night Ben but Tom wouldn't hear of it.'

The old man lay in the big bed, his ancient stethoscope resting on his chest. The skin of his face was like parchment, only his eyes were bright. Eyes that had looked on so much suffering, so little joy. Ben sat on the edge of the bed, taking the thin wrist between his fingers. He bent low to hear the whisper of the dying man.

'I'm fibrillating Ben. Had to see you before I go.'

An aching sense of grief and loss overcame the younger man, he fought to control the huskiness in his voice. 'You told me we should never listen to our own sounds Doctor.'

A faint smile creased the old man's face. 'Yes I did, didn't I? No matter now, lived a long life, no regrets.' His fingers lightly griped Ben's hand. 'Arrange things-must be cremated- ashes in the bush-Alice knows. Promise me Ben!'

'I promise Doctor. Please don't worry anymore. I promise.'

Ben made the necessary arrangements. After cremation in Brisbane, the party of friends returned to Myuna. The service for Dr. Coburn was the biggest event the town had ever witnessed. Carrying out the old man's wishes, he with Mick, dug the ashes around the base of an Ironbark sapling deep in the bush above the Chapel. Later a carved wood headboard would be erected which would itself eventually disappear into the soil.

Rest in peace, old warrior.

May, 1945

The town went wildly insane-the war in Europe was over! Japanese cities lay in smoking ruins, but what terrible losses must be borne to end this final chapter? The answer came in August with the atom bombing of Hiroshima and Nagasaki. Then in the sober light of final victory, Myuna with countless other towns, began counting their losses.

In late October, Ben received an official telegram-Have information. If possible see me by weekend. Signed DeVries, Major.

He found the lawyer busily clearing out his desk. They shook hands.

'Ben, glad you could come.' He waved his arm around. 'Applied for an early discharge. Can't wait to get out of here, back to Myuna and sanity.'

'I'm glad Pieter. Can we talk?'

'Come over to the Wentworth, I need a drink.'

Over a glass of whisky, Ben learned the fate of his adopted son and daughter. How Peter had died a slave on the accursed Burma railway, subjected with his mates to inhuman cruelty. And dear little Judy, yes she with other Australian nurses in a clearly marked Hospital Ship, torpedoed by the Japanese. Many had swum and waded ashore only to be shot or bayoneted in the water. By feigning death one Sister had survived, later to be found by a naval patrol, more disciplined than the Army, spending the rest of the war under great privation, in a prison camp. But for her evidence, the fate of these young women would never have come to light.

Ben slumped in his chair, his head in his hands.

'From my heart, I'm sorry old friend. I sweated over this but I thought it best, it came from me.'

'Thank you Pieter.' His voice came in a whisper. 'I must go, I must get back home.'

'Before you do, there is someone waiting to see you.'

Slowly Ben turned his eyes to where Pieter was pointing. A tall uniformed man strode towards them. It was Gareth.

'Hello Dad!' He shook hands with Pieter. 'Thank you for contacting me sir.'

Pieter rose taking Bens' hand. 'I'll leave you with your son Ben.'

Gareth pulled up a chair, close to his father. 'I know Dad. Major DeVries told me everything.'

Even as a child, Gareth had never been emotional, had shied from physical contact. A sense of calm came to his father. He looked into his son's face, he had changed, the youthful look gone forever. A face hardened by the suffering he had seen, except the eyes, the blue watchful eyes that would always look on his fellow man with kindness and understanding.

Gareth did not return to Myuna with his father. The town, now settled down, went about it's business. Pieter DeVries resumed practice and his daughter returned as building and business boomed. Everything must be done in a hurry.

In a private ceremony, attended only by close friends, Dave Truman married Beryl Carrol. Bernard Shey married Mary Flannagan in a civil ceremony in Sydney. Earlier he and Dave had called on Ben at the surgery, two young men whose eyes and voices still revealed the terror they had endured. Yes, they had been there in Beau fighters over Holland. They had been jumped by German fighter planes, Gerald's going down in flames, crashing in a ball of fire. Flying at tree top level they had escaped.

Ben thanked them, he enquired after Bernard's parents.

'Dad's all right Doctor, Mum won't forgive me for leaving the Church. After Mary and I are married, we will be making our home in Sydney, that's where the opportunities are.'

Then Hal Wynter came to see him and told him how Jack Rayward died. 'We were running through the white tapes, the passage the mine boys had cleared. Jack was near me, I heard him yell-Christ, I'm hit!-that's all I heard Doctor. Jack was dead when they found him.'

'Thank you for telling me, Hal.'

'I'm sorry about everything Doctor, nothing seems good anymore.'

'I know Hal, there is nothing we can say. It's a cross many of us must bear.'

The young man hesitated. 'Did you hear about George, Doctor?'

Ben nodded. 'Yes Hal, his father came to see me. From what I understand a great many Australians owe their lives to George.'

'The Germans shot him.'

'I know Hal, a terrible blow to his family. Fortunately, there are two younger boys.' He stood taking the proffered hand. 'Please come and see us Hal, you are always welcome at *Monaro*.'

Frances came back to him, begging him to hold her, forgive her.

'My dearest, dearest Francie. Forgive you, for what? My dearest wife, I am the one who needs forgiveness. You are the one with courage.' He silently thanked his maker, for this forgiving woman.

The younger Doctors were glad to be back, eager for work. At times they talked in terms Ben found hard to understand, but he was still the only surgeon.

'We can control infection now Ben. You can do procedures you would never dare before.'

Yes they still respected his skills, basic surgery hadn't changed that much, but still he must do that refresher course. Sydney hospital or one of the Veteran's Hospitals, but that could wait. He was not willing to leave home until things settled down.

Frances built her life around her husband and grandson. Gareth planned going overseas but for the time being was living in the house at Mosman with a bustling middle aged housekeeper to see to his needs. Les Haines, now a busy, much sought after builder, still attended to any maintenance required. The old gardener now retired, replaced by a young man glad of good pay and steady work, kept the grounds in perfect order.

Christmas Eve 1945 found the two old friends sitting where they had always sat, gazing out over the darkened land.

'How is Frances bearing up Ben?'

'How can you ever know another person's mind Pieter? Even those closest to you. We have been through a terrible period in our lives, although, thank God, she has courage enough for both of us.'

'Fortunately she seems very attached to your little grandson.'

'Her salvation Pieter, without Tom-God knows, I don't.'

They sat quietly for a moment.

'I swear this brandy tastes smoother, if such is possible.'

Ben smiled in the darkness. 'Only because it has been so long. They say everything improves with age.'

The summer of 1946 was hot and moist, ideal for cane The town prospered. Bob Martin came back eager to work. 'Lots to do around the place Doctor. Mick must have had his work cut out.' With a growing family and his wife pregnant again, Ben raised the man's salary considerably.

Captain Michael Flannagan and his younger brother, now wearing sergeant's stripes, were both with the occupying army in Japan.

Ben always enjoyed a few minutes with Mick on the two days his sulky trotted up the driveway. He knew Mick looked forward to their brief encounters. Carlo would leap nimbly onto the seat, happy to have his ears fondled. 'You did wonders with that dog, Mick.'

'He's come on good Doc, settled down now. Still watches everything that comes through the gates. Cottoned onto young Tom too. Nice little kid that, Doc.'

Ben nodded. 'I've been wanting a word with you Mick. No more cutting the grass or pushing the wheelbarrow, that's for Bob now.'

Mick exhaled a wisp of blue smoke. 'Think I'm gettin' too old for the job Doc?'

'We all are Mick. Just keep the drive clear like you used to. I'm talking as your doctor and your friend.'

'Sure you still want me to come up Doc?'

'I would miss you if you didn't. You're one of the family, you know.'

Mick drove on, a broad smile on his face.

Ben announced to his partners that he would appreciate it if they would look for someone to take his place. He was tired and when things were more settled, intended taking a trip overseas with his wife and grandson.

A telephone call from Gareth came through during surgery hours. Ben's heart lifted to hear his son's voice. Would he please come down as soon as possible. No, he could not discuss the matter on the telephone, just come.

What the hell was this all about? Must be more information as to Peter and Judy. Probably where they were buried. How to tell Frances? Perhaps something about the Mosman house. He would only be gone a few days.

She accepted his excuse. 'Hurry back Ben, it's lonely without you.'

Gareth met him at the station. 'Have a room for you at the Wentworth Dad, we can talk when we get there.'

Washed and refreshed, he met his son in the dining room. 'Well, here I am my boy. What is the mystery?'

'Lunch first Dad, then we can talk.'

Over coffee he regarded his son with growing impatience. 'Come on Gareth, out with it.'

'You have every reason to be annoyed with me Dad, but I took that chance.'

'Yes?'

'It's Gerald, Dad, he's alive-barely.'

Ben's face paled. 'Where? Where is he?'

'Out at Concord Military Hospital.' He gripped his father's arm. 'Dad, I was there when he came in. Please believe me, I couldn't tell you then, I had to find out his condition first.'

Ben felt numb. 'Tell me.'

'The details are sketchy. Apparently he was thrown clear of his plane-picked up by Dutch Resistance, more dead than alive.'

'Dear God!'

'They hid him in the basement of a farmhouse, terribly burned about the lower part of his body. His left leg has been amputated.'

The groan from his father was that of a man suffering beyond endurance. 'What butcher would have done that?'

Gareth's grip tightened. 'No Dad, they were wonderful people, they had their own surgeon. It was a competent job.'

'What else?'

'Metal fragments lodged in the pelvic bones and lumbar spine-inoperable. And Dad,' Gareth kept his voice steady, 'both lungs are heavily involved. All that time hidden in a dank cellar with little food- you can imagine.'

Ben buried his face in his hands, his voice barely audible. 'Oh God, oh my God, my son!' He looked up, his face haggard with his suffering. 'Take me to him.'

'Steady Dad, steady, he must not see you like this.'

Gerald was released into his father's care. The Air Force flew them to Evans Head then by Army ambulance to *Monaro*.

'I thought I would never come back here again Dad, but while Gerry needs me I will stay.'

Frances, restraining her tears, sat for hours holding her dying son's hand.

His voice came in a whisper. 'Glad to be home Mum, never thought I would make it.'

Only those close came to the sickroom. His wife with their little blonde daughter. He fingered her plaits. 'She is ours isn't she Dutchy?'

Dorothy had steeled herself not to weep. 'Yes darling, she is ours.'

Dave, Beryl and Hal came. Mick sat talking over old times. Carlo after an initial surge of madness, never left the bedside, having to be forcibly removed to be fed.

Gareth discussed the situation at length with his father and Ethel who insisted she nurse him. Gerald needed constant attention, having no control over his bodily functions. 'We are losing him Dad. Not that there was ever any chance.' He swore to himself-'He won't suffer by God, I'll see to that.'

Gareth sat with his brother in the small hours after Ethel had left. When the pain became unbearable he injected the merciful drug and waited until Gerald fell asleep. Often he coughed, a little blood oozed from the corners of his mouth. In his waking hours he told Gareth what he wanted-to lie in the tower and see the sun rise each morning.

'Don't know how Dad. We can't get him up the stairs.'

He told Mick.

'See the boys at the Slipway, Gary. They'll get 'im up there.'

To the men used to handling slings and ropes it was no problem. They rigged the necessary gear as their chippy removed the big window. An adjustable bed from the hospital went up first, then Gerald on a stretcher, slowly hauled into the safety of the tower. The window replaced, he lay propped up so that the whole world lay before him. Ethel enlisted the aid of a trained nurse, whose young legs made light of the steep stairs. Every day there were visitors. Dorothy spent each afternoon sitting, holding his hand.

Gareth came at midnight. The weather was cooler now, the sky blazed with stars. Gerald sank lower, heavily sedated he slept most of the time. A new moon grew larger, in the distance the sea shimmered, burnished silver to the horizon. In the silence Gerald whispered to his brother. 'The Captain comes some nights.'

'Yes, of course he does mate, of course he does.' Then he would carefully prepare the hypodermic. Carlo lay on the floor watching every movement.

Nights passed, the moon grew full, the sea shone brighter.

'Captain came last night Gary. Said the Brig's lying off the river.' His mouth trembled. 'You said you would never let me die hard, Gary. Promise me! You said to trust you.'

Gareth felt a cold hand round his heart. 'I promise Gerry, I promise.' He wiped the blood from his brother's mouth. 'Now it's time for sleep.'

During the early morning Gerald suffered a massive haemorrhage. Ethel with tears in her eyes, sponged the wasted face. He reached for her hand. 'Don't tell Mum or Dorothy, please Matron, they will only worry.'

Her voice trembled. 'If you say so dear. Now please lie still.'

She did tell Gareth and Ben. 'It's cruel, dear God, it's so cruel to see him waste away like this.'

Ben put his arm around her. 'There, there old girl. Without your strength we would all be lost.'

At midnight Gareth wearily climbed the stairs. To his surprise Gerald appeared wide awake, his voice stronger. 'Gary, could we have a drink?'

'You can have anything you like, little brother. Just name it.'

'Could we have some brandy?'

Gareth knew where the bottle was hidden. He poured into two small glasses. 'Would you like your injection first?'

'No, no, just hold me up so I can drink.'

He lay back. 'It burned all the way down Gary, but it was good.' His head turned to one side. 'I would like to sleep for a while now Gary.'

'Good boy.' He pulled the blanket up around his brother's chest. 'When you wake we'll see how you feel.'

He poured again from the bottle and stood gazing out over the moonlit countryside. 'Never seen it so light. Damn near read the newspaper.' He sighed, he was tired. The padded bench along the wall looked inviting. 'Gerry should sleep for an hour before the next shot, I'll just stretch out for a moment.'

Was it the owl hooting that woke him? He would never know. Gerald was smiling. The moonlight more intense, it's silver glow flooded the tower. 'Gerry, what is it, are you in pain?'

The answer came in a whisper. 'The Captain has come for me, Gary.'

There was a sudden rushing sound, Carlo was on the bed, licking his master's face. Suddenly he lifted his head. A howl, terrible, primeval, shattered the eerie silence of the night. Fear clutching at his heart, Gareth stood frozen. The dog leapt from the bed out the door. He could hear his claws scratching on the metal stairs, rushing downward. He heard himself whisper-Dear God Almighty! His trembling fingers reached out, feeling for a pulse, there was no pulse. Gerald had left with the Captain.

At last it was over. Another Wakefield in the soil by the Chapel.

Gareth waited a few days. The last weeks with his dying brother had shaken him more than he could ever have imagined. The pain in his mother's eyes haunted him. Never, never would he come back. Never would he marry. He had seen the agony his parents had suffered. No, not for him. Those last few hours with Gerald would remain with him forever.

Before leaving, he sought out Mick. He had always liked Mick. 'Thank you for everything, especially for looking after the outrigger Mick. I was a mean bastard you know, never let anyone else use it. I want young Tom to have it Mick.'

'Leave it to me Gary.' They shook hands.

Mick watched as Ben's car disappeared down the drive on the way to the station. 'Yeah, life can be a bastard. You can be dealt a crook hand all right.'

Ben returned to work. With the influx of returned servicemen and new settlers, his work load became heavier by the day. He reminded his partners of his request they find a replacement. They would, yes they watched the Journals. Most of the young men preferred the cities or went overseas. Many of the older ones had retired or stayed in established practices. Please, would he stay for the time being?

He and Frances talked long and earnestly late into the night. Again he suggested they leave *Monaro* and live in Sydney. Gareth was going away. The house in Mosman would be empty. Or, why not a long overseas trip? No. *Monaro* was their home, how could they leave it? Yes, they should have regular visits to Sydney and when Tom was older, a trip. 'He is so artistic Ben, like your father. Henri says he has a natural talent. They are teaching him French, a few words each time he has a lesson.'

'He is just a child Francie. Don't push him, let him be a boy. He needs to fish and swim.' He was about to say-like the others- but held his peace.

Frances would suddenly drop off, aided by a mild soporific, he determined he would wean her off that just as soon as possible. With sleep eluding him he would lie staring into the darkness, ghosts of the past drifting through his mind.

A week after his son's death he realized Carlo was not around. Mrs. Ellis had put his food out regularly where it remained untouched. Only one person would have a clue. Mick still put in his two days, Ben could set his watch by the sound of sulky wheels on the gravel. This morning he watched the old rig swing round the bend, half expecting to see Carlo on the seat beside his friend. 'Mick, I've been waiting to see you. Can't find the old dog anywhere. Have you see him?' He noticed the slight tremor in Mick's hands as he rolled the inevitable smoke. Not a good sign. A war, endless smokes and years of toil were taking their toll. Time for Mick to sit on his verandah and let the world pass by. How to tell him though!

'Meant t'tell you Doctor.'

Doctor? That was not Mick's style, Ben felt a sudden unease.

'Yeah, I found him all right. Didn't want t'worry you, all the trouble y'know. I'm terrible sorry Doc, couldn't say it before.'

'Thank you Mick.'

'Yeah, I was just waitin' the right time t'tell you. When Mrs. Ellis said he hadn't touched his tucker, I knew where t'look. He was dead Doc. In the same hole he dug behind the Chapel. Buried him there, hope that was all right.'

'Was he injured in any way?'

'Had a cut front leg, went through the kitchen window, Mrs. Ellis said.'

'Why do you suppose? He's never done anything like that before.'

Mick picked up the reins. 'Best I get goin' Doc. Sorry I had to tell you like this.'

Ben's voice faltered slightly. 'Thank you Mick, I am very grateful to you.' So Carlo was gone too, resting where he loved to roam. Guarding the forest, his forest with the goannas and snakes and the fat paddy melons.

CHAPTER XXVI

Christmas Eve 1950 found the two old friends where they had so often sat before. 'Good to see the lanterns again Ben.'

'Yes, there was a time I thought we would never see them again.'

'That's in the past thank God. Things will never be the same I know but it's good for the children.'

'Never seemed like Christmas without them.' Ben poured from the brandy bottle. 'Time passes so quickly Pieter. I feel my age these days, old as the hills.'

'You need a change. What about that trip you always promised yourself?'

Ben chuckled. 'Sorry I haven't mentioned it before-we are booked to sail from Sydney in April.'

'I'll be damned! You kept that close to yourself.'

'Tell the truth, it was a sudden impulse. Made the arrangements when we were in Sydney last month.'

'Just what you need. What about Frances?'

'Ecstatic. She thinks it's time Tom toured the great art galleries of the world. He is her whole life Pieter, trouble is she is trying to mould him into something he will never be.'

'What do you mean?'

'Oh you know, a concert pianist or even a famous artist.'

'And what do you think?'

'I've spoken to Henri Brelat who agrees he will be a first rate pianist but that is as far as it goes. The world is full of them.'

'You mentioned painting, art I should say, I suppose.'

'The same, he daubs. Colourful stuff, like my father used to do. But thank heaven, he is essentially a ten year old boy.'

'He and young Dorothy are good mates.'

'Yes, ever since Mick launched him in Gareth's old outrigger, they spend hours up and down the creek, fishing. Damn good fishers they are too!'

'How is the old boy, by the way?'

'Stubborn as ever. Finally managed to get him to see reason and I think he now enjoys retirement. Still calls in every Friday on his way to the pub, tells me the town gossip. Still cares for the four graves in the town cemetery.'

'That's Mick all right.'

'How is Dorothy? See very little of her these days.'

'She has taken the load off my shoulders Ben. Trouble is, I don't think she will ever get over Gerald. She is very moody at times. Still, she sees a lot of Hal Wynter, he was always very fond of her.'

'Will it come to anything?'

'God knows. He's a fine young fellow, but if there is anything doing I would be the last to know.'

For some minutes they sat in silence.

'Well, we have a new government. What do you think of Menzies and his colleagues?'

'The country has had a gutful of Socialism and shortages. Time will tell. It seems our fate is to be governed either by Socialists or Conservative toadies.'

'Ben, Australians get what they deserve. You once told me your grandfather said beer and sport are our gods.'

'Not mine old friend and I know not yours, but in general, I think he was right.'

'I wonder if the political situation would have been any different if your brother in law had lived?'

'Doubt it Pieter, Australians resist change. We have never had a leader who could inspire people, except Curtin perhaps. Someone who could stand up and say-This is your country, this is where you live. Forget the old world-You know as well as I do, there is a certain class who worship Royalty, a Royalty that scarcely knows we exist, much less cares.' He gave a short laugh. 'Sorry if I seem to be making heavy weather tonight.'

'You're not old man, you are merely saying what many think but haven't the intestinal fortitude to say.'

'Perhaps Pieter, but you know I love this country too much to leave, even when I despaired for the future. You meet so many good people, honest hard working, some without two bob in their pocket yet they give you a grin and say 'She'll be right Doc'.How many times have I heard that? Restores my faith, I suppose. But what sticks in my craw are these bloody toadies who call themselves British, never Australian, as if they were ashamed of the name. Yes, ashamed to call themselves Australians yet they make their wealth out of the sweat of underpaid workers.'

'Perhaps all these migrants may change things Ben.'

'I would like to think we could live that long. Anyway, to be honest, I don't much care. Too bloody old, leave all that to the younger generation. Be interesting to live to the year 2000, or perhaps it might not.' They both laughed.

'Dan's letter was a surprise. Growing oranges in California! Sounds wonderful.'

'Yes, happily married and released from his vows at last. I think he has Sean to thank for that. It was a long process but well presented as only Sean could.'

'Well some things have a happy ending. Ellen must be pleased.'

'Yes, when we eventually take our trip, we plan to visit them. They have two little girls and Jean's son, who he adopted, is now practicing as a lawyer in Los Angeles.'

'Good Lord! Isn't it strange how things work out? Real life is truly stranger than fiction.'

'Indeed. Do you hear from Gareth these days?'

'Oh yes, he's been back over a year now. Making quite a name for himself in his field.'

'Never comes up for a visit?'

'Doubt he ever will-that business with the Wells' girl and then Gerald.'

'Any lady friend on the horizon?'

'I've no doubt he has companions from time to time, but marry?' Ben shook his head. 'He's a sworn bachelor Pieter. He told me when I ventured the subject, that that is the way he wants to live his life.'

Ben stretched his legs and sighed contentedly. 'How's your glass Pieter?'

'I feel more relaxed by the minute Ben. Troubles seem far away.'

'That's the idea old friend. Pleasant isn't it?'

'You still have Mrs. Ellis, that woman's a born cook.'

'I'll be sorry when she decides to put her feet up. Thank the Lord she shows no sign of it yet.'

'Ethel finally gave in?'

'Yes, marvellous old girl. I only go down there occasionally. Faith has retired too of course. The new young Sister they got seems to know her job but whether she will stick it out remains to be seen. Most of them prefer the city.'

'What does she do with herself? Ethel, I mean.'

'Gardens, looks after the twins when Dave and Christine take the odd weekend. She reckons she is busier than ever.'

'I've been meaning to talk to you about Melbourne. What do you intend doing with the old mansion?'

'Your young brother is still there isn't he?'

'He certainly is. Still swears it's the best address in Melbourne.'

Ben laughed. 'I've always admired his style.'

'He is certainly meticulous regarding your interests. Ben, you could make a great deal of money selling property now.'

'No Pieter, you say it pays for itself, makes reasonable money, think I'll just leave it. Perhaps Gareth or young Tom will make use of it some day. As you well know, I am in no need of money.'

'I think, a wise decision. It can only increase in value. But what of the old place, *Monterey*? You must think about that, I really think you should.'

'No idea. Just leave as is until the present incumbent decides to move elsewhere. I believe there's a move afoot to preserve some of the better class old places. I could present it to the State.'

'Sound idea. I believe the big tourist Liners always pull into Melbourne for a couple of days, why not slip out and see for yourself?'

'By George I will! And look in on old Sean as well.'

Pieter held out his glass. 'I believe the expression the younger people use since the Americans were here is 'I'll drink to that!'

Inside the house, Ellen looked at Frances as voices echoed from the verandah. She smiled, 'I think it's time the gentlemen took coffee, lots of it and very strong.'

Later on the verandah. 'I envy you Frances-are you looking forward to your trip?'

'I am Ellen, especially for Tom's sake. It will be a wonderful experience for him.'

'What about school? He will miss a whole year.'

'I have spoken to Charles Cummings, although Tom is not ready for high school yet, he thinks a year out won't affect him in the slightest. In fact, he thinks it will be good for him.'

'Have you booked him into Gareth's old school. We booked little Dorothy into the Presbyterian Ladies College.'

'Oh no, I want him to go to high school here.'

Ben and Pieter exchanged glances. 'We will think about that when the time comes Francie.'

Later that night Frances brought the subject up again. 'You promised me Ben that I could look after Tom. Remember you promised.'

'Looking after, doesn't mean we should deprive him of a sound education, Francie.'

'There is nothing he could learn down there, he couldn't learn here. And I do need him Ben.' There was anguish in her voice.

He comforted her. 'Of course my love. Don't upset yourself. Everything will be all right.'

'He is such a lovable boy Ben. Did you know he has made his own little den in Abraham's old cottage?'

'Yes Bob told me. He helped to fix it up.'

'He asked me for Judy's photograph.' Her eyes filled with tears. 'He just looked at me and smiled and said-She had a lovely face didn't she Grandma? I worry so-if anything should happen to him.'

Ben took her hand in his. 'Don't be silly. Look when we step onto the Liner, you will forget all your worries.'

'He will miss a lot of school, do you think that matters?'

'Charles says he thinks children go into high school too early anyway. This trip will be a wonderful education for Tom. Now, do you want me to give you a sleeping draught?'

'No, you told me I must give up my crutches. Please bear with me Ben. I think about *Monaro* such a lot, Gareth will never marry and we don't know what Tom will do.'

'Francie, we don't own *Monaro*-houses own people and *Monaro* will own whoever comes after us.'

'It seems so sad, after all we have been through.'

'My dear, don't worry about it. I have made all necessary arrangements with the lawyers and with Gareth. He will see it goes to some worthy cause. Believe me, I have thought about it too but somehow I don't think it will ever come to that. Now, how about some sleep?'

'You are lucky Ben, you just have to close your eyes.'

He gave her a hug. 'If only that were true old girl.'

Christmas Eve 1958

Light blazed from every window of the house. Magic lanterns glowed amongst the trees, from inside came the sounds of youthful laughter.

'Like old times Ben.'

'Probably my age Pieter, I don't understand that blasted music they play. The women seem to enjoy it, frankly I am thankful for our retreat.'

'Times change Ben. The young don't understand our tastes as we seldom understood our elders.'

'You are right of course, but this, thank God never changes. Let me top up your glass.'

'Just think back over the years-the times we have sat here, the world at our feet. Some of the happiest moments of my life-what is left of it.'

'Don't talk like that Pieter, there are a few years in the old body yet.'

'You didn't seem so sure when you examined me last time.'

'I was merely warning you. Your blood pressure is on the high side, that's all. It happens to everyone, our arteries harden as we grown older.'

'Well, what did you mean telling me I must take it easy? I do so damn little as it is.'

'Leave the work to your daughter. Dorothy is capable of handling it, isn't she?'

'She is, but it's the usual bloody thing-men don't like dealing with a woman. They go up to Lambruk.'

'Well, why not advertise for a young bloke from the city? Damn it Pieter, you are wealthy enough to retire.'

'Habit Ben. Hard for an old horse to throw off his harness.'

'Know only too well, though thank God, I'm only called in occasionally and then strictly in an advisory capacity. When we go down to the city for school holidays I generally go out to the university to see what's new and Gareth keeps me pretty well informed.'

'How is he, still the dedicated bachelor?'

Ben laughed. 'Always will be. Y'know in his own quiet way, I think he is set on a Professorial appointment.'

'Knowing Gareth, I think he would be eminently suited. He has that dedicated air about him.'

'Probably, but I think he has a wait before him, there are few appointments available, we need more universities.'

'I believe Tom has been accepted for Medicine.'

'Against Frances' violent objections. I think what swayed her was the development of the Polio vaccine. She has lived with the dread of Polio ever since he was born.'

'You must hand it to the Americans.'

'We are talking too damn much and not appreciating this Cognac, hold out your glass.'

They settled back, fresh cigars glowing in the half light.

'Talking of America, Pieter, if I had young children, knowing what I do now, I would advise them to get the best degree possible and migrate. There is nothing here for them. We have talked of the future before, but beer and sport are still the gods, to hell with progress. Stand out intellectually and you will be chopped down to size, to the lowest common denominator.'

'Aren't you being a little too critical? You know as well as I do, there are many fine people in this country.'

'I know, but without a leader to inspire, I feel we will sink even deeper into apathy.'

'I agree I suppose. We have never produced a Lincoln. So what is the solution?'

'Damned if I know. I do know though, you and I are too old to worry, leave it to the young, it's their problem. To Hell with the future-you and I are here to drink to the Captain's memory and to a Merry Christmas and many more of them!'

Before Tom left for the city and his new life at University, Ben spent considerable time with his grandson. 'There is a place I want you to see before you leave Tom. A special place where I sometimes took your Uncle Gerald.'

The road south of Bangalow winds steeply upwards. Reaching the top, Ben turned into a little road leading to Possum Brush, then swung the car around facing the way they had come. Before them, over low undulating hills and rich volcanic plains lay the mighty Pacific Ocean. 'This is the furthermost Eastern point in Australia, Tom. Captain Cook would have seen all this as he sailed north.'

They stepped out of the car, breathing in the light air. A breeze faintly smelling of the sea stirred the bushes. 'Yes, your Uncle loved this place. He always said he would build his home here someday.' They stood in silence gazing out to the distant sea.

'Tell me Tom, and I know you will speak the truth. Do you want to study medicine?'

'I thought that is what you wanted me to do Grandpa.'

'What I want and what you want are two different things. There is no point in doing something if your heart is not in it.'

'Yes, I think I do. You said everyone should try his best to help others.'

'Your grandmother isn't too happy with your decision.'

Tom smiled and Ben thought how like Judy he is, same brown hair and green eyes.

'I love Grandma and would do anything to please her but I could never be a concert pianist. The teacher in Sydney said I play well but that is as far as it goes.'

'Well, there is a first rate instrument at Mosman you know, so you can play to please yourself.' He glanced sideways at his grandson. 'How will you like living with Gareth?'

'Pretty good, I reckon Grandpa. Uncle Gareth's a good sport, doesn't say much but you always know where you stand with him.'

'What about living away, will you miss *Monaro*?'

'Will I ever! But I'll come home for holidays, won't be able to wait until I get into the old outrigger again.'

Ben laughed. 'I think it's time we started back.'

Tom stood looking out over the rich country. 'I wonder what happened to the tribes that used to live here Grandpa.'

'I don't know. Old timers say they suddenly vanished-just picked up and silently disappeared.'

'Don't you think that's sad?'

'Tragic would be a better word. We have a lot to answer for.'

On the trip back Ben was surprised at his grandson's next question.

'Do you think there are any girls in the world who look like the captain's lady, Grandpa?'

Ben smiled. 'That's a funny question. I suppose it's possible. Why do you ask?'

'Well, she is so beautiful yet she looks sad. I wonder why.'

'I imagine it's the way the artist sees his subject Tom, and I think it is the way the viewer sees it. I'm sure she wasn't sad really.'

They drove on in silence. Ben thought to himself-Funny he should say that, I've often thought the same.

1959 proved an eventful year, bringing sadness and some joy.

Pieter DeVries, lawyer and attorney, Ben's oldest and dearest friend did not live to celebrate another Christmas, dying in his sleep just as the leaves of the Liquid Ambers were starting to turn. After a short period, his daughter Dorothy married an ever patient, ever attentive Hal Wynter.

Life went on. Ben feeling a great emptiness, grew ever closer to his wife. 'I feel so lonely Francie. Pieter was the only man I could talk to. I have nothing in common with the younger men and we are isolated from the average townspeople because of our position. It's a false position, Francie. Doctors know it but many play it for all it's worth.'

'Why not take another trip? We could go down to Melbourne. Ellen might come with us, I know she wants to see Sean and Pieter's brother again.'

He nodded. 'A good idea but wait until later in the year, Melbourne can be a cold hole in the winter.'

Although most of their mail came to the house, the occasional letter marked personal, found it's way to the surgery. Ben examined the heavy envelope, turning it over in his hands-quality paper, addressed in an obvious female hand, a female hand that brought a delicious feeling. He sat in his car slitting the seal with his penknife. Just a few words in mauve ink-Dearest Ben, As you will see from the enclosed photograph, things have turned out better than I ever dreamt. The doctors say the cause was anxiety. Affectionately, Jane. He examined the photograph, two happy healthy children, about a year apart. He sat for a long time, memories flooded back. He shook his head-No I'll never regret it, it was so beautiful while it lasted. How many men could ever have memories like mine?

Christmas 1965

Tom came home to *Monaro* with his grandparents after his Graduation ceremony.

'Do you know where you are going Tom?

'North Shore I think Grandpa. Hope so anyway, some of my friends hope to go there too.'

'Well you know it's a sort of slavery from now on. Long hours, little sleep and plenty of abuse.'

Tom laughed. 'So I believe, but for now all I want is to fish and swim. Is Dorothy home yet Grandma?'

'Yes, and she is such a pretty girl. You might have trouble having her to yourself this Christmas.'

Tom put his arm around her. 'Doesn't matter Grandma, so long as I have you and the old outrigger, I'll be happy.'

She smoothed his hair. 'Any nice young lady in your life yet dear?'

He laughed. 'Not yet Grandma, I'm still fancy free.'

This Christmas Eve, Ben kept a solitary vigil on the high verandah. Nothing had changed, the magic lanterns still diffused soft colours along the carriageway. Not yet completely dark, the sky had a mauve tint to it. Below the Frangipanis gave up waves of opulent perfume. He sighed. 'Damned hot tomorrow, probably another storm.' The tip of his cigar glowed, he poured from the dark green bottle on the little cane table. A sense of loss nagged at him. The injustice of it all, a man like Pieter gone, and no age really. And Dave, just when he was enjoying his well earned retirement. Life was bloody queer all right. What was the use of it all, so much anguish, so much hurt. As a doctor he was supposed to give comfort, to council wisely. Who the hell was to comfort him? *Monaro*, damn *Monaro*! It had brought him grief, grief he had had to hide. He would leave the place forever, only for the bonds that bound him to the place. His father, mother and his dear sons would keep him here until he joined them. At least there was Gareth, the son who would not come back, and Tom. Frances charges me with forcing him into medicine, perhaps I did. I can't tell. He is a gentle soul, a dreamer, ridiculously handsome. Medicine might force him to face the realities of life. Hope to God he doesn't become entangled in some ghastly love affair. Couldn't stand that. A chuckle escaped him-She would have to measure up to the portrait that hangs in the gallery, the mysterious captain's lady. The boy was besotted, possessed almost. A romantic all right, takes after my poor father. Well, that's how life is.

He refilled his glass, thank God he could still enjoy good liquor. What was it old Omar said? 'Come fill the cup, the bird of time has but a little way to fly.' Something like that-but oh, how true. He turned his head slightly, listening to laughter from inside. Thank God for Ellen and the girls and Hal, fine young man, hardly says a word, how war changes men. He drew on his cigar-Gareth really should make the effort if only for his mother's sake. Still he is his own man, very little sentiment in Gareth. And this pretty granddaughter of Pieter's, doing Veterinary Science-amazing! Young girls do everything these days and good for them! He settled back-ah, I can smell the coffee from here.

CHAPTER XXVII

The brief holidays passed all too quickly. Dorothy complained to her mother. 'Why did he have to be my cousin Mum? He is so beautiful.'

'Men are not beautiful dear, men are handsome.'

'Oh you know what I mean. Tom treats me like a boy. He's only serious when we go fishing. I wouldn't mind so much but when we go to the local dances he tries to avoid dancing with me and when he does he won't hold me like the others want to.'

'Tom obviously has more good sense than you have. Really Dorothy, you surprise me!'

'You know how all the girls are mad about him.'

'Perhaps, but you can never be, you are his cousin. I shouldn't have to explain further. Read your Bible or remember your lessons in genetics.'

Her daughter sighed. 'It's his last day tomorrow, we're going to the Chapel to put flowers on Dad's and his father's graves.'

Her mother turned away to hide the tears that came to her eyes.

'Mum, I'm so sorry!' She put her arms around her mother. 'You must have loved Dad very much.'

'Hush dear, don't say any more. Just make sure when you do fall in love, you know in your heart it is right.'

'You do love Hal, don't you?'

'Of course I do. He and your father were so alike. Hal has been a great comfort in my life.'

'Are you going to keep the practice Mum?'

'I don't know yet. If I do I will have to take in a male partner, women are still not accepted by everyone.'

Dorothy laughed. 'You should have seen the ribbing we got in First Year. Just three girls but we stood up to them. Now all they want is a date.'

Her mother looked at her lovely, smiling daughter. 'I'm sure they do, be sure to choose wisely.'

'I'll always be in love with Tom, the others are a pain.'

'Dorothy don't say that, even when you don't mean it. Now, please spend some time with your grandmother, she misses you.'

Mosman 1967

'So now Tom, residency over, you are legally entitled to practice Medicine. What do you intend to do?' Gareth sat with his nephew enjoying a cold beer in the shade of the Liquid Ambers.

'No idea Uncle. Bloody glad to be finished with that hospital. Reckon I'll take some time off, sleep for a month. Probably go up to *Monaro*!'

'Yes. Residents have a rough time all right. Only way to learn though, work under pressure, see all the latest procedures.'

"That why you stay in hospital work Uncle?'

'Partly, I have other plans of course, but they must wait.'

'Everyone reckons you're a top notch surgeon Uncle.'

Gareth smiled. 'Hope most of my patients share that sentiment. Anyway, forget Medicine for the moment. How do you like your new apartment?'

'Great Uncle. Terrific views, feels good.'

'Don't you miss the piano?'

'Hope I can use this one occasionally, music relaxes me.'

'You have the run of the house, you know that. It will be yours eventually as will *Monaro* and quite a lot of valuable property. I trust you will use it wisely.'

'I never think about it Uncle.'

'Well you should.' Gareth pushed back his chair. 'Come on, I'll take you to dinner at the club.'

Dinner finished, they retired to the lounge. 'Haven't had a call up for this Vietnam business yet?'

'Not yet, a lot of the other blokes have. They are not happy I can tell you.'

'Will you go if they call you.'

'I suppose so. Hardly worth the trouble fighting it.'

Gareth frowned. 'Bloody insane business. Wouldn't blame you if you refused. Hoped it would be all over by this.'

'You were in Korea weren't you Uncle?'

'Yes, and what the hell did that prove? Damn little, a country divided, kept apart by military might. Hardly a solution.'

'About half a dozen friends of mine have received their notices.'

'They must be desperate for medicos.'

'Apparently. You should have seen the things some of them did to get out of it. Swallowed their own blood then vomited it up, anything to make themselves appear unfit-bloody terrible, believe me.'

'Did it work?'

'Not that I know of. They were in, that was that. One of the Residents, a friend of mine, Sam Isaacs has been working on it since Fifth Year. His father is a Psychiatrist. He tried to pull a schizophrenic act used to come in just a raincoat, nothing underneath, had mood changes, all the classic symptoms.'

'I know his father, Dr. Isaacs well, he went to school with your Uncle Gerald. How did your friend make out?'

'Same as the rest.'

Gareth snorted with disgust. 'They'll never learn, our political masters. Australians will never accept Conscription. If the bloody fools had called for volunteers I'm sure they would have had all they needed. Well,' he stood, stubbing out his cigar, 'when do you leave for *Monaro*?'

'About a week I guess.'

'Come and see me before you go.'

A few days later Gareth arrived home to find his nephew at the piano. He stood listening at the doorway. Scherzo in B Flat Minor. Expressive, passionate, serene. How he loved this music! He walked quietly into the room. 'Hello there, didn't expect to see you so soon.'

Tom rested his hands on the keys. 'Been over most mornings after you leave Uncle. Yesterday you stayed longer than you usually do.'

'Why didn't you come in?'

'You were playing your violin, didn't want to disturb you.'

'Sorry I missed you Tom.'

'You're still pretty good Uncle, good enough for the Sydney Symphony I reckon.'

Gareth smiled. 'You know that's not true Tom, but thanks for the compliment. Anyway, I'm glad you are here now, I wanted to see you. Let's have a beer then I know a wonderful little Italian place for dinner.'

Over dinner they talked. 'You're going to *Monaro*?'

'Can't wait to get the outrigger out.'

'I envy you. When will you be back?'

'Friend of mine's father has a practice at Melvale. It's a group really. He wants me to go there for a week first. Good experience he reckons.'

'I'm all for it. Nothing like the real thing.'

'I'm a bit worried though, won't be like the hospital will it?'

'Go Tom for heaven's sake. You have to start some time. Hmm, a week eh, that means you will be back here next Friday?'

'About then.'

'Good, I would like a favour. Dr. Bailey-Stuart is giving a dinner party the following Friday.'

'The surgeon?'

'Yes, he could be very helpful to me. Could you put off *Monaro* for a week?'

'If you want me to Uncle.'

'You are very presentable Tom. Dinner suit by the way.'

'Oh hell!'

Gareth smiled.

Tom returned earlier than expected, Gareth found him waiting at Mosman. 'Everything all right Tom?'

'Wait until you hear Uncle! I'm the world's greatest bloody fool.'

'Sit down my boy. Have a beer.' He eyed his nephew closely. 'Well, out with it. What did you do, kill someone?'

'Might have been easier.' He stood gulping his beer. 'I tell you Uncle, I'll never do GP.'

'Go on.'

'I'm positive they trapped me. I made a complete fool of myself.'

'I find that hard to believe.'

'You might but it's true. I knew it wouldn't be like the hospital.'

'We all know that. What happened?'

'I tell you, it was a set up. You know, throw the new boy in the deep end, then piss themselves laughing.'

Gareth controlled his smile. 'I can't wait.'

'The old Sister, the receptionist, ushered in a girl about twenty, nice looking girl about to be married. Wanted the Pill and wanted to know all about, you know-sex, all that.'

Gareth fought to control his composure. 'I'm a surgeon not a physician, surely all you had to do was write a prescription?'

'Write a script? Like hell! The whole thing-pelvic examination, the lot.' Tom began pacing the floor. 'She got up on the table, pulled her dress up-God, I couldn't think! When I found my voice it sounded funny, a sort of falsetto-more of a squeak. I think I said 'would you please remove your hose?' Hose for God's sake, I couldn't even say panty hose. She just smiled at me and said- 'You do that don't you Doctor?'

No longer able to control himself, Gareth lay back convulsed with laughter. 'Oh Tom, Tom!'

'Go on Uncle, laugh. It wasn't funny.'

'Sorry Tom.' Gareth made a show of cleaning his glasses. 'I'm sure you handled the situation admirably.'

'Only just. I excused myself, dropped the bloody speculum, blundered outside and asked the Sister to come in with me.'

'Wise decision my boy.'

'Yeah, my first and last go at GP work. That afternoon I packed my bag, jumped into the Jeep and headed for Sydney.'

'Didn't you give an explanation?'

'No way, bugger them. I was too anxious to get out of there.'

'I think you should write and explain.'

'It's all right. The old man came out, sort of apologised and wished me luck.'

'What do you intend to do now?'

'Well, I reckon I'll go back to the hospital and try for my FRACP, remember you said I should.'

'If you do get your degree, what then?'

'Research of some sort, if I can get into it. Uncle, I can't deal with people.'

'I see. Well, come on I'll take you out to dinner.'

Dr. Bailey-Stuart's house stood in extensive grounds in leafy Killara. A butler ushered them in. Tom nudged Gareth. 'Jesus, Uncle, I've seen most of them at the hospital, they regard interns as a disease.'

'Relax, you are no longer a resident and these people are my friends.'

The host came forward with outstretched hand. 'Gareth, so good to see you. Ah, this is the nephew you have been telling me about. How are you, young man.'

Tom took the plump hand. 'Fine thank you sir.'

'Well come on, don't stand there, come and have a drink. I'm told dinner will be twenty minutes yet.'

Gareth merged into the crowd, all old friends and acquaintances. Tom stood cocktail in hand, not sure what he should do next. Marooned, ignored by the cream of the city's medical fraternity, he wandered through into the next room. Elegantly furnished, across a sea of carpet with the lid wide open, stood a Steinway Grand, inviting to be played. Not a soul in sight, he pulled the stool close, his fingers caressed the keys. Transported into another world, Chopin's Nocturne No 2, joyous, sensual, tender like gossamer, floated through the house. The hubbub ceased, suddenly he was aware people were standing watching him. He stood, a deep flush suffusing his face. Almost terrified, he stammered. 'I am sorry sir, I hope I haven't disturbed you.'

'Disturbed us? My boy, that was magnificent! Gareth, why haven't you told us your nephew is an accomplished pianist?'

Gareth smiled. 'I think he plays for pleasure only, James.'

'Young man, you must play for us after dinner.'

Left to himself again, Tom sat quietly idly glancing through some sheet music. He lifted his head, aware of a subtle perfume. A girl was standing looking at him. A lovely blonde girl, with laughing eyes and green jade ear rings. Her black evening gown clung to her slender figure. She held out her hand. 'I'm Leslie, Dad insisted I stay for the evening-I have to play Hostess.'

'Tom, Tom Wakefield. I came with my Uncle.'

She smiled. 'They are dear old souls, but really-well, you know.'

'Not much in common-know what you mean.'

'You play beautifully.'

He looked at her, he had never seen a lovelier girl. 'Only for pleasure. What about you?'

'I try but I'm not in your class.'

A muffled gong sounded. 'Oh Lord, dinner. I'm supposed to be gracious and make intelligent conversation. Come on Tom, you will have to help me.'

During the meal Tom surreptitiously glanced around at the affable, well groomed assembly, faces flushed with good food and wine. The conversation flowed smoothly-investments, cars, property, the burden of outrageous taxation. He raised his eyes to where Leslie sat, she smiled, his heart jumped. How beautiful she is. Her left hand rested on the table, a diamond ring sparkled on the third finger.

Later when the gentlemen retired for Port and cigars, he wandered through the French windows to the cool of the garden. He heard her light step and breathed the heady aura of her perfume.

'Far from the madding crowd?'

'Far enough for now. Who's the lucky man?'

She held out her hand. 'Mark is with the Navy. That rotten Vietnam business. He's a Gunnery Officer.'

'He is still a lucky man.'

'What about you Tom?'

'No one serious, guess I'm still looking.'

'That's hard to believe. Come on, tell me. There must be someone in your life.'

He laughed. 'There would be if you had a sister. Like you, I mean.'

She took his arm. 'Sorry Tom, Kathy is only twelve.' Suddenly she was serious. 'Ever since Mother died, I have had to take care of things.'

'I'm sorry Leslie.'

'Don't be. Dad's a dear. I could never let him down.'

'What about a career?'

'I am a physiotherapist. I work at the Children's Hospital three days a week. Do you like barbecues Tom?'

'I guess so, why?'

'The crowd I go with,' for an instant she seemed lost for words, 'they are really nice, Tom. Most of them have been involved in protest marches.'

'Everyone marches to his own drum, Leslie.'

'Are you going to Vietnam?'

'I don't know. I haven't been called up yet.'

'Will you go?'

'God knows. I'll wait until I see if they want me.'

'Look Tom, pick me up about eight tomorrow morning. We're using Daddy's boat. There is a lovely little beach along Pittwater. Just bring yourself and some white wine.'

'So long as you don't mind riding in my old Jeep. Don't worry, it's got a hood.'

She looked toward the house. 'I think the old dears are getting ready to leave. Come, you can stand by me as I act the gracious Chatelaine.'

The next morning she was waiting for him. She came running, a carry bag in her hand. He looked with pleasure at her slim brown legs, white shorts and Hawaiian blouse.

Breathlessly she opened the door. 'Daddy hates the people I get around with, I hope you don't.'

'Don't worry. I'm easy to get along with.'

'Do you know the way, to Coal and Candle I mean?'

'Sure.'

'We'd better get going then, they will be waiting for us.'

The day passed pleasantly, Tom refused to be drawn into politics. Would he go to Vietnam if called up? Didn't know, wait and see. Wouldn't he admit it was a rotten business? Would he blame anyone for protesting and tearing up their cards?

That was an individual decision.

'You don't seem to have an opinion Tom.' The group stood around as steak and sausages sizzled on the barbecue.

'If I have, I would prefer not to express it.' He smiled his disarming smile. 'What say we enjoy the day, forget the troubles of the world for the moment.'

Later frolicking in the water with Leslie, he confided. 'I'm afraid your friends think I am a bit of a square.'

'No they don't, they respect you because you don't thrust your opinion on them.'

'That's a relief.' He floated close to her looking up at the sky. 'Look at those clouds boiling up Les, looks like a storm coming. It's been so darn hot.' He was interrupted by a distant roll of thunder.

She swam lazily to the beach. 'Time to go everyone, storm coming.' She took Tom by the hand. 'I hate it when the water becomes rough.'

They pulled into the marina just as the storm broke. 'Please help me berth her Tom then the boatshed will take over. Just tie her up, that's all we need to do.'

Hand in hand, they ran for the Jeep. The storm broke violently, rain coming in sheets. 'Quick, get in made it just in time.'

She looked ruefully at her blouse. 'Just another minute! Just look at me.'

'Les, you're wet.'

She smiled pushing back her hair. 'Only damp.' She gave a slight shiver. 'Funny isn't it, how quickly it cools off.'

'Here, let me put this around you.' He leaned over and pulled a rug from the back seat. 'Can't let you catch cold.' Tucking it around her shoulders he leaned against her, his hand brushing her breasts. The nipples felt hard to his touch. 'Sorry Les.'

She sat still, smiling at him. 'Thank you Tommy.'

Wordless, he continued to wrap her closely in the rug. She gave a little gasp, arching her body. It happened spontaneously-they were locked in a passionate embrace. Her tongue found his, his hand explored her body. The rain drummed steadily on the roof. He fought free, looking into her half closed eyes. One of her ear rings fell to the floor.

'Les, forgive me. I had no right.'

Tears were in her eyes, she began to button her blouse. 'It's all right Tom. Please take me home.'

They drove in silence. At the house, she turned briefly and waved as the front door opened. He drove home cursing himself-What a rotten thing to do. How would I feel if someone did that to a girl I loved. Hell and damnation, I can't do anything right with females.

He showered long, the hot water soothing his anguish.

'It's only six o'clock and nowhere to go. What about that nice nurse, the dark one, a good sport and good company.' Idly he turned the pages of the phone book. Just look up her number, won't ring though. She wouldn't talk to me anyway. Probably thinks I'm some sort of sex maniac. She liked it though. I wonder-

Leslie answered the phone. 'Tom.'

'Leslie, let me get this off my chest-I feel a heel and I apologise.'

He heard her soft laughter. 'Whatever for?'

'I don't know what to say. I feel down in the depths. Les, I am desperate. Will you have dinner with me? If you say no, I will understand.'

Again the soft laugh. 'Don't be silly Tom, I would love to.'

'Pick you up at seven, okay?'

'I'll be waiting.'

Across the table they smiled at each other. 'My uncle introduced me to this place-do you like it?'

'It's very nice.'

'What about Chianti?'

'Whatever you like.'

'Les, I want to please you.'

'I love Chianti.'

They burst into laughter, then she was serious. 'Tell me about yourself Tom.'

'Not much to tell.' He gave only the briefest outline.

'Oh Tom, I am so sorry.'

'That all happened a long time ago. Never knowing my mother hurts sometimes but I was blessed with wonderful grandparents.'

'Your uncle is very nice.'

'Uncle Gareth, the crustiest bachelor this side of the black stump!'

'Since my mother died, I have been mother, hostess and I guess you could say, Chatelaine, so that it comes natural now.'

'What about Mark?'

'He is very special. Kind and generous, and very loving.'

'You must love him very much.'

She looked down, silent for a moment. 'Yes, I do.'

'That makes me feel more of a heel than ever.'

She raised her eyes, smiling. 'No you're not. You are sweet and gentle. I could easily love you Tom.'

He called the waiter.

'Let's get out of here. What would you like to do?'

'Whatever you like.'

'How about a drive across to Manly?'

'That would be nice.'

The week dragged. She had promised to have dinner Friday night but what the hell, he could never have her. He ached to see her, feelings he had never experienced before, a fever for which there was no cure. Why did he ever agree to go there anyway? Uncle Gareth of course. Well, he could hardly blame his uncle. Still, if he had never met her, he would not be suffering this misery.

When he was sure Gareth had left the house, he drove to Mosman. Sitting at the old Steinway, the music soothed him. Later, on returning home, he leafed through the mail in his letterbox. An official looking envelope. He turned it over. Doctor T. Wakefield. The message was brief-Report to Puckapunyal Army Camp, the date typed in. Well, that was it. A sense of relief, thank the Lord he had a couple of weeks before he had to front up.

Thursday he slept late. At Mosman, Mrs. Johns the housekeeper, met him at the door. 'Your uncle is in the drawing room, Doctor.'

Gareth was sitting gazing out over the harbour.

'Short list today, Uncle?'

'Sit down Tom, care for some tea?'

'No thank you.'

'North Shore has seen precious little of you, I phoned there yesterday.'

'Something has come up.'

'I see, perhaps you might enlighten me.'

Tom handed over the letter.

'When did this come?'

'Yesterday.'

'You might have phoned me.'

'I intended to, thought you might pull some strings.'

'I would never do that. It's your decision.'

'It's against my better judgement but I hate unpleasantness-demonstrating, hiding out, that sort of thing. Anyway, I won't be fighting anyone. I might even be useful.'

Gareth nodded. 'Yes, perhaps it's just as well. I had another reason for wanting to see you. You and Miss Bailey, she is engaged you know Tom. You could compromise the girl.'

'We haven't seen much of each other Uncle. All perfectly innocent.'

'I'm sure it is. Perhaps if you were to leave for *Monaro* immediately it might be better all round.'

'I want to Uncle, I plan to leave on Monday.'

'Well that's settled.' He smiled. 'Seeing you are unemployed, let me take you to lunch.'

In the afternoon, Tom phoned Leslie at the Children's Hospital. 'You haven't forgotten our dinner date for tomorrow?'

'Of course I haven't. Did you just phone me for that?'

'No, I got my call up notice yesterday Les.'

'Oh Tom!'

'We can talk about it tomorrow. Pick you up about six.' He desperately wanted to say 'I love you'.

All day Friday he was restless, the day seemed endless. At four in the afternoon, he stripped off and stood under the steaming shower. Hot water somehow eased the ache in his heart, relaxed his body. Through the noise of the water, the door chimes echoed through the unit. A hasty dry off, he donned his bathrobe-If they're selling encyclopedias, I'll bloody well kill them! Through the small space afforded by the safety chain, he saw Leslie smiling at him.

'May I come in?'

'Leslie? Oh yes, forgive me I'm not dressed.' He held the robe tightly around him. 'I was coming to pick you up at six, remember?'

'You don't mind my coming up here do you?' She gazed around. 'I like your apartment.'

'No of course not. It was, just sort of, unexpected.'

She came close to him, his heart thumped. 'Oh Les!'

Her fingers were undoing the tie of his robe. 'Unzip me, Tommy.'

Her dress fell to the floor, she was not wearing a bra. Her hands pushed the robe from his shoulders. He felt the nipples of her tight little breasts against his chest. His hand slipped down her back to the smooth silk of her panties, drawing her to him. Their lips locked in passion, he lifted her lightly as a child, carrying her into the bedroom.

The noise of the traffic in the street below, rose and fell as the afternoon shadows lengthened. From the bedroom in the quiet unit, came only the sound of their passionate whispering.

The proprietor of Guido's knew them by sight. Could they have a quiet table? But of course. With his affable Italian charm, he escorted them to a secluded corner. They sat in silence.

'Aren't you going to talk to me Tom?'

He reached over and took her hand. 'I love you Leslie, so terribly and I don't know what to say.'

'When you take me home tonight you are going to say goodbye to me, dearest, dearest Tommy, you know that.'

The proprietor, perceptive as his people often are, poured the wine. 'Please, do not bother to order now, drink, this is my best stock.' He smiled at them. 'It soothes the heart.'

'Les darling, how can I say goodbye? I love you!'

Gently, she pulled her hand away. 'I know Tom and I could love you.'

'It's Mark.'

'You know it is and you must know, being a doctor, Mark and I are lovers.'

He sat without speaking.

'You will always have a place in my heart Tommy. You are so gentle, you love a woman as she wants to be loved.'

He looked up. 'I love you Leslie, I will never love anyone else.'

'You will darling. You were made to love a woman.'

When they had eaten, Leslie asked. 'Are you going to take me for a last drive to Manly where we went before?'

He parked on the beach front looking out over the darkened sea. Elvis crooned softly on the radio. 'Would it be wrong if I held you one last time?'

She clung to him in answer. 'No darling.' She held tight to the hand that caressed her breast. 'Please Tommy, just hold me.'

In the hour before sun up, he drove past his uncle's house, stopping to slip a note into the letter box, then turned heading north through the sleeping city.

Throughout the long drive his thoughts were only of Leslie. A faint trace of perfume lingered to haunt him. How suddenly she had burst into his life. Not to ever see her again was unbearable. When, hours later, the familiar streets of Myuna came into view, a calm settled upon his troubled mind. Home. Home where every sight brought memories flooding back. The river was at full tide. Pelicans sailed majestically along the smooth water. A good time for bream, he would get amongst them tomorrow-might even try tonight. With quickening pulse he drove the winding road to *Monaro*, the gates were open, the gravel crunched under the tyres.

His grandparents were waiting for him by the little green gate in the wall. Of course, Uncle Gareth must have phoned them-but dear Lord, how frail they looked!

Mosman, 1973

Professor Wakefield looked closely at his nephew. Gone were the soft boyish looks, here was a lean young man whose eyes betrayed the Hell he had seen. 'Welcome home Tom.'

'Thanks Uncle. Glad to be back.' Hands in pockets, he gazed out over the glittering water.

'You seem preoccupied. Everything all right Tom?'

His nephew nodded. 'Just trying to adjust Uncle.' He smiled. 'Achieved your ambition at last.'

'If you call it that.'

'I am happy for you.'

'Thank you Tom, but we are not here to talk about me.'

'There is not much to tell Uncle.'

Gareth filled champagne glasses. 'Drink up, I am taking you to dinner.'

'Thanks Uncle but I don't feel much like going out, especially there.'

'Don't disappoint me Tom'

For the first time a faint smile crossed his nephew's face. 'All right, you always were persuasive Uncle.'

Guido's hadn't changed, Tom felt a sense of loss passing a certain secluded corner-two young lovers were holding hands.

'Feel like I have never been away.'

Seated at the table, Tom studiously studied the menu. The waiter poured a little wine for Gareth to taste.

'Tom, if you will put that cover down, I would like to talk to you.'

'Yes Uncle?'

'I was with your grandfather, I arrived in time. It was very peaceful. He was a great age you know.'

Tom fought to control his voice. 'What about Grandma, what will she do now?'

'Your grandmother is a strong resourceful woman Tom, she too is very old. You must see her as soon as you are able. Perhaps you do not realise what you mean to her.'

'I'll go as soon as I tidy things up here.'

'Any ideas for your future?'

'None, none whatsoever.'

'Well, before you go there are some matters we must discuss.'

'Thank you for having my unit kept in order.'

'You can thank Mrs. Johns for that. Ah, here's the waiter.'

'Uncle, do you ever, I mean have you seen Miss Bailey?'

Gareth sipped his wine slowly. 'I had hoped you might have forgotten her by this time, but yes, I do occasionally. She is married, quite the social butterfly.'

Tom smiled faintly. 'I hope she is happy.'

'I'm sure she is. Now what takes your fancy?'

When they had eaten, Gareth nipped the end of a long Havana. 'My one vice, at least my one unwise vice.'

'Never tried them Uncle, do they taste as good as they smell?'

Gareth smiled, drawing on the fragrant weed. 'Better, if such is possible.'

'You wanted to discuss some matters with me?'

'Purely business Tom. We have gone over the assets of our family before, you have a general picture of things. I think it time for you to take responsibility for these matters now.'

'I know nothing of business Uncle, you know that.'

'All you need to do is be advised by our solicitor and our accountant. There is property in Melbourne, some here and *Monaro*, and of course there are considerable funds invested.'

'I thought you handled all that sort of thing.'

'I have for a long time, now I think you should get used to it. You do understand?'

'Yes, I suppose so but I'd like to get away for a while. I've had a gutful of things generally.'

'Vietnam?'

Tom sighed. 'That amongst other things. I admit I learned plenty, but crawling round in the mud up there was no picnic. Then to come back here and be abused for something I had nothing to do with. At Central, a bloody stupid young girl spat at me! Why, for Christ's sake? Anyway, I couldn't get out of uniform quick enough.'

Gareth nodded. 'Hopeless business, tore the country apart. America too, apparently.'

'The whole damn thing was a mess. Hordes of reporters, most from countries that weren't even in the war. Some of them got killed, can't say much sympathy was wasted on them. They were so pathologically anti-American. One of the older American officers told me, had Macarthur been there, he would never have tolerated that sort of thing. I don't know of course, but I believe he was pretty ruthless.'

Gareth pulled on his cigar. 'I tend to agree with that officer you spoke to. I know Macarthur warned of the danger of wars in Asia, but of course he was long gone. No, if Macarthur had been around, Vietnam would never have become the quagmire it is. Anyway, it's time to put all that behind you. Go home to *Monaro*. What about an overseas trip, get yourself sorted out?'

'Yes I'm tired, very tired.' He grinned. 'First thing though, I must get some new clothes-nothing fits.'

'Well, I hope you don't go too soon. Spend a few days in Sydney, no doubt you have missed your music.'

'Yes, I wouldn't mind. They had a piano in the mess, must have come out of the ark. Couple of the blokes were pretty good musicians, one on sax, another the guitar. With a few beers we hammed it up-kept us reasonably sane.'

'I can expect you will be around for a few days then?'

'For sure. Must get the old Cherokee overhauled first thing.'

'About time you bought yourself a new car isn't it?'

Tom shook his head. 'I like the old girl, solid and dependable. Anyway Uncle, why don't you have a car?'

'Never have, never felt the need of it. Always use the one taxi company.'

They talked a little longer. When leaving, Tom promised to spend time at Mosman before he went away.

The next day he strolled along the streets of the city. David Jones of course! Should have just what he was looking for. There was a certain old world elegance about DJ's. He knew his grandmother always ordered from there. The first days of autumn had been anything but sunny, damn cold in fact. A light rain fell and a Southerly whipped along the tight streets. It was a relief to enter the warm cocoon of the big store. The ground floor was strictly for women so he wandered toward the escalators-Tailoring Department, second floor.

Someone touched his arm. 'Tom!' That familiar perfume, he turned slowly.

'Tom, I can't believe it's you.' They both laughed a little. She said. 'It's been a long time.'

He drew a long breath. 'How is life with you Les?'

She took his arm, he felt the soft pressure of her expensive fur.

'DJ's have a nice little coffee shop, please Tom?'

They sat facing each other. 'You look thin Tom, was it very bad?'

'Bad enough. What about you Les. I hear you are married.'

'Yes, and a mother too.'

He took a deep breath.

She laughed. 'She is just twelve months old-were you worried?'

He bluffed. 'Of course not. Are you happy Les?'

She looked down. 'Yes I am, really Tom. You came into my life when I was lonely.'

'I think we both were.'

She slipped out of her coat. 'I often think of that last night together, when we drove to Manly.'

He smiled. 'And Elvis sang 'Are you lonesome tonight?'.'

'Yes.' Tears welled in her eyes.

'Don't Les. That's history now.'

'Have you found someone, Tommy?'

'Not much chance of that.'

'Because of me?'

'Because of a lot of things.'

She took his hand, holding it to her cheek. 'Dear Tom, dear gentle Tom.'

'Les, please don't.' He took her hand in his. 'Someone might see us.'

'I don't care.'

'I do, for your sake.' He looked around. 'Some of these old gossips would have a field day. Come on, no tears.' He rose and helped her into her fur. 'Bet you have a luncheon appointment.'

She regained her composure, opened her purse and had a look in a tiny vanity mirror. 'You always were the sensible one. You're right, I must go.' For a moment their eyes met. 'Goodbye Tommy.' She walked rapidly to the door, turning for a moment to wave.

He lingered over his coffee, a sense of elation filled him. The spell was broken, that episode was history now!

The rain cleared, warm autumn days returned. Tom stood at the wide windows studying the surging harbour traffic.

'So you leave tomorrow?'

'About midnight Uncle-best time to travel.'

'I see. I must say you look more relaxed these days.'

'Yes, it's the thought of getting away, work out what I want to do.'

'You will keep in touch?'

'Of course I will.' He sat down. 'You asked me to take some of the family responsibility the other night.'

'I hoped you would.'

'I'll be glad to Uncle. Can it wait until I come back?'

'Of course. You have made up your mind to go overseas, have you?'

'I think so, but a spell at *Monaro* first.'

'Excellent idea. While on the subject of responsibilities, anything you want to know?'

'I don't think so.' He paused. 'Yes one thing, what happened to the old mansion in Melbourne?'

'*Monterey*? Wonderful old place. Your grandfather made that over to the National Trust.'

'I'm glad. It would have been tragic for it to go for development.'

'There is plenty of development around it. The old place stands out like a beacon.'

'Nothing much changes around here Uncle.'

'No, I suppose not Tom, we just all grow a little older and I hope a little wiser.'

'Well, I'd best be going. Please keep an eye on my unit Uncle.'

'I'll leave that in the capable hands of Mrs. Johns.' He took his nephew's arm. 'I hope you won't waste your training as a doctor Tom, and the experience you gained in Vietnam.'

'No chance of that. I'll be ready for work when you see me again.'

They shook hands. 'Good luck my boy and a safe journey wherever you go.'

CHAPTER XXVIII

Monaro

'Nothing looks the same Grandma. The town has changed, I didn't even see anyone I recognized.' He smiled down at the frail face he loved so well. 'Only *Monaro* is the same-it never changes.'

'*Monaro* will be yours dear, your grandfather made sure of that.'

'I'm so sorry Grandma, terribly sorry. I should have been here.'

'Hush, you must not dwell on things that can't be helped. Your grandfather's dearest wish was that you might have children to keep and love *Monaro* as we have done.'

Her eyes searched his face. 'Have you found someone Tom?'

'Let's have a cup of tea, in fact I could do with some lunch. I'll tell you all about it before I go again Grandma.'

An hour later he took her arm. 'Come and show me the garden.' Arm in arm they walked slowly amongst the familiar shrubs. 'Mrs. Ellis' daughter looks after things now I see.'

'I am well cared for dear, your uncle sees to that.'

'Who looks after the grounds now Grandma?'

'Bob Martin's son. He is a landscaper and has people working for him.'

'Whatever happened to old Mick? I'll always remember Mick, he was very old when I last saw him.'

'Mick passed away dear, he had cancer of the lungs. Your grandfather made sure he did not suffer.'

Tom sighed. 'I will never forget Grandpa as long as I live. He was so gentle, I know how he must have felt.' He turned to face her. 'I am sure I would have done the same Grandma.'

She smiled. 'You are very much like him my dear, I hope you always will be.'

He breathed the air, filling his lungs. 'It's wonderful here, the air is like wine. I want to take the old canoe and go fishing tomorrow.'

Frances smiled. 'Perhaps you had better call on your cousin first. She returned from overseas just last month.'

'Dorothy, you mean Dorothy is here? That's great we can go fishing together.'

'It might be wise to ask her husband first.'

'Husband, she's married? Who to-is he a Yank? I know she was in America.'

'You don't seem to approve dear.'

'It's not that I don't approve Grandma. Just seems-well, it's a bit of a shock, that's all.'

'Dorothy grew up, just as you did Tom.'

'Well, who is he, what's he like?' He sounded slightly aggrieved.

Frances allowed herself a smile. 'He is a very nice young man, a Veterinarian, like Dorothy. No, he is not an American, he is from Sydney.'

Early the next morning Tom stood outside the DeVries house, listening to the chimes of the doorbell. A grey haired woman answered the door. For an instant she looked startled, then flung her arms around him.

'Tom, Tom my dear, you have come home!' She turned calling to her daughter. 'Dorothy come quickly, see who is here.'

Dorothy came to the door, her satin dressing gown belted around her. For a moment she stood staring, then dropping the hairbrush from her hand, she rushed forward and flung her arms around his neck. 'Oh you beast, Tom Wakefield, why didn't you phone? I look terrible!' She stood back, surveying him. 'All right, now explain yourself. Better still, come in, I want you to meet someone.'

A tall thin, tousle haired man emerged from the bedroom, an infectious grin on his face. 'What's all the commotion?'

'Martin,' she dragged Tom forward, 'this is the brute I've told you about. Never phones, never writes letters, just turns up when you least expect him.'

Both men laughed and shook hands. 'Don't believe a word of it Martin.'

Her mother interrupted. 'These two haven't had breakfast yet Tom. You will stay and have a cup of tea, won't you?'

'Thanks Aunt, I'd love to.'

Breakfast was a riotous affair. Dorothy was ecstatic, sitting between the two men she loved, she kept up a constant chatter.

Tom thought-thank God no one has mentioned Vietnam.

Martin sat back looking at his wife who barely had time to finish her meal. 'Now if I can get a word in edgewise,' he grinned, 'thank you Tom. I believe you and my better half are great fishermen?'

'Well,' Tom drawled it out, 'if you don't mind baiting someone's hook for them, yes. There's plenty of good Perch along North Arm.'

'You're a spoilsport Tom Wakefield!'

They all laughed.

'Any chance of wetting a line while you're here?'

'Any chance? I can't wait to get amongst them. I suppose you have heard about the old outrigger?'

'Often. Will it hold three?'

'Takes four with ease. What about tomorrow?'

Dorothy broke in. 'What about today?'

'Why not?' Tom looked at his watch. 'Tide will be full at one twenty-pick you up at twelve.'

The days passed too quickly. On Sunday afternoon, Tom walked with his grandmother to the Chapel, carrying armfuls of flowers. They sat a while in the cool amber light. With a sigh, she took his hand. 'Come dear, I want to talk to you before you leave us again.'

Tom's heart ached as he looked at her, at the thin tranquil face. Before you leave us again-yes, this one he loved so much and those sleeping in the walled garden outside.

The track through the dense bush had been widened and fenced on either side with fine bird wire so that she might walk alone to the Chapel in safety.'

'Are you happy dear?'

'I think so Grandma. I'm restless but I am truly happy when I am here. I love *Monaro*, it is part of me.'

'I worry Tom. Your uncle has never married, I hope you will and have children. It was your grandfather's dearest wish.'

'Don't worry Grandma, even if I don't find someone to love, I will still marry a nice girl so you will have a brood of great grandchildren.'

She stopped, holding tightly to his arm. 'Tom you must never marry unless you love. Promise me. I have seen marriages like that, it brings only tragedy and unhappiness.'

They continued walking. 'All right Grandma, but I might end up a bachelor like Uncle Gareth.'

'It would be better than being unhappy and bringing unhappiness to another my dear.'

In the still of the night, he would make his way to the tower. Always he stopped to gaze into the face of the captain's lady. How lovely she was. Could anyone look like that in real life?

At breakfast he told his grandmother of his plan to go overseas. 'Uncle Gareth agrees. Help me sort myself out before I settle down. I think I have to go, really.'

She slowly put down her cup. 'Is there something you haven't told me Tom?'

'I was in love Grandma. I thought I was anyway, but she belonged to someone else.'

'Are you still in love with her?'

He shook his head. 'No. I will always be terribly fond of her, but you know, even if she had been free-we were opposites. I would have made her unhappy. The life she leads would never have suited an old slow coach like me.'

She smiled at him. 'Thank you for telling me Tom.' She sounded relieved. 'Have you decided where you are going?'

'Grandma, that is something I wanted to talk to you about. I think I'll go to America first, to Boston. See in I can find out anything about the captain and his lady-their descendants, I mean.'

'Your grandfather tried after the First War dear, and there was absolutely no trace of anyone of that name. Any descendants have disappeared long ago. An old clerk gave him the name Carrington but there were dozens in the phone book.'

'Pretty hopeless I know.' He smiled. 'But I'll have a look just for the heck of it. Grandma,' he bent down to stroke a sleek Persian cat, rubbing itself softly against his leg. 'I didn't know you had a cat.'

'No dear. Mrs. Coburn's daughter brought her to keep me company. She is a lovely creature. One day I will tell you about her famous ancestor.'

He held her veined hand in his. 'Dear Grandma, there are so many stories I want you to tell me.'

Boston, August 1973

'Dr. Wakefield, I'm afraid there wasn't much to go on. The Law firm you mentioned has long since ceased to exist.' The Pinkerton man sat opposite Tom in the lounge of his hotel. 'I've checked out every Carrington in this town, every known connection-nothing.'

'You've done a good job Mr. Berry. I'll be leaving the end of the week. Let me have your account and I'll settle up.'

'Thank you sir. Sorry I couldn't have been more helpful. If it's convenient I'll drop in my written report tomorrow.'

'That won't be necessary Mr. Berry, not much point really.'

'As you wish Doctor. I suggest you leave your address though, in case anything turns up from one of our agents.'

'Right. Care for a drink?'

'Thank you, no sir. Never drink on the job, agency policy.'

Tom smiled as the earnest little man took his leave. When he had gone, Tom thought over his stay in Boston. Very conservative, much like parts of England as he remembered from those years long ago when his grandparents had taken him overseas.

Well, that was that. Might as well book a flight to London, make a round trip of it.

Friday came, his last day in Boston. Might take another taxi ride around the suburbs. Those high brick fences with privet hedges, conservative all right, a look of old world elegance.

The phone rang. 'Sorry to disturb you Doctor, there is a person in the lobby wishing to see you.'

Tom smiled, Mr. Berry no doubt. The desk clerk prided himself on instinctively knowing a gentleman when he saw one-any other man was a 'person'.

'Thank you, I will be right down.'

Mr. Berry sat rotating his hat between thumb and forefinger. He rose as Tom walked in.

'Sit down Mr. Berry, sit down.'

The agent came to the point. 'Doctor, Pinkerton's pride themselves on their efficiency. When I left you last, I felt strongly we must have missed something.'

'I am sure you did your best Mr. Berry.'

'Please Doctor.' He held up his hand. 'I enlisted the help of my superior and without going into detail, I think we have come up with something.'

'Sounds very interesting.'

'Truth is Doctor, we have many points of contact.' He handed Tom a typed sheet of paper. 'Under our noses all the time. It seemed so difficult at the time, now it seems so obvious.'

Tom studied the paper. 'But this is not Carrington-the name you have here is Paget.'

Mr. Berry nodded. 'Women take their husband's name Doctor.'

'Good Lord, of course! Just where is this address?'

'About the best part of the city, you might say the 'old money' part.'

'I see. Well, I suppose it might be worth a visit. Thank you Mr. Berry.'

In the early afternoon, dressed in slacks and sport jacket, Tom hailed a taxi. Damned if he was going to dress up. If he was shown the door, he might as well be comfortable. He gave the driver the address. 'Know where that is?'

'Sure, no trouble. Big Shot country.'

Half an hour later, after driving away from the city through tree lined streets, the taxi stopped before massive iron gates. 'You said thirty four.'

'Right. You wait for me here, I shouldn't be long.' Tom walked up the gravelled drive to the large brownstone house. He felt a sense of nervousness. They will probably think I'm mad or even something worse.

A maid in black uniform with starched white cuffs and collar answered the door. 'Yes sir?'

'Is Mr. Paget in?'

'No sir, Commodore and Mrs. Paget are in the city today sir.'

'I see. Is any member of the family at home?'

'No sir, Mr. Richard is away in the Navy and Miss Helen is at the University.'

'At the University of course. Well, thank you, I may call later.'

The taxi driver looked inquiringly. 'Back to town now, chief?'

'Do you know the way to the University?'

'Sure, everybody does.'

'Okay, let's go. Right to the office.'

Tom sat back wiping his brow. What the hell am I doing? Probably some domehead with glasses.

He waited impatiently as the woman at the desk answered the phone. His smile, which usually brought female attention, had little effect on this prim, efficient woman.

'I am looking for Miss Helen Paget, can you tell me where I might find her?'

'You have just missed her by five minutes. She called in here on her way.' She melted a little at his dismay. 'If you hurry you might catch her at the car park.'

Tom jumped into the cab. 'Where the hell is the car park?'

'Just along the road here.'

'Hold it here, wait for me.' On the footpath, a slim girl was waiting to cross the road. 'Surely it must be her!' She wore a simple white dress, her honey blonde hair held back with a thin ribbon, in a ponytail. Under her arm she carried some books. His gaze took in her slim brown legs and white sandals, one foot slightly raised as she waited the chance to cross.

Tom was slightly breathless when he reached her. 'Miss Paget?' He fumbled for words. 'They told me at the office, I might find you here.'

She turned a cool gaze on him. He was dumbstruck-the portrait- those eyes, those beautiful brown eyes, the clear whites. The same soft generous mouth. 'Oh Miss Paget, I have been looking for you!' He suddenly felt very foolish.

She continued to regard him curiously. 'Are you from the University?'

'No, no I am not.' He tried to smile, adding lamely. 'I'm from Australia.'

'Oh!'

'Miss Paget please, may I talk with you? My name is Tom Wakefield.'

She smiled a little. 'Australia is a long way from here Mr. Wakefield, it must be very important.'

'It is quite a long story. Is there some place we can talk, have you time for a coffee?'

'If you wish.'

'Thank you. I won't be a moment. I'll just pay the taxi driver.'

'My car is over there.' She pointed to a blue Oldsmobile roadster.

The coffee shop nestled amongst others in a little village like area shaded by great spreading trees.

'What a pleasant place.'

She pulled into the curb. 'Yes, a favourite meeting place for students.'

They made small conversation while the girl took their order. 'Would you prefer a cool drink Mr. Wakefield?'

'Coffee is fine. Please call me Tom, Mister sounds so formal.'

'All right, if you call me Helen.'

They smiled at each other. 'Did I startle you when I came rushing up from the taxi?'

'Not really.' She blushed. 'A little surprised that's all.'

Tom's heart beat faster as he looked at her. Her clear, ivory skin with little makeup, the sweet curve of her lips, those lustrous brown eyes that still regarded him with some curiosity.

'I couldn't recognize your accent, I knew it wasn't English.'

'I was worried you might think I was trying to accost you and call for help.'

She looked at him, smiling gently. 'That thought never entered my mind.'

'Your own accent doesn't seem quite American, Helen.'

'I suppose not. I have lived most of my life in France. My father was the Naval Attache at the American Embassy in Paris. I went to the American School there and later to the Sorbonne. We have only been back here this last year. The house we are living in now belongs to my grandparents on my father's side. They live in Florida now.'

Tom put down his cup. 'Well, I guess I had better start, as the saying goes, at the beginning.'

Her eyes seldom left his face as the story unfolded. Refilled coffee cups stood unheeded. When there was no more to tell, he took from his pocket a colour photograph of the captain's lady.

Helen gave a little gasp. 'That's Mother's necklace! Tom, it's the most wonderful story. All those years ago-what relation would I be to her?'

'I can't say Helen, perhaps your mother might know.'

'Tom, please excuse me for a moment.' She went to the cafe telephone.

He looked after her as she made her way through the tables-She is not wearing a ring. I pray, oh Lord I pray she is not engaged. That doesn't mean she isn't though. There must be someone.

She came back to the table. 'Tom, I have just spoken to my mother-would you mind coming home with me? Could you stay for dinner? Unless,' she hesitated, 'unless you have another engagement.'

'Another engagement? Oh Lord no. But look, sports jacket and slacks, what would your parents think?'

'We are not very formal at our house Tom.'

Helen's mother met them in the drawing room. A gracious, well groomed woman with few of her daughter's features. She extended her hand. 'I am so pleased you found time to come and see us Dr. Wakefield. From what Helen has told me, I am fascinated to hear more.'

Tom smiled as he took her hand. 'Please call me Tom, Mrs. Paget. And time is not a problem.'

'Helen tells me you have not long returned from Vietnam.'

'Yes, that's right.'

'Dear oh dear, here I am talking and we are all standing. Do sit down.'

An hour later, with the photographs still in her hand, she sat with tears in her eyes.

Helen comforted her. 'Please Mother, don't be upset.'

'I'm sorry, please forgive me. She must have been so lonely, so far away from her family.'

'I don't think so Mrs. Paget. Apparently they were very friendly with the local Anglican priest, Father Trendel. He managed their affairs and according to what my grandmother knows, they were very happy.'

'I am so glad you came Tom. I have tried at various times to find out about my predecessors but always there has been a wall. Now I know a little anyway.' She looked at Helen. 'You are so like her dear.'

At the sound of an opening door, they looked up. A tall grey haired man in naval uniform entered the room. He looked surprised. 'I'm sorry I didn't know we had a visitor.'

His wife rose to greet him. 'John, this is Dr. Wakefield. He is from Australia.'

'How do you do sir?' The Commodore's grip was firm.

'From Australia eh? Always glad to welcome an ally.'

Over dinner the conversation continued. 'Had a spell in Vietnam, Doctor?'

'Almost two years sir.'

'Glad to be out of it no doubt.'

'Yes, very glad.'

'Our son, Richard, is in the Navy. Expect him home this fall. I've no doubt he feels the same.'

Dinner over, the Commodore folded his napkin. 'Well, no doubt you all have much to talk about. If you will excuse me, I have some papers to attend to.' His smile was friendly. 'Trust we will see you again Doctor. How long do you plan to spend in Boston?'

'About another week sir.'

'Fine, fine you are welcome anytime.' He paused at the door, 'when you are ready to leave, our gardener, who passes as our chauffeur will see you back to your hotel.'

'Thank you very much sir.'

Mrs. Paget looked at her watch. 'And you must excuse me for a little while. There is so much I want to ask you Tom. If you are not busy tomorrow, perhaps you could come over. Some of Helen's friends come for tennis on Saturday, do you play?'

'Whenever I get the chance.'

'Well, I must leave you now and get on with my phoning.'

Left alone together, Helen seemed suddenly shy. 'I hope you don't mind Tom, Mother does rush a little. If you have something planned-.'

'Not a thing, I would really like to come.'

She smiled a little. 'Come before lunch, can you manage that?'

'Of course.'

For what seemed an eternity, they sat without speaking. He thought-how beautiful she is. He fought back a desire to reach for her hand.

A faint smile hovered about her lips. 'You seem far away Tom.'

He smiled, shaking his head, looking beyond her into the next room. 'I was admiring your piano. Do you play Helen?'

'A little, do you Tom?'

'I try.'

'Will you play?' She smiled again. 'Please.'

'If you like. I'm a bit rusty though.'

Ten o'clock struck. 'Good Lord, the time! Your parents will kick me out.'

'Oh Tom you play so beautifully, the time has flown. Come I'll ring for the gardener, he will drive you back to your hotel.'

At the doorway, as the car drew up, she again seemed withdrawn. He longed to take her hand. 'Goodnight Helen, thank your mother for me.'

'Goodnight Tom.'

He sank back into the comfort of the Cadillac- 'She is friendly, polite, yet somehow aloof-good Lord, I wish I knew what she was thinking! She seems so shy-perhaps she has had an unhappy experience. Perhaps there may be someone else in her life, if only I knew. But then, what did I expect, we only met yesterday?'

That night he tossed, haunted by dreams of *Monaro*, of the captain's lady, of Helen. Morning came, he shopped for a tennis outfit then took a taxi to the brownstone mansion.

He had not realized how extensive the grounds were. A panic seized him when he saw the crowd of young people. He stood uncertain. Helen came smiling to meet him. He felt the same weakness whenever he saw her.

She took him by the hand. 'Thank you for coming Tom. Come and meet some of my friends.'

Later someone called to her. 'Please wait for me Tom.' She turned to a tall well built young man. 'Steve, please look after Tom until I get back.'

The young man held out his hand. 'Steve Carter, didn't catch your full name Tom.'

'Tom Wakefield, Steve. Glad to know you.'

'That accent Tom, what is it, I know it's not English.'

Tom laughed. 'Australian. Guess you don't meet many around here.'

'You're the first. Noticed the Virgin Queen brought you along. Known her long?'

'Ah-sort of family friends.'

'She's a knockout.'

'She certainly is. I haven't been here long Steve, why the Virgin Queen?'

Steve Carter laughed. 'Oh that. Well, I know for sure many have tried Tom but none have succeeded. But good luck to you. Come and have a beer.'

Helen stood surrounded by her friends. 'Where on earth did you find him? He's gorgeous! Do you own him? Boy, guys like that shouldn't be on the loose.'

She smiled. 'He knows the family. He is just visiting.'

'What does he do?'

'He's a doctor. Really, I don't know him very well.' She blushed deeply.

They gathered closer. 'Honey you're blushing. Does he know?'

Sunday came, there was nothing to do. He strolled on the Common, taking little interest. After lunch he rang-Helen was out. Of course she would be, a popular girl like that. He rang again at five. She answered the phone.

'Helen, it's Tom.'

'Tom I looked everywhere for you yesterday. Whatever happened?'

'Steve gave me a lift back to town, you seemed busy.'

'Oh Tom I am sorry, I missed you.'

'Helen,' his heart pounded, 'would you have dinner with me?'

She answered softly. 'I would like that Tom. When?'

'Monday. Would seven be all right?'

'That would be fine Tom.'

Monday night he sat talking to Mrs. Paget, waiting for Helen to come down. At her light step, he looked up.

She stood for a moment, smiling at him. Her gown clung to her slender figure, her hair, swept back from her forehead, fell in a slight wave onto her shoulders. Small gold ear rings gleamed in her ears. 'Hello Tom, am I late?'

He could hardly find his voice. 'No, no of course not. I have a taxi waiting outside.'

At dinner, he ate little. He wanted to ask so much, but words would not come.

She talked about her life in France-how she loved Paris. Had he been there?

When he was very young. He ventured, would she be going back there?

Perhaps, she wasn't sure. Would he be leaving soon? He must have many interests.

Their eyes met, his heart turned over. He wasn't sure just when the conversation continued. Polite, almost stilted, not like that first day in the coffee shop. She seemed reserved, he thought. There just has to be someone else, probably someone in France. After all she has spent most of her life there.

In the taxi home, they barely spoke. She hesitated a moment as the driver stood by the open door, then her smile, her murmured thanks.

He sat back with eyes closed as the taxi turned down the gravelled drive. Why oh why hadn't he walked to the door with her? It would have been so simple, just a natural thing to do. Just take her hand in his.

Later at the hotel, he sat at the bar, drinking a little too much, thinking of all that had happened since that first fateful day in Boston-Good Lord, how close he had come to leaving! Then finding her, it seemed almost a miracle. She was so beautiful, so gentle, so like the portrait. The portrait that had fascinated him since childhood, he remembered his grandfather smiling and calling him an incurable romantic. Perhaps he was, perhaps if he was more forthright, he would tell Helen how he felt, but would that be wise? She may already be in love with someone. Because he had come so far, she was just being nice to him. Yet that day in the coffee shop it had been so relaxed, so normal, he even felt she liked him a little. He certainly did not understand women. With Leslie it had been different. 'Dear Les, I hope she is happy, I wonder if we will ever meet again.' He sighed deeply.

The barman looked at him curiously. 'Another one sir?'

'No, no thanks.' He pushed a note across the bar. 'Think I'll call it a night.'

Next morning he phoned early, arranging to meet Helen for lunch at the coffee shop.

It was crowded. She smiled a welcome. Would he mind if her friend joined them, it was so hard to find a place this time of day.

No, of course he wouldn't mind.

She introduced an attractive, brown haired girl. 'Tom, this is my friend, Ann Fulton.'

The girl smiled. 'I met you on Saturday Tom, do you remember me?'

'I'm sure I do Ann, but you must forgive me if my memory appears a little vague.' He grinned. 'There were so many pretty girls there.'

Ann laughed. 'Are all Australians as diplomatic as you Tom?'

The hour passed pleasantly. Both girls were doing an Arts course, both in their final year. Ann's husband was in Vietnam, a Navy pilot.

Did Tom think the war would end soon?

He was sure it would, it couldn't go on much longer from what he had seen.

Ann excused herself, there was someone she must see while she was there.

Left alone, they fell into easy conversation. 'I like your friend.'

'Ann is nice. She worries so Tom, her husband hasn't had leave in over a year. Last time Ann had to go to Tokyo for just two weeks. It's not fair.'

He nodded. 'I can understand how she feels. It's a rotten business.'

She looked at her watch. 'I'm sorry I can't stay Tom, Ann is waiting for me. I must rush.'

'Helen,' he hesitated. 'I see the Boston Pops is in Concert. Would you care-I mean are you free Friday night?'

She coloured slightly, smiling at him. 'Thank you Tom, I would like to very much.'

He felt a flood of relief. 'Pick you up about seven, we can have dinner first.'

She was gone. The young waitress hovered about him. 'More coffee sir?'

He nodded, smiling at her. 'Yes, just top it up please.'

Alone he wondered-What the hell do I do with myself? The days are empty until I see her again. Suppose I could do the rounds of the hospitals-He imagined visiting medicos, especially those who had served in Vietnam, might be politely welcomed. He dreaded the thought of questions he might be asked-what had he seen in Vietnam, his opinion of treatment of wounds in the field. No, he decided to give that a miss. Never be a bloody surgeon anyway. One thing they wouldn't want to know about, one thing that still haunted him-the endless stream of body bags he had seen. Yes, only those who had never been there, wanted to know about it. If Ann, that gentle, worried friend of Helen's only knew what happened to poor bloody pilots shot down over hostile territory. Well, she would never know from him anyway. He wondered if any war in history had so divided people, had caused so much grief and hatred.

He asked the waitress to phone a taxi for him. On the way back to the city, he thought-Why not hire a car, drive around, see the countryside? Soon get used to driving on the right side of the road. Again his mind dwelt on all that had happened. Depression seized him-I can't go on like this. I just can't bring myself to say the words I want to say. What on earth can she think of me? I swear I will tell her Friday night. If she is offended, if she rejects me, I'll leave. The only decent thing to do. Oh Lord, if only Grandma were her for me to talk to. Dear wise, old Grandma, will she still be there when I get home again?

He looked out at the city buildings. 'Drop me off at the nearest hire car firm please.'

Thursday at the University cafeteria Ann, the only one in whom Helen could or would confide, confronted her. 'Are you going to tell me?'

Helen looked down. 'Oh Ann, does it show?'

'It does to me. Is it serious?'

She shook her head. 'I don't know. I think he likes me but I just don't know.'

Ann took her hand. 'Helen, I hope I am your best friend. Please be careful, I couldn't bear to see you hurt.'

'He must like me a little, he asks me out. He is so gentle, he seems shy with me.'

'Honey, I can't help you there but if a woman's instinct means anything-the way he looks at you, I'm sure he is head over heels in love with you.'

'Ann, please don't laugh at me, I just feel I have been waiting for him all my life. Does that sound silly?'

'I would never laugh at you. All the time I have known you, you have seldom had dates, yet everyone knows there is not a man on campus who wouldn't sell his soul to have you.'

Helen looked down again. 'And I know what they call me, but I could never do what they want.'

Ann spoke gently. 'I know. I hope you never will. Helen, just be careful. That's all I ask. If Tom cares, he will tell you.'

Friday afternoon, Tom considered it wise to return the hire car. It had proved an interesting experience. A bit hair raising at times, definitely need more practice. He smiled to himself, some of those other drivers he had encountered must have come close to heart failure. Well, let them try driving on the left side of the road. Still they all had been remarkably courteous, even the motor cycle policeman who had pulled him over and who, after inspecting his international driving licence, had insisted on guiding him back to the hire car company. 'Best take a taxi Doctor, you'll live longer that way.'

Later in his hotel room, Tom dressed carefully. He was glad he had packed his dinner suit and reserved a table at the restaurant where they first had dinner together.

The hotel doorman recognized him coming from the elevator and at Tom's signal whistled a taxi. On the way to the brownstone mansion, he sat back, his mind alternating between excitement and nagging doubt. Suddenly they were there. He told the driver to wait.

Helen met him at the door. With racing pulse, he returned her smile of welcome, wordlessly taking her arm, he led her to the waiting taxi.

At dinner she smiled at him across the table. 'Tom, you seem far away sometimes, please tell me what you are thinking about.'

He shook his head. 'Sorry Helen, nothing really just enjoying the evening.

She coloured slightly. 'Are you thinking of home?' He failed to notice the gentle rise and fall of her breast as she thought-or of someone you miss?

He desperately wanted to say-I am thinking of you, how much I am in love with you. How to tell you.

Instead he told her more of his life at *Monaro*, things he hadn't spoken of before, of his cousin, the old outrigger canoe and how they used to go fishing together.

Her eyes seldom left his face. 'Oh Tom, thank you for telling me.' She sighed. '*Monaro* must be a wonderful place. Your cousin Dorothy, how I envy her-a veterinarian!'

'She loves animals Helen, that's all she ever wanted to be.' He smiled. 'I'm sure you two would get on very well together.'

Later in the theatre, he gave himself up to the soothing charm of the music, breathing in the faint perfume clinging to her, so close to him.

The evening ended as had the first. He walked with her to the wide entrance to the house. He hardly recognized his own voice. 'Goodnight Helen.'

Her heart beating rapidly, she stood for a moment in the light filtering through the glass panels of the door. 'Goodnight Tom, thank you for a lovely evening.' She turned quickly, her latch key in the lock.

The taxi driver, who had discreetly kept his gaze ahead, opened the door for him. 'Back to the city sir?'

So that was that. Speeding through the night, he made his decision-I have given myself up to day dreaming, well, tonight was the end. She obviously doesn't feel anything for me.

Letting herself into the house, Helen was surprised to find her father sitting reading. 'You are up late Dad.'

'Just a little, I have been waiting to talk to you.'

She stood at the foot of the staircase waiting.

For a moment he seemed lost for words. 'This young man you have been seeing, I hope there is nothing serious in it.'

Helen remained silent.

'Nothing against him you understand. I have met many Australians, no finer people, but my dear you are our only daughter and,' he added lamely, 'he appears much older than you.'

'Just nine years Dad, one less than you and Mother. Anyway, you have nothing to worry about, he is not interested in me.' With that she ran quickly up the stairs.

In his room, Tom glanced at the clock. Almost twelve thirty-Hang the time I'll call her now.

The phone had hardly rung when it was picked up. Her voice sounded strained. 'Tom, it's you.'

'Yes, did I wake you?'

'No, I couldn't sleep.'

'I just rang to tell you I have decided to leave for England next week.'

There was silence. 'Helen, are you there?'

'Yes.' Her voice came in a whisper.

'As it's Saturday tomorrow, I thought we might go for a last drive in the country. I'll hire a car.'

'Please don't do that Tom, let me call for you.' She hesitated. 'If that will be all right?'

'Of course. About ten?'

'Yes, that's fine. Good night Tom.'

Replacing the phone, he sat back thinking of all that had happened. It seemed like a dream, and now it was all ending. On the edge of sleep, his eyes closing, he murmured-For all my life I will think of her, for all my life I will be in love with her.

Next morning he was waiting as the blue Oldsmobile pulled into the kerb. She was wearing the same white dress as on the day he first saw her, her hair tied back in a ponytail. He smiled a welcome. 'Thanks for coming.'

She returned his smile. 'Where would you like to go?'

'You're the driver.'

'I know some lovely country, have you time Tom?'

'All day, every minute of it.'

With the city far behind, they sped through rolling hills, along avenues of spreading trees that met in overhanging canopies.

They were both silent, staring ahead barely exchanging a word. Past a cluster of signposts, she turned off the paved road along a leaf strewn lane. Rounding a bend, a gate loomed ahead.

'This place belongs to a family friend. So long as we close the gate we can go through. It is really beautiful Tom.'

Through the trees the lane led to a small grassed knoll, high above the surrounding country. She parked in the shade.

'Please bring the rug Tom, from here you can just sit and look down on the world.'

He followed to where she stood waiting.

'Here is the best place, under this tree.' She sat with her knees drawn up, her hands clasped around them. 'It is lovely here don't you think Tom?'

'Very.'

She looked away. 'When are you leaving?' Her voice barely a whisper.

He did not answer. They were very close. Gently he held her to him. She was trembling, slowly she fell back into the circle of his arm. She lay quite still, her eyes half closed, lips slightly parted. Everything seemed to be happening in slow motion. He kissed her soft yielding lips. She smelled of flowers. Her eyes opened wide, she was smiling at him. They kissed again, a long lingering kiss. He felt faint, his heart pounded. Fearful of rejection, his voice came low and husky. 'Helen, I love you. I've loved you from the moment I first saw you. Please, please say you will marry me.'

A sob escaped her, two tears rolled down her cheeks. His heart turned over. 'Helen, darling Helen what have I said?'

Her arms stole around him, drawing him to her. 'Oh Tom, why did you take so long? I've been so miserable. I thought there must be someone else.' She was between laughter and tears. 'If you hadn't asked me, I would have been an old maid. I could never marry anyone else.'

For the next hour they sat close together talking, loving and planning. Then hand in hand, stopping every few steps to gaze at each other in wonder, they made their way to the blue roadster under the giant Sycamore.

First Published in Australia 1993

Printed by Caprice Lithographics Pty Ltd
Sydney Australia

ISBN 0 646 15315 3